John Wright

THE DETECTIVE LEN MORGAN SERIES

~~~

A Scent of Suspicion - #1

His Father's Sons - #2

A Passion for Revenge - #3

CHAOS ...*and Cops*! - #4

Insania Interruptus - #5

In Pursuit of Phantoms - #6

~ ~ ~

A Really Bad Day for Henry
...a really nasty short story.

(All of the above listed titles are available in paperback for $9.95 each at createspace.com.)

John Wright

A Scent of Suspicion

Written by
John Wright

Book one of
The Detective Len Morgan Novel Series

Published in 1999 by John Wright

~

Re-published 2012 by John Wright

~

©2012 by John Wright

~

Cover Photography by John Wright

~

All rights reserved. No part of this book may be reproduced without written permission, except for brief quotations to books and critical reviews. This story is a work of fiction. Characters, businesses, places, and events and incidents are either the product of the author's imagination or used in a fictitious manner. Any resemblance to actual persons, living or dead, is purely coincidental.

This book was printed in the United States by **CreateSpace**;
(http://createspace.com/)

To purchase additional books: visit **CreateSpace eStore**,

ISBN-13: 978 - 1484074022
ISBN-10: 1484074025

Dedication

*To Ruth Rounds, my patient Grammarian and Editor,
Gayle Maurer, my Graphics Cover Design Artist,
Ray Hoy, a Formatting Genius with the patience of Job,
Beth, the Internet 'Chat' friend I never met in person
but, who along with my dozens of Internet friends,
originally prodded me into writing fiction,
and
to my precious feline friend, Jasmine.*

John Wright

Table of Contents

Len Morgan Series	pg. 3
Prologue	pg. 11
Chapter 1	pg. 13
Chapter 2	pg. 19
Chapter 3	pg. 34
Chapter 4	pg. 48
Chapter 5	pg. 55
Chapter 6	pg. 65
Chapter 7	pg. 79
Chapter 8	pg. 95
Chapter 9	pg. 106
Chapter 10	pg. 120
Chapter 11	pg. 136
Chapter 12	pg. 150
Chapter 13	pg. 162
Chapter 14	pg. 173
Chapter 15	pg. 189
Chapter 16	pg. 199
Chapter 17	pg. 211
Chapter 18	pg. 228
Chapter 19	pg. 242
Chapter 20	pg. 257
Chapter 21	pg. 271
Chapter 22	pg. 287
Chapter 23	pg. 298
Chapter 24	pg. 315
Chapter 25	pg. 331
Chapter 26	pg. 344
Chapter 27	pg. 363
Chapter 28	pg. 376
Preview Book #2	pg. 393
About the Author	pg. 394

John Wright

Prologue

Day 1, Van Nuys, CA, Wednesday morning, June 5, 1996...

The big man sat astride her naked body and gripped her throat tightly as he raised the gleaming blade. Entangled in the soiled bed sheets and exhausted from her futile efforts to struggle free, she confronted the incredible mind-wrenching horror of her inescapable end.

"Goddamn whore!" He screamed, driving the blade deep into her chest. As it pierced her racing heart, her lifeblood spewed forth and splattered her bosom, and the sheets grotesquely with mixed patterns of dark droplets and rivulets.

Enraged, he continued to plunge and withdraw the blade. In a final screaming frenzy, he ripped and slashed at her milk-white flesh, cleaving it from her ribs.

"It's my money, bitch!"

Finished, he slumped. Perspiring and wasted physically, his savage energy seeped from his pores like the blood that flowed from her massive wounds. He casually wiped the blade on his trouser leg and rose from her lifeless body. Rubbing the back of his sweaty neck, he looked into her once bright eyes, eyes that now stared vacantly at nothingness. He pocketed the knife and exited the dimly lit room.

John Wright

Across the San Fernando Valley in Granada Hills…

In the old but comfortable, upscale condominium complex, Villa Casa Grande, the heavy smoke wafting from the smoldering butt-filled ashtray caused Homicide Detective Lieutenant Len Morgan's burning eyes to water. Brackish tears formed and ran down his unshaven cheeks. Exhaling the last drag, he stared at the live cigarette in his hand, then he coughed and mashed it out, "Enough, dammit!"

He sat up abruptly in his bed, his body awash with perspiration. Len Morgan looked at the trembling hand that held the cigarette seconds before; it was empty. The rancid ashtray was nonexistent.

My God! he thought, *I've been having that dream again!* Confused, he shook his head in disbelief. Having the discipline to quit cold turkey, he'd smoked his last cigarette three years ago.

Reluctantly crawling out of bed, he went into the kitchen and re-nuked a cup of day-old coffee. Sipping it slowly, he coughed, "Shit! Enough of that!" Still coughing, he headed for his awaiting wake-up shower.

Len Morgan stood six feet-three inches tall and weighed a trim two hundred-twenty pounds. With just a smattering of gray beginning to show in his thick dark hair, he didn't look forty-six years old.

He lived alone in Villa Casa Grande, but on occasion, he had the company of a female companion of several years,

Gabrielle Beliveau. A wealthy Bel Air resident and professional cellist, she would sleep over when her string ensemble was not touring the country.

Shaved, dressed and more ready to face the day, he poured himself a half-cup of the cold remaining brew and drank it in one swallow. *Ugh!* He thought, *it still tastes shitty, worse than what they brew at the precinct. Oh well, duty calls.*

Pocketing his shield and holstering his weapon, he reached for the telephone and pressed the memory-digit number for his long-time homicide partner, Detective Sergeant Jeffrey "Robbie" Jeff Robinson.

The voice on the other end of the line answered, "Hello, Jeffrey speaking."

"Hey, Robbie, are you on your way or should I walk?"

"Walk? When did you ever? On second thought, maybe a little walking would do both of us some good."

Smiling, he could hear Jeff Robinson chuckling on the other end of the line. As he listened, he stared out at the hazy morning sun that reflected off the nearby rooftops. "So Robbie, since I nearly poisoned myself with my own coffee, I'll get a fresh cup at old Jim's down the block. Pick me up there, okay?"

"Sure thing. Colleen says 'Hi'. See ya'."

Outside in the wide carpeted corridor, he disregarded the awaiting elevator and instead headed toward the winding stairway that led to the ground floor. Passing by his neighbor Sara Dunlap's unit on the way, he heard the familiar sounds of loud, angry shouting spilling from under her door.

Damn, they're at it again, and bright and early too, he mused, trying desperately to ignore their loud arguing. *Sara sure picked a loser in that one.*

He was still muttering to himself as he entered the familiar surroundings of Jim's Corner Coffee Shoppe. "What a piece of shit…."

"Say what?" Jim asked from behind the counter, looking over his shoulder at his longtime friend and neighbor.

"Oh, nothing, Jim. I'm just muttering to myself again," Len answered, noting that he had been deeply involved in his neighbor's personal affairs, at least to the extent of mumbling about them. "I had something on my mind that's none of my damn business. Know what I mean?" he asked, pulling a couple of dollars from his pocket.

"Uh … no," Jim said, handing Len a thick paper-cup filled with steaming black coffee. "…but, I don't do a whole lot of that knowin', ya' know what I mean?"

"Yeah, Jim. So when are you going to get rid of that silly New Jersey accent?" Len asked, grimacing as he carefully sipped at the scalding brew.

Jim replied in his thick, deep voice, "New Jersey? Are you talkin' to me? This here is how I talk, okay? Moreover, for your information, I ain't from Jersey. I keep tellin' you I moved here from Brooklyn when Mister O'Malley and them bums came out here. Can't you remember anything?"

Len snorted and handed him two dollars, "You tear me up, my friend. See you tomorrow, maybe."

"Yeah, yeah, yeah," Jim grunted. "Hey! Be careful out there!"

With impeccable timing, Sergeant Jeffrey Robinson parked the big Ford Victoria police cruiser at the curb as Len stepped out of Jim's Corner Coffee Shoppe.

A bright African-American, Jeff Robinson was ten years younger and taller than Len at six feet four inches. He was also a bit overweight. His wife Colleen confessed, *"I feed him too well, too often."*

Jeff Robinson and Len had been a Devonshire Hills precinct homicide team for twelve years. Although the opportunity had been frequently available for Jeff Robinson to advance, he'd decline and choose instead to remain with Len.

Getting in the cruiser, Len said, "Hey! Right on time, partner. Did you run some lights again?"

"Yeah, a couple, but I stopped for one I usually ignore. There was a shiny Black-and-White cruiser sitting there today. It didn't seem like a professional thing to do, you know, to run a traffic light in front of a fellow cop. Anyway, there's always tomorrow."

"Good luck with that," Len said, buckling his seat belt.

"So, are you surviving with Gabrielle out of town?" Jeff Robinson asked, looking over his shoulder waiting for the traffic to clear.

"Later…"

"Yeah, later," Jeff Robinson mumbled, grinning as the big car jumped out into the traffic. At the same time Len attempted desperately to avoid spilling old Jim's steaming coffee and scalding himself.

"So hey, pal, can we give it a break? Either avoid some of the damn potholes or pull over for a sec and let me pitch this shit?"

"What's your problem? Did you fall out of the wrong side of that empty bed of yours this morning?"

"No, but I am becoming increasingly pissed about the mess my young neighbor lady has gotten into with her worthless *Cholo* boyfriend," Len explained

"What about her boyfriend? What's got you so worked up?"

"He's a fuckin' jerk. Argue, argue, argue … all the goddamn time yelling and arguing; even this morning as I left to meet you. It's getting tiresome, okay?"

Len stared at the still steaming black liquid as he tried to keep it from spilling in his lap. "Besides those two going at each other constantly, this coffee of Jim's is always too damn hot to drink, and, besides that, it tastes shitty. Gabrielle has me spoiled with the good stuff she brews. This *is* really bad."

"Sheee! You're beginning to sound like some old married guy. I can remember when you thought Jim's coffee was the cat's ass. Is this a sign of our changing times partner?" Jeff Robinson asked as he pulled the Ford into the Devonshire Hills precinct's underground parking area.

Ignoring Jeff Robinson's question, Len got out of the car and pitched the remaining coffee across the shiny parking garage floor. Wadding up the empty paper cup, he arched a *three-pointer* toward the trash barrel twenty feet away.

"Three!" he yelled, his left arm stretched high as he bounced lightly on his toes, exhibiting a magnificent two inch vertical leap ala pro basketball standout and former Detroit Piston, Bill Laimbeer.

"Yeah, three," Jeff Robinson mocked when the paper projectile found 'nothing but net' as it entered the trash container. "You are pretty agile for an old white man. What are you, a cybernetic Magic Johnson now?"

"Yes-s-s-s!" Len said, satisfied with his athletic prowess. "Actually, a *Magic Morgan* now. Somewhat lyrical, huh?"

Grinning, Jeff Robinson replied, "Yeah, Magic Morgan my ass."

They exited the elevator on the second floor and pushed open the heavy double glass-doors leading into the homicide department squad room filled with desks, detectives and busy staff.

Walking through, Len and Jeff Robinson exchanged hellos, smiles, and friendly backslaps with their fellow detectives and uniformed associates working the day-watch.

Len enjoyed it here in the early morning when the atmosphere was light and loose before the deadly seriousness of what they did for a living caught up with them. The room echoed with laughter now: many were making jokes and sipping hot coffee, fresh out of the department's old coffee maker labeled, *'Property of La Brea Tar Pit'*. In Len's opinion, the precinct coffee tasted worse than old Jim's.

The noise and chatter were music to his ears. Here was where he belonged. At times, he questioned how he would ever handle the quiet solitude of sailing the sea on his thirty-nine foot, 12-meter, vintage Bermuda sloop after retiring. It would be in stark contrast to this. *Oh well, time enough to figure that out later,* he always said. *Today it's police work; tomorrow it's time to sail the ocean blue.*

"Hey Dutch! Get any *strange* last night?" Jeff Robinson shouted at his cantankerous superior officer, Captain Elmer 'Dutch' Ryan, as they walked past the open door to the similar glass enclosed office the two detectives shared.

Ryan glared back at Jeff Robinson from across his cluttered desktop and snarled, "Bag it, smart ass! Go find a crime to solve or something!"

In their glass-enclosed cubicle, much like Captain Ryan's office, Len sat down hard in his swivel chair and laughed at Dutch's crude behavior. "That poor old bastard needs a rest, Robbie, some time off to kick back in the shade, that or a projectile bowel movement, something. I truly hope I die before I become one of those ... a foul mouthed old Homicide Captain."

Jeff Robinson laughed as he hung up his coat. "For sure. Before that, you'll probably become a foul mouthed *young* Homicide Captain."

Len was the only Lieutenant in the Valley West Devonshire Hills precinct homicide unit. Jeffrey Robinson was one of two Sergeants: the other being a blond female of Russian heritage, Svetlana Belanova, former ballerina and a nine-year veteran of the department.

"So," Jeff Robinson said as he sat down at his desk. "What's all this shit again today that's got your undies in a twist?"

Len sighed and exhaled a long breath. "About my young neighbor lady?"

"Yeah, her, what's her name."

Frowning, Len looked across the desks at Jeff Robinson, "Forgetful? *Her* name is still Sara Dunlap. And for some reason, when our paths cross, she reminds me of Melissa, my first wife."

"Okay, but is that the problem?"

"No, I'll get to the problem. Whatever, it makes me uncomfortable whenever I meet her outside or passing in the hallway. Mostly the problem is knowing what a total piece-of-shit her *Cholo* boyfriend is."

"Who is he?" Jeff Robinson asked, interrupting. "Have you ever pulled his sheet?"

"A sheet on her current choice of male companionship? No, to my knowledge he's just a worthless Latino street bum named Armando."

Len's telephone rang, "Detective Morgan here. Yes, sir, we'll be right there." Hanging up, he looked at Jeff Robinson. "Put your coat back on partner, it's crime solving time again."

2

Still Wednesday, day 1...

Detectives Morgan and Jeff Robinson entered Captain Ryan's office, closed the door behind them and sat down. The two glanced at each other briefly, waiting for Captain Elmer 'Dutch' Ryan to speak.

"Well, boys. It's good to see you today," Ryan said, grinning, faking congeniality. "We got us a nasty Code-187 this morning. The homicide took place early this morning in the shit-district of our beautiful Valley. Here is the info, all that we have anyway. Get on your horses and see what the uniforms have, okay? Well ... get outta' here!"

"Thank you, sir," Len replied, reaching for the note from across the Captain's cluttered desk.

"Go solve a murder, then I'll accept your thanks!"

"Yes, sir," repeated, nodding to Jeff Robinson to head out.

In the garage below, Jeff Robinson muttered as he slid into the driver's seat, "What a goddamn sweetheart; he needs to get more than rest. If ever I get like him, so help me, just shoot my ass off. Got that, Len?"

"I hear you," Len said as they sped down Devonshire Boulevard and onto the exit ramp that led to the eastbound freeway.

Minutes later, they pulled into the parking lot of the less-than-elaborate Valley Arms Hotel. Greeted by the flashing lights from a pair of shiny Black-and-White cruisers parked nearby, they parked where they could. The Crime Scene

Investigative crew and Medical Examiner's contingent was also on the scene.

Walking through the shabby hotel's entrance and across the small unkempt lobby, Len stopped and asked a uniformed officer, "Where's the victim?"

"Second floor, sir. Up the stairs and to the left," he said, pointing.

Len hit the stairs running. That was a mistake: his left knee buckled unexpectedly, which caused him to grasp the handrail to keep from falling.

"Hey! You all right?" Jeff Robinson asked, alarmed.

"Damned old knee, it never ceases to surprise me." Gritting his teeth, Len slowly stood erect. Grimacing, he flexed the sore knee with some difficulty and began the climb again, slower this time, limping up the old, threadbare stair steps.

Upon reaching the top, his mind began to race, ticking off the usual questions: *Who's the victim? How did it happen? Will anyone know anything?* All questions of which his mind sought answers daily. *Sometimes,* he thought, *this is a totally shitty way to earn a living.*

"Hi, Al," Len said, still grimacing as he limped toward Command Sergeant Alvin Berry, who stood in the second floor hallway. "What have we got?"

"Hey. Hi Len, Jeff. What'd you do, bud? Stub your toe on what's left of the carpeting?"

"No, it's an old college football injury, a long stupid story. What gives here?"

"Well, we got a dead female, a prostitute, mid-to-late thirties, real good-looking little girl, or she was once. She's badly messed up guys, just so you aren't too surprised when you view her."

"Got any gloves, Al?" Len asked, peering past the Sergeant into the crowded room.

"Smithy, gloves? Booties?" One of Berry's younger uniformed officers quickly produced two pair of latex elastic gloves and boots. Len and Jeff Robinson pulled them on and entered the stuffy room where the bloodied victim's body was lying on a blood soaked bed. The ME was making his preliminary examination and a CSI photographer was busy taking still photos of the crime scene.

"Damn!" Jeff Robinson said, turning his face away. "What kind of crazed bastard would do this to another human being?"

Covering his mouth and nostrils with his handkerchief, Len responded, "He must not have enjoyed her company, huh? That or the high price of female companionship these days."

As he stared at the victim, he noted the abnormal amount of blood and gore splattered and cast about the room, especially on the bedding and the cheap carpeting.

"One thing for certain, she didn't have a chance to struggle. It appears that she died on the spot, Robbie, and quickly too. Most of this cutting and ripping of flesh looks to be post mortem to me. Some psycho has a definite problem with women, or at least with this particular woman."

Len looked back and discovered that he was talking to himself. Jeff Robinson was outside, standing in the hallway retching at the rancid, heavy odor of dried blood and the ugly sight of spilled organs and exposed ribs.

"What a mess," Len muttered under his breath. "Any witnesses, Al? Anything at all?"

"No eyewitnesses. We did find a bloody kitchen knife in the back alley. The CSI guys have that; they'll check it out in the lab. We have uniforms out canvassing the other tenants and the neighborhood. We also have a lady friend of the victim, her neighbor. She rents a room down the hall, her 'place of business', you know. Anyway, she reported it to 9-1-1."

"Are we almost through here, Jim?" Len inquired, impatiently looking at Dr. James Franklin, the Assistant Los Angeles County Medical Examiner.

The ME nodded as he removed his plastic gloves and closed his case. "We'll be gone as soon as we get the victim bagged and on the gurney, Lieutenant." Finished packing his equipment, he left the room.

"Al, does everyone else have what they need? Forensics? Photographers?" Len asked, rapid fire, not really expecting an answer. "I've seen all I need, except where is this neighbor woman? I want to speak with her."

"She's outside in one of the squad cars. We took her preliminary statement earlier. CSI is going to be here for a while longer though, lifting prints, and taking hair and fiber samples. I'll hang with them. Lookin' at this place, they may need a truck before they're finished. Follow me," Berry said as he turned to leave the room.

"Robbie, are you all right?" Len asked. Jeff Robinson was still in the hall at the top of the stairs. "You're white as a ghost."

"Right, and you can screw your white ghost. Yeah, I'm okay," he said, removing his plastic throwaway gloves and booties. "If I live to be a hundred I'll never get used to that shit. Sometimes I wonder why I'm in this business at all. I can't stand that kind of mess!"

"None of us can," Len said, favoring his sore knee as he made his way down the stairs. "But someone has to do it. Right?"

"Yeah, yeah ... cake, baby, just a piece of cake."

The two accompanied Sergeant Berry outdoors to a nearby squad car. Len peered inside at a traumatized woman seated on the hard plastic rear seat.

"Good morning, Ma'am, I'm Detective Morgan, Devonshire Hills Valley West precinct. This is my partner, Sergeant Jeff Robinson. Do you mind if we ask a few questions?"

Heavily tanned with long dark hair, she could have played the part of a Hollywood "B" movie slut: a hooker and not a happy hooker at that. As she slowly attempted to exit from the rear seat of the cruiser, her short, tight-fitting leather skirt made preserving her dignity impossible.

As she squirmed her way out of the car, she did her best to avoid disclosing the fact that she was absent any undergarments. Her low cut blouse, damp with perspiration from the growing morning heat, added to her discomfort. It clung to her capacious, unsupported breasts and outlined her prominent nipples.

"Ma'am," Len said, doing his utmost to concentrate only on her eyes, "please, what is your name?"

"Let me interrupt for a second, sir," a young uniformed officer said as he handed a small notepad to Len. "I took her preliminary statement earlier. Here it is, sir."

"Thanks, Officer." Len nodded and smiled at this obviously nervous rookie. *Probably on his first murder case,* he thought, opening the notepad.

"Ma'am, it says here your name is Gloree … Gloree Marie-Saint?" He looked curiously at the nervous, distraught female standing in front of him. "Seriously, is that really your name?"

"Captain Morgan…"

"No, ma'am, it's just Detective Morgan. Please go on…"

"I'm sorry, Detective, no, my real name is Gloria, not Gloree."

"I understand. Do you mind if I call you Gloria?" he asked, speaking quietly in an attempt to calm her shattered psyche. "And what is your real last name, Gloria?"

"Mitchell, Gloria Mitchell. Am I in trouble here Detective, considering what I do for a living?"

"No, Gloria, you aren't in any trouble with us, unless you're the one who murdered your friend."

Upon hearing those unanticipated words, Gloria Mitchell broke down and collapsed backward against the squad car. Jeffrey Robinson, who was closest, caught her just as her knees buckled, "Someone? Get some tissues and water!"

"Please sit down in the front seat out of the sun, ma'am," Len suggested. "Or if you like, we can leave here and go somewhere else, somewhere quiet where we can talk. Maybe you'd be more comfortable at the precinct? Afterward, we can have you driven wherever you want. Don't be concerned about that."

"Oh, yes, please." She began to sob again and took the bottle of water offered by the young police officer. "Thank you. Yes, anywhere, Detective, this is too ghastly here."

Jeff Robinson turned and headed toward their cruiser with Len and Gloria Mitchell following on his heels. At the same time, the ME's contingent brought the victim's body from the hotel.

"I have a hint how you feel, ma'am," Jeff Robinson said, as he opened the rear door for her. "This ain't a fit place for normal folks right now."

Before Len could get in the cruiser, a stout, older man in a baggy suit approached. He panted heavily as he trotted laboriously across the hot asphalt parking lot, a notepad in one hand and a micro-cassette recorder in the other.

"Len, Lieutenant Len Morgan? Got a minute?"

"Oh great, here comes one of our fearless defenders of the first amendment, the local press sleaze." Len stopped beside the passenger side door. "Hi, Seymour, long time. I thought you'd died and gone to reporter heaven or whatever the hell it is. What's up?"

Out of breath and perspiring heavily, the old man stopped and rested a sweaty palm on the front fender of the cruiser. He put his micro-cassette and notepad inside his jacket and pulled a grimy white handkerchief from his back pocket. Wiping his sweaty face, he labored between deep breaths, "I heard you boys had a murder here this morning. What can you tell me, and who's that woman in your cruiser?"

"Well, Seymour, your 'Dick Tracy' police scanner must be working just fine today. Yes, we got us a murder, and all I can tell you is that the victim was a female, name unknown to us at this time. It looks like she was stabbed to death and we have no suspects currently. As always, we'll be more than happy to cooperate with the press and broadcast media in our usual manner. We'll have a press conference when we have any definite information to release."

Nodding toward the nervous female in the cruiser Len added, "This lady back here? She's my dear cousin, Lili, visiting from Ohio. I hope you caught all of that on your micro-cassette. We gotta' go. Get out of the sun, too, you look like shit. Bye-bye."

Len got into the cruiser and slammed the door shut, leaving a frustrated Seymour standing in the hot parking lot. "Get us the hell out of here, Robbie. That fat maggot makes me ill."

The ride back to the Devonshire Hills precinct was somber: no one uttered a word. The only sound was the occasional squawk and static of the police radio, interrupting the silence as they made their way across the hot Valley.

Once there, Jeff Robinson parked inside in the cool shade of the underground facility. The three of them got out of the cruiser and walked to the elevator for the ride to the second floor.

"Len, shall we use the Interview Room?"

"No, let's use our office. It's more relaxed, informal."

Leaving the elevator, they entered the squad room that had been so vibrant and alive earlier, so full of cheer.

What a difference a few hours makes, Len thought as he opened the door to their office, bidding Gloria Mitchell, aka Gloree Marie-Saint, to enter.

"Please have a seat, ma'am. Detective Jeff Robinson, would you bring some coffee and cold water please? Ma'am, we're going to have our Staff Assistant tape record your statement. It's policy. Do you understand what we have to do?"

"Yes, I understand, Detective." She sat quietly as he reached for his intercom.

"Room service," Jeff Robinson announced, pushing a small serving cart into the office. "We have hot black coffee, at least that's what they said it was, and we have ice water, a whole pitcher of it."

"Much obliged," Len replied, nodding at Jeff Robinson. "Please accept our hospitality, Miss Gloria. Coffee? Water?"

"Thank you, Detective," she said, smiling nervously, reaching for a glass of water. "This is some improvement over the parking lot at the hotel. Thank you, you are both so kind."

A rap on the doorjamb interrupted the conversation. In walked a tall, smartly dressed Asian-American female, Mariko Tanaka.

"Hi, Miss Tanaka," Jeff Robinson greeted, rising to his feet. "Coffee, ice water?"

"Thanks no, Detective Jeff Robinson. I just finished my morning break," she replied. Smiling, her sparkling white teeth contrasted with her complexion. She placed the cassette recorder on Len's desk, took a chair and crossed her legs.

"Miss Tanaka will read the Miranda to you, Miss Gloria, explaining your rights. We take this precaution in the event that you might become a suspect. Do you understand this? Do you feel comfortable answering our questions without benefit of legal counsel? If so, Miss Tanaka will be taking some informational data from you."

"Yes ... yes, I have nothing to hide," she answered nervously.

Len cleared his throat and stood unexpectedly, "Please excuse me for a couple of minutes, I'll be right back."

Jeff Robinson nodded. Gloria Mitchell sipped from her water glass and returned Miss Tanaka's smile.

Len returned a few minutes later and took his place behind his desk facing Gloria Mitchell. Jeff Robinson rose to adjust the mini-blinds to soften the bright morning light. "Is that all right? Can everyone see okay? Miss Tanaka?"

"Yes, that's fine," Mariko Tanaka said, nodding and adjusting herself in her chair, crossing her legs again.

"Let me see, Miss Tanaka, what do we have here?" Len asked as he took her legal pad. Scanning it, he quietly repeated the data taken earlier, "Gloria Ann Mitchell, born on four, June, nineteen sixty, Bloomington Heights, Indiana. Current address is Sepulveda Boulevard, Van Nuys. Uh ... we won't list your occupation, ma'am. We'll show you as unemployed and looking for employment, okay?"

"Fine, yes, that's fine," Gloria Mitchell answered, obviously relieved.

"All right, now tell me, what is your friend's name?"

"Her name is Lorena Jeanne Reynolds; at least that's what she told me. Heaven only knows what her real name is. She used the name Noreen le Rae with her clients."

"Fine, we'll have that checked out. Please go on. What other friends or clients did she have that you are aware of? You know, tell us whatever you can about the victim. Take your time, and if you need a restroom facility, Miss Tanaka will be happy to show you the way. We want you to be relaxed, Miss Gloria, it's important that you recall all of the information you can related to the victim. Ready?"

"Yes, I understand, Detective. I've only known her about three years. We are … we were neighbors, I mean in a professional sense, you know; we both rented suites on the same floor of the hotel."

"Yes, Miss Gloria, suites … so do you have any knowledge of who may have been with her earlier today?" Len asked, rubbing his chin.

"I don't know who might have been with her; all I can say is that I stopped by her room this morning to see if she wanted a hot coffee or anything else from the store. I was going down to the corner Seven-Eleven for some stuff. When I didn't get an answer, I tried her door, it was ajar and I entered. I immediately smelled a man's cologne or after-shave lotion. It was a strong, heavy scent, not a feminine fragrance at all. Definitely not Noreen's, she couldn't wear perfume: allergies I guess. Then I … I … saw her lying there."

"Take your time, Miss Gloria."

Len waited a few moments and then asked, "Do you have any idea what brand cologne or after-shave it was? Have you ever smelled it before?"

"No, not really," she answered, "but if I ever smell it again, I'll know it. I do believe that for sure."

"Miss Gloria," Jeff Robinson inquired, "do you know if Noreen had any enemies, or a pimp that may have been a problem for her?"

"No, not that I know of. She was a quiet girl, never had a pimp or any pimp problems. She pretty much minded her own business."

"Miss Gloria, do you know any of her clients by name, or profession, or if they have businesses or are prominent names locally?" Len asked, "Anyone that might stand out?"

"Well, I know she once had a big thing going with that furniture warehouse guy that's on TV all the time. He's the old guy that wears those white cowboy hats in his commercials. He was one semi-regular client that she mentioned. She said when he visited he always left his hat in his car so no one would recognize him."

"Cowboy Faron, the Furniture Baron," Jeff Robinson remarked, grinning. "Old Cowboy, who would have thought?"

"And she had another local businessman, an art collector or dealer that came by about every month or so. He came on to me once or twice a year ... I didn't like him at all."

"Why?" Len asked, more curious than anything.

"He was really mean and kinky, and big too. He was weird."

Len leaned back in his swivel chair and stretched his long arms out above his head. "Do you remember his name?"

"No, only, that he was really quiet and sullen but demanding and arrogant too. He could have a mean temperament, especially if he didn't get what he wanted, or get it the way he wanted it. Come to think of it, he used a dreadful cologne."

"Really?" Len replied, obviously becoming interested in this man. "Do you think it matched the scent that you experienced in your friend's room?"

"I'm sorry, Detectives. I really don't remember."

"Okay, we'll check out the local art dealers and museums and see if we can find this individual."

"Ma'am, might you know where his place of business is located?" Jeff Robinson asked, shifting in his chair. "And you said he was big? Like fat? Or are you referring to his genitalia?"

"Oh, no," she said, apologizing and blushing slightly. "He was just physically bigger, a strong man. And no, I don't know where his business is located."

Continuing she added, "Then, Noreen had another guy that she was hot on. A local radio news talk-show producer named Tommy Breen. He works at KGNZ Talk Radio."

"KGNZ Talk Radio?" Miss Tanaka injected. "I caught that show after I arrived at the precinct this morning."

"What time was that, Miss Tanaka?" Len asked, interested in her information.

"Oh, dear, let me think. I got here at seven-forty ... it was after that."

"When we get an estimated time of death, we can check out Tommy Breen," Len said. "Miss Gloria, is there anything else you can recall that might help us?"

"No, not that I can recall."

"Again, do you have any idea at all who she was with last night?"

"No, I don't know that," Gloria Mitchell answered, wiping some tears from her thick mascara featured eyes, now churned into a dark muddy mess. "I know that she was supposed to have an overnight trick, but I didn't see who it was."

"Fine, I think that's enough for now," Len said, getting to his feet. "Sergeant Jeff Robinson, please drive Miss Gloria wherever she wants to go. Just give him an address, ma'am."

"Thank you, Detective Morgan, you're a decent man," Gloria Mitchell replied as she stood to leave. "Thank you all," she repeated, nodding at Jeff Robinson and Miss Tanaka. Taking the lead, Sergeant Jeff Robinson escorted Gloria Mitchell from the office.

Still standing, Len said, "And thank you, Miss Tanaka, or should I call you Mariko? As your time allows please have a staff steno convert this recording to written notes and then to hard-drive for our electronic files. And assign a case number too?"

"Certainly, Lieutenant Morgan, and please feel free to call me Mariko."

"Thanks. Before you dash away, do you have a minute?" Len asked as he sat back down. "You hired in here recently and I've never taken the opportunity to get acquainted. Do you have some spare time right now?"

"Sure," she responded as she settled back into her chair. "What would you like to know?"

"Well, everything," he said, grinning. "I do know that you graduated summa cum laude ten years ago from Notre Dame du Lac in Indiana with a degree in law so my curiosity is why are you employed in what I'd consider menial labor in our little homicide department?"

Mariko Tanaka smiled broadly. "Detective Morgan, I intend to make law enforcement my life's work. What better way to learn the ropes than to begin at what some might describe as 'the bottom'?"

Her remark caused Len to laugh aloud. He rose from his chair and took a seat on the corner of his desk. "Excuse me, Miss Tanaka, but do you consider our homicide department as 'the bottom'?"

Smiling again, she responded, "At one time when I first hired in I might have thought so, but every day is full of so many unexpected surprises. Working at this level my education is broadening rapidly. No offense intended, sir."

"What did you do after graduating from Notre Dame?"

"Well, I took the summer off and got in some much needed rest here in California with my two older sisters. We live together in Studio City. My college education began at UCLA. Afterward, my wonderful father pulled a couple of strings and I enrolled at Oxford University in London for a year, then back to Notre Dame where I received my juris doctorate."

"Whoa, quite a broad education, I'd say." Len responded.

"Yes. But well worth it."

"What did you do before coming here?"

"I worked two years for the ACLU in the District…"

"The district? In DC? Washington?"

"Yes. Then a college friend referred me to an appellate court Judge in Chicago. I spent four years there as a research clerk and para-legal until he retired in November of 1992. During that time, I took the Illinois bar, passed it, and received my license to practice law. Thanksgiving was coming up so I flew back to California to 'thaw out' during the holidays."

"Timing is everything, yes?"

Mariko Tanaka smiled, "Yes. While in California, I received a telephone call from an all-female law firm back in Chicago offering me a job. They were located in the Sears Tower and represented mostly Democratic state and local politicians."

"How did that work for you, representing politicians?" Len asked, returning to his chair behind his desk.

"I guess it was okay, the pay was good. I think the senior partner may have attended college with Hillary Rodham; every office came furnished with her picture."

"Interesting…"

"You think? Well, I worked there several years until the morning following the disastrous 1994 midterm elections when Speaker Gingrich and the Republicans won about everything in sight. I was working on a brief in my small office and listening to the 'I-man' on my radio. It was late morning and the place was like a tomb; too much commiserating and late night drinking I guess while watching their clients losing their jobs the night before. As Imus broke for a commercial they played Willie Nelson singing, 'Turn out the lights, the party's over'."

With that, Miss Tanaka laughed aloud, "I thought it was funny."

Len smiled, folded his arms and waited to hear the rest of her story.

Gathering herself, she said, "My office door was open and the senior partner-bitch walked in looking like death warmed over. She told me I could 'quit all the uncalled for laughing anytime and turn off the damn radio'."

"And you did what?" Len asked, folding his arms across his chest.

"I complied. I finished the brief, and then typed out my notice of Intent to Quit. It was November again so I sold and gave away my small collection of furniture, jumped in my little lease car and motored back to the Valley."

"That was abrupt, but the timing worked out and you were here with your family during the holidays again. So, what did you do after that?" he asked.

"You are one curious gentleman, sir. I moved in with my two sisters and helped them in their boutique in Studio City. I took the California bar exam during that period, I passed it and hired in here a month ago. Satisfied?"

"That's one remarkable history. Moreover, you are slightly older than I presumed too, but you certainly don't show it. So, what are your real plans, Miss Tanaka? I don't see you being here forever."

She smiled and adjusted her skirt that was creeping up her thighs, "No, this is a stepping stone, and I come from a good gene pool; none of us in my family show our age. What are my plans? I am looking at maybe going over to the DA's office one day: maybe even becoming the DA. Assistant DA Marcia Clark is taking a temporary work leave; maybe she will retire and leave an opening. Maybe later I'll seek the office of State Attorney General. All in good time, sir."

"You have your sights set high enough, Miss Tanaka. And please, forget the 'sir' routine, call me Len. Now, your name appears to be Japanese, but you don't look Asian."

"Yes, my father, Michio Tanaka, is Japanese and a law professor at UCLA. My mother is Samoan. Does that satisfy your curiosity?"

"Ah… Professor Michio Tanaka is your father? I remember him well from my early days at UCLA; a gentleman and a gifted educator. Too, I notice that you aren't wearing a ring. Tell me, are you 'taken' or seeing anyone?"

"My, my, Lieutenant Morgan," she said smiling demurely. "You're certainly a curious chap."

"I'm a detective, Miss Tanaka," Len replied, returning the smile. "I have an inquiring mind."

Miss Tanaka smiled in return. "Obviously. For your information, no, I'm not 'seeing anyone', but I do have my eyes on a possibility." With that, she asked, "Is there anything else today?"

"No, not really, except I think the individual you are 'eyeing' is a very fortunate fellow. Thank you, Miss Tanaka," Len said as he got to his feet, "I appreciate your taking this time with me."

"Not so fast, Lieutenant, if you have the time, please tell me a little something about you."

"Really? Me? I'd be happy to." And he sat back down.

"I'm a Midwestern meat-and-potatoes farm boy from Wisconsin. I grew up on my grandparents' farm. The military listed my dad as MIA in the Korean conflict following General MacArthur's invasion of Inchon, so Mom and I moved in with her folks. Granddad taught me how to farm and to sail; that's the current love of my life. I married young and we had a baby girl. My wife died in an auto accident soon afterward…"

"Oh, I'm so sorry," Miss Tanaka said, interrupting.

Continuing, Len said, "My sister-in-law and her hubby, both wonderful people, adopted the baby and I came out here and enrolled in the LA police academy, later in community college, a few semesters later at UCLA where I received a degree in law enforcement."

Miss Tanaka smiled and nodded in agreement.

"I remarried after that, it didn't work out so we divorced soon afterward … amiably I might add. She is still a good friend today."

"How good?" Mariko asked, smiling inquisitively.

"Not *that* good…." Len answered, almost choking on his words. "She's a local defense attorney and widow of one of my best friends. Her name is Carole Bullock."

"I've heard of her…"

"Moving along," he said, "as a kid, the 1960s Dragnet television series with Jack Webb as Detective Joe Friday, totally consumed me. My life's ambition was to become a Los Angeles cop. That dream came true twenty-five years ago."

"Interesting, and you've been here since?"

"That's right, anything else? If you don't mind, Miss Tanaka, we can continue this chat later over coffee. Right now I have to catch a murderer."

"Continuing anytime is fine," she said with a smile, tucking her note pad under her arm and reaching for the cassette recorder. "Thank you for the chat, Lieutenant Morgan. Good luck now." Still smiling, she returned to her desk.

Len watched her as she left. *How fortunate we are*, he thought.

Still Wednesday, June 5...

Alone in his office, Len leaned back in his swivel chair and wondered which of the three individuals named by Gloria Mitchell might be the type to slaughter a woman.

The ringing of the telephone broke his train of thought. It was Assistant Medical Examiner Franklin. "Len? These are preliminary findings, more to come. The estimated time of death was thirty minutes either side of five-thirty this morning. The cause of death, in layman's terms, was an initial puncture of the heart muscle by a long, narrow blade knife; probably the bloody knife found in the back alley, it fits the wound perfectly."

"Okay, so it's the murder weapon?" Len suggested.

"Almost a certainty. After the initial wound to the heart, you saw the result of the multiple slashing strokes across the throat, chest, and abdomen. Death was almost instantaneous, which explained the condition of the body and the blood soaked bed."

The ME continued, "Our computer search has failed to reveal any modus operandi to similar crime scenes on file in Los Angeles or in Southern California. Records are currently being sought from our neighboring states and FBI files."

"The blood type on the kitchen knife found did match that of the victim," the ME added. "Our autopsy is still in progress. We didn't find any usable fingerprints on the knife, just smudges. I hope that CSI, still at the crime scene, can ascertain something usable. When more information is available I'll let you know and send a written report."

"Thanks, Doc, I appreciate your prompt action on this matter. I know how busy you folks get down there. Thanks again, I'll talk to you later." Len hung up just as Sergeant Jeffrey Robinson arrived.

"Hey! I called KGNZ Talk Radio earlier," Jeff Robinson announced. "Talk-show producer Tommy Breen was at the radio station before five o'clock and his program aired live until nine.

He didn't leave the station until nearly eleven. What does that do for him?"

"It leaves him out of the loop for one thing," Len answered. "But I still want to talk to him, to maybe glean more information about the victim; you know, the normal stuff."

"Okay … but on the way out in the elevator we did have one little issue, unless you are aware of it already…"

"Issue?" Len exclaimed, interrupting. "What issue? What are you talking about?"

"We ran into Detective Lanny Boyle from vice. He recognized our witness and wanted to know what the hell she was doing in homicide. I suggested that he talk to you if he had any questions. He wasn't too happy with me or my answer. Did he find you?" Jeff Robinson asked

"No, and if he does, he won't be happy with me or my answer either. What was Miss Gloria's reaction?"

"She became really shook up, panicked, maybe thinking he was going to put a pinch on her. I got her to calm down afterward and she's cool now."

"Good, good job. So, Jeffrey," Len said, grinning, "how broad is your knowledge of fine furniture? You and Colleen have a house full and did you buy any of it from Cowboy Faron, the Furniture Baron?"

"You know, I really don't like it that much when you call me Jeffrey. I always end up with some nasty-ass job or a stupid errand to run. What is it this time?"

"I'd like you to visit the Furniture Baron's outlet," Len answered. "Check him out and see if he knows any of the victim's friends or customers. Pull sheets on him, and the radio news producer guy too. We'll need lots of paper in this case-file fast. If Dutch gets a burr in his ass we'll have ours covered for a while. Also, the murderer needed a way to and from the murder scene. Delegate Miss Tanaka to obtain copies of all taxi fare records for the six hours prior to and after six o'clock today."

"Check. I'm on my way."

"And Robbie, when you are talking to Cowboy Faron, see if he appears physical enough to have possibly done this thing? As you know, this perpetrator must have been a big, crazed bastard."

"Got it," Jeff Robinson said, "And I'll take a run back over to the crime scene too, to see if CSI has found anything useful."

"Never mind that, Robbie, I'll go back over."

Len organized his small desk and then went out to the squad room to see if anyone had a spare car--no takers. Visiting the motor pool, he checked out a cruiser and drove back to the Valley Arms Hotel.

As he climbed the winding hotel stairs again, he paused for a moment on the first landing and rested his aching knee. "Too many stair steps today. Damn."

Command Sergeant Al Berry, still overseeing the operation, met him again on the second floor.

"Al, did you take lunch?"

"Uh … no," Berry grunted. "I can't eat during one of these grisly messes, Len, it's too crazy. I just wait until I'm home, showered and cleaned up. You know."

"Yeah, figures." Len placed his hand on Berry's broad shoulder and asked, "Do you have time to go over a couple of details with me?"

"Sure, no problem. Where do we start?"

At the same time the CSI forensics team was still in the hotel room nitpicking, intently going over the carpeting and bedding for stray hairs and fibers, seeking an errant clue that could be instrumental in identifying the perpetrator, to place him in that room.

"Berry, who were the first officers on the scene after the hooker discovered the body and called 9-1-1? Are they still around?"

"I think it was the young rookie, uh … you know, the fresh-lookin' kid you got the initial report from this mornin'. He and his partner were on traffic patrol when the call hit the streets. They were less than a block away."

"Curious. So, why did the rookie take the statement from the hooker? Why not his partner, the obvious veteran?"

"The older vet stood by the door," Berry explained, chuckling. "Guardin' the place, not lettin' anyone in. You know, protectin' the crime scene until the criminologist teams and the ME arrived. That left the rookie to take her statement. What's true is, the vet knew if he took the statement he would be in paperwork up to his ass for a month of Sundays. Clever old fart, huh?"

"Apparently," Len said, chuckling. "Where are they now, back on the streets?"

"Probably, or gettin' some cop food at the local doughnut shop. That's where the VWPD lives," Berry joked. "You know the routine, if you need a cop in a hurry, don't call 9-1-1, call The Donut Hole in Chatsworth."

"No shit. Well, I'll have Dispatch get them back here. I have a question for whichever of them has a good nose, whichever of them is the bloodhound."

Still favoring his sore knee, Len went back down the stairway and radioed Dispatch. The vet and the rookie were quickly located and ordered back to the hotel. Len also caught Jeff Robinson on the radio en route from the Furniture Baron's outlet. "What did you come up with, Robbie? Anything we can use?"

"Well, the furniture Baron, Cowboy Faron, is old enough to be your daddy, that's one thing. If he had a hankering for a filly like the victim, all the good it probably did him was in his mind. Also, he couldn't rip his way out of a wet paper bag if he had help. Anyway, he furnished us with a few referrals from the victim, some of her associates or friends she'd sent to the Baron's outlet to make furniture purchases. I have those names and addresses in my pocket. What's new with you?"

"I'm waiting for those two traffic officers we met to get back here so I can verify again what they might have smelled in that room. After that, I'll meet you back at the precinct."

"Do those traffic cops know you're driving on the public streets, probably with an expired operator's license, huh, Len? Len? Do they?" Jeff Robinson asked in mock seriousness.

"I don't know, Robbie, unless you told 'em."

"Right," Jeff Robinson snorted. "Leave you alone for a minute and dementia sets in."

"Anyway, get back to your desk and work on those referrals. I'll catch you later. Clear."

"See ya', bye. Clear."

At that moment, the rookie and the vet pulled into the hotel parking lot. Len stepped from his cruiser and waved them over, "Stay in the car where it's cool boys, this will only take a minute. Which one of you went into the victim's room first?"

The veteran officer looked at his young partner before answering. "We sort of entered simultaneously, sir, or Duane here was just a step behind me. We went in together, why?"

Len leaned his forearms against the roof of the cruiser and asked, "Did both of you catch a scent of cologne or after-shave lotion when you entered the room?"

The veteran officer shook his head slowly, trying to recall. "Not me, sir, not that I can recall. I guess I was too busy looking at the victim."

"Sir, Lieutenant Morgan," the rookie spoke. "I noticed the odor but I thought it belonged in the room. You know, like the old stories you hear of 'smelling like a two-bit-whore'. I smelled something like a heavy, sweet perfume, or maybe it was after-shave. Yes, sir, I did."

"Good. That's good, officer. You say it was heavy, sweet?"

Concentrating, the young officer said, "Well, sir … to me it was noxious. Really sweet if you know what I'm saying, like lilacs or some other flowery fragrance, but heavier."

"Sounds disgusting," Len said. "I'm sorry, Officer Duane, I can't read your name-tag from here. Do you have a last name?"

The well-built young rookie appeared to be in his late twenties, with dark hair and eyes and a smile that radiated. "Officer Duane Josephs, sir. Obliged to help you, sir, thank you."

"Josephs, huh? How long out of the academy?"

"Not long enough, sir," Josephs' partner volunteered, laughing at his homemade joke at the rookie's expense.

"That's true, sir," added the rookie, who aimed a solid backhand shot at his partner's shoulder. "Not long enough."

"All right," Len said, standing upright. "Thank you both. You boys get on outta' here. Be safe; write those citations. And Officer Josephs, you'll probably be hearing from me again."

The vet and the rookie waved a half salute and drove away.

Len turned back and saw Sergeant Berry leaving the hotel and waved goodbye, "Thanks again Al, I'll give you a sparkling commendation in my report."

As he drove back across the Valley to the precinct, Len found himself wondering if his operator's license really had expired. *What a cruel joke that would be,* he thought.

He returned the cruiser to the motor pool and took the elevator upstairs to his office where he found Jeffrey Robinson busy on the telephone, "Hey, partner, what's happenin'?"

Hanging up the phone, Jeff Robinson replied, "I got your rap sheets on Faron and Breen, nothing much there, clean, ordinary stuff. Here, see for yourself."

Len took a seat behind his desk and examined the papers. He looked at them carefully, rubbing his chin as he did, this time feeling the beard stubble peeking through. *Shaving at five o'clock in the morning makes for a grubby detective by mid-afternoon.*

"Robbie, did you contact Breen, the radio guy?"

"No, I've been workin' on the names Faron gave me, the referrals from the hooker and the furniture purchasers. Do you want me to call him?"

"No, I'll call him if the number you have is still current." Reaching for his phone, he entered the unlisted number. Len idly tapped his fingers on his desk as he waited while the telephone continued to ring on the other end.

"Hello," a man's voice answered.

"Hello, Tommy Breen? This is Detective Lieutenant Morgan, Devonshire Hills, Valley West precinct."

"Who? How did you get my number?" Tommy Breen demanded. "Why are you calling me?"

"Let me repeat, I'm Homicide Detective Morgan, Devonshire Hills precinct. We have a fresh homicide on our hands, Mister Breen, and we'd like to ask you a few questions."

"Homicide? What homicide? How am I involved? What is this … like, you know, a joke?"

"Mister Breen, I don't joke all that much about homicides. We have a murdered hooker in the Sepulveda district. We have information from a reliable source that you knew her. We merely want to speak with you, that's all."

"Hooker? I don't know no hookers," Breen said excitedly, "You know … like I don't know any hookers!"

Len sighed. "Mister Breen … a highly reliable source has named you as a frequent client of the murder victim. I must advise you that giving me false or misleading information is a prosecutable offense. Do you get my drift, Mister Breen?"

"Yes … sir. I know that," he said, swallowing hard. "Do you, you know … know the victim's name?"

"Yes. We know the victim's name, Mister Breen," Len said, shaking his head in mock desperation as he looked across his desk at an increasingly interested and amused Jeff Robinson. "Sir, will you be coming in here voluntarily or must we send a car?"

"Uh … when do you want me to come in? Like today?"

"Yes. *Like* today would be just ducky, Mister Breen, within the hour in fact. Ask at the front lobby for Detective Morgan, Homicide Unit. All right?"

"Yes, sir, I'll be right over. It may take some time, like the afternoon traffic … you know."

"Yes, I know. *Like* the afternoon traffic in the Valley is always tough, but drive safely. We'll be waiting for you."

Slightly annoyed, Len leaned back in his swivel chair, stretched his arms out behind his head and looked across the desks at his partner.

"Tell me, why do some folks have to make things so tough on themselves? He could have answered any question I had on that phone and been done with it. Instead, he got his dander up and tried to be a smart ass."

Jeff Robinson smiled. "But, you enjoyed your little power trip didn't you? You know you did."

"Eh ... I suppose. Maybe. Do you think it was my inner-child wanting a piece of the so-called free press? Wanting to give them some of the same shit they tend to give us at times?"

"Well, you asked him some basic questions, the one word answer variety," Jeff Robinson suggested. "Instead, he elected to avoid them. Now he gets to sweat it out. Further, he gets to visit us and experience our world famous hospitality and our fabulous three-day-old high viscosity coffee. You gotta' offer him the coffee, Len."

"That could border on the cruel and unusual," Len said, snickering at Jeff Robinson's suggestion. "Take my calls, I gotta' pee again; too much coffee today. I'll be right back."

"Sure," Jeff Robinson answered.

Returning minutes later Len sat down just as Jeff Robinson discovered something of interest in the yellow pages of the Valley directory.

"Hey, Boss! Here's an art museum out on Ventura. What do you think? Something to look into tomorrow?"

"Sure. Call the place. Make certain the owner or manager will be there first thing. Maybe we'll check out some rare art treasures."

"Gotcha."

At that moment, a slightly built, bespectacled little man knocked on the jamb of the open door and peeked in.

"Yes?" Len said, looking up.

"I'm Tommy Breen," the little man said nervously. "Are you Detective Morgan?"

"Yes, come in, Mister Breen," Len said, smiling and standing. He gestured toward an empty chair next to his desk as he keyed his intercom. "Miss Tanaka, will you join us again, and bring in the cassette recorder? Thanks."

Len looked at Tommy Breen, "Please have a chair, sir. Sergeant Jeff Robinson, would you pour Mister Breen some coffee?"

"Oh, no thanks," Breen protested as he took a seat.

"But we insist." Jeff Robinson said, smiling broadly, as he filled a mug with the hot steaming brew from a nearby cart. "I'm Sergeant Jeffrey Robinson, Mister Breen. We tune in to KGNZ; 'Good News' radio all the time. You folks do a fine job!"

"Thanks," Breen said, looking suspiciously at the hot steaming coffee placed nearby on the corner of Len's desk. "It's a pleasure to meet you too … I think."

Miss Tanaka entered quietly, handed Len the recorder and resumed sitting in her previous chair.

"Mister Breen," Len said, staring incredulously at Jeff Robinson, who was still smirking. "Uh … we called you in because a reliable source named you as a client of a Noreen le Rae, the victim of a grisly murder this morning in the Sepulveda district. Can you elaborate on, or describe for us, the depth of your relationship with Miss le Rae?"

Breen's jaw dropped and his complexion suddenly turned pale. "What? Lorena? Murdered? Oh, no, it can't…" his voice trailed off.

Saying nothing, Len leaned back in his swivel chair and quietly watched the visibly shaken radio producer and waited for a further response.

"I … I didn't … know; like you know. I don't…" Breen stammered.

Still not speaking, Len waited, keeping his focus on the devastated Mr. Breen. Jeff Robinson sat quietly, watching Len who quietly continued to watch Breen fidget.

With tears welling in his eyes, Breen finally replied, "Officer! I can't believe this is happening! You can't possibly suspect me. I mean, do you? I couldn't, you know … murder anyone."

Remaining silent, Len didn't respond.

"Lorena was my ... my ... she and I had a good thing, you know, we really enjoyed our time together. We were more than ... shit, I can't believe this." As he sobbed, he reached in his pocket for his handkerchief.

Jeff Robinson leaned forward in his chair slightly, staring at Len in anticipation of a response of some kind.

After several more seconds, Len broke the silence. "Mister Breen, we don't suspect you of anything. Especially the murder of your friend Noreen, or Lorena, as you refer to her. Take your time. Would you like some cold water, a cigarette, anything?"

"Oh, man," Breen said, shaking his head in disbelief. "When did this, you know ... happen? Where did it happen?"

"She was murdered in her hotel room early this morning while KGNZ Talk Radio was broadcasting your show. We've checked you out. You're in the clear. Are you familiar with the hotel?"

"Yes, I know where she lives...."

"Mister Breen, we need to know everything about Noreen, or Lorena, that you are aware of. It doesn't matter how tiny or insignificant, everything, okay?"

"Well," Breen said, "you know ... we were lovers, we had been for the last couple of years."

"And?"

"We were lovers. That's it. She, you know ... she loved me too, but she wouldn't take my money though. I really loved her, but I couldn't be open and public about it. I would have been, you know... ostracized, probably ruined professionally, like if the other radio stations had ever found out. I may be out of work if this conversation ever hits the streets."

"We're sorry for that," Len said as he looked at the distraught little man. "Obviously, we don't have a way to put a lid on everything that goes on in this town as you well know, but we'll do our best to keep your name out of the news."

Continuing, he asked, "Mister Breen, do you know of any of her other clients or customers besides yourself?"

"No, not really," Breen answered, taking a short sip of the hot, day old coffee. Choking on it slightly, he said, "She never, you know … we never discussed her profession."

"So she never mentioned any of them to you?"

"No, never. All I can add is that she was planning to get out of the business soon. She had been putting most of her earnings away, investing it she said. She was going to move up to the Bay area soon and open a bed-and-breakfast with a friend of hers, Gloree Saint-James or somebody, you know … as soon as they saved more money."

"Gloree Marie-Saint?" Suddenly interested in this new information Len nearly left his chair. His abrupt outburst startled Miss Tanaka.

"Tell me more about Gloree Marie-Saint, Mister Breen," Len insisted, settling back into his chair. "Please continue."

"Yeah. Well, I think that was, you know, her name. They were tight, close friends. I guess as close as two friends in that business can be. Who knows? What a damn shame," he said, looking at the floor. "I just can't believe any of this is happening."

"What more did she ever say about her new business venture in the Bay area?"

"Nothing except that she was eager to move."

"Did she ever mention how much money she and Gloree were putting away or needed to open; anything like that?"

"Detective, all she said was, you know … that it wouldn't be too long before she could go legit… you know … her and Gloree. Like getting out of it… the business."

Len glanced at Jeff Robinson, then back at Breen. Abruptly pushing his chair away from his desk, he stood. "Thank you, Mister Breen. You've been extremely helpful here today. We're deeply sorry for your loss, so please accept our condolences and our sincere apologies for having to break the news of this tragedy to you like this."

"Detective, it's probably better to find it out from you than to, you know … to suddenly have it handed to you, live, or while on the air," Breen said as he got to his feet. "I don't know what I would have done in that case. Thanks again."

"I suppose," Len replied, nodding soberly in agreement. "That would have been a terrible shock, and uncomfortable for sure. Have a good day, sir, and be careful driving in your frame of mind. We'll be in touch if need be, like there are things we still don't know, you know?"

"Uh ... yeah." Breen said, looking quizzically at Len. "Well, okay ... goodbye." Then, nodding at Jeffrey Robinson and Miss Tanaka, Breen left the room.

Jeff Robinson again stared incredulously at Len. Shaking his head, he said, "Damn, man, you are really something else, you know? Like, you know?"

"Robbie, don't let our Miss Gloria get out of the city. Have her brought in right now!" Len demanded. "The lying whore! This is taking a devious little twist. And too, you know ... like if Breen had said 'you know' and 'like' one more time I'd have put the cuffs on him."

Miss Tanaka, standing now, stifled a laugh.

"Check," Jeff Robinson said, biting his tongue, the telephone already in his hand. "Are you thinking Gloree, or whatever the hell her name is, was involved in this now?"

"Robbie, the taxpayers pay us a lot of money to be suspicious assholes. There has to be a batch of money involved here if two ladies of the night are going to open a new bed-and-breakfast business in San Francisco; it sure as hell can't be done with pennies.

"And, if one person instead of two is privy to a large batch of money ... that makes twice as much for the one. Damn right, the bitch is involved! She has some additional questions to answer. So, she doesn't like our lockup or Vice Detective Boyle? Okay, fine. Maybe we'll lock her up anyway. At least that will keep her in town and we'll know where she is."

Jeff Robinson nodded in agreement.

"Find her, Robbie get her back here!" Len ordered.

Jeff Robinson nodded again and telephoned Command Dispatch to issue an immediate APB for Gloree Marie-Saint, aka Gloria Mitchell.

Turning to his Staff Assistant, Len said, "Miss Tanaka, please request the DA to obtain a warrant for any bank records or any financial information connected to both Noreen le Rae, aka Lorena Reynolds, and of Gloria Mitchell, aka Gloree Marie-Saint. Thanks."

"Yes, sir," she responded and went back to her desk.

With Jeff Robinson off the phone and Ms. Tanaka busy at her desk, the room was quiet now. Staring blankly at one another, Jeffrey Robinson and Len Morgan sat not moving. "Call it a day? Give it hell tomorrow?" Len suggested, looking back at Jeff Robinson.

"You bet, Boss. Is ol' Dutch still here? Do we need to feed him any paper work today?"

"Screw Dutch," Len whispered as he stood and reached for his coat.

"Not me, you screw him. I'm saving myself for my Colleen."

As they left the office for the parking garage, Len smiled. "Still tryin' to make a baby, huh?"

"Yep," Jeff Robinson answered as he got the car. "We try and try and try."

"Maybe if you'd stop wearing those silly designer condoms you could get her pregnant," Len suggested, still smiling.

Jeff Robinson laughed. "Yeah, but what about the disease risk? If I contracted an STD and was disabled or worse, what would you do for a partner?"

"STD? From your wife? Mercy, you are impossible," Len snorted as he buckled in. "Anyway, I've already found my next homicide partner: that Duane kid from Traffic. A green-as-grass rookie with a brain."

"That's bullshit too," Jeff Robinson grunted. "You could never get through a day without me and you know it."

"Yeah, I guess," Len sighed. "Besides, the rookie doesn't know the way to my condominium and I'd be put through that basic training process again. Forget it. You're safe for now."

Jeff Robinson pulled the big Ford cruiser up in front of Len's building. "Well, get out, asshole, I got *work* to take care of on the home front. See you in the morning."

"Later," Len said, laughing as he departed.

He entered into the foyer of Villa Casa Grande and checked his mailbox. He sorted out the junk mail and threw it in the nearby refuse container.

Home at last, home at last, he sighed. *Now for another boring evening of network TV to put me away until five-thirty tomorrow morning.*

Opting to take the wide carpeted stairs that led to his second floor abode, he noted that his knee felt almost normal again. "Damn football," he grumbled.

As he walked past Sara Dunlap's unit, the commotion and loud arguing that had been going on that morning had stopped. The only sound he heard was his own breathing after climbing the stairs, that and the soft sound of the carpeting beneath his shoes. He put his key in the lock, let himself in and disarmed the security system.

Wonder of wonders, the old system is actually working today.

Not hungry, he tossed his coat on the sofa, kicked his shoes off and sat down, stretching out in his favorite chair: an over-sized, well-upholstered soft leather recliner: a Christmas surprise from Gabrielle.

Len chuckled to himself, remembering how they had attempted to make love in it the night it was delivered, it didn't work too well he remembered. *So I carried her into the bedroom and we completed what we had started.* Reliving that blissful night in his mind, he smiled sleepily as his eyes became heavy and drowsy. Soon he was dreaming.

Late Wednesday, end of day 1, June 5...

Startled from a sound sleep, Len sat bolt upright in his recliner. "What the hell was that?" He listened intently, thinking he'd heard a gunshot. Still mentally thick and drowsy from the nap he wasn't certain what he'd heard, if he'd heard anything at all.
BAM!
There it was again! Not a gun shot, but something hard hitting a wall in Sara Dunlap's quarters next door, followed by the too familiar sounds of loud screaming and yelling followed by yet another loud crash!

"That's enough," he muttered, leaping from his chair.

Leaving his condominium he ran next door to Sara's where the arguing and noise from inside were becoming louder and more pronounced. Len concluded that it was her boyfriend, Armando. His voice was unmistakable; Sara was crying.

Hammering on her door with his beefy fist, Len shouted, "Sara! Armando! Open this door! Right now!"

His pounding created a sudden, complete silence from within, no further sounds of violence, no further arguing heard.

"Sara, I know you're in there and I know who's with you!" Len shouted. "Now open this goddamn door or I'll break it down and arrest both of you!"

The door opened and a pale, meek Armando, obviously shaken by the unexpected interruption, greeted Len. "Hey, man, chill. Everything's cool...."

"Oh, screw you!" Len grunted and let fly with a left hook that caught Armando squarely in the mouth. The force of the blow sent him lurching backwards. His head glanced off the edge of Sara's heavy wooden coffee table on his way to the floor.

"Where's Sara?" Len shouted, standing over him. "…I said, where's Sara?"

"I'm back here, Len," a tear filled voice answered from the dark hallway to his left. "I'm right here. Make him go away, please make him leave."

Len looked at Armando, who was still on the floor. With his blood pressure rising, Len merely pointed at the open door.

Armando slowly got up from the floor. Feeling his bruised jaw, he said nervously, "Chill, dude, I'm outta' here…."

"You can shut the hell up while you're at it!" Len roared, clenching his fists, resisting the urge to pummel Armando's face again. "Now get out!"

A terrified and much subdued Armando nodded and hastily left. Len slammed the door behind him and turned to the weeping Sara.

"Sara, what's going on here?" he asked, looking at her bruised face. "That piece of shit struck you, didn't he?"

Standing in the dark hallway, she covered her face with her hands and sobbed. "Len, he's been terrible the last three days. Tonight was the worst, I can't believe this…."

Len went to her and carefully put his arms around her shoulders, he held her tightly, soothing her as best he could, rubbing her back through her soft, chenille robe.

"Sara, come over to my place and I'll fix you a stiff drink, or some hot tea or chocolate, something to allow your nerves to settle. What the hell time is it anyway?"

Still sobbing, she said, "Oh, Len, you're too sweet. You don't need to look after me, I'll be all right."

Len glanced at his wristwatch, it was 8:30 "No, Sara, please now… you're coming over to my place for a while and at least get calmed down. Come along."

With her eyes swollen from the crying and her lower lip split from one of Armando's blows, she managed a crooked smile, "Thanks, Len, I'm okay. Just let me sit down and catch my breath."

Len sat down beside her on the sofa.

"I'm sorry, Len," she said, embarrassed. "I'm just jumpy. It's been terrible the past few days; I didn't know where to turn or what to do."

"Well, it's over now, I'll personally guarantee that."

"I hope I don't need to see a doctor or go to the ER. Do I? Am I really messed up?"

"Let me see." He took her chin in his hand and slowly turned her head to the right and back. "He got you pretty good, Sara. You have some bruising and discoloration, that bottom lip is split a little. Damn it! I should have just gone ahead and arrested him. I can have his ass in jail in ten minutes on a 235 if that's what you want!"

"Len, no. I don't want him arrested. All I want is him out of my life, gone."

"That's easily enough arranged," Len said, "I still wish I'd arrested the bum."

Sara looked hard into Len's blue eyes, then moved forward and lightly kissed his cheek. "Thanks, my hero," she whispered.

They sat quietly for a few seconds, then Len broke the silence, "Sara, do you mind telling me what caused this ruckus?"

"Oh dear ... where do I start? Well ... I've dated Armando for some time, but lately he has been an impossible jerk. Second, he doesn't have a job or any way to earn any money so his income is spotty, putting it mildly. That's his problem, and mine."

"What did he want? Money?" Len asked.

"No, not really. He wanted me to arrange for him to get a major credit card through my bank where I work as a commercial account manager. He said that with a major credit card he could make deals: deals that required quick cash. Quick turnover, low risk, quick profit deals he called them. He never explained what they were; you know, the deals ... drugs or what."

"Where does he live?" Len asked.

"I don't know exactly, somewhere near Chatsworth, or in Canoga Park west of here. He hangs out in a pool hall down on Sherman Way. That's where he and his Cholo friends do their thing, I guess."

"Anyway," Sara continued, "tonight I told him it was impossible for me to arrange a credit card. It was simply out of the question."

"And?"

"And he freaked out. He's been pissed at me for the last three days, you know the routine. We bitches are expected to roll over and die if we don't perform as expected. Now he says I don't love him. Well, now I realize that maybe I never did. He only wanted me around because I had money and would pay for our dates. It was always about the money."

"Screwin' loser. Sorry, Sara. I deal with these sorry assholes nearly every day of my life, they're worthless. Are you certain you don't want to press charges? I can still have him picked up. He'll do time, I guarantee that."

"I don't want him arrested, Len, I just want him to leave me alone. I don't want him over here anymore, ever."

Len nodded. "He won't bother you anymore, Sara, believe me."

Looking more at ease, Sara smiled, "Thanks Len, you are a dear. I'm so fortunate to have a good neighbor like you. You go home, I'll be fine. Thanks for intervening."

"Anytime," Len said. "Sleep well."

As he left, he thought, *Why didn't she want that scumbag arrested? People, I'll never figure them out.*

He went to his bathroom, brushed his teeth and undressed. Stark naked after having tossed his clothes on the chair, he dove into the cool sheets of his awaiting bed to sleep, and to dream the dreams usually reserved for younger men.

Day 2, Thursday, June 6...
Morning came too soon. Len was still groggy when he called Jeff Robinson to verify his ride to the precinct. "Hey! Robbie, hurry up! I may fall asleep down there on the street. Get your big butt over here."

"Yo ... I'll be right there. See ya, bye."

Jeffrey Robinson pulled up in front of the condominium right on time.

"Must have shined that traffic light this morning, huh?" Len asked, getting into the big Ford cruiser.

Jeff Robinson nodded and winked.

"Robbie, I've got an extracurricular chore I need to handle before we go to the precinct. Drive over to Bugsy's Pool Hall on Sherman Way."

"Say what? Did old Bugsy produce a suspect?" Jeff Robinson asked as he pulled away. "Someone else to add to our murder suspect list?"

"No," Len muttered as he stared out the window watching the storefronts flying by. "It's a personal thing, nothing to do with Bugsy or suspects, just a piece-of-shit *Cholo* pool hustler who was beating on my neighbor last night. I want to reintroduce myself to his ass, unofficially of course. Get my drift?"

Jeff Robinson smiled and nodded, "Uh … I think so."

As they parked in front of the pool hall, Len unbuttoned his suit coat and removed his gun and shield. Stowing them carefully in the glove compartment he said, "Robbie, make sure this cruiser is locked." Satisfied, Len got out of the car and strode into the smoke-filled pool parlor. Jeff Robinson followed.

"Hey, Bugs, long time!" Len said, greeting his old friend. "How's it going? You stayin' outta' trouble?"

Bugsy, the wrinkle-faced owner of the old pool-billiard parlor looked up from his morning Valley Press newspaper and smiled a toothless smile. "Len! Long time, son, how'ya been?"

"Fine, Bugs, just fine. Listen, there's probably a punk I'm looking for and he may be in here … yeah, there he is, Armando. I'm going to have a 'fatherly' chat with him, citizen to citizen," Len explained.

Leaning closer to Bugsy, Len whispered, "He's probably not going to be back in here spending his time and money for a while, okay Bugs?"

"Hey, just do what you have to do, son. He's a pissy little weasel anyway. Makes no never mind to me, take him down for all I give a shit."

Leaving Jeff Robinson behind, Len strode to the back of the poolroom. The place reeked heavily of stale tobacco smoke and spilled beer. *Lord, what a helluva place to visit before breakfast.*

"Hey!" Len yelled at a very confused Armando, who saw him approaching, "Let's smoke...."

"Wha... what?" Taken by surprise by Len's sudden appearance, Armando quickly looked around to see if his *cholo* buddies were available to lend some possible support.

"Armando, what do I have to do with you?" Len asked, a sweet fake smile plastered on his face. Still smiling, Len stepped in front of Armando, who was slouched on the corner of a pool table, his hands jammed deep inside his baggy pants.

"Hey cop, I'm minding my own business here. Anyone can see that. Right *muchachos*?" he asked, smiling weakly, faking bravado to his pals.

"Really, Armando?" Len reached for a pool stick from the table to his left, "Mind your business on this!"

In one sweeping motion, Len swung the heavy end of the wooden cue stick from the smooth green tabletop and struck Armando solidly across the side of his head, knocking him to the floor. The force of the blow caused the stick to break in half; the butt-end flew across the nearly empty room and clattered noisily to the floor. Len stood menacingly over the fallen Armando, and then he turned and glared at the *cholos* who stared back at him in silent disbelief.

"*Ven aqui, Vatos*," Len invited, gesturing menacingly with the splintered end of the cue stick. "*Por favor*, I'd be more than happy to give you some lumps too."

They collectively shook their heads and backed away; leaving Len with a terrified Armando sprawled on the floor with his head bleeding.

"Get up you piece of dog shit, I'm not through with you."

Len reached down and grabbed a fistful of Armando's baggy plaid shirt. He easily lifted him and threw him back against a pool table.

"You're worse than dog shit, you stupid bastard, you're day-old dog shit. You're worthless, you make me sick!"

Armando cowered, confused and wide eyed, paralyzed with fear. Len merely glared at him and whispered quietly, "…just one more thing."

"Yeah, wha…what?" Armando was barely able to look at him.

"Stay away from Sara Dunlap! If you value your shriveled *cojones* you'll stay the hell away from her or I'll be back and stuff this stick up your silly ass. *Comprehendes*?"

Armando nodded. Len looked back at the still startled *cholos* and smiled. Satisfied, he turned away, buttoned his coat and nodded to Jeff Robinson to head for the door.

"Thanks Bugs, I needed that," Len said. Patting Bugsy's shoulder, he handed him a crisp one hundred-dollar bill and the splintered end of the cue stick. "This is for any damages, and for your recollection of what never took place here. See you around, thanks."

In the car, Jeff Robinson broke the silence. "Day-old dog shit? Very impressive. Good work in there too."

"Screw you, Robbie. It just came out of my mouth. Dammit! I hate scum like that. He beat up my neighbor Sara Dunlap last night. Day-old dog shit is too complimentary. I almost think I wanted to kill that little bastard just now."

"Right," Jeff Robinson observed, nodding in agreement. "…and that's always a good way to start the day too; expose your latent psychotic tendencies early on and get it over with. But right this minute, with you sittin' there all calm and smiling, if you had a candy sucker in your mouth and a snap-brimmed velour hat you'd be Telly Sevalas, huh? So screw this shit, Len, I'm starving. Let's radio in then go somewhere and get some eggs and toast before we visit that art museum. Sound like a plan?"

"Yes!" Len readily agreed, adjusting his coat and seat belt. "I'm hungry as hell too, let's do it!"

"So, 'Telly'," Jeff Robinson continued as he made a left turn toward Ventura Boulevard, "where shall we stop? At Abbe's, Soleh's or Lenny's?"

"It's Denny's, idiot!" Len snorted, correcting him. "Stupid shit, you're as goofy as that old woman in their TV commercial."

Thursday, day 2, 8:30 a.m., June 6...

Leaving Abbe's Deli and removing the toothpick from his mouth, Jeffrey Robinson asked sarcastically, "Did you get enough to eat? Man, you're such a pig! It was an embarrassment sitting in the same booth with you."

Len merely snorted and grunted contentedly as he rubbed his hands over the front of his belly he intentionally extended for Jeff Robinson's benefit. As Jeff Robinson got behind the steering wheel, Len unwrapped a mint and asked, "Where exactly is this art museum?"

"Right here in Tarzana, a few blocks west on Ventura. Think we'll score?"

"Who knows? Do we know if Gloria Mitchell has been found and in custody? We need to talk to her and fast," he said, adjusting his seat belt. "She wasn't exactly honest with us, and after we tried to put her at ease. Pity."

The westbound drive on Ventura Boulevard was smooth and quiet; most of the traffic was eastbound this time of day. With a squawk, their radio barked. Len picked up, "Morgan here, what?"

"Lieutenant Morgan, this is Dispatch. We have Gloria Mitchell in custody. What's the charge? Clear."

"Good work. For openers, start with falsifying a statement made to a peace officer. That'll keep her until we can get back. Clear."

"Will do, sir. Clear."

"Damn antiquated police radios and stupid pagers. When will Dutch ever get personal radio-phones for us?" Len implored, placing the microphone back in its cradle. "I mean, it is 1996 isn't it?"

"Yes, it is, and it sounds like Gloria Mitchell didn't flee the nest after all. Now she can partake of our fine accommodations," Jeff Robinson remarked, as he parked in front of the Western Museum of Fine Art.

"I wonder if Vice Detective Boyle had anything to do with locating her. Anyway, we're here, Boss, let's rumble."

Inside the museum, the large showroom was void of people, staff or customers. Adorning the walls were a variety of attractive hangings: paintings and fabrics with no particular genre or scheme.

A quiet voice from behind asked, "Yes? Is there something in particular that I can show you gentlemen this morning? I'm Laura."

Turning to face the voice, Len removed his shield from his coat pocket and showed it to her, "Yes, Laura, I'm Detective Morgan, with the Devonshire Hills Homicide Unit and this is my associate, Sergeant Jeff Robinson. Are you the manager?"

"No, Detective, I'm merely a sales associate. Dominic is the manager, he's over there. Hello, Detective Jeff Robinson. I believe we chatted on the phone a day ago, right?" Jeff Robinson smiled and nodded in agreement.

"Homicide?" Dominic quizzed as he slowly approached. He raised an eyebrow and ran his hand through his greasy hair. "Who died?" he asked.

"A young woman," Len answered as he sized up Dominic. "She was murdered recently. Maybe you can furnish us with some information, such as the name and address of the owner of this business."

Dominic, a gaunt, dark skinned man, looked nervously at Len. "Why is the owner of this establishment any business of the Homicide Division?"

Irritated and resisting the opportunity to make Dominic wish he'd never asked the question, Len explained quietly, "Dominic, we're chasing a loose lead. We can determine the ownership of this business easily enough, but since we're here, wouldn't you like to cooperate with your local police department?"

Recognizing his mistake, Dominic shifted his feet and ran his hand through his hair again. He took a deep breath and replied, "The principal owner is Mister Duard van Haan. I'm sorry for appearing rude, but Mister van Haan is a very private person and likes to keep it that way. He's not here now; actually he rarely visits. In fact, most of my contacts with him is via telephone. May I ask if Mister van Haan is in some kind of trouble?"

"You say that you're the manager of the museum and a Mister van Haan is the owner?" Len asked, removing one of his departmental calling cards from its case and handing it to Dominic.

"Yes. I've been Mister van Haan's manager since we opened in nineteen eighty-two."

"Then you must know Mister Van Haan very well. Does he live locally?" Len queried, putting his card-case back in his coat pocket.

"I know him only as an employer," Dominic answered, again shifting his feet and going back to his hair with his hand. "Not socially at all, only professionally. Yes, he lives locally."

"Where is his residence, Dominic?" Len continued, curious as to why Dominic appeared so nervous.

"He lives in Beverly Hills, actually north of Beverly Hills, on Benedict Canyon Road."

Finally, Len thought, *an extended answer.*

"Dominic, you have been very helpful today, thank you. We won't detain you further this morning. Miss Laura, good-day." Nodding to Jeff Robinson, he headed toward the front door.

"You're welcome," Dominic said, shifting his feet one final time as he ran his fingers through his hair again. "Goodbye."

In the car, Jeff Robinson snorted. "Did you get a hint that he was trying not to soil his BVDs?"

Len roared, laughing loudly, "What makes you think he didn't have a pant-load?"

"Yeah, maybe that's what all that shifting of the feet was about, and in front of that nice lady too."

The telephone rang on the private line at the huge limestone mansion in North Beverly Hills, "Hello," a stern male voice answered.

A nervous voice on the other end replied, "Duard? It's Dominic. Is that you?"

"Yes?" was the answer in Beverly Hills. "Who else would it be? What do you want, Dominic? I'm busy."

"Duard, there were two homicide detectives here just now. They asked questions about you and some woman who was murdered a day ago."

"Questions? What questions?" Duard van Haan asked, becoming more impatient.

"Well, they asked me who the owner of the museum was, basic questions. I told them nothing at all," Dominic said, lying blatantly. "I just wanted you to know that. You know how nervous I am around the police. I was nervous, Duard."

"Never mind, Dominic," Duard reassured him. "It's probably nothing. Now go back to work. Sell something for a change!"

Duard van Haan rolled over in the big bed and kissed his naked partner: a fair faced, smooth skinned young man. Holding him close to his bare torso as their lips parted, van Haan drew the cool satin bed sheets around them.

Outside the Art Museum in the car, Len radioed Command Dispatch. "This is Lieutenant Morgan. Please patch me to homicide Staff Assistant, Mariko Tanaka.

Seconds later, "Miss Tanaka, Lieutenant Morgan here. Please take this name: Duard van Haan, owner, Western Museum of Fine Art, Ventura Boulevard, residence, Benedict Canyon area, Beverly Hills. I want every word you can print on this guy. Also, did records ever verify who in the hell the victim was? Her real name and address? Confirm the same data on

Gloria Mitchell for me too. Again, as usual, first thing this morning will be soon enough for me, okay? Clear."

"Uh, D-U-A-R-D ... Duard...." Miss Tanaka repeated, slowly spelling out the first name. "And what did y'all say his last name was again?" she mocked in a slow, faux drawl.

Bewildered, Len pressed the microphone tightly against his chest and stared at Jeff Robinson in frustrated desperation. Then acknowledging her silly mind game, he laughed. "Miss Tanaka, you caught me that time. Now get busy! Clear."

"Ain't she the beat?" Jeff Robinson said, chuckling as they continued the drive back to the precinct. "And so damn sweet too. If I wasn't a married man I'd...."

Interrupting, Len asked, "You'd what?"

"Oh, doctor!" Jeff Robinson began, "I'd ... oh, never mind!"

Len laughed aloud at Jeff Robinson's obvious embarrassment.

"You have a nasty mind, Detective Morgan," Jeff Robinson observed, feigning anger.

Later, at the precinct, Mariko Tanaka met Len and Jeff Robinson before they reached their office. She handed Len a sheaf of papers and said, "There you are Lieutenant Morgan, this morning, just as you requested."

"My goodness," he replied, delighted. "Miss Tanaka, I do owe you."

"Yes, you do!" She winked and walked away.

Jeff Robinson watched as she left and smiled. "Mm-mmm ... lookin' good."

"Detective, your libido is showing."

At that moment, Captain Elmer 'Dutch' Ryan's voice roared from his office behind them. "Morgan! Jeff Robinson! Get your skinny asses in here and close the door behind you!"

Captain Ryan sat at his cluttered desk and waited for them to enter. Red faced, he had his Irish up this morning. Jeff Robinson closed the door and took a chair beside Len.

Ryan leered at the two of them and angrily asked, "What in Holy-God's-Blessed-Name have you two assholes been doing this morning?"

"Conducting basic departmental police business, sir, it's called investigating," Len answered flatly.

"Hah! Investigating my ass," Ryan fired back. Standing, he yelled, "what in hell are you two doin' going to a respectable man's place of business and harassing his employees? Answer me that?"

"Are you talking about a routine visit to the business place of a possible murder suspect, Captain?"

"You know damn well what I'm talking about," Ryan roared. "You and Jeff Robinson were at the Art Museum on Ventura this morning, harassing Duard van Haan's manager and his employee. I want that shit stopped! Now!"

Len turned his head and stared out of the glass office windows at nothing in particular for a moment. Then he took a deep breath and looked back at Ryan, who had resumed sitting in his chair. "Captain, with all due respect, sir...."

"Shut up!" Ryan interrupted, "Damn it, don't you understand English? I want you two to stay away from van Haan and his business. Starting now!"

Len stood abruptly and looked down at the angry little man seated behind the desk. "Captain, sir ... I don't know what your problem is, sir, nor do I much care, but I'm a veteran homicide detective doing my job. If you're telling me *not* to do my job, simply reduce it to writing and my shield will be on this shit-piled desk in a flash."

Captain Ryan, remaining silent, glared back at Len.

"I do what the taxpayers of the Valley pay me to do," Len articulated. "I solve murder cases. To do that, I ask questions of people: some innocent people, some not so innocent. We don't predetermine the difference; we just ask the goddamn questions."

Jeff Robinson shifted uneasily in his chair and stifled a cough. Ryan then glared at him.

Len continued, "If you're ordering me to stop doing my job, just spell it out on that Division letterhead. Until then, stay the hell out of my face, sir."

Looking daggers at Len, the Captain's face flushed. He snarled, "Well, you better damn well know who you're dealing with. This van Haan has powerful friends in high places. He's rich and well connected. He's a major player in the mayoral and city commission electoral campaigns. He's not one to trifle with, so if you like this goddamn job so damn much, you'd better be right on this guy or you may be walking the streets writing parking tickets."

"Is that all, Captain?"

Ignoring the question, the Captain rose and strode out of his office, leaving Len and Jeff Robinson behind.

"Suppose that was a yes?" a grim faced Jeff Robinson solicited.

"Screw him, Robbie, and with your big, ever tryin' dick!"

"Aaghtk!" Jeff Robinson gagged, clutching his throat. "No thanks!"

Back in their office, Len pored over the papers handed him by Miss Tanaka. Jeff Robinson was on the telephone when a uniformed female officer appeared at their door, "Excuse me, Detectives, I have the prisoner from lockup."

Len looked up and saw Gloria Mitchell, puffy eyed and outfitted today in a dismal colored, city issued, shapeless prisoner's dress; totally out of character.

"Thank you, Officer," Len said, nodding. "Come in, please take a chair."

Gloria Mitchell sat down; her eyes began to tear. "Why am I back here? Why was I arrested? You said I wasn't a suspect. Now I'm in jail and can't post bond. Will you tell me what's going on?"

Len handed her a partial box of tissues and signaled for Miss Tanaka to join them. Replying coldly, he said, "Miss Mitchell, you were read your rights earlier, do you have an attorney? If not, do you want one appointed and present before we talk?"

"No," Gloria Mitchell answered, sobbing, wiping at her cheeks with the tissue. "I'm not guilty of anything, I don't need an attorney."

Miss Tanaka entered again with the audio recorder in hand and took her previous seat.

Len began, "Miss Mitchell, earlier we asked you for any and all pertinent information regarding the murder victim, Lorena Jeanne Reynolds. After you left us, we were surprised to learn from a reliable source that you and Miss Reynolds were planning to open a bed-and-breakfast business in the San Francisco Bay area. May I ask why you didn't think that information was pertinent to this investigation?"

She looked away, and then nervously looked down and started sobbing. Between deep breaths, she wiped at her eyes again with the wrinkled tissue, "Detective, I didn't think that kind of information was important to your murder investigation. Yes, we were both getting out of the business. We have money saved."

"I guess so," Len said, interrupting, as he reached for the copy of a newly arrived bank memo. "Quite a lot of money, it appears in a joint bank account with the victim. Can you explain the amount?"

"We had been saving for a more than a year. We each put in as much as we could spare. She kept the bankbook, I never knew exactly how much was in the account, but I did know it was growing."

"Yes, it grew a lot," Len replied, looking directly into her eyes, then back at the bank memo. "The balance was \$128,716.47 as of yesterday. Not really enough to murder for, or maybe it is enough to murder for?"

"How much? My God! I had no idea," Gloria Mitchell murmured, her shocked voice trailing off at the disclosure of the amount. "Detective, I didn't have anything to do with her murder, I swear it. You have to believe me, I didn't murder her!"

"Miss Mitchell, that remains to be seen, I'm sorry. Is there anything else you forgot to mention? What else are you withholding? And what is your connection with Vice Detective Boyle?"

Hearing his name, she burst into tears. Len looked inquisitively at Jeff Robinson, who answered with a shrug of his shoulders.

"Ma'am, take your time," Len said quietly. "When you're ready, please tell me about your involvement with Detective Boyle."

Finally regaining her composure Gloria Mitchell explained, "He pinched me a year ago one night down on Sepulveda Boulevard. It was late and he put me in the front seat of his car. He said he was going to take me to jail on prostitution charges. On the way he pulled off onto a side street and propositioned me, saying if I'd 'do' him, he'd let me off and not press charges. I didn't believe him, but since we weren't that far from the Valley Arms Hotel at the time, I suggested doing him there instead of in his car. He readily agreed." She paused, breathing more normally now, she sat and stared at the floor for a few seconds.

"Go ahead, Miss Mitchell, whenever you are ready," Len said.

"Oh, Lieutenant, it was so scary! When he parked in the lot, I jumped from his car and ran into the hotel. I guess he was too surprised to react quickly and I made it to my room before he got to my floor. I was so scared I could barely breathe. I locked my door and hid in my closet, but I could hear him pacing up and down the hall. Finally he left."

"And?"

"And I haven't seen him since until in the elevator with Detective Jeff Robinson. Will I be going to women's prison now, Lieutenant Morgan? Am I in more trouble for running away from a vice detective?"

"Hardly, Miss Mitchell, don't worry about Mister Boyle, he's the least of your problems. Let's get back to your current situation and your involvement with the murder victim." Solemn faced, Len looked directly in her eyes. "Are you certain you don't want a public defender assigned to you?"

"Am I being charged with murder?" she asked, her clasped hands shaking as she tried to compose herself.

"No, not yet." He sat quietly, looking at the growing piles of paper on his desk. "We're attempting to get a handle on why your friend was murdered. If we knew why, it would give us some direction. Personally, I don't think you did it. Obviously, when we determine why she was murdered, the list of possible suspects will narrow. I strongly believe that $128,000 may have been a possible motive. It's the only thing about this case that makes sense to me."

Leaning forward in her chair, she beseeched, "Who else do you think would have known about the money?"

"That's a good question, Miss Mitchell," Len observed, "If I knew the answer my life might become more simple."

"So can I be released now? May I go home?"

"Certainly, but be aware that if you go back out on the street, you may be inviting another murder … your own. My suggestion is that you allow us to detain you in protective custody until we feel it's safe for you to leave. If you want a court appointed attorney now, he or she can have you on the street in a matter of minutes. It's your choice; you're free to go, or to stay. Do you understand?"

Taken aback, Gloria Mitchell asked quizzically, "Who would want to murder me?"

Len looked at her, "I wish I knew that answer. Perhaps the same individual that murdered your friend … if it's about the money."

She swallowed hard and nodded, "I'll stay here then."

"No, not here," Len explained. "We'll move you into a Safety House, a secured house here in the Valley. You'll be well protected by two plainclothes cops, one being a policewoman."

Len looked up at the female officer, who had waited quietly during the interrogation. "Officer, please take Miss Mitchell to the Command desk. I'll call ahead authorizing her release. Thank you again, Miss Mitchell, we'll be in touch."

She smiled a tight, closed mouth smile, and attended by the female police officer, left the room.

"Robbie, please call Watch Command and make the arrangements for Gloria Mitchell to pick up her clothes and any personal items from the hotel. Call Beck or Farley at the East Valley Safety House; let them know she's on the way. If our murderer wants her too, he'll have to look damn hard."

"Gotcha', Boss," Jeff Robinson replied.

"Oh, Robbie, let's get cute here ... contact the DA and get a wiretap on Miss Mitchell's telephone. I want to know who is calling her and why. We may snag an unsuspecting predator."

"Great idea, will do!"

"And Mariko," Len said, turning his attention to his Staff Assistant. "Will you get Detective Boyle from Vice on the phone for me? Thanks."

Len watched as Jeff Robinson began his telephone calls. Len also noticed he had referred to his Staff Assistant, Miss Tanaka, as Mariko again. Just then, back at her desk, she signaled that he had a call.

"Hello? Lanny? Len Morgan here, could we meet for five minutes over a coffee in the cafeteria? Great. See you there."

Jeffrey Robinson sat unmoving, his head buried in his paperwork, ignoring Len as he departed their office, but wishing he could be a fly on the wall in the cafeteria.

Thursday, end of day 2, June 6...

At home hours later, following a solitary dinner of steak fajitas at the El Vaquero Cantina on DeSoto Avenue, Len checked his incoming telephone messages. Seeing the blinking red light, he pressed the *Play* button.

"Len," Jeff Robinson's recorded voice said. *"It's four thirty-five. Gloria Mitchell is in the Safety House in Sherman Oaks. She's settled in, comfortable and willing to stay put. Call me when you get home if you aren't too late. Colleen and I are going to bed early tonight. Ciao."*

Len looked at his wristwatch, it was 8:15 p.m. *Shoot, it's not that late. What the hell.* He picked up the telephone, and then hesitated, thinking of his partner and Colleen.

"No," he said aloud, exhaling a small sigh, "you guys go for it. Make a baby. There's plenty of time for cop work tomorrow."

Day 3, Friday, 6:55 a.m., June 7...
The telephone was ringing as Len walked across his bedroom, tying his silk tie. "Hello, Morgan here," he answered, adjusting his shirt collar.

"Hey! Are you ready?" It was Jeff Robinson.

"Robbie, hi. I'm in the middle of dressing, but come get me. Maybe we'll hit Abbe's again, or how about Soleh's? I'll buy."

"Hey, fine. See you in a flash."

The sound of Jeff Robinson's horn outside caught his attention as Len locked his door, *Right on time, as usual. Good old Robbie. And the knee feels just fine today. Great!*

They exchanged hellos and the usual friendly sarcastic barbs and headed to Soleh's Deli, where they ordered bagels, cream cheese, and thick egg-and-onion omelets with hot black-coffee.

"Robbie, run it all past me again, what have we got on this murder case and our primary suspect." Len pushed his cup toward the edge of the table in anticipation of a refill from their regular waitress.

"Well, right now we have a portion of the financial scoop on van Haan. We know he's the principal owner of an apparent low profit art business, yet he appears to rake in outrageous money. His local bank account has a large balance and we haven't determined if he has any European or offshore accounts or not. Miss Tanaka is working on that."

"Mariko came up with all of that info?" Len asked as he sipped his coffee and noticed, too, that he again referred to Miss Tanaka as Mariko.

"What about the hookers' joint bank account? Anything strange there?"

"You mean strange like a pattern as far as deposits, deposit dates, that type of thing?"

"Yeah, like I said, anything out of the ordinary?"

"You bet. Going way back and up through last month there were large deposits made to the account on or about the fifth of every month. Major bucks each time."

"How major? It must have been thousands of dollars to generate the balance I saw on that memo."

"Yes. Five thousand large every month," Jeff Robinson said, touching his mouth with a napkin.

Len whistled, "Five grand?"

"That, plus her 'business earnings', but, every month a $5,000 cash deposit was made. No checks, nothing traceable, always cash. Go figure? It seems like the IRS would be getting curious with that kind of money showing up regularly."

Len shook his head in amazement. "I guess. Damn! You gotta' be one hot hooker to have a john that regularly coughs up $5,000 every month. So, here's an obvious question: was she murdered on the fifth of the month for a particular reason? Like it was the blackmail payday? Or is that too coincidental? That's sure a lot of money every month. You say we don't have a paper trail?"

"Nope, nothing, each deposit was made in cash."

Len sat quietly, his brain buzzing. *How in hell could a hooker get that kind of money, and get it consistently if it wasn't extortion or blackmail?*

"Robbie, we don't have a smoking gun, but we might have a motive here. It's called 'kill-the-bitch-and-keep-the-cash'. And that motive is aimed right at our guest in the Safety House. What do you think?"

"Makes sense to me. But another question or two has entered my mind. Off topic, how do hookers file income taxes? You know, it still seems to me that the IRS should have flagged this joint account for investigation or for an audit, huh? I sure as hell would if I were an IRS Special Agent. Do you suppose the hookers had a CPA or some kind of tax preparer that created some kind of a tax shelter?"

"Great question. If they don't have a CPA, they might get an unexpected visit one day … well, Miss Mitchell might. Lorena Reynolds already did. Are we ready to boogie?"

"Not quite. Did you buy the coffee yesterday, or did Boyle?"

Len laughed and shook his head. "You know, young Detective Boyle became truly agreeable during that quick cup of coffee. I related a dumbass yarn to him about a dumbass cop who lost his stripes for 'negotiating' a tryst with a dumbass hooker. He said, *'That must have been one dumbass cop'*. I agreed. That was it. Now, are we ready to boogie?"

"You bet," Jeff Robinson said, nodding his head and smiling. "Where to, Boss? A visit with Mister van Haan?"

"You're reading my mind."

"Hell, that's no big thing," Jeff Robinson quipped.

"What's that?"

"That mind of yours. Let's go."

"Lead the way, partner," Len replied.

The silver-gray Ford Victoria cruiser stopped in front of the ornate iron-barred security gate outside the Benedict Canyon limestone mansion. Jeffrey Robinson pressed the security alarm button, spoke, "Good morning," into the intercom and waited.

A proper male voice answered, "Who is it, please?"

"We are Devonshire Hills Valley West precinct homicide Detectives Morgan and Jeff Robinson. We wish to speak to Mister Duard van Haan if he's available." The massive wrought-iron security gate swung open quietly.

"Apparently he's available," Jeff Robinson ventured.

"Not too shabby," Len remarked, as Jeff Robinson slowly maneuvered the cruiser up the winding, palm tree lined drive to the front entrance of the huge limestone mansion.

"This isn't the old Howard Hughes estate is it?" Jeff Robinson asked as he parked the cruiser in the shade of a tall, well-trimmed eucalyptus tree.

"No, the Hughes estate is across that ravine, right over there. See the cluster of larger red-tiled roofs. Look to the right of that pair of small red-tiled roofs on the crest of that steep ridge, that's it."

"Oh, yeah. That's huge too isn't it?"

The butler opened the massive front door and bid them to enter. "Please wait here for a moment, the master will be right along."

The two detectives waited patiently in the bright, sun-drenched foyer, admiring the wondrous artwork hangings that covered every available space on the finely plastered, stark white walls.

"Good morning, people," a man's voice said from the opposite side of the foyer.

Duard van Haan, a stout, well-built middle-aged man of medium height approached them smiling. His sparse, nearly transparent closely clipped hair gave the impression that he was balding. His cold, steely-blue eyes nearly matched the color of his silk robe.

"I'm Duard van Haan, and you are?"

Len handed Duard van Haan a departmental calling card, "Mister van Haan, I'm Detective Lieutenant Morgan and this is…"

"…and this is *Mister Tibbs*!" Duard van Haan said, interrupting, smiling again, his cold blue eyes looked directly at Jeffrey Robinson. "Lieutenant, this is Mister Tibbs isn't it?"

"I'm *Sergeant* Jeffrey Robinson," a highly serious, tight-lipped Jeffrey Robinson emphasized. "You may call me *Sergeant* Jeff Robinson, Mister van Haan."

"Oh dear … I'm so sorry," van Haan answered, feigning politeness. "I was merely attempting to be light. Levity, you know?"

Neither Len nor Jeff Robinson responded. Len continued. "Mister van Haan, we're sorry to bother you at this hour of the morning, and we don't want to waste your valuable time, but we need to ask a couple of questions."

"Detectives, the earliness of the hour is nothing. However, you were fortunate to catch me here this late, I'm usually busy at my office by this time," van Haan responded. "I had something to handle first."

"That's good to know. First," Len showed van Haan a recent morgue photo of the victim, "do you know or recognize this woman?"

Van Haan took the morgue photo of Lorena Reynolds and examined it closely. He handed it back and said flatly, "I'm sorry, Detective; I've never seen this woman in my life. Am I supposed to know her? She looks like a common street walker to me, and a dead one at that."

"So, you're saying that you never had any dealings with her?"

"Never. Do you have reason to believe that I may have?"

Len took back the photo and stared hard at this arrogant man. "No, Mister van Haan, we have no direct knowledge that she may have been connected with you. We do have information from a reliable source that this woman did have contacts with an art curator operating in the Valley. Since we don't have a name to go on we are asking you and the others in the art community if they are familiar with this person."

"I see," van Haan reflected. "Now let me understand this clearly. Because someone told you this dead hooker had an involvement with an art curator, you are asking me if I knew her?"

Len stared questioningly into the eyes of the heavily built man. "Sir, you just said hooker. Before that, you said streetwalker. Why?"

"I'm sorry, Detective, as I said before, she looks like the type. Look, I can't help you further; I have pressing business to handle. Jerome will show you out."

"Duard?" a young male voice called out from the upper floor, "How much longer are you going to be? I'm lonesome."

"Not long, I'll be right there," van Haan answered as he looked in the direction of the stairs.

"Just one more thing, sir," Len requested. "Can you tell us where you were in the early morning hours of June five?"

"Detective Morgan, is it? I usually leave here for my office in the Valley every day at five-thirty sharp. I was probably there until mid-morning. Good-day."

"Thank you, sir, if you remember anything else that might be pertinent, please give us a call?" The request fell flat. Van Haan was already walking back toward the massive winding stairway as Jerome appeared to escort them to the front door.

Outside, Len preemptively offered, "Yes, I wondered about the dainty male voice plaintively calling out from upstairs too. And yes, *Mister Tibbs*, I noticed his cologne. It was dreadful."

"Screw him," Jeff Robinson snapped as he settled into the cruiser. As they left the property and turned west, he looked at Len and asked, "Can you believe that cologne? It would make a Parisian whore smile with delight. And that little wimpy voice from upstairs; 'Duard, I'm lonesome'," Jeff Robinson mimicked.

He continued, "Was that the 'pressing business' he had to 'handle'? No pun intended. Suppose he likes *handling* young men? That voice didn't sound too feminine to me."

"Yes, that voice," Len said, smiling slightly. "It was wimpy. And Robbie, just because he mistook you for Sydney Poitier, don't be so thin-skinned, I'd have been complimented."

"Screw you too," Jeff Robinson snarled, staring out across the ravine.

"Hey! Don't be so quick to get out of the neighborhood," Len said, looking around. "I want to locate a good vantage point for a stakeout if we need one. I want to know everything this man is doing from now on. Besides his strong cologne, he's big and well-built enough to be our man."

Len continued, "...and he was convinced the victim was a hooker. Huh? Did you notice, too, he avoided a direct answer to my last question? He never admitted where he was the morning of the murder, only that he leaves for work at five-thirty and was probably in his office until mid-morning. Slippery bastard."

"Screw him," Jeff Robinson muttered. "Kiss my ass, 'Mister Tibbs'."

Smiling at his partner, Len reached for the radio microphone and asked Watch Command Dispatch to contact Mariko Tanaka. "Miss Tanaka? I need a progress report on the bank and business records we sought on Duard van Haan and his Great Western Museum, plus the taxi records I asked for earlier. Prepare a request to the DA for a wiretap warrant and warrants for disclosure of additional information such as overseas bank records, plus van Haan's business records."

"First: progress is slow this morning, Lieutenant," Miss Tanaka answered, chuckling. "Second, you repeated yourself. You said business records twice."

Len paused for an instant and chuckled too, then he resumed, "…including all International Parcel and FedEx deliveries."

Returning the microphone to its cradle, he looked over at Jeff Robinson and asked, "Now what? Why are you shaking your silly head?"

"Naughty, naughty, you didn't say 'please' to Miss Tanaka, and you didn't say 'Clear' when you concluded your radio conversation. That's a ton of demerits."

"And who's keeping count? Anyway, we need to convert to cordless UHF radio-phones someday, or to cellular phones. This Shield-714 stuff is dated."

"True, but I'm still keeping count. With those demerits you've been accumulating, your lieutenant's job is in jeopardy. I'll accept your position now, I've decided that."

"Take it, if I have a job after Dutch learns we actually set foot in van Haan's house, if either of us still has a job that is."

"I'm telling you, Len, ol' Dutch needs some rest, or a lot of time in the shade. He's really been on edge lately and may have forgotten whose side he's on."

"Tell me."

The two detectives returned to the precinct. Len, with the dozens of computer printout sheets from Officer Tanaka in hand, headed directly to Captain Ryan's office.

"Captain, sir, just hear me out before you start yelling," Len implored as he entered the Captain's office.

"Certainly, and thanks for knocking first. It always reflects good social graces and quality upbringing, right Detective?"

Ryan said sarcastically, looking up from his hopelessly cluttered desk. "I already heard that you were at van Haan's today, so this better be damned good, Morgan," Ryan said, glowering as he leaned back in his swivel rocker.

Len took a chair. Seeing no available space on the Captain's cluttered desk, he placed the collection of paperwork on the floor. Taking a deep breath, he spoke, "Captain, I want your permission to put a stakeout on van Haan's house and his business. I smell a rat, literally. His cologne is a major factor. I'll explain that later. To start with, this man is too wealthy to be making an honest living peddling faux art. Especially the type he features in his museum. I have a motive for the murder of the hooker too--blackmail. I believe I have our prime murder suspect right here in these papers. I need your approval to proceed."

Dutch Ryan sat and quietly studied Len's face.

"Well?" Len asked.

"Blackmail?" Ryan asked, seemingly interested, as he ran a hand through his thinning hairline. "How so?"

"The dead hooker; I think she must have played a part in some of his sexual dalliances, although he was with a young man upstairs at his house today."

Ryan's face lit up, and after attempting first to stifle a laugh, he broke down and laughed aloud for several seconds.

Len paused and looked quizzically at a totally out of character Dutch Ryan. "Why are you laughing, sir?"

Dutch Ryan leaned back in his swivel chair and stared at the ceiling for a few seconds. He recovered eventually and wiped at his eyes. "Excuse me, Len, I've been acting like a total bastard lately; you boys may have even noticed that. I'm sorry, it's a personal thing, but this Mister van Haan sounds like he would fit right in with my own fucked up family." Ryan broke out laughing again. "Any lesbians in the mix?" he asked, wiping his eyes with the back of his hand again, brushing the tears away.

"Sir?" Len questioned, not certain if he recognized this man who looked remarkably like his normally nasty Captain.

"He's not a Roman Catholic too, is he?" Dutch asked, feebly attempting to get serious. "My whole damn family was absolutely weird, Len. Now, you can see where I came by it growing up with my so-called spinster Aunt Sarah, her so-called bachelor brothers, except for my old man. Then there was my promiscuous mother who abandoned us, my younger sister and me, when we were kids."

Dutch Ryan pushed his chair back, stretched his arms above his head again and continued. "I never married or even dated, Len. My dad was an Irish beat cop in the Bronx, and he raised me and Rose, my sister, with some assistance from Aunt Sarah and, of course, the Nuns. I was a slow learner as a child. My speech patterns were stubborn and slow to mature so I got stuck with the nickname 'Dutch'. Do you see why I'm so damn strange and cranky? As I said, I never married, probably because I didn't want to be guilty of polluting the gene pool."

Ryan took his handkerchief from his pocket and wiped at his eyes, still damp from laughing. "Okay, enough of this hilarity; please go on. Explain blackmail."

Len chuckled, never having seen Dutch Ryan in this jocular mood before. Then he continued, "Well, sir, if Lorena Reynolds and van Haan were fucking regularly, maybe, during some unintended pillow talk she discovered how he was making his real money by using his Art Museum as a front. We know she was putting away one helluva lot of cash every month until two days ago. The murderer may have opted not to play anymore and killed her, or he had her killed. 'Nothing personal, just business'."

"Makes a lot of sense. So, what's all this horseshit about cologne?" Ryan asked, becoming more serious as he rocked slowly in his swivel chair.

"It goes back to the crime scene, sir. The victim's room reeked of heavy perfume, or cologne, according to two different witnesses, a traffic cop and Gloria Mitchell, the other hooker. Both were at the crime scene soon after the murder took place."

Confident that he was getting through to the Captain, Len continued, "Van Haan's cologne smells like a cheap whore's dream. Robbie and I can attest to that based on our meeting with him today."

"So what else do you want from me?" Ryan asked, surprising Len with his quiet, professional attitude.

Stammering, "Uh ... sir," Len answered. "I'll need wiretaps, a double stakeout, and maybe LAPD's SWAT, that's all."

"Whoa!" Ryan roared with his face slowly breaking into a genuine smile. "What in hell are we going to do here? Start World War Three?"

Len smiled too. He retrieved his papers from the floor and stood, feeling relieved at Dutch Ryan's comical retort. "I certainly hope not, sir, but I don't know what we're going to run up against. This has all the earmarks of a major crime bust as well as a murder case. It could get nasty. What do you think, sir?"

"Len, please wait, sit back down," Ryan said as he got up to adjust the window shade from the late morning sun. "Do you know Luis Campanera? United States Treasury Special Agent?"

"I've met him socially several times, but I don't know him personally. Why? What has Treasury got to do with anything?"

Smiling again, Ryan sat back down and continued. "Treasury sent a little pup in a nice pinstripe suit over here earlier this morning. He marched in here big as shit, probably when you were at van Haan's mansion. He didn't leave too damn happy, I'll tell you," Ryan said, savoring the moment and his own salty remark.

"What's the connection, sir?"

"The connection is that Treasury has been watching van Haan too. They agree with you that he is just too damn fat to be making his money legally. Treasury's mistake, when they discovered you two sniffing around, was to come in here and order me to take you and Robbie off the case and to leave *their* van Haan alone." Ryan smiled and waved his right arm in a small circle above his head.

"Ordered? They ordered you to stop a murder investigation?"

"Son, they tried. Shit! I ate his goddamn lunch!" Ryan roared. "No damn way would I take any shit from some pantywaist federal prick in a pinstripe suit. We're investigating a murder case, I told him. Hell no, we won't get out of their way!"

Ryan winked, "But I did say we'd consider coordinating any future efforts with them if we could work with Luis Campanera. He got Campanera on the telephone immediately. They agreed."

Len sat dumbfounded. *So, Dutch chewed up a federal officer, spit him out and got what he wanted; cooperation from the feds.* "Sir, what's next? I'm confused now."

Ryan handed Len a business card. "Call Special Agent Luis Campanera at this number, he has their stakeouts in place as we speak; that's how they knew that you and Robbie were on the prowl. We'll only observe for now and move in later when it's within our jurisdiction. Campanera has the wiretap warrants, too, in effect since this morning. Our CSI Director Warren and his techie people in Command are patched into the fed's wire. This is a joint effort between them and us now, to nail some bastard's balls to the wall."

Len rose and extended his hand, "Thank you, sir, I believe we'll get him for you."

Just as Dutch stood to shake Len's hand, veteran Detective Paul Tobin and his young partner, Detective Fred Cooper entered the office.

"Hi Dutch," Tobin said. "We've got us a real nasty mess over there, sir. Are we interrupting?"

"No, not at all. Sit down boys, you too Len. You need to get the scoop on this one too."

The three detectives took chairs and Paul Tobin spoke first. "We got there, to the RFK Junior High School, and conducted short, low intensity interviews with the twenty-three students who were in the room at the time of the shootings. CSI forensics took what prints they could from the doorknob, but it's unlikely they'll get anything useful."

Len interrupted, "What shootings took you to RFK Junior High School?"

"Well," Paul Tobin explained, "a young, alleged to be, Latino kid entered a classroom early today and ordered one of the students to stand up. When he did, the Latino kid pulled a gun from under his shirt and fatally shot the other kid point blank. The attacker fatally shot the teacher too when he tried to subdue him. Both shooting victims were pronounced dead at the scene."

"Jeez wept!" Len uttered, slumping back in his chair. "And the shooter escaped?"

"Yeah. For sure no one got in his way, and the hall monitoring cameras were malfunctioning otherwise we'd have made him on video. The entire classroom emptied and the screaming kids scattered throughout the school."

"Unbelievable," Dutch muttered.

"It took some herding, but we do have about two dozen eyewitnesses, all minors obviously. Some were friends of the dead kid. It traumatized most of them beyond the point of giving us any good information. The Principal has the school on Lock Down for the rest of the day and all of the parents have been notified to pick up their kids at day's end."

Detective Fred Cooper spoke, "As Paulie said, after the shootings, the kids fled the classroom, freaked out, I guess. The school authorities had a helluva time locating all of them. Then the parents were notified."

"Good." Captain Ryan pressed his intercom button. "Miss Tanaka, would you bring your pad and join us, please?"

Miss Tanaka entered the room and Detective Paul Tobin jumped to his feet, "Here, Miss Tanaka, take my chair."

"Thank you," she said, taking a seat and adjusting her skirt. "What's up, Captain?"

"Miss Tanaka," Dutch began, "this is in regards to the shootings today at the RFK Junior High School. I want you to prepare formal requests to the parents of those children in the room where the shootings took place. Explain our situation and ask permission to speak with them and their children;

together. Advise them we can have a school counselor or our police psychiatrist on hand, if they wish, or any other professional counselor of their choice. Am I going too fast?"

Miss Tanaka looked up, "No, sir."

"Also, include a request for permission to use any of the children willing to assist our computer graphics composite artist. Place my Robo-signature at the bottom. That's all, Miss Tanaka, thank you."

"I'll have these ready for you as soon as possible, sir." She departed and went back to her desk in the squad room.

"Captain, the school has provided us with the addresses and phone numbers of the parents of the kids. Anything else?" Paul Tobin asked.

"Yeah, you boys go back to the school and chase down today's absentee records from all of the area's schools in the shooter's age group. Then get the most recent school photos of all of those students not in attendance today. Contact the school counselor at RFK Junior High and see what we can do to find out who the young victim's close friends were, to see if we could determine a possible motive. The victim must have really pissed off someone to warrant his shooting in broad daylight. See what all of that yields and let me know. Oh … I doubt anyone will demand that you produce a warrant for that information, but if they do, let me know that too. Now go!"

"Right, Captain. We're on it." Paul Tobin said, rising from his chair. "Come on Coop, let's go to work. We'll see you later, Len."

Len stood, shook their hands, and nodded in agreement. "Yes, later. Good luck, you two."

He turned and looked at Dutch Ryan. "Man, that's nasty, Dutch. What a mess, especially in front of all those youngsters. They'll be scarred for life."

"I guess." Sighing, Dutch added, "Mother Mary, save us all. Where do these punk *cholos* get off, putting a cap into another kid in a classroom? I can't stay abreast with the times anymore. Anyway, get in touch with Luis Campanera and see what you two can work out on this van Haan thing. That case will probably put you in this chair."

"Sir?"

Ignoring Len's question, Dutch Ryan looked away, toward his outside window. "We'll take some time to sit and talk about that subject later, alone. When we do, I'll try to make some sense about why I've been so damn crabby lately. Now go to work, son. Catch your murderer."

Still Friday, day 3, June 7...

Len entered his office and punched Jeff Robinson's shoulder as he walked past him, "You aren't going to believe this shit, partner..."

Jeff Robinson looked up, "I see your meeting with Dutch went serenely enough. I even heard him laughing in there, what's with that? He ain't sick is he?"

"Seriously, he may well be," Len answered as he sat down. "That was something he started to touch on but dismissed it quickly, saying that it's for another time. Afterward, I actually think he was close to apologizing for being such a flaming-ass prick."

"Really."

"Did you hear what went down at the RFK Junior High School earlier?" Len asked.

"Yeah, Miss Tanaka told me. Damn messy," Jeff Robinson said somberly.

"No shit. Anyway, on our case, Dutch says that the Feds, the Treasury Department, have had a tail on van Haan too. They saw us visit the Museum and probably his house. So, in a nutshell, Treasury is going to be *our* backup. They've got him wiretapped, tailed, and ready to stake out. Now we've become a major player in their plan, compliments of Dutch. How wild is that?"

"No shit!" Jeff Robinson exclaimed, leaning back in his chair, "So the feds are thinking van Haan is involved in some kind of high-roller money operation?"

"Must be, and now we'll get to play in the same league as the feds, at least for a while until we prove our case or get blown out of the water. The only thing we have to do is not interfere with their game plan. We need to contact Special Agent Luis Campanera and arrange a meeting for later. Ready to function?"

"Yeah, I'm ready!" Jeff Robinson replied. "So, we're going to be working with Luis?"

"Yes, according to Dutch. His deal with the feds was that Luis had to be our main man. It should work out okay," Len said, reaching for his telephone. Entering the number from the card Dutch gave him, Len waited as the phone rang at the federal building in West Los Angeles.

"Yes, this is Detective Len Morgan…"

"Yes, Detective Morgan, Special Agent Campanera is expecting your call, will you hold, please?"

"Sure," Len replied, surprised at the personal reception. Luis Campanera answered his telephone and, after a friendly exchange of platitudes, the two agreed to meet later that day in his office.

Westwood Federal Building…
The elevator stopped at the tenth floor of the federal building. Len and Jeff Robinson stepped into a wide, well lit room and were greeted by a pleasant receptionist who directed them to Luis Campanera's office suite.

"Hello! Are you in here, Luis?" Len asked, as he and Jeff Robinson entered an empty reception area through an open door.

"Back here, yes. Come in," a voice answered from a room in the back. "We've been expecting you. We've been doing some initial brainstorming."

The conference room was long and narrow and enjoyed a broad northern exposure of the Santa Monica Mountains on the near horizon. Tastefully outfitted, the room housed a dark wooden conference table attended by a dozen finely upholstered chairs. The obligatory faux painting of President Clinton hung on the far wall. To Len's wonderment, a familiar looking female sat at the table along with a male Asian-American agent.

Special Agent Luis Campanera, in his shirtsleeves, stood at the whiteboard. Campanera, less than six feet tall and with a slightly protruding stomach, smiled broadly as the new arrivals came in.

"Good morning, Luis," Len said as he and Jeff Robinson shook Special Agent Campanera's hand. After glancing suspiciously at the female again, Len smiled and said, "Good morning everyone else."

Campanera spoke. "Len, Robbie, it's always good to see you both. Please, let me introduce you to Special Agents Laura Andrews and Andy Chiu. I think you both met Agent Laura at the art museum. They comprise my new special task force I put together hours ago. Agents, I'd like you all to meet my good friends, Detectives Morgan and Jeff Robinson. They are with the West Valley, Devonshire Hills Homicide Unit. Len, Agent Andrews is our plant inside the art museum. She hired on with van Haan a week ago and keeps us abreast as to what our man may be doing."

"I see. I thought for a moment that van Haan may have installed a plant within your ranks." Smiling at Len's comment, the group exchanged handshakes.

Campanera began, "Before today, treasury agents across the country had been working independently on various aspects of the van Haan case and other similar cases. Each agent covered a particular area of expertise. Our team consensus is that van Haan is probably laundering money and dealing in illegitimate forgeries of stocks and bonds."

Continuing, Special Agent Campanera said, "One of our special agents, whose expertise is illegally earned money, says van Haan has varying involvements in some small businesses in California and Nevada, none of which are profitable.

Frankly, we think his income comes from laundering, pure and simple. We also think he moves a lot of dirty money, some of it through his non-profitable businesses. Non-profit being a generic term, he's not showing a profit on his books. Assuming that he uses his museum as his front, he probably keeps a percentage of the laundering traffic as his take. It's simple as hell. If you move a lot of money in and out, you get to keep a lot of money. Maybe skim a little extra too?"

Len and Jeff Robinson nodded, listening intently at the new information.

"One of our special agents, out of the Washington, D.C. office, suspects van Haan may be running counterfeit paper too." Campanera added. "Not only laundering and moving illegitimate cash, but also counterfeit stocks and bonds, possibly from North Korea. There has been a rash of ersatz paper of all descriptions on the west coast during the past year. His bank account balances have increased during that time too. Lastly, one of our southeastern district agents thinks there may be a connection with the Russian Mafia."

"The Russian Mafia?" Len asked. "That's interesting. So, Luis, how did Treasury happen on the scene?"

"The Internal Revenue Service became suspicious since van Haan does a ton of cash transactions, but his businesses always show a loss. Most intriguing, he uses a Wilmington, Delaware, CPA to do his tax preparation. That same CPA is also suspected of having Russian Mafia connections and has been high on the FBI's radar for a while."

"Wow!" Jeff Robinson exclaimed.

"So he was handed off to you to infiltrate his operation here in the Valley and confirm what the hell he was doing?" Len asked.

"Yes … that's about it." Campanera answered. "And we no more than set up our surveillance when you boys showed up. That caused us some major dismay and Dutch was contacted to rein you and Robbie in."

"Fat chance, huh, Luis?" Jeff Robinson replied, smiling.

Campanera laughed. "Yeah, our rookie field agent was definitely taken aback by Dutch's salty response. All for the best though, seeing how it has worked out."

The group sat quietly for a few seconds with no one responding.

Len spoke first, "Is van Haan suspected of laundering drug related money? If so, does this money originate from the Columbian or Mexican drug or child trafficking cartels? Or Chinese Tongs?"

"We suspect maybe some of it is drug related, but have no positive proof of its origin. The FBI, DEA and ATF are investigating that. A recent report compiled by an international study group strongly suggests there are Russian criminal factions and other foreign terrorist entities making deep inroads into South American and Mexican drug trafficking. It's fast becoming a damn mess, Len."

"I agree, Luis, but fortunately for Robbie and me, that's a federal problem. Anyway, how much do any of you know about him or his habits? Who are his friends, if any, his women, hookers or male playmates, does he have any professional associates?"

"Please, one question at a time, Lieutenant," the bespectacled Asian-American special agent said. "I'm Andy Chiu. We're just delving into those areas. All we have so far is that he's mostly a loner. His friends are far and few between … or is it few and far between? Is that right?"

"Close, Andy," Campanera said, winking while the others chuckled. "You could say that van Haan's friends are sparse. Forgive Andy, he's a newbie in the states and our old clichés are not his forte."

Slightly embarrassed, Andy continued, "In the past, his women acquaintances were prominent, high class call girls. He spent a lot of time in Tahoe, Reno and Las Vegas. He showed an occasional propensity for slim, good-looking boys too. He openly exhibited bisexual tendencies until the AIDS epidemic found the light of day. Beyond that, we don't know much. Maybe you can help us in that department."

"We don't know much either," Len said, reaching for his briefcase. "But we suspect he may have lowered his standards as far as his choice of women. Financially speaking, Andy, a day ago we received printouts from the bank where he has his personal and business accounts, probably much of the same info you've collected."

"Beyond that," Len continued, "we have nothing, especially anything that gives us a profile on his sexual preferences. We know that our murder victim was not a high-class Tahoe or Vegas type; at least her domicile didn't reflect that. When we visited van Haan's mansion we strongly suspect that he was entertaining an impatient young male friend."

"Wonderful," Campanera remarked sarcastically.

"Well, that's about all we know for certain, except that he smells," Len said

"What?" Campanera asked, looking mildly amused.

"Luis," Len answered, smirking, "he stinks, reeks. Trust me."

"What the hell are you talking about?"

Len explained to the assembled agents how the murder scene reeked of after shave lotion or cologne and of their odiferous experience during the interview at his mansion.

"Amazing," Andy Chiu said. "Do you have any idea what brand he uses?"

"No, not a clue. If we could get our lone character witness close enough to get a whiff, we'd be closer to linking him to the victim. So far I haven't figured out a way to make that happen."

"I have!" Jeffrey Robinson announced excitedly as he leaped from his chair. "I've got it!"

Heads turned in unison to hear what Jeff Robinson had to say.

"Listen … two of our traffic cops got a whiff of the same cologne in the victim's room as did our character witness. Y'all will love this; all we need to do is contrive a harmless traffic incident and let those same two traffic cops stick their respective noses into his car window!"

"No shit," Len replied, looking at his partner in amazement. "Now why in hell didn't I think of that? How easily the simple things elude us. What type of harmless incident do you want to create that isn't considered entrapment? A casual hit-and-run?"

"No," Jeff Robinson snorted, resuming his seat. "You know that traffic light I complain about? The one that gives me fits every morning. We can have a traffic technician rig a signal light on one of those several lights van Haan passes through every morning on his way to work. When we see him coming, we trip it so that he can't avoid running a 'Red'. See what I mean? A piece of cake, a potential traffic citation."

Impressed with his partner's idea, Len settled back in his chair and smiled, enjoying the approving nods from the federal agents.

"Robbie, that's pure genius." Campanera said, in obvious agreement with his unique plan.

"You know," Len said, "it may just work. He's not a rocket scientist; he mistook Robbie for Sidney Poitier earlier today."

"What?" Campanera asked, "Poitier? What's that all about?"

Self-consciously shifting in his chair, Jeff Robinson explained, "Yeah, the poor dope called me 'Mister Tibbs' earlier."

Laughter broke out in the entire group.

After it subsided, Campanera said, "Len, you can get the schedules for the surveillance teams from Andy. Arrange a shift schedule with your people and we'll get busy catching a criminal."

"Fine, Luis. Here, Andy, here's my card with the homicide department fax number. Send the schedules over when you get them formatted."

Turning to Campanera, "Luis, it has been good seeing you again, and, as always, a pleasure to be working with you."

"Same here, Len, Robbie," Campanera said, shaking their hands.

Andy Chiu asked, "Lieutenant Morgan, Luis, excuse me for interrupting, what was the name of the murder scene witness? I need it for my profile on van Haan."

"Gloria Mitchell, Andy." Turning back to Campanera again, Len asked, "Curious, how long have you had van Haan under surveillance? Before last Wednesday?"

"Surveillance? Full time started a morning ago. Why?"

"Damn. Van Haan indicated that on Wednesday, the morning of the murder, he went directly to his office at five-o'clock. But if you weren't tailing him until a day ago, you can't verify that."

"Yeah … sorry, we can't be of any help on that one."

The two homicide detectives left the federal building as the afternoon rush hour traffic began its slow departure out of West Los Angeles. "Len, you know all of the shortcuts out of here, you and Gabrielle spend a lot of time in Los Angeles. Direct me to a back way so I don't have to grow old commuting to the Valley."

"Well, take Wilshire and go west to the northbound 405," Len advised, grinning, awaiting Jeff Robinson's response, "…that way you'll miss the major portion of the slow northbound traffic."

"Hey, the 405 is what I want to avoid. It's gonna' be packed this time of day."

"Probably not as packed as your 'short cut'. Everyone uses the canyon roads across the Santa Monica Mountains to avoid the rush. It's like Yogi Berra's remark about that posh restaurant in Kansas City, or wherever it was."

Jeff Robinson pulled the big Ford cruiser onto the ramp leading up to the 405, "Okay, I'll bite. What? What did Yogi say?"

Settling back, loosening his tie, Len replied, "Yogi said: 'No one goes there anymore, it's too crowded'."

"That's it? Yogi Berra said that? Shit … Philosophy-101, huh?"

"Yep. Now, please take me home."

On the I-405 and going uphill, leaving the Los Angeles basin behind Jeff Robinson asked, "What's your thinking on the possible Russian Mafia involvement if it turns out to be factual?"

"I was just mulling that over. It sounds far-fetched as hell to me, but it might be for real. Even so, how does it connect to the murder of a hooker? I don't see it, but I'm convinced if we are going to nail van Haan, we'd better find some concrete evidence soon or the feds will get him first."

Jeffrey Robinson dropped Len off in front of his condominium complex, waved goodbye and sped away.

Villa Casa Grande, Granada Hills...
As Len entered his living room, the rich aroma of Gabrielle's favorite brand of Irish Crème coffee filled his nostrils.

"Hello!" he called out in complete surprise. "Do I have unexpected company?"

"Hi, Len," Gabrielle's voice answered from the back hall. "I'm back here getting dressed."

In the hallway outside his bedroom, he felt the humidity created by her recent shower. "Are you decent?" he asked, removing his coat and tie. "Hi sweetheart, talk about a pleasant surprise," he said, entering his bedroom where Gabrielle was busy buttoning her blouse.

"Oh, Len, I desperately need a hug!"

They embraced and held each other close for a few seconds. "What are you doing back in Los Angeles, and are you packing?" he asked, obviously confused at seeing her suitcase lying open on his bed.

"Yes." She smiled nervously and looked into his puzzled face as she tucked in her blouse. "I just flew in and endured a horrid taxi ride from LAX. Let's go out for dinner, shall we?"

Still looking at the suitcase, he shrugged. "Sure. Where?"

"To that restaurant on La Cienega, the little cafe we like, you know, with the outdoor patio and the vine covered trellis?"

"The place with all the neon lighting, the fifties motif and Bill Haley music?"

"No, not 'Ed's', the one closer to Wilshire Boulevard. It has red awnings or canopies out front."

"Oh yeah … I remember. I'll put my tie back on and unplug the coffee pot. When you're finished packing, we can leave."

Len carried Gabrielle's luggage to the elevator that would take them to the subterranean parking garage. In the elevator, he said, "I'm curious about your unexpected arrival. What happened to the seven-week tour you began four days ago? Did you get a cancellation or something? And why are you removing your things from my place?"

"Oh, Len, it's a combination of several things. My real estate agent called me in Durham last night and said she needed my signature if I approved a proposed purchase offer on the house. I asked if a fax would suffice. She apologized but said it would be better if I could be here to sign it in person. You know how fussy some of these Bel Air real estate agents are."

"Your real estate agent? What agent?" Len asked, becoming more confused. "Are you selling your house? Where are you going to live?"

"Len," Gabrielle answered, "let's eat first, then I'll explain it all afterward, okay?"

"I guess," Len said, shrugging. Still perplexed, he left the elevator and walked across the glistening concrete floor toward his car.

"Poor little car," he said quietly, getting into his snappy black Audi S4 Turbo sedan. "You never get to stretch your little tires and run the roads anymore. Let's see if you'll start." Len buckled his seat belt and turned the ignition switch. The car responded immediately.

The traffic on the Simi Valley Freeway was light and the two of them sat in silence as he wove the Audi through the remains of the early evening traffic to reach the southbound 405 and back into the Los Angeles basin. His mind was in mass confusion.

As he drove, Len recalled the last morning they were together; it was four days ago. He had awakened early, responding to 'Nature's call'. Gabrielle had stayed overnight and was still sleeping soundly in the middle of his bed. Getting up, he remembered having glanced at the time on the clock-radio.

It was just past five o'clock, he thought. *I got up, tiptoed to the bathroom, and relieved myself. Finished, I recall drawing a glass of water, drank it and returned to the warm bed and Gabrielle. I put my arm around her shoulders and pulled her close. She murmured softly, we kissed and fell asleep.*

Gabrielle must have responded to the radio later. She woke me up saying she had to shower and get out of there or miss her flight to Atlanta.

When she stepped from the steaming shower, her youthful looks confirmed the fact that she was seven years younger than me. After drying from her shower, she said I was amusing, passionate and lovable too. "I'll miss you, dearest," and she went into the kitchen.

She brought back the coffee and we discussed her upcoming seven-week tour with her Southern California String Ensemble.

I remember her saying it was "...a surprise visit to the Clinton White House, if the ship of state was still afloat when they reached Washington, D.C." Then she said her taxi would arrive soon and she finished dressing.

His thoughts continued, *That took place just four days ago; it's funny how quickly things can change. Four days ago she looked back at me as she entered the taxi that misty morning; she smiled and waved before disappearing in the fog.*

Speeding down the I-405 San Diego Freeway, alone in his thoughts of happier times, a familiar yet uninvited feeling began to consume him. *I wonder if I'll ever get used to being alone,* he thought, glancing across at Gabrielle, still sitting silently and staring ahead into the dark night.

As they sped toward Los Angeles for dinner, her troubling behavior was boggling Len's mind, causing that lonely, empty feeling to creep into his consciousness again. *Weird, because she's sitting here beside me.*

Reaching Westwood, Len took Wilshire Boulevard East to La Cienega Boulevard and the awaiting restaurant. "Well, look at that," he said, "a parking place out front. Isn't that providence?"

" 'Go for the front row', as you always say, Len."

The two entered the cafe and opted for seats outside under a heavily vine-covered patio trellis. They ordered from the list of light dinner specials and ate, not conversing or looking at each other.

Len sat and stared at the menu, not really reading the words. He recalled his first meeting with Gabrielle. It began that morning three years ago on her meandering front porch as he investigated a celebrity homicide near her Bel Air home. *Yeah, her charm, auburn hair and those flashing green eyes did get my attention.*

He also recalled how they hit it off immediately and later began to date regularly, enjoying each other's company and close physical relationship often and profusely until now.

Len broke the awkward silence, "Gabrielle … what? Please talk to me. You return unexpectedly, pack your clothes, and disclose your covert plans to sell your house, and then this complete silence. Is it my toothpaste?"

Gabrielle smiled nervously and reached across the table for his hand, "No. It's not you. I've just had so much happening in my life lately. It's not you, Len."

"Then what is it?"

"Please, I understand your confusion, but this is a sad time for me, and for us."

Len touched his napkin to his mouth and looked directly at her, deep into her eyes, "A sad time? Us? Why is that?"

"Len, we've been together a long time and when our relationship was new and fresh it was perfect. Perfect for both of us at the time." She hesitated, and then added, "But times change."

"And the changing times make our relationship less than perfect?" he asked. "These several years have been less than perfect?" he settled back into his chair and rested his hands atop his thighs. "What's so imperfect with our relationship?"

"It's going nowhere, Len, that's what. I still love you, but not like a deep, lasting love. I loved you for all of the good times together through those years."

Gabrielle stopped speaking and took a moment to gather her thoughts. "I know you're not willing to venture into a permanent, long-term relationship." She continued, "You've said as much yourself. And at first, I didn't want that either."

"But now it's different?" Len wiped his sweaty palms on his napkin and reached for his water glass: his mouth was suddenly parched. "Now you want an enduring relationship? And you said loved? Past tense?"

"Len, there is so much more that I want in life now. I don't know where to begin. Yes, it is different. I've changed and I want a commitment. I know you aren't ready for that … not now, or ever." Gabrielle sat quietly and looked away at the resplendent vines covering the trellis. "And yes, loved, past tense. I have met someone else."

The words, *someone else,* struck him with the force of a George Foreman uppercut. Completely stunned, he sat silently weighing those words over again while resisting the fleeting impulse to upend the table and send it flying across the room.

He sat his water glass down and touched the napkin to his mouth again. "So," he raised his eyebrows and paused, his words came slowly, "…you want our relationship to end, to terminate, is that it?"

Tears appeared on her cheeks as she looked back at him. She swallowed hard and whispered, "Yes, I do. I'm sorry."

Len reached into his pocket and handed his handkerchief across the table. He forced a weak smile and wiped his sweaty palms with his napkin. "Gabrielle, you know I've always been agreeable to anything. It's always been that way with us. It's … it's just so damned abrupt!"

The ensuing silence was deafening. After a moment, he gathered himself and spoke again. Carefully choosing his words and with his voice nearly breaking he asked, "As adults in an imperfect world, is this where we simply shrug and say 'That's life?' Well, sometimes life absolutely sucks."

Gabrielle nodded.

"If you're finished with dinner, I'll drive you home. Are you ready?"

She turned her head away and again stared at the vine-covered trellis. Releasing his hand, she whispered, "Yes. I'm ready. Please take me home."

She glanced furtively at him, dabbing at the mascara smudges on her cheeks with his handkerchief, "Don't hate me?"

Len hung his head, "Hate you? Don't be silly." his voice broke as he stood. He reached into his pocket, removed several large bills and tossed them on the table. "I'm well beyond hating you."

"I guess that's fair. Would you like me to explain further about my decision? May I?" she asked.

"Sure, why the hell not? Fill me in on the way back," he muttered flatly, exhibiting no emotion.

As they drove away from the café, Gabrielle, with tears starting to form, began to explain, "I met a man on the tour several months ago, a New England gentleman from Boston. He followed our tour from city to city and attended every performance. He overwhelmed me with attention: flowers every day, dinners at the finest restaurants and the like. We didn't have sex at first…"

Len took the cue and noisily cleared his throat, hoping to avoid hearing the intimate details.

"Last evening he proposed, he asked me to marry him; immediately. I accepted."

Len nodded and cleared his throat again while noticing that he was gripping the steering wheel too tightly and exceeding the posted speed limit. Relaxing his foot from the accelerator, he replied, "And … ah, first, allow me to clarify something, our nights ago you slept in my bed. Now, tomorrow you are flying back east to get married to a Bostonian. Is that what you're telling me?"

"You make it sound so … so shabby; so common."

"Shabby and common are your words. My intention was to merely seek clarification."

Gabrielle remained silent for a few seconds. Taking a deep breath, she added, "The house sale is nearly complete, and this will be my last night in Los Angeles."

"I see."

After several more minutes of deafening silence, Len pulled the Audi up to her security gate and punched in the entry code sequence. He parked in front of the mansion, gathered her luggage and accompanied her to the front door for the final time.

"Do you want to come in?" she asked, "For a coffee or…"

"No," he whispered quickly, his throat beginning to tighten. "Let's end it here. This is…"

"I know, I am so sorry … goodbye, dear Len."

Len nodded and turned away in order to hide his imminent tears. Upset that he was having such a strong, emotional reaction, he quickly left the porch and got into his car. Old memories filled his mind as he looked back at her a last time. She stood alone, silhouetted in the bright doorway. He swallowed hard as the hot acrid tears of pain and sadness flowed freely from his eyes.

"Dear Len? Bitch."

He hit the accelerator and sped out of the gateway into the awaiting comfort of the dark night. He sought to distance himself as quickly as he could from this deep, bitter hurt.

Day 4, Saturday, 6:00 a.m., June 8…
Len spent a tormented night sleeping fitfully. When he awoke, it was early afternoon and his bedding was a hopelessly tangled mess on the floor. Deciding not to spend the day at home alone, brooding, he ate a bowl of cold cereal, dressed in his faded UCLA University sweats and drove across the Valley to his office.

His previously troubled mind cleared somewhat as he drove. Looking back, many things took on a clarity that hadn't been there the night before.

Gabrielle wanted to get married all these years and I've been too busy or feeble-witted to see it, he thought. *I never wanted to remarry, not then, or now, or to her.*

The very thought of ever remarrying again made him uncomfortable based on his tragic history with Melissa, her unexpected death and his short marriage to Carole. *So, maybe this is all for the best; she gets what she wants, a loving husband, and old "Dear Len" remains single. When I get to the office, I'll call her, apologize for being such an egregious asshole last night, and at least wish her good luck.*

Arriving in the VWPD homicide squad room, he waved a quick "Good afternoon" to Sergeant Svetlana Belanova and Wolf Mueller, handling the last hours of the weekend daywatch. At his desk, Len called Gabrielle's home number. The telephone rang incessantly. *Damn! She must have left town already.*

Disgusted with himself, he attempted to bury his thoughts in his work. He began by examining the pile of taxi records that Mariko Tanaka had accumulated. He looked through them meticulously, page-by-page, entry-by-entry.

So, he thought, *three different taxis delivered passengers to the Valley Arms Hotel in the twenty-four hour period before the slaying of Lorena Reynolds. Five taxis picked up passengers in the four hours following the approximate time of the murder.* Len logged this data in his PC and made printed copies for Miss Tanaka and Jeff Robinson to examine in further detail on Monday.

He looked outside; it was dark. Svetlana and Wolf had left and he was alone. Out of curiosity, he retrieved Detective Paul Tobin's latest status report from his computer on the RFK Junior High classroom murders. Len noted that the young victim's name was George Stamos, age 13, and he lived with his parents in Woodland Hills. The other victim was a male teacher, 37 years of age, married with three children, and commuted from Thousand Oaks.

What a goddamn waste, Len thought. *Who could do a thing like this? More, why?*

The case records showed that Paul Tobin had interviewed two students, the total of George Stamos' closest friends. They both indicated that George was a quiet, studious type whose main interest was in Algebra: factoring polynomials.

Not usually a hot topic of teenage conversation these days, Len concluded. The statements from the students shed no light on the shootings.

Len continued reading: three RFK students received permission from their parents to assist the composite artist in the rendering of the perpetrator's face.

"Great!" Len said aloud, and switched applications and opened an art file. In seconds, the composite image of a young man's face appeared on his monitor screen.

Len studied the facial features; *He looks like any other normal Latino youngster, maybe about high school age. Average: except for his sharp pronounced nose, shaved hair on the temples, the rest combed straight back on the top. Hmm... nothing extraordinary, no tats, scars or missing teeth.*

I'm curious if the other school pictures we requested gave us anything, or if we're attempting to match this sketch electronically with any other area school's photo records, maybe even our mug books. I'll leave a note for Paulie.

Stretching and yawning, Len said aloud, *"Shit, I'm bushed. Time to go home; this aching body needs some sleep."*

Day 5, Early Sunday, June 9...

It was just past midnight when he left the precinct on Sunday morning. At home, he showered, changed his bedding, and slept.

Upon awakening later, he drove to Marina Del Rey to relax and spend the rest of the day on his sailboat. He puttered around doing some menial in-cabin cleaning and polishing. When the marina's convenience store opened, he purchased a can of paint remover, a couple of dishtowels and a large bag of cat chow. His task today was to remove the gold-leaf script that read "Miss Gabrielle" from the heavily varnished transom.

While he worked on removing the script, he enjoyed the companionship of a longhaired white feline stray he called

'Cat'. Curled nearby, sleeping mostly, Cat would awaken occasionally to yawn, and then resume napping.

Len, like his old renovated thirty-nine foot Bermuda Sloop, needed some tender loving care. On this particular Sunday, the sloop and Cat were the perfect therapy to help him put Gabrielle's abrupt departure out of his mind.

I wish I could have reached her on the phone to apologize for being such a jerk. Oh well. I can drive past her place, get the phone number of her real estate agency and get in touch with her through them. Rethinking that he concluded, *or perhaps not.*

When he finished with the removal of the gold leaf, Len stowed his tools below deck in the cabin and locked the boat securely. Giving Cat's fuzzy chin a parting scratch, he opened the bag of chow, dumped it into a large plastic bowl he kept handy and placed it on the aft deck.

There, Miss Cat, that should hold you for a while. Now keep close guard, don't let any vermin aboard.

Totally relaxed, he strolled leisurely to the parking area where he'd left his black Audi. *What a beautiful day, I love it down here*, he thought, enjoying the last few minutes of this peaceful time at the marina.

As he opened the car door, he noticed his pager's tiny red light blinking furiously. *Shit! I forgot to clip it on my waistband again.* The VWPD Watch Command Dispatch number appeared when he activated the pager.

Okay, what did dispatch want with me at one-thirty on a Sunday? Curious, he ran quickly to the marina general store to the nearest payphone.

Earlier, day 5, Sunday, June 9...
The sweltering midday sun shone unmercifully, choking the San Fernando Valley on an otherwise uneventful, quiet Sunday. A smattering of fair weather clouds laced the sky back dropped against a bright blue as the small white sedan stopped at the curb in front of the drab stucco cottage.

A pizza delivery man got out of the passenger's side of the car and took the service walk to the cottage's front door. Atop his right hand was a large pizza box that he carried like a serving tray. He rang the doorbell and waited patiently, humming a nameless tune. His brilliant red and blue satin jacket gleamed luminously in the bright sunlight.

A man's voice from inside the cottage responded through an intercom system, "Yes? What is your business?"

"Your pizza, *monsieur*," the distinctive European voice of the delivery man answered.

"Pizza? We didn't order any pizza. Sorry, you must have the wrong address," the voice on the intercom responded.

"But, *pardonne moi, monsieur*," the delivery man said, looking at the address label on the box. "This delivery label reads twelve-seventeen. That's the number of your house, no? That is what the label on this box reads."

"Yes, this is number twelve-seventeen, but no one here ordered a pizza."

Confused, the pizza man checked the delivery address label again and suggested, "*Mon ami*, one moment? I'll have to throw this pizza away when I get back to the store. You are welcome to have it, free, no cost. Why let a perfectly good ham and pepperoni pizza go to waste? It is yours if you want it."

The voice inside didn't respond immediately. Then, "You say it's free? You'll just give me the pizza for free?"

"*Oui, monsieur*. It is yours if you want it."

The pizza delivery man heard a security bolt release, then the massive wooden door swung open, revealing an older man wearing a white shirt and dark slacks.

"*Merci, mon ami*, you have made a fateful decision…"

SPLAT! SPLAT!

The silencer-equipped pistol hidden beneath the pizza box spewed forth its ugly message of death into the unsuspecting man's chest. The force of the impact knocked him backwards onto the floor. The gunman pitched the pizza box into the room and quickly entered the cottage. He stepped over the dead man's body and holding the pistol with both hands, moved cautiously toward the back of the cottage.

Close behind, the driver of the small white sedan entered the house and quickly closed the entry door.

The gunman entered the kitchen and surprised a matronly looking woman dressed in a white cotton blouse and dark slacks. Shocked at the sight of an armed stranger in her kitchen, she instinctively reached for the snub-nosed revolver clipped to her waist. It was her last move.

SPLAT! SPLAT!

Two more bullets soundlessly found their target and the woman fell heavily to the hard kitchen floor.

"I've got her! She's back here!" a voice yelled from a room in the rear of the cottage. The gunman ran into the center hall of the dwelling. The voice was that of his driver who appeared, forcefully dragging Gloria Mitchell out of a bedroom. She resisted like a wild woman, screaming at the top of her lungs.

The gunman struck her with a hard backhand blow across her temple with his weapon. Rendered unconscious, she slumped, supported by the driver.

"We must get her out of here," the gunman insisted. "Quickly!" The driver nodded.

Taking hold of her arms, they lugged her to their car parked at the curb and clumsily pushed her into the rear seat where she slumped to the floor.

"Wait, *mon ami*," the gunman ordered in his thick accent, "there is something I must do."

He ran back into the cottage. Seconds later he returned and sat in the rear seat guarding the slumped form lying on the floor. The small white sedan sped away, leaving two people dead inside the white stucco cottage.

Across the Valley at the VWPD Dispatch desk, a small red light blinked rapidly accompanied by a nagging, persistent buzzing. The chief dispatch officer turned in his swivel chair, "Uh, oh ... East Valley Safety House. What did you do, John? Forget to close the front door again?"

The officer turned back to his computer keyboard, initiated a few sharp keystrokes and then looked at a television monitor mounted at ceiling height on the enameled concrete block wall. The screen was a flurry of gray speckles and lines that moved vertically from bottom to top. He pressed another key and the picture stopped scrolling. In seconds, the monitor replayed what the security cameras at the Safety House had recorded moments before.

The dispatch officer watched the screen as Officer John Farley casually approached the door and pushed the intercom button. He watched while Farley apparently conversed with whomever was outside. As Farley opened the door, the monitor showed a tall man in pizza delivery garb, burst through the door, preceded by what looked like a pizza box, which he threw across the room exposing a gun in his hand. Farley's body fell to the floor.

The dispatcher watched incredulously as the gun-wielding man stepped over Farley and disappeared off screen. A second man entered carrying a gun. After he closed the front door, he disappeared off screen following the first man.

"Holy-Mother-of-God!" the dispatch officer whispered, crossing himself. His wide eyes stared in utter disbelief at the scene playing on the monitor. It took him several seconds to regain his composure. Upon doing so, he keyed the large microphone located on the desk in front of him.

"Attention all units, we have a Code-three! Repeat, Code-three! Proceed to the Devonshire East Safety House. Officer down, condition unknown, possible Code-187! Repeat, Code-three!

Proceed to the Devonshire Safety House east. Officer down, condition unknown, possible Code-187!"

At Marina Del Rey, Len placed a quarter into the pay phone and called Watch Command Dispatch. Grumbling again about the lack of a cell phone as he waited through a couple of rings.

"Valley West Police dispatch,"

"This is Morgan, Devonshire Hills Homicide. I was paged earlier this afternoon, what's up?"

"One minute, Lieutenant, Chief of Detectives Rogers wants to speak with you."

Puzzled that the Chief was on duty on a weekend, he waited on hold.

"Len? Clara Rogers here ... where are you? We're having a really bad afternoon today."

"I'm at Marina Del Rey, Chief, what's happened?"

"We lost the East Valley Safety House this afternoon," she explained, "during the commission of an apparent abduction of your female witness after the brutal killing of Officers Farley and Beck. From all appearances, it looks like a professional hit. Both officers were shot twice in the chest and twice in the back of the head."

"Holy shit," Len murmured. "Excuse me, ma'am ... my language."

"Can you explain what is going on?" she demanded. "What makes a common hooker so important, Lieutenant? I'm told that this was supposed to be an ordinary protective custody confinement. Now I have two dead cops in the morgue, one with a widow to console. It's a damn shame. Those officers were decent folks. They'd paid their dues and were on Safety House duty to finish out their time until retirement. Safety House is a goddamn oxymoron at this time; safe my ass."

Standing in the hot afternoon sunlight, Len was stunned at the grievous news. At the same time, it was apparent that Chief Rogers was taking this hard. Age wise, he guessed Chief Clara and Officer Beck to be relatively close in years.

"Chief, I'm beyond sorry. This is unbelievable. How can I be of any assistance? With the widow, or the families? I'll do anything, let me know?" Len tried vainly to be of some comfort as he stood, sweating profusely, in disbelief of what he had just heard.

"Len, did you have any suspicions that someone would try to remove her from our custody? And another thing, how did anyone know she was there?" the frustrated Chief asked.

Len stammered and pinched the sweaty bridge of his nose with thumb and finger. "No ... no ideas, especially on how anyone would know. I suspected that someone might want to get to her, that's why we confined her."

"I've asked the FBI to assist us, with the kidnapping aspect, of course, and more because two of our cops were murdered. Neither the FBI nor I think we'll be asked to raise any ransom, but something about this stinks to high heaven."

"I agree, Chief. We had her telephone line tapped, maybe the FBI can look into that, it might lead somewhere."

"I'll pass that along. And you asked what you can 'do for me'? You can make sure the detectives Dutch Ryan sent out there are capable enough to find this cop killer, that's what. I want the dirty scum that did this; bring 'em in here. Now I've got to notify some family members. Later."

Len placed the receiver back in its cradle. Benumbed by the events, he stood and stared at nothing in particular for a few seconds. Taking a deep breath and inhaling the salty Pacific air, he turned and ran quickly to his car.

His mind raced as he ran. *Who could get into the Safety House and abduct Gloria Mitchell? And why? Unless they were breaking her out. And why the execution style murders? What kind of message was that supposed to send?*

No logical answers were forthcoming as he sped north on the 405-freeway and into the summer heat of the Valley. When he arrived at the Safety House, he had to park a block away because of the gathering congregation of police cruisers and ME vans. He walked through a crowd of uniformed cops gathered outside on the lawn and entered the front door. Yellow police tape stretched throughout the interior of the house.

"Who's in charge, Officer?" he asked of the stocky uniformed cop standing inside the entry.

"Detective Sergeant Belanova and Detective Mueller, sir. You'll find them in the kitchen."

Frowning, Len looked uneasily at the tiled floor with the narrow white tape outline that marked the position of a previously fallen cop, then at the huge meandering dark bloodstain, then back at the stocky young officer. "I don't have any booties with me…"

The officer nodded, "It's okay, sir. Forensics have finished, you can go back to the kitchen."

Len nodded grimly and walked to the rear of the cottage. "Lana, Wolf, I just heard. I was at the marina messing with my boat all day and I left my damn pager in my car. Chief Rogers said you were here. What have you got?"

"Two good cops are in the morgue," Sergeant Svetlana Belanova whispered, obviously shaken but collected enough to be concise. "Both of them were killed by shots to the chest, and then shot twice post mortem, execution style in the back of the head; clean and efficient, like an afterthought."

"Or a calling card," Detective Wolf Mueller suggested as he entered the kitchen from the back yard.

"FBI?" Len asked. "Any trace evidence? Did forensics find anything useful?"

"Spent cartridges from a nine-millimeter," Mueller answered. "Not another damn thing except a pizza box. CSI is testing for latent prints from the shell casings, the door hardware and the box. The FBI came and went already. Right now they're probably with Chief of Detectives Rogers, or Dutch, looking through whatever you and Robbie have in your files relevant to Gloria Mitchell."

"Who is this Gloria Mitchell anyway?" an agitated Svetlana asked. "We heard she was a hooker, a friend of the murdered hooker in the case you guys are working. Is that right? Another hooker? Is a hooker so goddamn hot that busting her out of slam is worth killing two cops? Unbelievable!"

"Yes, it is unbelievable, Lana. To explain, the first hooker and Gloria Mitchell were business partners, so to speak," Len said. "I ordered her confined here to keep her alive, away from whoever may have killed her friend. That didn't work out so well. I wish there was some way to determine if she was abducted, or if she walked out arm in arm with the shooter."

"Shooters, plural," Belanova corrected, dabbing at her mascara smeared cheekbones. "There were two of them. Dispatch has it on video tape, compliments of the in-house security system."

Len looked around the room. He spotted two surveillance cameras mounted above the kitchen cabinets and presumed the entire house must be similarly equipped.

Belanova continued, "Anytime the entry doors open the cameras activate and the pictures are transmitted to Watch Command where they are recorded. So, two guys walked in, shot Farley and Beck and schlepped your hooker out the front door. The shooter, a tall light-haired type, revisited the house. He rolled Farley over and gave him two in the head, then disappeared off camera where another camera saw him repeat the procedure with Beck. Unbelievable!"

Len shook his head in disgust, "Guys, look, I'm sorry. Investigating any murder is total shit, especially when it's two cops you've worked with; then it's even worse." He paused, hearing only the strained breathing of the three of them, then he asked, "Is there anything I can do for you?"

"No."

"Okay, I'm gonna' beat it back to the precinct and see Dutch, if he's still there."

Len strode into the homicide squad room and went directly to Captain Dutch Ryan's office. The door was open and Dutch was sitting behind his desk sipping bourbon and water from a small glass. Although it was Sunday evening, the recent events of the afternoon demanded his presence. Len knocked softly on the oak doorjamb, "Dutch, got a minute?"

Seeing Len, Dutch smiled. "Len, come in," he said, letting out a heavy sigh. "For you I have all night. Come in and have a seat. Care for a drink? You've been to the Safety House?"

"No, thanks, and yes. I just left Lana and Wolf. They're distraught as all hell, but I'm sure they'll be okay. You sent the right team, Dutch."

"I sent the best team that was available," Dutch said, leaning back in his swivel chair, looking tired and much older. "You and Robbie have more than enough to handle with your hooker case. Paulie and Coop are interviewing half of the RFK Junior High School student body. What are your thoughts about this so-called abduction? Is Gloria Mitchell part of it, or was she actually abducted?"

"I'm at a total loss, Dutch … Lana said the video tape replay showed Mitchell unconscious and being dragged out the door by the two shooters. If she was part of the escape plan, they went to great lengths to make it appear to be an abduction. If she wasn't, who knew she was there? And what makes her important enough to kidnap, not to mention the blatant execution of two cops? Why her?" Len asked, frustrated by the current events.

"I saw the tape replays a few minutes ago," Dutch said, his voice breaking slightly. "I get cynical as hell when cops are killed. I nearly puked when I saw that tall bastard back into the kitchen, rolling Lynda Beck over and … damn … and put two caps in her head. I nearly bought it, son," His fabled hardboiled image softened. "…and Miss Mitchell looked unconscious on that video."

Len took a deep breath and responded, "I don't know if I ever want to see those videos, Dutch. I don't think I need that. Let's change the subject. Did the FBI visit you today or did they contact the Chief?"

"Both, first they met with Clara Rogers, then came here. Pecking order you know, we have to be politically correct. You know the routine," Dutch snorted, a major amount of sarcasm in his raspy voice.

"What was the end result of the FBI visit, and who was it? Anyone we know?" Len asked, shifting in his chair.

"I didn't know him, a nice fellow though. Just a minute," Dutch answered, opening his center desk drawer.

"Is there any cold water left in your fridge?" Len asked.

"There's bottled water, juices, soft drinks, better bourbon too: a new bottle of 'JDB'. Help yourself to anything. Get another water for me too while you're in there, I'm parched."

After unscrewing the cap from the water bottle, Dutch removed a calling card from his center drawer, it read:

J. Fulton Smith, Chief Special Agent
United States Department of Justice
Federal Bureau of Investigation

Los Angeles, California

"I've never met him before; you?" Dutch asked, handing the card to Len.

Len looked at it, feeling the embossed printing on its face, "Nope, never. Nice quality card though. When are we going to get some like that, Dutch? And cell phones too?" Len asked, smiling as he offered to return the card.

"Your ass, and keep the card, you may need it later," Dutch said as he poured another splash of bourbon into his glass. "I pulled your files on Gloria Mitchell. I made J. Fulton copies of what you and Robbie compiled. Then we went downstairs and watched those damn tapes. Three different cameras caught those two bastards. How brazen can it get, blowing away two cops while the video cameras played on?"

Len shook his head and took a long drink of his bottled water.

"Agent Smith had Watch Command make copies of the videos," Dutch explained. "He's going to have still shots made of the best available frontal and profile facial views of the shooters and run a make on them. Smith will Fed-ex what he has back to us tomorrow morning. Obviously, the Feds will work the abduction angle; our team will apprehend the murderers."

Len grunted, and, finished with his water, took the empty plastic bottle over to Dutch's recycle bin.

"One good thing did come out of this for you," Dutch said, his tired eyes twinkling a bit.

"I can't begin to imagine what that would be, sir. What is it?"

"The newspaper and TV folks will be concentrating on Svetlana and Wolf instead of you and Robbie. I know that'll break your heart."

"True. I'm not much of a fan of our protectors of Free Speech, but, if Beck and Farley could be brought back, I'd gladly deal with the media. Lana and Wolf will do a great job for you, Dutch. I admire both of them."

"As do I. We got a helluva prize when Svetlana gave up an aspiring career with the Russian Ballet to join our force. And Wolf, he has one calculating mind, though he does his best to hide that attribute."

"For two nationalities that historically have little in common, those two get along fabulously, at least that's my opinion," Len added.

"Yes, very much so." Dutch pushed his chair back, placed the empty glass in his desk drawer and got to his feet, stifling a yawn. "Len, drag me out of here and point me in the direction of my car. I need some sleep; I don't know when I've been so damn tired."

"I hear you, let's go."

Len flipped the light-switch turning off the lights on the way out and the two veteran detectives left for their respective cars.

Day 6, Monday morning, June 10...

Len Morgan and Jeff Robinson skipped breakfast, but rode to the precinct together as usual. Missing this day was the usual teasing and kibitzing. Jeff Robinson had heard about the Safety House shooting on the Sunday Evening News Hour. He knew both of the slain cops personally and listened attentively as Len filled him in on the particulars.

"Lana and Wolf are handling the case and a Special Agent of the FBI, J. Fulton Smith, is assigned to it. When we get to the office, I'd like you to contact him and volunteer our help or assistance in locating Gloria Mitchell and her abductors."

"Sure."

"We desperately need her testimony regarding the cologne if we are going to hang anything on van Haan, Robbie.

She's about all we have, other than Josephs' nose. Oh ... one other small item," Len added looking to his right, staring at nothing. "Gabrielle broke off our relationship last night. She's getting married to some well-to-do easterner she met while on tour."

Jeff Robinson looked at Len in disbelief, "Len ... I don't know what to..."

Len waved him off. "It's okay, Robbie. Really, it's okay."

Back at the precinct, Len sat at his desk reading a memo from the District Attorney's office stating that the ME had released Lorena Reynolds' body to her family. They were having it flown back to New Lebanon, Tennessee, for burial services on Wednesday afternoon, June 12. Hearing Dutch Ryan calling his name, Len rose and headed to the Captain's office.

"Good morning, Len. I have the ME's report here. Take it with you; nothing new. They did determine the knife found in the alley was the murder weapon. Also, I want you to catch an early plane Wednesday morning and arrange to be at Lorena Reynolds' memorial service. Call ahead to the Nashville or New Lebanon PD and inquire about the prospects of hiring a police photographer to surreptitiously take photos of the attendees at the funeral service."

"Do you think our murderer may show up for the funeral, Dutch?"

"Murderers are known to, as you've seen in the past few years."

Len nodded in agreement.

"While you are there, make yourself known to all of the victim's family; be visible. Make them aware of who you are and that we're doing all we can to apprehend the perpetrator. Some positive public relations can't hurt, especially in this case."

Len agreed again. "Will do, Captain."

Returning to his desk Len called the airlines and made his reservation. He would be flying out of LAX Wednesday at 6:20am on flight #237.

He then called the New Lebanon Constable's office to inquire about a photographer. "We have a good one, a reliable young man who's usually available at a moment's notice," advised the Deputy. "If you want, I can locate him and see what his schedule is and call you back,"

"Great! I'll await your call."

Now I call that efficiency, Len thought. *I've never been to Tennessee either. I wonder if everyone there wears ten-gallon hats and writes country music. Whatever, I need a break to get away from all this personal shit, to get away from home for a day.*

His telephone rang. "Morgan here."

It was the New Lebanon Constable's office calling back. "Your photographer/driver will be waiting at your arrival point holding a sign with your name printed on it. Also, Constable Othel Baine would be pleased to meet briefly with you."

"Fine," Len said, "I appreciate your help with this, Deputy, and for the Constable's hospitality as well. Thanks again."

That is efficiency. Maybe Tennessee won't be so bad after all.

Just then, Dutch stuck his head in the door, "Len, get Robbie and meet Svetlana and Wolf at the refuse collection center in the North Valley off the Golden State. East Valley PD reports a Code-187; a female's body shot twice in the skull. This doesn't look good."

Dutch turned to go back to his office and bumped head-on into Jeff Robinson, nearly knocking him down.

"Whoa! Excuse me, Robbie, I'm sorry, son. You and Len are outta' here again. Good luck," he said, patting Jeff Robinson's shoulder as they parted.

"What's that all about?" Jeff Robinson asked, reaching for his coat.

"It appears that our executioner has struck again," Len answered as they hurriedly left the squad room. "This time it's a dead woman left in the city dump. Pray it isn't Gloria Mitchell."

"No, I meant Dutch's attitude. Is he sick?" Jeff Robinson asked as they ran to their cruiser.

"Oh, Dutch? I don't know. He's been a prince since he bit the ass off that Treasury agent. Don't knock it, partner,"

Len cautioned, out of breath, winded by the run from the elevator through the parking garage.

"Right, it's just so unlike him," Jeff Robinson said.

In the garage, they came upon Vice Detective Lanny Boyle, who was taking a smoke break. "Hi, guys, what's up, another crime to solve?"

Len stopped, considering an answer. "Lanny, what's on your immediate agenda, right now ... anything pressing?"

Boyle took a final drag on his cigarette, butted it in the sand-filled bucket and answered, "No. It's a quiet day on our end. What's up?"

Len looked tentatively at Jeff Robinson, who cocked his head and shrugged as he fathomed what Len was about to suggest. "Lanny, we just got a call about a dead female's body in the refuse collection center in the East Valley. There's a strong possibility that you might be interested, if you get my drift, or you might not ... your choice. Care to ride along?"

Lanny Boyle looked into Len's eyes, eyes as penetrating and serious as he'd ever seen them, and they had worked closely together years before when Len was assigned to the Vice Squad. "Uh ... yeah, thanks, I will ride along. Do you mind if I light up?"

"I mind, Lanny. If you can wait until we get to the refuse center, help yourself there," Jeff Robinson suggested.

"Will do."

Getting into the cruiser, Jeff Robinson asked, "Are we in a big hurry?"

"Not that big, Robbie. I doubt the body will mind if we get mired in traffic."

The three detectives sped easterly across the Valley to the Golden State I-5. They exited at an off-ramp that led to a narrow gravel service road that accommodated one of the Valley's huge refuse collection centers.

"Dutch said the victim had two wounds in her skull, Lanny. It sounds like our Safety House shooter's work to me," Len suggested as they approached the center.

"And that's where Gloree, the hooker, was abducted from?" Boyle asked. "The hooker that you and I had a discussion about?"

"The very same, Lanny," Len answered. "If this body turns out to be her, you might realize some closure; one less hooker for Vice to bother with."

"Yeah. Thanks, Len, I appreciate you and Robbie asking me along."

"Here we are, gentlemen, and try not to breathe the air," Jeff Robinson announced as he stopped the cruiser at the wire-mesh gate attended by a young uniformed East Valley police officer.

Len lowered his window and flashed his shield, "Which way, Officer?"

"Straight ahead, maybe a thousand meters, sir. Just over that rise. You'll see the others parked to your right. Be careful not to stray off the roadways or trails. You may get stuck."

"Thanks, Officer. Okay, Robbie, let's rumble."

Upon reaching the crime scene, Jeff Robinson parked behind a Valley East PD cruiser. The three detectives got out and joined the assembled officers and criminologists gathered around. Seeing Devonshire homicide Detectives Svetlana Belanova and Wolf Mueller ahead, Len hailed them. "Hello again, people, and you all know Vice Detective Lanny Boyle?"

"Yes," Mueller retorted, nodding at Boyle. "We gotta' quit meeting like this, Lieutenant Morgan."

"What have you got, Lana?" Jeff Robinson asked as he looked inside the taped off area in the direction of the ME who was huddled with his mobile team.

Svetlana Belanova stared at the backs of the men clustered inside the secured area and replied, "We got a naked dead woman, bound and gagged with duct tape and shot twice in the base of the skull, one shot high, the other low; the same bullet pattern as Beck and Farley. It may be your abducted hooker, guys. What was her name? Mitchell?"

"Yeah, Mitchell," Len replied. "Naked? And left in the city dump … that's an attention-grabbing twist."

Vice Detective Boyle shuddered slightly in the damp air and reached for a cigarette.

The other detectives stood and quietly made small talk while the ME and his staff completed their preliminary investigation. Arising, the ME turned and approached Len and his compatriots. He removed his latex gloves, placed them in a plastic baggie and handed it to one of his staff members.

"Hey! Morgan, Robbie, Svetlana," Dr. James Franklin, the Assistant County Medical Examiner greeted, as he extended his hand. "Good to see you as always, although the setting and the air quality could be better."

"What have you got, Jim?" Svetlana inquired.

"Similar shot pattern to the skull as the two officers at the Safety House, Lana, except this definitely was an execution style killing. Point blank, lots of GSR, wrists taped behind her back and her mouth gagged with duct tape. Warner at CSI may be able to lift a usable print from that when we get her back to the lab."

"She looks beat up, or is it just the soil from this shitty place?" Svetlana asked, as Detective Boyle moved in closer to Svetlana to hear more clearly what the ME had to relate.

"No, I haven't seen evidence of a physical beating … there are no other wounds on her body. Her knees and upper arms show a heavy layer of soil residue from this location. It appears that she was on her knees when she died and then fell over. It's safe to conclude that the killer finished her off from behind."

"What a goddamn animal," Len muttered. "Is that all you were able to determine, Doc? Did CSI get any footprints or tire marks? What about the time of death? Can you speculate?"

"Slow down, Lieutenant," Franklin said, sighing. "We've determined quite a bit so far, but nothing that's useful for you as yet; no footprints, and no tire tread indentations, not in this stuff.

"Well?"

"As I said, with her wrists having been taped, it's my unofficial opinion, this woman may have been held captive...."

"And?"

"…and subjected to vaginal and anal copulation pre-mortem, several times based on the amount of dried secretions visible. That's unofficial. When I get her back to the lab I can be more specific."

Len frowned, nodded and looked away. Lanny Boyle shook his head in disgust, mashed his cigarette out on the soggy ground and stared into the distance.

"As far as the time of death," the ME continued, "her body temp and the amount of blood pooling in her extremities, indicates that she died sometime between midnight and two o'clock this morning. Until we can get her back to the lab, I can't be more precise than that. The good news is that the trash rats and wild dogs hadn't discovered her."

"Well, that's a big plus," Svetlana said, derisively.

Len shook his head, "Ugly. Thanks, Jim, you guys never cease to amaze me."

Gripping Franklin's hand and squeezing it, Len added, "We'll see you later. Excuse me; I want to view her before your boys close that body bag."

"Sure. I'll have more information available for all of you by mid-afternoon at the latest. Stop by, or call," he said and returned to his field staff.

Len, accompanied by Detective Boyle, joined his trio of detectives in the secured area where the ME's staff was in the process of arranging the dead woman's body in the plastic body bag.

Len looked down at her cold, ashen face. It was Gloria Mitchell. "Shit," he muttered softly. His eyes fixed on her, recalling the first time he'd seen her. "She was semi-attractive once, even with her scant business clothes that were too short, or too tight, or both. This is just too damn bad. No one deserves to die like this, and then be left in a stinkin' dump for rat food. What a screwin' mess this is becoming."

Svetlana and the other detectives stood silently and watched the ME's assistants zip the body-bag shut and move her body onto a gurney. Lanny Boyle stepped away from the group, turned his back and with his hands placed on his knees, vomited discretely.

"Ballistics should show us conclusively if the same weapon that did in Beck and Farley also killed her," Svetlana offered, wiping at her eyes. "I guess there's nothing more we can do out here, huh? Back to the drawing boards?"

"It certainly looks like it," Detective Wolf Mueller replied. "This is mind messin'. How in hell did the killer know where she was in the first place? Then why did he kill her after he abducted her? And naked? Hands taped behind her back? Damn!"

"Good questions and damn few good answers, Wolf. So, what are you two doing for the rest of the morning?" Len asked quietly.

"Back to canvassing the Safety House neighborhood and looking for anyone who might have seen something, anything. Care to join us? It's loads of fun," Svetlana said, chuckling sarcastically.

"I'm not doing anything particularly special this morning, are you, Robbie?" Len asked, looking at his partner who was still staring at the lifeless body bag.

"Uh … no. But I thought I might take a break from our normal laugh-a-minute-schedule and volunteer to do some canvassing too," he answered, placing his hand on Svetlana's shoulder. "If it turns up anything that will help us find that sorry sonnuva-bitch, I'll help. Count me in."

"Okay. Then Robbie, ride with Lana and Wolf," Len suggested, "I'll drop Lanny off at the precinct and catch up with you."

The several detectives nodded in agreement and returned to their respective cruisers. Leaving the odiferous refuse collection center behind, they headed out in a two-vehicle caravan: one car headed toward the East Valley and the Safety House, the second car made a non-conversational trip back to the precinct.

Later, back together, the four homicide detectives split up and completed a non-productive neighborhood canvass. Meeting back at the Safety House, they decided to visit the

ME's lab to determine if Dr. James Franklin had made any further discoveries.

The Coroner's chilly lab reeked of cleansers and exotic chemicals. The stark white-enameled walls, accompanied by the spotless stainless-steel tables, gleamed under the bright overhead lights and gave the impression of a hospital surgical room.

"This place gives me the willies every time I come here," Jeff Robinson remarked as he and the others entered the room.

"It has to be the white walls," Len suggested, "what else?"

Jeff Robinson smirked and quickly looked away, attempting to conceal his amusement at his partner's inane remark.

Assistant Medical Examiner Franklin was in his glass-enclosed office and waved to them as they approached. Len asked, "Jim, can you spare us a minute?"

"Certainly, please come in, all of you. Have a seat. Bring in some of those folding chairs from the examining room; I don't have enough in here."

The group settled in and Franklin explained, "The victim died at approximately one-thirty this morning. Death was immediate. CSI says they pulled one good print from the duct tape used to gag her. They sent it off to the FBI for a comparison check. Further examination disclosed that she'd engaged in vaginal and anal intercourse with more than one individual before her death. It's impossible to say how long before, but I can affirm that it was within hours. The act did not appear to be forced or that she was physically abused."

Len, shifted in his chair. "Jim, leaving the details of the pre-mortem fucking aside, did forensics match the slugs previously obtained from either Beck or Farley?"

"Yes, our curiosity was at a high level too, so we couriered the slugs to CSI as soon as we retrieved them. Ballistics indicated that the same weapon killed all three victims. You have an executioner out there, gentlemen: an assassin."

"Great." Sergeants Belanova and Jeff Robinson muttered in almost perfect unison.

Len cleared his throat and asked, "Were you able to establish the blood type, or DNA, of the individual she'd had intercourse with prior to her death?"

"Blood type, yes, but we experienced an anomaly at first. We obtained two distinct types. One was type 'B', the other was 'O' positive. Two different technicians were doing the blood testing using the semen specimens. Each one obtained a different blood type. We had, if you'll excuse the expression, *seminal soup*."

Taken by surprise at that remark, Jeff Robinson coughed. "Sorry," he said, "that's a new one."

Doctor Franklin smiled and continued. "It took us several more attempts, with vaginal cavity and anus swipes, to determine that we had two distinct blood types, ergo, two different sexual partners. As an aside, we also ran dry semen samples taken from her thighs. One could speculate the dried semen on her leg would be representative of the individual that indulged most recently. This is unofficial speculation of course. I'd guess, and again I stress the word guess, that the victim had engaged in consensual intercourse several times before her death. I repeat unofficially, and it appeared to be voluntary with no signs of forced penetration."

"Again, multiple sex partners aside, Jim, did you discover any evidence of drugs or narcotics in her system?" Len asked, becoming irritated.

Looking through his notes, Dr. Franklin said, "No, only some caffeine. She ingested some small amount of coffee or cola earlier. No barbiturates or narcotics; apparently she led a clean, drug free life. Also, she had eaten pizza earlier that evening."

"Well, there's a damn break!" Jeff Robinson remarked sarcastically. "Now we can show pictures of our suspects to seven thousand pizzerias in the greater Los Angeles area and maybe someone out there will recognize them."

"Sergeant Jeff Robinson?" Dr. Franklin said, "I merely attested that she had eaten pizza a few hours before her death, I meant nothing beyond that."

Discomfited, Jeff Robinson held his head in his hands for a moment, "Doctor Franklin … I was totally out of line and I apologize. It's that we have four homicide cases, all becoming complete dead ends: two dead cops, earlier a hooker, now this. We had Miss Mitchell scheduled to be a state witness. Now she's history. The frustration level here is enormous. Again, please forgive me, sir."

Nodding his head, Dr. Franklin said, "Apology accepted, Sergeant Jeff Robinson. We get frustrated in this department too. You've suffered losses. Unlike you, we haven't lost any members of our department, but I'm still deeply saddened. No offense taken, Sergeant."

Jeff Robinson nodded, rubbed his neck and stared at the floor.

Suddenly Len's pager went off. Looking at the caller ID and then across Dr. Franklin's desk at the telephone, Len asked, "May I, Jim?" Franklin nodded as he passed the instrument to Len who entered Watch Command Dispatch's number. "Lieutenant Morgan here, what's up?"

A strained voice on the other end of the line relayed a terse message, "*Lieutenant Morgan, we have a Code-187. Proceed to Officer Borys Svoboda's residence at 7998 Oakdale, in Winnetka. Watch Command Officer Berry needs assistance, sir; Officer down, two bullet wounds to the base of the skull. The apparent murder weapon is at the scene next to the body. Additional units and CSI are in progress. Clear.*"

Stone faced and not uttering a word, Len handed the telephone back to Franklin and exhaled a loud sigh. "Saddle up, everyone. It's not over yet and it's getting uglier by the hour. We have another officer down. It appears the executioner has struck again."

The three detectives sat dumbfounded as they heard Len's words. Their collective mood didn't improve either.

"He's killed another cop?" Mueller asked, stunned by the news. "Dammit!"

"When will this bullshit ever end?" an angered Svetlana Belanova asked as she grabbed her folding chair and physically threw it out the doorway where it clattered loudly across the examining room floor before striking a bench and coming to rest.

"I may as well follow you folks," Franklin said, ignoring Svetlana's outburst. "My pager will be going off in a minute too." He reached for his telephone as the four detectives departed and pressed the intercom button, "Attention, everybody, we have another homicide run."

The two unmarked police cruisers arrived at the small stucco-plastered house in Winnetka and parked behind the CSI van and two Black-and-White squad cars sitting at the curb with their rack lights flashing.

On the way to the house, Seymour, the old newsprint reporter, and his cinematographer approached Len. "What can you tell me about this rash of shootings, Lieutenant? This is how many? Four? Six?"

Agitated, Len stopped, looking at first to blow off Seymour but then he gathered himself. "Seymour, I'm not keeping count. Any shooting is one too many and I don't know as much about this one as you do; you got here first. Check with Watch Command Public Relations in the morning. Maybe we'll have some of this sorted out by then."

"That sounds like a long-winded 'no comment' to me, Lieutenant. We go to press before Watch Command can give me anything. I need information now, tonight," Seymour stated, becoming irritated.

"Okay, you want 'long-winded'?" Len snapped, ready to leave old Seymour standing in the dark. "Tune in to Geraldo, maybe he can be of some help. 'No comment' or not, I have nothing for you, but thanks for asking, good night."

Inside, the same stocky officer that he'd seen previously at the Safety House met Len. "Officer Meeker is it?" Len asked, looking at the officer's nametag. "This is getting to be a habit. Where's the victim?"

"Straight ahead, sir. On the kitchen floor. CSI is still checking for evidence so don't touch anything."

"Gotcha ... thanks, Meeker."

Len entered the small kitchen. Command Sergeant Alvin Berry, his old friend from the Lorena Reynolds' hotel slaying scene, was there. It was evident that Berry had been weeping. He stood leaning with his back against the counter top, keeping a silent vigil over the uniformed body of his fallen friend, Officer Borys Svoboda.

Svoboda's body lay face down in a pool of blood on the kitchen floor with one shot to his chest, two bullet holes in the base of his skull. A nine-millimeter Glock-20 handgun, apparently discarded by the killer, was beside his body.

"Well, this sure as hell sucks, Al, who found him?"

"His brother Stash, Stanislaus, whatever," Al Berry indicated, wiping at his right eye. "Stash is in the front bedroom. He said he came over to get Borys and the two of them were going to do supper at Red Lobster. Stash said he saw a white car leaving when he came around the corner. At least it appeared to be leaving from here, he said. When Borys didn't answer the door, Stash said he walked in and found him in the kitchen. Blood was trickling from his wounds; he hadn't been dead two minutes."

"Bastard!" Len swore, his teeth clenched in frustration. "You called EMT for Stash?"

"Yeah, they should be here by now. The ME too."

"We just left the Medical Examiner's office, he's on the way. Did Stash touch the gun or anything else that you know of?"

"He told CSI that he only touched the phone," Berry replied. "He called 9-1-1. It took him a while to make them understand what happened. It wasn't so much the language barrier, he was just so rattled. Dammit, this really sucks. You know?"

Len nodded. "Did Watch Command dispatch put out an APB or a BOLO for any white car with a single occupant?"

"I don't know. I haven't talked to 'em."

The Emergency Medical Team arrived and Detective Mueller motioned them into the front bedroom where Stanislaus Svoboda was sitting on the edge of the bed sobbing uncontrollably.

Svetlana Belanova and Jeff Robinson left him and joined the others in the kitchen.

"Al, if you want to split, we'll stay here with CSI and wait for the ME to arrive," Len suggested, placing his hand on Berry's shoulder. "No need for you to be here, okay?"

"No. I'll wait until they get here, Len. It's my job, you know?"

"Then you'll go home?"

"I will if you order me to," Berry replied, staring back at Len through his bloodshot eyes.

"Sergeant, consider it an order. After the ME arrives, you go home. Agreed?"

Berry nodded his head. "I need a beer, excuse me, sir?"

He opened the refrigerator, removed a cold can of beer and popping the top, sat down hard in one of Svoboda's kitchen chairs. He sat silently and stared at the floor as he rubbed the cold aluminum can against his clammy forehead.

"Ya' know that beer looks good to me too," Len said as he opened the refrigerator and took out what was left of a six-pack. He removed a can for himself and handed the remaining three-pack to his fellow detectives. "Lana, Robbie, Wolf, care to toast a fallen friend?"

Assistant Medical Examiner Franklin and his field staff arrived shortly afterward. The CSI forensics crew finished their work and, along with Sergeant Al Berry, left for home. Detectives Morgan, Jeff Robinson, Belanova, and Mueller followed soon afterward leaving the Medical Examiner and his team to complete their work.

Before he left the small house, Len instructed the forensics technician, Look through Borys Svoboda's desk or anywhere else where he may have letters or other pertinent communications stored. Look for anything suspicious. I have an ugly gut feeling about this. I want anything you find. Call me later on my pager, okay?" The forensic technician nodded and Len departed with Jeff Robinson.

10

Monday evening, June 10...

"So, what do you suspect?" a sullen Jeffrey Robinson asked as they drove across the darkening Valley. "Why do you want forensics to toss Svoboda's place?"

Len took a deep breath. "Svoboda was in Dispatch, right? We've been wracking our brains since Sunday at the Safety House trying to figure out how those two killers knew of Gloria Mitchell's whereabouts. Now we have another cop with two holes in the back of his head. This doesn't look good for Svoboda."

"How? Where does he fit in?" Jeff Robinson asked, becoming agitated.

"Let's presume for a minute that the killers had a mole in the department, Robbie, one who knew where their quarry was. They would have no trouble picking a good time to knock off the Safety House and abduct her. Make any sense?"

"A 'Mole'?" Jeff Robinson responded, a growing edge in his voice. "You've been reading too damn many Robert Ludlum mysteries, man. Do you suspect Borys? Do you think he was a mole, or whatever you call it?"

Len ignored Jeff Robinson's question.

"Dammit, Len, Borys was a good guy!" Jeff Robinson said sharply. "And he was a good cop. He took the same oath you and I did. Give him some credit, or at least respect the dead!"

"Robbie, I'd suspect you in these circumstances if you were lying on that floor. I'm sorry, but I'm at the point in this case where everyone looks suspicious." Finished speaking, Len sat motionless and quietly stared straight ahead through the windshield of the cruiser.

"Well, thanks a lot, friend," Jeff Robinson uttered, a sharp, sarcastic bite in his voice.

Len's head snapped around, "Robbie! Put your emotions and loyalties aside for a minute and look at the facts! Two men actually broke into a departmental Safety House and abducted a state witness. Who told them she was there? Who knew? The only people who went there were cops. The only people who knew she was there were cops. Who else besides a cop could have told the two killers where Gloria Mitchell was confined? It had to be a cop, worse yet, one of our own!"

Sullen faced, Jeff Robinson took a quick glance back at Len, then back at the road.

"I know this is a hard pill for you to swallow, Robbie," Len continued, "…but a mole, or if you prefer, a dirty cop, told whoever hired the shooters. Believe whatever shit you will, but a dirty cop told someone exactly where Gloria Mitchell was confined. There it is, shitty as hell. I'll stake my reputation on that scenario as being factual, like it or not!"

Several seconds of silence passed. Neither one speaking until Jeff Robinson said softly, "Uh, Len. You'll probably want to join Colleen and me for supper tonight, right?"

Len stared back at Jeff Robinson in utter disbelief. Then he smacked him with a hard backhand across the shoulder. "Partner, you crack me up. You're a rare case. Sure, let's eat."

Day 7, 7:55 a.m., Tuesday morning, June 11…
When Len and Jeff Robinson arrived at the precinct, the mood in the detective's squad room was unusually somber. The hushed conversations revolved mostly around the recent execution style murder of Officer Borys Svoboda.

Len went immediately into Dutch's office. "Dutch. I received a phone call at home last night from forensics before they left Svoboda's house. They relayed the contents of a telegram to me, one found in his desk, one from his mother in Poznan, Poland."

"And?" Dutch queried.

"The telegram, which CSI had translated into English, related that a strange man contacted Borys' mother that day implying that her son Borys was in major trouble; if he didn't cooperate fully as he was ordered, he'd never see his mother alive again. Svoboda's mother apparently went ballistic with fear and wanted to know what was happening."

"What the hell?" Dutch asked, taken aback by the contents of the telegram.

Len continued, "I had Watch Command ask for a subsequent search of his phone LUDs last night and they show that Svoboda made a return telephone call to his mother within the hour upon receipt of that telegram. The call lasted for about forty-five minutes. That's it. What do you think?"

"I think Borys was the victim of extortion, plain and simple, and he did what he had to, to protect his mother. That's what I think."

Made aware of this startling information, Dutch Ryan summoned his homicide detectives together in the squad room to apprise them of the telegram's contents.

"I know the press and TV news hounds will be all over this particular murder like stink-on-shit," Ryan explained in his inimitable fashion. "And they will try to make out that Svoboda was dirty. Oh … for you younger detectives, stink-on-shit is the same as green-on-grass."

The assembled group chuckled softly at their Captain's salty remarks.

"Anyway, I wanted all of you to know that whatever Borys Svoboda did, even if it inadvertently caused the deaths of our fellow cops and abduction of the victim at our Safety House, in Borys' mind, he did the only thing he could do."

The assembled detectives nodded their heads in silent agreement.

"It makes me sick to say this, too, but we will request his most current bank records. We have to verify if he's recently come into any unaccountable funds. Holy-Mother-of-God, please help us all if he accepted any money from those bastards." Taking note of the collective reaction of his assembled detectives, Dutch concluded, "That's all, girls and boys, let's go to work."

Len and Jeff Robinson returned to their office and sat quietly. Len pulled his center drawer open, removed a calling card and tossed it across the desks to Jeff Robinson. "Would you call this fellow, Robbie? See if he has made the bastards in the still photos from the Safety House videos. Excuse me, I need some coffee."

"Who is J. Fulton Smith?" Jeff Robinson shouted at the disappearing Morgan. "Is he the FBI agent who was looking for Gloria Mitchell? And bring me a cup too!"

When Len returned with the coffee Jeff Robinson was talking with Special Agent Smith. He placed a cup of the precinct coffee on the corner of Jeff Robinson's cluttered desk and sat down to eavesdrop. Listening to one-half of the conversation, Len waited for Jeff Robinson to finish. Hanging up, Jeff Robinson said, "Well, surprise, J. Fulton is a nice guy."

"Why would you have reason to think he would be anything else?"

"His name, J. Fulton ... the 'J' abbreviation first ... it looked like a sissy name to me and I don't happen to like sissies."

Len snorted and nearly choked on the hot coffee, "So, what did you determine from J. Fulton?"

"A bunch of good stuff. He forwarded electronic copies of our boy's still shots to CIA and Interpol. Interpol sent back confirmation identifying the tall, light-haired shooter. Hang on to your hat, partner, I'm gonna take you for a wild-ass ride here." Jeff Robinson took a quick sip of his coffee and referred to his scribbled notes. "This bastard is a ruthless international hit man, a notorious terrorist who uses several aliases. Known mostly as Yves-Gaston Giroux, his nationality is possibly French, Belgian, or French-Canadian. He has suspected ties to every mob or gang related syndicate in Europe and in Russia."

Jeff Robinson paused and waited for a response.

"No shit?" Len murmured. "Russia? An international hit man? What the hell gives?"

Jeff Robinson nodded and continued. "Agent J. Fulton suggested the CIA and even the Israeli Mossad might have hired him and his gun at times. Interpol has filing cabinets full of his exploits. This is one bad-ass dude, my friend."

Len sat quietly, absorbing Jeff Robinson's every word. "That's fascinating. Is there more?"

"Yeah. You won't like this either. Giroux's modus operandi is always the same. His signature is two well-placed rounds in the back of the head."

"You're right, I don't like it. What else?"

"Agent J. Fulton has it from a couple of their associates in Moscow that Giroux always leaves his weapon lying next to his last hit once his contract is completed, like some kind of ego trip calling card."

"Huh?"

"You know, like the burglar in the Pink Panther movies would always leave a white feather? This bastard also leaves the unspent clip inside the piece."

"Why?"

"I dunno … but if you count the number of rounds shot into his victims, and the number remaining in the clip including the chamber, it totals one full clip."

"You're kidding."

"Dead serious, Len, and this you will especially not like: more on his modus operandi. He shows up bare headed, no gloves, day or night, showing no respect or regard for any security cameras or witnesses, never attempts to conceal his identity, leaves fingerprints all over the place and seemingly evaporates into the ethers."

Jeff Robinson stopped, took a deep breath and a swallow of coffee. Totally stunned by this outpouring of new information, Len sat patiently, choosing to listen.

Jeff Robinson continued, "No one has yet laid a hand on him for any of his alleged exploits. There's hard evidence all over the European continent, but no one has yet been able to touch his ass. It's like he doesn't exist. A phantom."

Len, still silent, stared at Jeff Robinson, becoming nearly mesmerized at his telling of the strange legend of Yves-Gaston Giroux.

"So, Robbie, if he left his Glock at Svoboda's he must have fulfilled his contract. Let's remember to have forensics check the clip to determine how many rounds were left. May I see one of those still photos?"

"Yeah, here." Jeff Robinson removed one from his center desk-drawer and tossed it across the desks.

Len stared at it, intently concentrating on the photo. Suddenly he reacted and slammed his palm hard on his desktop. His face flushed, he stared hard at the photo of Yves-Gaston Giroux. Suddenly he jumped to his feet! "Just a damn minute!" he shouted, startling Jeff Robinson, who was in the middle of a swallow of coffee. "I know this bastard!"

"What?"

"I swear ... we were classmates at the academy twenty-five years ago! Where are the videos from the Safety House, do we have a copy here? I want to see him in action, I'm certain that I know this asshole!"

"I'll shit-sure get you a copy. First, you'd better relax, go take a pee or something before you embarrass yourself," Jeff Robinson implored, reaching for his ringing telephone as Len strode out the room.

"Miss Tanaka," Len said, approaching her desk, "please contact an old police academy friend of mine, Royal Canadian Mounted Police Commander Lawrence Fitzhugh, in Ottawa. Have him call me ASAP."

"Commander Fitzhugh, Royal Canadian…" Mariko Tanaka repeated, writing his name on a pad.

"Well," Len interrupted, "I think he's a probably a Commander by now. Anyway, then contact the LA Police Academy and have them send over glossy prints of my entire graduating class; the class of seventy-one. And don't laugh at the pictures either, Miss Tanaka, one day you'll be old and ugly."

Mariko Tanaka chuckled. "Anything else?"

"Yes, have the police academy provide copies of all admission records of any foreign exchange students from France, Belgium or French-Quebec Province, same graduating class. If anyone calls looking for me, I'll be downstairs retrieving a video from Watch Command."

At that same moment, the voice on Jeff Robinson's telephone conveyed, *"Watch Command Dispatch here, Sergeant Jeff Robinson. Werner's Motel on S. Van Nuys Boulevard reports a Code-187 in one of their units. Gunshot wounds to the back of his head."*

"Holy shit!" Jeff Robinson exclaimed. "This is unbelievable. Have forensics and the ME been notified?"

"They're rolling as we speak, sir. Anything else?" the dispatch officer asked.

"Yes. Radio Sergeant Belanova and Detective Mueller and have them meet Morgan and me there. That's all. Thanks."

Jeff Robinson slammed the telephone down, grabbed his coat and ran into the squad room. "Len, where are you?" he shouted.

Hearing him, Mariko Tanaka answered, "He's chasing down a video. It'll take him five minutes, Robbie."

"Right. Tell him to be ready to leave, pronto. I'll be back in a flash." Jeff Robinson turned and headed for the Men's Room just as Len returned to the squad room. "Len!" Jeff Robinson shouted over his shoulder, "Another body, same MO; let's roll."

"I just heard … let me get my coat."

The big silver-gray Ford cruiser crawled slowly through the non-rush hour traffic on the Valley's crowded surface streets. "I find it simply fascinating how all the 'Sunday drivers' manage to congregate on these surface streets at mid-morning," Jeff Robinson observed, obviously frustrated with the slow moving traffic.

"Yeah, they're all out here because they secretly know we don't need to see another dead body. You said you invited Belanova and Mueller to meet us? Did one of them lose a bet and it's their turn to buy donuts?"

"Just helping out, this is probably another murder to add to their caseload."

"True. I wonder if this is another contract for our international friend. This is too weird. Oh … I asked Miss Tanaka to contact a friend of mine in Ottawa, a good friend in the Royal Canadian Police Force. He attended the LA Police

Academy the same time this Giroux character and I did. Both were on the foreign exchange program."

"Is your friend a one of those famous pony-riding red-coated Canadian Mounties that always gets his man?"

"I can't say. Maybe Ottawa is too cosmopolitan for the horseback cops. Seriously, I'm going to ask him to do a background search for me. I can't recall that much about this Giroux, but I do recall he was supposedly from Quebec. I remembered listening to the way he pronounced it, with a hard 'Q', *ka-bek*, not like you and I would say it, *kwa-bek*."

"Interesting, which is right?"

"Hell if I know, nor do I much care, but that's where he said he was from. I hope the Academy has his old admission records on file. Mariko is running those down. If he used an alias, fine. How many future cops were from Quebec in that graduating class?"

"So, you think he may be in Canada now?"

"He's somewhere, Robbie. Wherever he is, I want his ass. Hey! There's the Werner Motel," Len said, pointing across the intersection. "Park behind one of those TV satellite trucks and leave our lights flashing; block his ass for a while."

As Len headed across the crowded parking lot toward the motel room he recalled that he had called Mariko by her first name again. *Strange, this becoming a habit.*

The small parking lot was jammed with Black-and-White squad cars, a CSI van, the Medical Examiner's hearse, and two local TV remote vans. As he approached, Len was greeted by a young TV newscaster and his cinematographer, "Lieutenant, what can you tell us about this shooting? Is it possibly the act of a serial killer, sir?"

"Serial killer? I doubt that's likely. And about this killing? M'man, you know more about it than I do, I just arrived. More news at eleven," Len answered, patting the newsman on his shoulder. "Stay in touch, we'll release something later."

"On this killing or on all of them?" the young reporter persisted.

"That depends on a number of things, but hang in there. We'll have a statement for you later, trust me. Now I have to go to work."

"What's up, guys?" Jeff Robinson inquired as he and Len joined Detectives Belanova and Mueller inside the motel room.

"Same ol' shit, different flies," Sergeant Svetlana Belanova said, shrugging as Len entered the crowded room. "Two bullets in the back of the skull, one high, one low, exactly like the city dump killing. The motel housekeeper found him thirty minutes ago and nearly shat her oversized panties. There he was … naked, with his head and shoulders stuffed down between the bed and the wall. All she could see was his bare ass, his limp 'Johnson' and his dangling *huevos* staring at her when she entered the room."

"Yeah, there he was," Mueller volunteered, "…naked as a plucked chicken. And he'd been fuckin' recently too. The ME suggested that he might have been shot just as he was getting it…."

"Never mind!" Jeff Robinson interrupted, grimacing at Wolf. "Do we know who he is?"

Belanova shook her head, "There's no identification anywhere, but he sure resembles the second shooter on the videos from the Safety House."

"I thought so too," Mueller said. "Have you seen the empty pizza boxes, Len? Apparently, they ate pizza for dinner last night. 'Spose it was Gloria Mitchell's last supper too?"

Feigning a high degree of intellect, Jeff Robinson touched his forehead with the back of his hand. "Whoa, this is becoming elementary, 'Doctor Watson'! My highly trained deductive mind tells me the shooters were holed up here, kidnapped Gloria Mitchell and brought her back…"

Interrupting and thoroughly unimpressed, Mueller added, "Don't forget to mention they all ate pizza and diddled a lot too, *Sherlock*. If forensics finds the roll of duct tape they gagged her with, we're making progress."

"They already found it," Len said. "Along with the clothes she was wearing when they abducted her."

"If Giroux leaves his gun after his last hit," Jeff Robinson continued, now becoming serious, "then this dude must have been offed before Svoboda."

Looking at the victim, then at Svetlana, Jeff Robinson explained, "Help me count: two, four, six, eight shots at the Safety House, two more with Gloria Mitchell, two with this guy, then three in Svoboda. That's fifteen shots fired. A Glock-20 clip holds twenty rounds … the weapon Giroux left at Svoboda's should have five rounds left unfired."

A CSI officer came out from the bathroom and hearing Jeff Robinson's conclusion, said, "Right you are, Sergeant. There were five unspent rounds. What's the connection?"

"Yeah," Belanova said, "and you keep mentioning this name 'Giroux'. Who's that?"

"Yves-Gaston Giroux, the famous international terrorist. He was one of Morgan's old police academy buddies," Jeff Robinson explained, "and probably our executioner."

"Oh, butt off, *shvartze*," Svetlana muttered, irritated at Jeff Robinson's seemingly idiotic explanation. "Who is he really?"

"Hey, *rashka*, he is really Giroux, a hired European gun." Jeff Robinson replied. "Two slugs in the back of the head are his trademark, his signature, and he always leaves his piece at the scene of the last hit of a contract. The rounds left in the gun added to the slugs in his victims equal a full clip. Since the clip left in the piece found at Svoboda's had five rounds left unfired, it's obvious to me that he's Giroux and his contract is fulfilled."

"Fascinating. A European hit man? Or a maybe a copycat?" Belanova questioned. "Why? What the hell made your hooker so important that it took an international hit man to take her out? This is not believable."

"Unbelievable as it sounds, Lana," Len added, after quietly listening to their exchange, "that is what we are facing." Turning to the CSI officer, he asked, "Did the ME estimate the time of death, Officer?"

"Ball park, Lieutenant? Last night, maybe early evening, according to the ME's assistant, sir. When they get him in the lab, they'll give it to you in hours and minutes. Oh, the woman's panties show evidence of dried vaginal secretions too."

"I guess that makes sense," Len commented. "Gloria Mitchell was apparently being used as a convenient receptacle in addition to whatever it was they really wanted from her. Thanks, Officer."

Continuing, Len instructed, "Lana, Wolf, please hang around here and wrap it up. Don't get too chatty with the media out there, but be polite; we'll give them a statement later. Personally, I think our man Giroux has flown the coop; his contract is complete if Robbie's theory is accurate. Anyway, get whatever information you can from the motel office on the license plate from the white compact. Put an APB on the plate, it's probably stolen, probably the car too. Have a ball."

"You too, Len, Robbie," Belanova said. "Later."

On the drive back to the precinct, Len ran the sequence of recent fast-moving events through his mind. *None of this makes sense. They abducted Mitchell Sunday afternoon. Took her to a motel room, ate pizza, drank coffee, and engaged in a lot of sex. Then Giroux offs his accomplice while he's enjoying some "strange," apparently to lower the risk of apprehension? Then he kills Gloria Mitchell later in a garbage dump, and murders Svoboda and leaves his gun. How in hell does Gloria Mitchell fit into this picture?*

"I don't get it," he said aloud.

"Don't get what?" Jeff Robinson asked, looking curiously at his partner. "What ain't you getting? Enough good steady sex? What?"

Len shook his head, as if to clear it, then he turned and stared out his side window, "Nothing, I get nothing. Forget it."

They rode along in silence for a while, then Jeff Robinson asked, "Why did you invite Lanny Boyle to the refuse collection center?"

"Hmm? Oh … I knew he had more than a passing professional interest in Miss Mitchell and when I saw him in the garage, the thought struck me. As I mentioned to one of you, it might have given him some closure."

"You worked with him in vice before you transferred to homicide, right?"

"Yeah, we worked together a couple of years. Vice wasn't my bag, too much undercover shit for me."

Jeff Robinson, silent for a few seconds asked, "What kind of a name is Lanny? Do you know his real name?"

Len snickered, "Yeah, I know it; it's Lance."

"Lance?"

"Yeah, Lance Boyle."

"Oh..."

Back in their office, Len called the airline as Dutch had suggested to verify his flight to Nashville and to get his seat assignment. United Global Airlines guaranteed him an aisle seat and breakfast on the Denver flight, with dinner on the return flight back to Los Angeles.

Maybe lunch in Tennessee then: real food sounds great. I need to get out of this madhouse for a day ... before another body shows up.

Mariko Tanaka called Len on his intercom, "Boss, Officer Svoboda's bank accounts showed nothing suspicious, no unusual deposits. Also, the academy is sending over the photos and admission records from your graduating class. The preliminary findings indicated there was no Giroux in your graduating class."

"What?" Len questioned, obviously agitated. "That's wrong, Mariko. I remember him clearly. He absolutely graduated with the rest of us."

"Let me finish, Boss, there was a Jean-Luc Gerot from Quebec enrolled. He spelled it, G-E-R-O-T. Is that close enough?"

"Gerot, not Giroux?" he said, using the same pronunciation for each. "Yes, yes, that's real good. Get what you can on him. Do we have any word from Lawrence in Ottawa?"

"Nothing yet. I'll let you know."

"Thanks for the update on Svoboda, too," Len said as he slumped back in his chair to contemplate the bizarre chain of events of the last couple of days and compose some loose mental notes for the upcoming news conference.

Contemplating too, that Miss Tanaka was calling him Boss and he was calling her Mariko.

His intercom buzzed again bringing him back to the world of the living; it was Mariko Tanaka, "Boss, I have Commander Fitzhugh on line three, hold a second, please. Go ahead, Commander."

Len picked up his phone, "Lawrence? Hey!"

"Len Morgan? My God, chap! What a complete surprise! What's going on in Los Angeles? Too many crimes out there and you need help?" Lawrence Fitzhugh asked as he laughed at his jab.

"Lawrence! You sound great! So where's your horse? And that red blazer and silly hat? You know, we're planning the New Year's Day Rose Parade already and I thought I'd invite you."

"Wonderful, we'd love to be there! I'll bring the entire squad, ponies and all!"

"Seriously, Lawrence, I know you must be busy, but we have a serial-murderer on the loose and I think he may have been a classmate of ours from the academy."

"You don't say. Who is it?"

"Do you recall a French Canadian by the name of Jean-Luc Gerot, spelled, G-E-R-O-T? He was a tall, fair-haired fellow. Quiet, as I remember, a loner, he kept to himself mostly. Any recollections?"

"My God, that was twenty-odd years ago. I'm sorry, I don't remember him. That doesn't say I won't recall later, after we hang up, 'ey? What do you have on him?"

"We suspect that he's committed several execution style murders here, strange scenarios. The FBI looked at our surveillance videos and suggested that we may have an international hit man in town: one Yves-Gaston Giroux."

"Giroux? Bloody shit! I know about *that* Giroux fellow, but he spells his name differently. He's reported to be French-Canadian or Belgian. Whichever, he's one nasty bloke, let me tell you. He has no qualms whatsoever about a hit either. I know he's personally accounted for assassinations numbering in the hundreds: women, children, he doesn't care. The terrorist Carlos received the most notoriety, but Giroux has killed more people, and single handedly too, not using bombs or explosives."

"Unbelievable..." Len muttered.

"So you really think this Jean-Luc academy fellow is Yves-Gaston Giroux, 'ey? Why?"

"Why, Lawrence? Because they look alike, not to mention the name similarity, and our guy uses the identical MO you just described. The academy is sending admission files and photos to me today, maybe tomorrow morning. We also have glossy stills the FBI generated from some videos. I can fax or email all of this to you. In the meantime, would you have time to check out Jean-Luc Gerot at your end? I can't give you much more, but I do recall him saying that he lived in Quebec."

"I can provide you with all the time and manpower we have at our disposal, especially to locate a man of Giroux the terrorist's caliber. Anything else?"

"Yes, I'm going to be in Tennessee tomorrow. Take my home telephone number and let me know if you dig up anything. Leave a message on my machine; I'll call you Thursday, okay?"

"Sounds good. Maybe later we can chat about old times, 'ey? Compare war stories someday, what do you think?"

"That would be great. Let's make time."

"Fine," Fitzhugh replied, "talk to you later. Goodbye now."

Len hung up, feeling good about his old friend in Canada. Leaving his desk, he went into the squad room to Mariko Tanaka's desk and advised her of the content of his conversation.

"Please fax copies of the academy documents to Ottawa when they arrive along with the glossy stills provided by the FBI. Thanks, Mariko."

Jeff Robinson reappeared and Len brought him up to speed.

"Care to help me do a news conference? The departmental spokesperson is out of town today and she asked if I'd fill in."

"No damn way. That's your forte, smooth talking devil that you are. I'll stand in the back though and watch you prevaricate."

Reporters, cameras, and floodlights packed the news conference room when Len entered and took his place behind the deputy departmental spokesperson. While waiting for his turn, Len listened to the usual mundane reports of break-ins, car thefts, et al. The assembled news gatherers were becoming noisy and impatient by the time Len got to the lectern.

"Good afternoon, ladies and gentlemen." Adjusting the microphone to his height, he began, "Most of you know me; for those of you who don't, I'm Len Morgan, Detective Lieutenant, Homicide Unit. Today I'm filling in for your usual host and I don't have a prepared statement so I'll attempt to take your questions from the floor. Please be gentle."

The chatter and ensuing noise level in the room became intense. Len saw a familiar face and pointed his finger in that general direction, "Seymour, it's good to see that you survived your recent jogging regimen, please go ahead."

"Lieutenant, the community is in shock. In the past week, besides the shootings at the RFK Junior High School, two hookers, three cops, and an unknown male subject were brutally murdered. All but those shot at RFK were shot twice in the base of the skull as well as somewhere else.…"

"Seymour," Len interrupted, "…is there a question in there?"

Seymour paused, and then asked, "Yes, how are these murders connected?"

Raising his hands in an attempt to get some order in the room, Len answered, "Seymour, I'm not as certain as you that these killings are connected. Next, over there…"

"Lieutenant, it appears that these last murders could be a crime of passion; I mean with the naked female found in the dump, and then today, the naked man in the motel. Have you considered passion as a possible motive?"

Seeing an opportunity to divert the media's attention away from the real motive, Len replied, "Well, there you go. We can't keep anything under wraps around here, can we? To answer your question, I can't speak to that, sir. If I speak further I may be guilty of aiding the perpetrator with privileged information, information we want to keep secure for ourselves and the staff of the District Attorney's office. Next, right here…"

"Lieutenant, are you implying that these were crimes of passion? I mean these killings appeared to be gangland, or Mafia type hits. Explain the passion connection."

"That's easy. Many Mafioso's have primal urges too…"

The reporters assembled in the room broke into loud laughter.

Len continued. "Many Mafia Dons have families, huge families, ask Puzo, or Coppola."

Again, more laughter.

Len continued, "If you think these recent killings appear to be execution style slayings copied after past Mafia or gangland hits, that's your prerogative. Further, I can't speak to that. Sorry. Next…"

"Lieutenant, do you have any new leads or suspects in tow?"

"Yes, and no. Next…"

"Sir?" Petitioned the same questioner, "Yes and no?"

"Yes to the first part of your question, no to the last. One last question, folks, I'm starved…"

"Is money an issue in these murders?"

"Money?" Len shrugged. "I fail to see what money has to do with naked people being shot in the head. If any of you do, please, you're welcome to come up here and explain it to the rest of us. Thanks folks, we'll keep you informed as more things develop. See you later."

Len stepped off the podium and pushed his way through the loud chattering crowd, fending off more questions with a smile and pleasant *No comment* responses. Jeff Robinson opened the door to the hallway and the two of them headed for the parking garage.

"Man, what a silver-tongued obfuscating devil you are. Crimes of passion? My ass."

"Hey. They opened up that one, I didn't. And when did I *obfuscate* about anything?"

"You were damn close, especially on that last question, the one about money."

"Not even close, Robbie. I asked a question in answer to his question. So the *putz* didn't want to step up and elaborate. If he had, my ass would have been grass. Agreed?"

"That's what I thought I said." Jeff Robinson said, winking and punching Len's shoulder.

"Ouch!"

Day 8, Wednesday, 6:00 a.m., June 12...

Jeffrey Robinson volunteered to drive Len to LAX for his post-dawn flight to Nashville. In his usual fashion, they arrived just in time at 6:10 a.m. with Len boarding his flight at the last possible second.

I need this trip, Len thought, handing his boarding pass to a flight attendant at the gate. *This is the perfect change of pace I need to get Gabrielle out of my mind and to get refocused on these cases.*

Flight #237 to Denver left Los Angeles a few minutes late at 6:35 a.m. Breakfast was served and the plane landed at the Denver International Airport during a torrential rainstorm, but right on time. With several minutes to kill before his connecting flight to Nashville, Len wandered through DIA and took in the sights.

So this is the fabulous DIA, lovingly referred to as the Denver "Imaginary" Airport. Such a deal with big white leaky tents for a roof. Those five-gallon capacity plastic buckets preventing the raindrops from reaching the granite floors lend a nice touch too; who'd a thought? And what's with that big green wooden barricade fence over there?

He glanced at his watch and headed toward the gate for his Nashville flight. *If I arrive on time, I'll have forty-five minutes to reach the funeral home. That's tight. I hope the New Lebanon PD located a good driver.*

Len's flight arrived on schedule at Nashville International Airport at 2:15 p.m. He left the jet bridge and looked for anyone holding a card with his name penciled on it. There it was. He waved at the cardholder and shouted at him over the bedlam in the concourse, "Hi, I'm Len Morgan."

A short, bespectacled young man approached. He looked average enough, except for a ponytail that extended from the backside of a bright blue Chicago Cub's baseball cap. He tucked the placard under his arm and extended his hand. "Detective Morgan? I'm Colt. I'm been assigned as your driver and photographer."

"Pleased to meet you, and I'm very glad you're here to rescue me. Colt, you say? Is that your surname or given name?"

"Just call me Colt, sir."

"Okay, then Colt it is. You may call me Len. Excuse me for a moment?" Looking around, he located a telephone booth where he began scanning through the local white pages.

"What are you lookin' for, Detective?" Colt asked.

"Colt, I need to locate the Winters and Sons Funeral Home. I've misplaced a note I had with the address and telephone listing. We called ahead yesterday and explained that you and I would be attending today's service. We received permission from the immediate family and from director Winters to take some pictures. We assured everyone that your filming would be done in good taste, as inconspicuously as possible, and with the utmost respect for the family and other mourners in attendance. Ah ... here it is, Colt, the address. Do you know where this is?"

Colt looked at the phone book listing Len indicated. "Winters on Crabapple Tree Road? Let me think ... yes I do, they're not all that far away."

"Good. So, are you a driver first, then a photographer, Colt?" Len asked as they made their way through the foot traffic in the concourse. "Do you work for the New Lebanon PD, or are you an independent?"

"Independent photographer, full time, but because I'm drivin' first today, I said I was your driver first. As a professional photographer, I work for the Nashville PD almost exclusively. Not that much for the County Sheriff or New Lebanon's police department. As an independent, I do my own photo finishin' too, in my own lab, the works. Why do you ask, sir?"

"No reason, just a detective's natural curiosity and attempting to make idle conversation."

Colt nodded.

A few seconds later Len commented, "What a beautiful day you have here in Nashville; is it always like this? There's not a cloud in the sky."

"Let's cross the street here, Lieutenant. I'm in that parkin' structure yonder. Where're you wantin' to go first?"

"The funeral home first. I want to speak with the family of the victim before the three o'clock service starts. Then afterward let's visit the local Police Chief or Constable, whichever, in New Lebanon. I have to pay my respects, a professional courtesy. You know … and you can take our picture."

They entered the cool shade of the parking structure and walked briskly to the end of the building. Colt gestured in the direction of a shiny Black Jeep CJ-7 with a black fiberglass top, "There she is, isn't too fancy, but I reckon it gets me where I need to go. You can put your stuff on the back seat. I cleaned it out so you could have some place for your luggage."

"All I have is my brief case, Colt, but thanks."

Speeding down Interstate-40W and leaving Nashville, the pair passed the time in silence until Colt casually remarked, "There's one."

"One what?" Len asked, confused, looking around, unaware of what one his companion was referring.

Colt pointed to his right, "A cloud, there's a cloud yonder."

Len bit his tongue to keep from laughing at this newly found protégé. *For sure, this kid may be certifiable.*

They exited Interstate-40 at Crabapple Tree Road and minutes later were at the Winters and Sons Funeral Home.

"Here we are with time to spare. We were nearer than I thought," Colt said proudly as he pulled into the drive. Getting directions from one of the funeral home attendants, Colt parked the shiny black Jeep in the back lot with the shiny black funeral vehicles.

"Look, it kind'a fits right in with them others. Good thing I had her washed," he said with a broad smile.

Noting Colt's first smile, Len nodded, smiling as well.

Colt grabbed his 35mm SLR camera, zoom lens and tripod and locked the Jeep. "So, what procedure do you want me to follow, Detective? Regular closeups of everyone, or just certain people, what?"

"I want closeups of all of the big males that arrive. We've determined that our suspect is a large, strong man. Add to that, I want pictures of the victim's immediate family. That's it. Oh ... afterward, a picture with the New Lebanon Constable. Don't let me forget. Professional courtesy again."

"Okay," Colt said, attaching the zoom lens to his camera. "Do you want me to make slides or prints later?"

"Black and white or color glossy prints in eight by ten would be perfect."

"You name it, you've got it. No problem, sir, I'm locked and loaded."

They entered through the main entrance of the funeral home and paused in the quiet, well-appointed foyer. Len rang a small bell and waited. Seconds later a thin, gray-haired man wearing a black suit and tie entered from a room off the main corridor.

"Good-day, gentlemen, I'm Bernard Winters, Funeral Director. Are you with the Reynolds family or are you guests?"

Len handed Director Winters one of his calling cards and extended his hand, "I'm pleased to meet you, Director Winters. I'm Detective Lieutenant Leonard Morgan, Devonshire Hills Precinct, Los Angeles. This is Colt, my associate and photographer."

"Oh, yes, Detective, one of your California people did call earlier. We're all ready for you. Follow me, gentlemen, I'll show you what we have. It's a small space, well concealed from the mourners by flowers and located several feet behind the closed casket."

They followed Director Winters to a narrower corridor that led to the back of the chapel where he introduced them to a small but operable space. Well concealed behind a white lattice backdrop, as Winters suggested, it held several large floral arrangements.

"This is perfect," Colt said, as he situated the tripod and attached the camera. "I should be able to shoot unnoticed through the lattice and flowers as long as more flowers don't arrive at the last minute and block my view."

"That won't happen," Director Winters assured him. "Any late arriving flowers will be placed on the floor at the ends of the casket. So, gentlemen, I'll leave you to your business. Is there anything I can get for either of you? Coffee, iced teas?"

"Thank you, no, sir." Len replied, "but could you alert me when the deceased's family members arrive. I want to introduce myself and pay my respects."

"Certainly, it's no imposition at all."

The first arrival appeared to be the victim's mother: a matronly woman, accompanied by a small-framed teenaged girl. With them was a well-built young man, more than six feet tall, Len guessed, maybe two hundred-twenty pounds and in his early twenties. The young man appeared glued to the side of the teenaged girl.

As requested, Director Winters notified Len and escorted him to the chapel to meet the victim's family. As he approached the trio he was taken aback briefly by the complexion of the two women. Their skin, tanned lightly, seemed to have a glow, probably created from exposure to the warm Tennessee sun. Each was wearing lightweight, inexpensive, predominately black dresses with large bright flowery prints. They also wore a small veil under the brims of their black straw hats. Black shoes and matching purses completed their ensemble.

Like my Grandma Min used to wear, good common folks.

Getting her attention, he extended his hand to the older woman, "Good afternoon. I'm Detective Morgan from Los Angeles. My sincere condolences, ma'am. Are you the mother of the deceased?"

The woman looked Len squarely in the eyes while gripping his hand firmly, "Yes, I am, and tell me again, why are you Los Angeles Police here today?"

Taken slightly by surprise, Len responded, "Ma'am, as one of our officers must have explained on the telephone, we're investigating your daughter's case. Unfortunately, some perpetrators often attend the funeral of their victims. We don't want to intrude on your grief in any way, ma'am, but we may just discover something that could be beneficial in solving the crime. With your permission, may I stay for the service? I'll remain in the back out of sight."

"Yes, yes, Detective, please do stay, and please excuse my rudeness. I don't know where my head is today. I guess I'm just a tired old woman with the responsibility again to raise another young'n. My first attempt was a failure; she's in that pine box over there. Little Laureen here, my granddaughter, will be my second try. This is not how I wanted my life, or Lorena's, to end up. Please stay," she said quietly, wiping at her heavy lidded eyes with her lace hankie.

"Thank you, ma'am."

"Detective, you can call me Ide, short for Ida: Ida Hackett. And this is Laureen, Lorena's fifteen-year-old daughter. This is Laureen's boyfriend, Aubrey Jim Hunnicutt."

"Pleased to meet y'all," Laureen said softly, lightly taking Len's hand. Len noted that her ample physical attributes more than belied the fact that she was only fifteen years old.

"My pleasure, Miss Laureen, perhaps under different circumstances. And, Aubrey Jim is it?" Len looked at the young man, concentrating on his face as they shook hands. "Didn't I see you on the United Global flight earlier today?"

Aubrey Hunnicutt was a striking young man: tanned, tall and muscular. His short blond hair glistened against his tanned skin.

He replied, answering brusquely, "You kin' call me Aubrey, but I prefer A.J. Yeah, I was on flight #237 this mornin'. What about it? Were you on it too?"

"Yes, and here I am. Did you fly in from Denver?"

"No, from Los Angeles. I attend Cal Southern University out there. I flew in today for the funeral."

"Cal Southern? Good school. Athletic scholarship?"

"Yeah, I got me a full football scholarship after I graduated all-state, all-conference from Brentwood Academy here last spring. I'm livin' on campus in the athletes' dorm. We're doin' summer practice and stuff now."

"Brentwood Academy? I understand they have quite a football program. What position do you play?"

"Runnin' back. Tailback mostly, but the dumb coaches have me practicin' at linebacker now. I hate it."

"Cal Southern is well known for their award-winning tailbacks," Len commented. "I played high school varsity football in Wisconsin and later was a walk-on at UCLA where I injured my knee during a heavy scrimmage. That's a story for another day."

"What position did ya' play?"

"Wide out."

Hunnicutt's young face took on the beginnings of a sneer. Half-smiling, he asked, "So how'd ya' blow out a knee? Were ya' out of shape or somethin'?"

As Len stared hard at the young man, his mind raced through several scenarios seeking an answer for this brash kid's question. "No, not exactly, Aubrey," he replied shrugging. "One of the defenders rolled up the back of my leg in a pile-up. In shape or not, you know the consequences."

Hunnicutt looked down at the carpeting and exhibited his partial sneer again. With an arrogant chuckle, he turned and joined Laureen.

"Don't pay him no never mind, Detective," Laureen suggested, smiling as she put her arm around Hunnicutt's waist. "Aubrey Jim's so into himself right now, goin' to that ritzy college, livin' high on the hog in Hollywood an' that. He's a good man though, most'a time anyways."

Len smiled, noticing her heavy accent. "Thank you, Miss Laureen. We all get into ourselves occasionally. Thanks, anyway."

He returned his attention to Ida Hackett as the young couple turned and moved a few steps away. Len extended his hand again to Ida Hackett and squeezed it warmly, "Mrs. Hackett, I'm sincerely sorry. If we can be of any help with anything, feel free to call us. Here, this is my card with all of our telephone numbers listed. Call us collect any time. We'd be obliged to assist you and your family in any way possible."

"Well, Detective, there is one thing we'll soon be needin' some help with," she suggested, "…the matter of Lorena's bank account. How do we get a hold of all that money she'd put up?"

Upon hearing that question, Aubrey and Laureen, standing nearby, quickly turned and rejoined the couple.

Noting what appeared to be a keen interest in all that money, Len paused before answering. "Well … contacting her bank would be my first guess. Do you have an attorney?"

"Why, no. Why would we need an attorney? It's our money now ain't it?"

"Most likely, but you'll still need one," Len answered. "This is probably a probate court matter. The money is in a joint account in two names, your daughter's and that of one of her friend's. Unfortunately, her friend died earlier this week. To date, we haven't established if either had a will or if her friend left any heirs. Regardless, before anyone collects anything, the account will have to go through a probate process. If either died intestate, without a will, it will prolong the matter. It's normally quite a lengthy process."

Aubrey Hunnicutt's eyebrows furrowed and his face took on a sudden sullen expression. His eyes narrowed as he glared at Len.

"Damn! I knew it!" Laureen hissed. "It's always somethin'!"

Ignoring their various displays of emotion, Len continued, "With the money in a joint account, Mrs. Hackett, all of their respective heirs have a bona fide claim of ownership. At the very least, I believe, to that portion, or percentage, which each depositor contributed."

As he spoke, he noted the radical change in everyone, including their facial expressions and body language. "I was a law major in college, but I'm not an attorney. You will definitely need to hire one."

Ida Hackett nodded, and then looked at the floor.

"Well, I must get back to work," Len concluded. "Again, my sincere condolences Mrs. Hackett, Laureen, Aubrey." Len extended his hand, but Aubrey turned away, ignoring the gesture.

The younger couple joined hands and walked away, leaving Ida alone to follow behind them. She breathed a deep sigh and slowly approached the closed casket in the flower-filled chapel where her once beautiful daughter lay, concealed in quiet repose.

Joining Colt in the shadows behind the flower-covered latticework, Len whispered, "I want some really good shots of the young athletic looking fellow sitting with the young girl."

"Gotcha', Len," Colt whispered.

Feeling a bit shocked when called by his first name, Len nodded. *Yep, Colt's ice is finally out of the pond, he's thawed out, "Now ain't that the beat?" or whatever it is that Robbie says.* "Funny, that," he said.

"What say?" Colt asked.

"Oh, nothing, Colt, just thinking aloud about something I remembered. It's nothing."

Less than a dozen neighbors and distant relatives attended the service. The local Pastor rambled on endlessly with his eulogy, maybe in part to make up for the lack of mourners Len guessed.

Ten minutes into the service, a tall, stoop-shouldered man entered the chapel. In his late fifties, he was balding slightly and his face was well weathered and tanned below his brow line.

He carried an old slouch hat in his hand, his new blue chambray shirt buttoned at the collar, but with no tie. His well-worn dark blue suit-coat was clean, the same with his bib overalls.

    He approached the front of the chapel hesitantly. As he reached the front row, he stopped, glancing first at the pastor, then at the closed casket. The pastor stopped speaking and gestured to the man to come forward. He nodded appreciatively and gently placed a callused hand on the wooden casket. He stood quietly, looking at it for a moment, then brushed at his eyes and turned away. Before sitting down, he nodded to Ida Hackett and Laureen Reynolds. He took a front row seat across the aisle.

    Young Laureen rose from her seat, leaving Aubrey Hunnicutt with her grandmother, and went across the aisle and sat with the tall man. She reached for his hand at the same time.

    Watching attentively, Len's attention returned to Ida. He watched as her expression hardened into an icy, unseeing stare. Aubrey Hunnicutt, sitting alone sneered silently and continued to look at the floor.

    Interesting. Might that be the estranged husband/father figure? If he is, he doesn't appear to be especially welcome here today.

    At that same instant, two good-sized men in dark blue suits and hats entered at the rear of the chapel. They removed their hats and took seats in the back row.

    If I were watching a cheap Hollywood detective thriller, I'd wager on those ol' boys being local cops. This is becoming even more interesting.

"Colt," Len whispered as quietly as he could, "get several pictures of the tall man that just came in, plus those two gents in the suits sitting in the back row, okay?"

    "I got 'em already, Boss," Colt whispered.

    "Good man," Len whispered, squeezing Colt's shoulder.

    When Len concluded that the long service was nearing the end, he excused himself, and, leaving Colt, took the back corridor into the foyer leading from the chapel where the mourners and attendees would be exiting. He took a place in the wide hallway and studied the faces of the mourners as they departed, looking for a sign of anyone who might be considered a killer.

The two big men were already in the hall and took positions facing the open doors. They sized up Len and quietly exchanged a couple of words between them.

The small procession of mourners emptied the chapel quickly. Laureen and the tall man followed Ida Hackett with Aubrey Hunnicutt bringing up the rear. As the small group approached the doorway, the two men in the blue polyester suits suddenly moved in and grabbed the tall man by his arms.

Surprised, he attempted to jump back and jerk free. His momentum caused the younger of the two men to trip and fall backwards into the chapel, collapsing a couple of folding chairs as the two of them landed on the floor.

Astonished, Ida and Laureen screamed out, causing the last of the departing mourners to turn in an effort to see what was going on. Director Winters, totally speechless, stood beside the women and watched the unexpected fracas.

Len, astonished as well, found himself inadvertently blocked out by Mister Winters. Belatedly, he pushed past him in a feeble attempt to separate the struggling men. The two men wearing suits, upon subduing the tall man, produced handcuffs and lifted him to his feet.

Taken by surprise, Len watched helplessly in a state of mild shock. Ultimately, his wits returned. "Excuse me, gentlemen! What are we doing here?"

"Who the hell are you?" the younger of the two men questioned, between deep breaths and catching his wind. "…and whose business is it anyway?"

Len produced his shield and handed the older man his calling card, "I'm Detective Lieutenant Len Morgan from Los Angeles. I'm investigating the murder of the deceased. Is this man the estranged husband?"

Producing his star-shaped shield, the older of the two men spoke, "I'm Inspector Isaac Caldwell and this is my partner. We have a warrant for this man's arrest. He's to be incarcerated in the county jail overnight pending a child support hearing before our local magistrate. Is all that satisfactory enough, Mister?"

"You say you are arresting him for nonpayment of child support? Seriously? In a funeral home?"

The older law officer nodded, still studying Len's card, "Yes, and this is Junior Levon Reynolds himself, the estranged husband of the deceased. Say, ain't you a bit far outside your jurisdiction, Lieutenant?"

"My jurisdiction takes me wherever I think a murder suspect may be hiding, Deputy."

"That's *Inspector*, Detective," the older man corrected.

"My mistake, Inspector," Len said. "...and you do know that murder has no jurisdictional barriers or statute of limitations, right? So, are there any other charges against this man? When is the hearing?"

"The warrants are for nonpayment of child support. They usually hold these kind of hearings on Fridays. That's the day the Circuit Judges set aside for this kind of non-calendar action."

"This Friday, tomorrow the fourteenth?"

"Yes, sir. And until then, ol' Junior here will be our guest if you need to speak with him. Right, Junior?"

Junior Levon Reynolds stared at the floor. Laureen stood close beside him and held his arm tightly; tears flowed freely down her cheeks.

It's apparent that she really loves her father, Len thought, looking at the two standing close together. *Obviously, she didn't feel quite the same for her deceased mother.* "I'm on a tight schedule, Deputy Caldwell..." Len began

"Ahem, it's still *Inspector* Caldwell, sir."

Len stopped speaking for an instant, then he gathered himself, "...with your permission, *Inspector* Caldwell, I'd like to speak with your prisoner and ask him a question or two, outside the chapel of course."

Caldwell smiled. "I personally don't have a problem with that, do you Junior? You know the routine, you can have an attorney assigned to represent you and talk to the detective later if you like, or you can answer any of his questions now," the older lawman explained.

"Hell, ask away," Junior Reynolds said as they left the funeral home. "I ain't got nothin' t'hide, and I ain't guilty of no murder neither."

Outside under the brilliant blue-sky, the unseemly group gathered on the lush, well-manicured front lawn of the funeral home. Len looked pathetically at the tall stoop-shouldered man in handcuffs who was grieving for his wife.

Colt, who approached with camera and tripod, stopped nearby to load new film.

Len asked, "Junior, where were you for the last week or so?"

"Now, Detective," Junior Levon Reynolds answered, squinting his eyes from the bright afternoon sun, "I've been right here in Tennessee … how could I be anywhere else? Hell, I got no money, no car, nothin' but a tired ol' jack-mule. I hitchhiked and mostly walked to get here today. I been on the damned road since near five this mornin'. I sure as hell didn't have the where-with-all to fly out west and murder Lorena, now did I?"

He hung his bare head, his shoulders convulsed and he began to sob, "Sweet Jeez, help me…" Then, looking hard at Len he asked, "Why ya' accusing me? I didn't do nothin'!"

Ida Hackett's face softened. She handed Junior Levon Reynolds his rumpled slouch hat that she'd retrieved from the floor inside the chapel. "Here, son. A man needs his hat," she whispered. Her voice broke as she placed her hand on his shoulder.

Reynolds took his hat, and looked appreciatively at his former mother-in-law. "Thank ye', Ide."

Laureen grasped her father's arm even tighter and continued to glare at the two deputies. "Why's he have to go to jail?" she asked Caldwell. "We don't need his money none!"

Aubrey Hunnicutt's expression hardened abruptly when he heard Laureen's words and he stared at her curiously. Len caught the change of expression too, but quickly turned his attention back to Junior Levon Reynolds.

Inspector Caldwell looked sympathetically at the young girl. "It's the law, Missy. We're just doing our jobs."

"Well, Deputy Caldwell…" Len began.

"Uh ...Inspector, sir." Caldwell corrected.

Ignoring the interruption, Len continued, "...as I was going to say, that's all I need from this man." Looking at Junior Levon Reynolds he added, "Junior, I wasn't accusing you. I know you didn't murder Lorena but I did have to ask." Thoroughly irritated, Len turned abruptly to Colt, "Let's saddle up and get the hell outta' here."

Turning to Ida Hackett and Laureen, he nodded, and ignoring Aubrey Hunnicutt, strode quickly toward the parking lot and Colt's shiny black Jeep.

As they left the funeral home, Colt spoke, "Sir, I got pictures of the impromptu action inside as well. Do you want prints of..."

"Yes!" Len interrupted brusquely. "I want prints of every goddamn thing you have. When will they be available?"

"Today, if you don't mind spendin' some time at my studio. I'll develop and print today."

"Great, do it, Colt, and I ... I apologize for biting your head off. Those two deputies pissed me off; arresting Mister Reynolds inside the funeral home like that ... it was unprofessional as hell and totally out of line. I'm sorry I yelled at you."

"Not a problem. I thought what the deputies did was dumb too."

"If you can get the prints done for me today I'll catch a red-eye flight home tonight. Do you want payment now or do you want to bill the precinct?"

"I'll bill later, no hurry. Besides, this has been a right inter'sting day. I thought so anyways. Not the same ol', same ol' stuff I usually get stuck with. Know what I'm sayin'?"

"I think I do. It was an interesting day for me too, Colt, highly illuminating. Oh, when you total your bill, include an extra twenty-percent."

"Sir? Why?"

"Why? Because you earned it."

The unlikely pair then left the Winters Funeral Home behind and drove into New Lebanon, a small village located outside of Lebanon, Tennessee. Still rankled by the past events at the funeral home, Len wanted to make his official visit to Constable Othel Baine's Police Department a short one. Some Tennessee law officials were not high on his list of favorite people and it was beginning to show.

Still Wednesday, June 12, day 8...

Len and Colt entered the Constable Othel Baine's small stuffy office. A tall, ruddy-faced, well-built man in his mid-forties, he stood and extended his hand.

"Obliged meetin' ya', Detective. We don't get too many official visitors around here. Please, take a chair."

As Constable Baine came around from his desk to shake hands again and pose for the *photo-op,* Len spoke, "Constable Baine, thanks again for taking the time to see me. My official visit in your beautiful state is complete. I want to thank you and your deputies for their cooperation and to personally invite you to stop in at the Devonshire Hills Precinct if ever you visit Los Angeles."

The invitation nearly proved to be a mistake.

"Ain't Los Angel-ees known as the land of fruitcakes and wing-nuts, Detective Morgan? I always heard it was," Constable Baine drawled, returning to his antique desk where he sprawled comfortably in his leather-upholstered swivel chair. He paused briefly, then switched sides of his mouth with his chew, and smiled. "But, you know…" he continued, again pausing for effect, "I can't say that with any amount of certainty m'self 'cause I ain't ne'er been to LA."

Then he reached for an empty aluminum soda can he kept handy and drizzled some tobacco juice into it. He wiped at his chin with the back of his hand and smiled broadly again, "Fu'ther, I ain't fixin' on goin' neither, but we thank ye' for the invite."

Ever the comedians, even in Tennessee, Len thought, forcing a smile, but as with his earlier encounter with Aubrey Hunnicutt, several dozen thoughts raced through his mind as he sought the proper reply to the Constable's mocking remarks. Settling on the most diplomatic, he sighed. Standing, shaking Constable Baine's hand again, he responded, "Probably a good choice, Constable. Probably a good choice."

Day 9, Thursday, June 13...
Having caught a redeye direct flight out of Chicago's O'Hare International bound for Los Angeles the night before, Len landed at LAX in the dark of early morning and took a taxi home. Wasted, he slowly climbed the winding stairs to his empty abode. Inside, he checked his telephone messages.

Bingo! Lawrence must have called back.

Pressing the *Play* button Len heard Lawrence Fitzhugh saying: *"Len, we struck bloody gold, in a way. Call me when you get home. No, wait ... if you're late, call Thursday in the morning, my time."*

Len removed Colt's photos from his briefcase and went to his bedroom. Stripped naked, he fell into his cool sheets and was sleeping before his head struck the pillow.

Later that morning, Thursday, June 13, Devonshire Hills Police Precinct...
While his partner was at home sleeping in, Sergeant Jeffrey Robinson met for a second time with Special Agent Luis Campanera and his agents in Westwood. As Campanera explained, "...the packages coming and going from Duard van Haan's art business were not large. Some of the incoming packages and crates looked like they might contain artwork, but there were too few of them; the amount of artwork-sized

shipments didn't come close to matching the volume of the smaller sized packages."

Using the Treasury Department's stakeout facilities offered by Special Agent Campanera, Len and Jeff Robinson planned to put in four hours of surveillance daily. Len's trip to Nashville altered that plan so Jeff Robinson sent Detectives Paul Tobin and Fred Cooper in their stead.

The substitute Devonshire Hills detective duo began their stakeout in the posh residential area across the ravine from van Haan's hillside mansion. There, they got a good fix on van Haan's punctuality along with his comings and goings and made written notes they later turned over to Jeff Robinson.

Early that afternoon, having finally aroused, a very exhausted Len Morgan arrived on the job. He poured a cup of cold precinct coffee and reviewed the stakeout team's notes with Jeffrey Robinson. Detectives Tobin and Cooper noted that van Haan consistently left his house at precisely 5:30am in his Mercedes S600 sedan affixed with a personalized out of state license plate that read: VH-1.

"Look at that fancy license tag," Jeff Robinson commented, reading over Len's shoulder. "Do you think he has a clue what it really means? VH-1?"

Len stifled a yawn. "Well, I sure don't. What the hell does it mean?"

"What? You don't know?" Jeff Robinson grunted in disbelief. "Man, you white guys ... VH-1 is the big time cable TV musical/video entertainment network. Their ads say, *'Your favorite TV shows, music videos, celebrity news and stuff'*. Don't you know anything?"

"About what? Music? Yeah, I know a little about *real* music, like concerts in halls where people wear tuxedos and black ties, not in manure strewn cow pastures wearing old plaid shirts, loose-laced Nike high-tops and baggy pants slung below their ass."

Jeff Robinson snorted.

Len continued, "So you think van Haan is an inner city rapper now and hangs with the likes of Milk Chocolate Ice,

Beagle Sniff-Butt, or some other hip-hop gangsta' dudes like that? What time did you say it was?"

"You're too much," Jeff Robinson said, still snickering as he continued reading the reports. "Still half asleep and it ain't five o'clock yet. Look there, Len! Traffic Division is also on to van Haan. They've made his morning route: same trip every day. Bingo!"

Len's mind was preoccupied, still semi-numb from jet lag and a lack of enough rest. He blinked his eyes to recover and let his weary mind zero in again on Jean-Luc Gerot, possibly the terrorist assassin Yves-Gaston Giroux.

Also, Len's telephone conversation with Commander Lawrence Fitzhugh early this morning aroused his interest. Fitzhugh had explained, "*I checked out our Jean-Luc Gerot. His father is still alive and living in Quebec, same address for years and years. Checking our operator's license records, it shows Jean-Luc Gerot last residing in Vancouver, British Columbia. I've been authorized to tap the phones of both his father and the Vancouver residence. Oh, Gerot has a younger sister named Marie. She's living in Quebec with dad, maybe seeing after the old man. I'll keep you informed. For your information, my Mounties, Scotland Yard and the Home Office are working in tandem with this. They want him too. We've put a cute little bloody name on this new top-secret file: we call it Snakebite. Like that, 'ey? Later, chum, we'll continue to forge onward. Call if anything comes up.*"

Jeff Robinson's voice interrupted Len's train of thought, "Len, we have his early morning travel routes now, every day, same time, same routes. Hey, are you awake? Are you okay?"

"Yeah, I'm fine, Robbie, just daydreaming, thinking some … I'll be all right. What time is it again?"

"Boss, I know it must be tough," Jeff Robinson consoled, pausing a second, looking at his watch again and then at his weary partner. "It still ain't five o'clock. Okay, tomorrow we do it."

"Sorry, Robbie," Len said, stifling yet another yawn. "Tomorrow is when we're pulling him over? Is that what we're doing?"

"Yup. Big doins' tomorrow."

"Good, I hope Josephs and the old vet don't contract sinus infection. We need their noses." Len stood slowly and stretched his tall, six foot-three-inch frame. "Is this stunt of yours a first? Pulling a suspect over to see what he smells like?"

"May well be; I hope they recognize the scent. I know I shouldn't be prejudiced, it ain't right, but van Haan really pisses me off. I'd like to collar him myself, know what I mean?"

"I believe I do. He's not that high on my list of favorites either. Is it five o'clock yet?"

"Yes, finally," Jeff Robinson answered, sighing and rolling his eyes.

"Already?" Len asked, suddenly energized. "Doesn't time fly when you're doing things you like to do with people you love?"

"I wouldn't know," Jeff Robinson lamented incredulously as they left their office for the elevator. Serious again, he asked, "Do you think your Mountie friend will get him? That telephone call from him this morning sounded promising."

"Let's hope he helps us get our man, only time will tell. Let's go, I'm beat."

Morning, day 10, Friday, June 14, 5:30 a.m., in Benedict Canyon...
Unlike its nearby sister streets-- Beverly Glen Boulevard, Laurel Canyon and Coldwater Canyon-- Benedict Canyon is more narrow and meandering. A scenic two-lane paved ribbon, it snakes through the fabled hills connecting west Los Angeles and the San Fernando Valley. The I-405 San Diego Freeway is full of traffic at rush hour, or any hour, so these surface streets can make life tolerable at times for the local commuters.

Duard van Haan strode from his front doorway and got into his awaiting Mercedes S600 sedan. He left his mansion and drove north to Mulholland Drive. From there, he went down the hill on Beverly Glen Boulevard and into the teeming Valley. The traffic light on the cross street two blocks north of Ventura Boulevard was showing 'Green' as he approached. Slowing slightly as he always did, he then accelerated to cross through the intersection. As he did, the signal flickered on 'Caution' for a split second then turned 'Red'. Unable to react quickly, he ran the light.

"Damn it!" he cursed aloud, slamming a big fist hard against the steering wheel. "That was a fast signal change!"

A short block later, as he neared Ventura Boulevard, he heard the soft moaning of a police siren behind him. He looked into his rearview mirror and saw the dreaded red-and-blue flashing rack lights pulling in behind him.

"Shit!!" he cursed. "First a fast light, now a damned traffic ticket."

He turned onto Ventura Boulevard and pulled the big Mercedes sedan over to the curb. Sullen faced, he lowered the driver's side window and watched in his rear view mirror as a young police officer approached.

"Good morning, sir," the officer greeted as he leaned over and looked through the open window. "We stopped you because you ran a traffic signal a couple of blocks back. May I see your operator's license, vehicle registration, and proof of insurance, please?"

Van Haan reached inside his suit jacket for his wallet, protesting loudly as he did. "Officer, that light changed much too quickly, it malfunctioned or something. I don't recall it even going to Caution. It went immediately from Green to Red."

"Really?" Officer Duane Josephs replied as he looked carefully at the driver's license. "I'll contact traffic maintenance division and have someone take a look at it. Please wait here, Mister van Haan, I'll be right back."

Van Haan sat and stewed impatiently while Josephs went back to the cruiser. His partner, the old vet, waited patiently, standing guard near the Mercedes' right rear fender.

Officer Josephs returned to van Haan. "Thank you for your patience, sir. You have a clean slate. Here is your license, vehicle registration, and proof of insurance. Have a good-day now."

"But, what is the ticket going to cost?" Van Haan asked haughtily, as he returned his license to his wallet and put the other documents back in the sun visor pocket. "I feel like having my attorney fight this."

"Ticket, sir?" the young officer questioned. "I wont be issuing you a ticket this morning. You're free to go, sir."

Taken off guard by Officer Josephs' unexpected words, van Haan stared skeptically at him.

"There is one thing, sir," Josephs said, leaning over and getting closer to van Haan's open window. "I don't want to sound oddly inquisitive, but could I trouble you for the brand of your cologne or after-shave? I'd really appreciate it. Is that too personal a request, sir?"

"What?" Van Haan questioned in utter disbelief. "Why in hell would you want to know that?"

"Well, sir," the young officer explained quietly, getting ever closer to the open window. "It's my partner back there. He's … you see, hygienically disadvantaged, sir."

Van Haan stared incredulously at the young police officer. "Say what? What in hell are you saying?"

"Sir," the young officer said, speaking even more quietly and getting still closer to van Haan, "…he smells. Obviously, he doesn't bathe that often and I have to ride with him all day in this Valley heat. I can't handle it. I thought if maybe I bought him something, like some good cologne or aftershave, it might help. See what I'm saying?"

Van Haan began laughing aloud, roaring and pounding the palms of his hands on his steering wheel. Gathering himself, he said, "So, Officer, let me see if I have this straight. I am not getting a traffic ticket, and you want to know the brand of my cologne?"

"Yes, sir. And, it's not a trade-off. You said the traffic signal malfunctioned; I believe you and I radioed Traffic Control to have it inspected. I wasn't going to write a ticket after your explanation. You can drive away right now. No problem. But, sir, I would appreciate your help," Officer Josephs entreated, straightening up and standing erect at the open window of the Mercedes.

"Officer … your last name, what is it? Josephs?" Van Haan squinted, reading the shiny metal name tag pinned on the young officer's blouse. "If you can afford it, go over to any good outlet on Rodeo Drive in Beverly Hills. Buy your smelly partner a bottle of *Suspicion*."

"Thank you, sir…"

"You might pick up some good quality deodorant bar-soap for him as well," van Haan suggested, tight lipped, his eyes fiercely cold. "Now, I'm very late. Excuse me please?"

Officer Josephs nodded, stepped back and with a half salute, smiled at van Haan as the power window closed. The big Mercedes sped away and disappeared into the early morning traffic.

Josephs turned and winked and pointed a finger at his chuckling partner, "Radio Detective Morgan, 'Stinky', I believe we have our man."

Across the Valley, Len and Jeff Robinson arrived at Abbe's Deli for breakfast at the same time they received word from the two traffic cops. Before departing from the cruiser, Len dispatched them to Giorgio's in Beverly Hills to purchase a bottle of the highly odoriferous *Suspicion* brand cologne.

Returning to their office, Len and Jeff Robinson stared at the pile of paperwork deposited on their respective desks. A message requesting an immediate return call to a Deborah Rosen, Assistant District Attorney, caught Len's eye first. The balance of the papers amounted to redundant forms and bank ledger sheets with much of the same data received earlier from the Treasury Department.

"I wonder what this Rosen person has in store for us, Robbie. Do you know who she is? I don't recognize her name."

"Nope, that's a new one on me. Maybe she heard you were an available bachelor again and wants to join you tonight for wine and dinner?"

"Stow it!"

"Whoa, excu-u-u-u-se me, bro."

Len quickly caught Jeff Robinson's eye, winked and reached for his telephone. After calling Deborah Rosen's number, he waited patiently, pawing through some of the clutter on his desk.

"District Attorney's office."

"Yes, I'm returning a call from Deborah Rosen. My name is Detective Len Morgan, Homicide Unit, Devonshire Hills."

"One moment, sir, she's expecting your call."

"Detective Morgan," a pleasant but firm, female voice said. "Thanks for the prompt return of my call. I have some late arriving information regarding a current murder investigation you are working: a female victim known as Miss Lorena Reynolds, aka Noreen le Rae?"

"Yes, that's our case, Miss Rosen. It is Miss isn't it?"

"Yes, close enough. We've been able to research and locate Miss Reynolds' next of kin. They are all out of state, living in New Lebanon, Tennessee. The late Miss Reynolds is survived by a fifteen year old daughter, Laureen Reynolds, a sixty-six year old mother, whose name is Ida Hackett, and an estranged or ex-farmer husband, Junior Levon Reynolds, whereabouts currently unknown."

"Ms. Rosen, may I interrupt? I recently attended Lorena Reynolds' funeral in Nashville and personally met everyone you have named, including Junior Levon Reynolds. The local Sheriff's Department apprehended the poor bastard inside the funeral home and took him into custody. Anything else?"

"Oh, I wasn't aware of that. Apprehended him for what?"

"Nonpayment of child support."

"Okay. Well, here's something else that might interest you: a big fat $100,000 insurance policy. It's a term policy naming the daughter, Laureen, as the beneficiary. Besides the term insurance policy, we were obliged to advise the mother and daughter of the bank account held jointly with a Miss Gloria Mitchell. I understand Miss Mitchell is currently in protective custody in a Safety House in Sherman Oaks?"

"Miss Mitchell *was*, past tense, in protective custody in a Safety House until last Sunday afternoon. Physically abducted by a pair of gunmen, her body showed up in a garbage dump two days ago. Also, the Reynolds family is aware of the joint bank account. In fact, they made a point to ask about it when I met with them before the funeral service. That joint bank account is causing quite a ruckus. The amount of money in it may have had something to do with the murders of both Lorena Reynolds and Gloria Mitchell. The Reynolds family didn't mention a life insurance policy, term or otherwise. I wonder if it's double indemnity if the insured was a murder victim."

"I don't know how the policy reads; only that one exists. The survivors, namely the daughter Laureen and the mother of the deceased, should move to obtain their legal rights to that joint bank account as soon as possible. If the other holder of the account is deceased, that will definitely complicate matters for everyone's next of kin."

"I discussed some of that with the relatives prior to the funeral service," Len explained.

"Another question while I have you, just how good is the case you are building against your prime suspect, a Mister Duard van Haan? Our office appears to be in the middle of some heavy political pressure. His attorney has made several inquiries starting with the Mayor's office and it has trickled down to us; the pot is beginning to boil."

"How good is this case?" Len paused a moment, stifling a chuckle. "That's a good question. We have some circumstantial evidence, more just confirmed by one of our uniformed police officers today, evidence that could possibly place our Mister van Haan at the scene on the morning of the murder; I say possibly. Do we have an open and shut case here? Hardly. Today we verified the one slim lead we've been working and beyond that, our joint surveillance with the United States Treasury department hasn't turned up anything useful as far as linking him to the murder. I wish I had better news for you and the District Attorney. Another couple of days may turn up something more useful."

"This sounds exceptionally weak to me, Detective. Why is Treasury involved? And do you have any other suspects in tow?" Rosen asked.

"No, not a damn one," Len replied, as he looked across the desks into the face of a concerned Jeffrey Robinson, who sat slumped in his chair. "But as I said, a day or two more and that may change. Treasury has been watching van Haan for some time; he's possibly running bad money and ersatz paper too."

"That's interesting." The phone went silent for a moment. "What does your department have on the assassinations of the Safety House personnel and the other police officer in his home?"

Len sighed, "We have two of our best detectives working those cases along with the murder of Gloria Mitchell. No concrete leads, except we may have discovered the identity of the perpetrator. He's possibly an international terrorist."

"What? An international terrorist? What kind of bullshit is that?"

"Excuse me, ma'am, but we'd be happy to share what bullshit we have. I am serious."

"Okay, I'd be more than happy to look at it. What does your department have on the RFK classroom shootings?"

"We've hit the wall, ma'am. The only witnesses are two dozen young teenage kids. They were too traumatized to be of any help. CSI came up empty at the scene except for four 22-caliber shell casings. We did generate a reasonable likeness of the perpetrator from two or three of the kids who could describe him to our departmental sketch artist. Beyond that, nothing."

Assistant District Attorney Deborah Rosen sighed heavily, "Well, okay, go for it, Lieutenant Morgan. Please stay in touch."

"My God. What a delightful conversation that was," Jeffrey Robinson said, staring across the desks at his frustrated partner. "Although I could only hear your half of it. We really don't have jack-shit on van Haan, do we, or on much of anything else?"

"Just the fact that van Haan smells, he likes strange pussy and has butt-boys visit his house, none of which are capital crimes," Len replied. "And the other cases are stalled out too. Sonnuva-bitch!"

"BFD."

"Yep." Len agreed. "Okay, I'm going now."

"Where?"

"To the powder room to pee a lot. Maybe I'll upchuck too, just as a matter of principal. I'm as convinced as you are, Robbie, van Haan is our man, but when you look at the evidence, we haven't any. Shit!" Len slammed his fist hard on his desktop, stood and strode past Jeff Robinson into the squad room.

He returned later with two cups of hot precinct coffee and rejoined Jeff Robinson, who asked, "Well, if it isn't van Haan, who in hell are we looking for?"

Before he could answer, an excited Mariko Tanaka burst in. "Len, Robbie! Dutch is at Cedars Sinai Medical Center! He's in critical condition! It's his heart!"

Len and Jeff Robinson left the coffee on their desks and hurriedly grabbed for their coats. "When?"

"We just got the word from ER at the hospital. When he didn't show up for work today we were curious. When we didn't hear from him later, and his pager or phone didn't respond, we sent a Black-and White to his house. It's horrible! The officers found him lying unconscious on the kitchen floor! When the EMT crew arrived, they said it was a miracle he was still alive. He's still unconscious; it looks bad guys."

"Okay, let's all try to be calm for a second," Len said, taking a deep breath. "Now what the hell can we accomplish if we all run over to Cedars ... besides becoming a nuisance and feeling good about our being there? To hell with that, let's go!"

13

Still Friday, June 14, day 10…

The Devonshire Hills Homicide trio made a record-setting trip south out of the Valley to the Cedars Sinai Medical Center. With full siren, flashing lights, and the capable driving skills of Sergeant Jeffrey Robinson they were in west Los Angeles in thirty minutes, all the while Len was receiving occasional updates from Watch Command radio passed along by the hospital.

Jeff Robinson parked the cruiser and the three of them ran into the center, going immediately to the Cardiology Unit registration window, where the receptionist directed them upstairs to the cardiopulmonary waiting room.

There, Len stopped at the nurses' station. "We're from Valley West PD, is Doctor Ira Malcolm expecting our arrival?"

The aide smiled, "Yes, Doctor Malcolm has a couple of stops to make first, but he will be with you shortly. Please take a seat. If you like, there's coffee or sodas to your left behind that partition."

"Thanks, that sounds good." Len slumped into a chair and somberly pondered the situation. What they learned so far was that Dutch Ryan was currently in surgery receiving a catheter angioplasty procedure to relieve major blockages in the arteries near his heart.

At that moment, Dr. Ira Malcolm entered the waiting room. He acknowledged the trio with a wave of his hand and stopped at the nurses' desk to handle some details. Finished, he turned and introduced himself.

"Good afternoon. I'm Doctor Malcolm."

"Good afternoon, Doctor. I'm Len Morgan, these are my associates, Miss Tanaka, and Sergeant Jeff Robinson. We work under Captain Ryan's command in the Valley West Devonshire Hills precinct. How is he doing, sir?"

Nodding, Dr. Malcolm explained, "We were touch and go for a bit. Your Captain was unconscious upon admittance, but thankfully, he came around in the ER. When he was somewhat stabilized, I discussed his situation with him and suggested that we do a temporary catheter procedure, an angioplasty, to which he readily agreed. Are you at all familiar with that procedure?"

They nodded their heads in response.

He continued. "Later, when his physical condition is improved such that we can operate, we'll probably do an open heart and by-pass several of his major arteries; it depends on what we find during the angioplasty. The open-heart procedure looks like weeks down the road so I strongly recommend that you make whatever arrangements are required in order to allow your department to function without him. The worst is behind him so there's no need to worry. If he'd arrived any later, we may have lost him. Any questions?"

"Doctor, for my part," Len said, "I'm so thankful and satisfied that he's in capable hands. When will he be out of surgery? An hour, two hours? We'd like to see him if that's possible."

"He won't be all that long now. Let me see, what time is it? Okay, he's been in for about thirty minutes, I'd give it another hour. However, he'll not be in any condition for visitors today. If you care to wait anyway, feel free to do so. We'll keep you apprised of his condition if there are any changes."

"Doctor, you said he may have to undergo a bypass. Is 'may' the operative word here?" Jeff Robinson asked.

"Yes. We'll see how he responds to the angioplasty. In some cases, that's all that's required for patients to return to normal health. We'll do some other tests when he's stronger and make a determination at that time. Are there any further questions?" Dr. Malcolm asked, getting to his feet.

"None, thanks, Doctor," Len answered. "Thanks again for everything that you and your staff have done."

"Oh, yes," Dr. Malcolm added, "one other thing; he asked us to contact his niece in Chicago. We did, and as soon as she can make arrangements she'll be here in California."

"Fine, thanks again, Doctor," Len said.

"Boss, I'd like to stay around for a while. You guys can leave when you want, I'll catch a taxi," Mariko Tanaka offered.

"No, I'll stay too. Robbie, if you want to split, I'll see that Mariko gets home."

Jeff Robinson shook his head, "I'll stay for a while. I can't just dash away and abandon the two of you. Besides, I'd like to see how Dutch does too."

"Fine," Len said, loosening his tie and rubbing the back of his neck. "Is anyone hungry besides me? I think I'll visit the cafeteria and grab a quick bite."

"That sounds good," Mariko said. "If you don't mind, I'll join you. Robbie? Hungry?"

"I'll wait here while you two fill your faces," Jeff Robinson said, smiling and stretching out his legs.

Leaving Jeff Robinson behind, Len and Mariko summoned the elevator and rode it down to the cafeteria.

The two returned an hour later from their afternoon lunch and resumed a quiet vigil alongside Jeff Robinson. Mariko took a seat next to him and placed a comforting arm across his shoulders. "Any news?"

"Yeah, guys. He's in the recovery room now, sleeping. Everything went well, really well. The fact is they finished with the rhinoplasty sooner than they thought. Now we just have to wait for him to wake up."

Mariko and Len suddenly burst out laughing at Jeff Robinson's faux pas.

"What? What's so damn funny you two?"

Still laughing, Mariko, having regained some partial control between fits of giggling explained, "Robbie, he didn't have his nose repaired, they repaired his arteries; it's called an angioplasty. Jeez."

"Oh," Jeff Robinson said quietly, causing both Mariko and Len to laugh again.

Another hour passed and it was obvious to Len that his partner was having a difficult time waiting for any news that might be forthcoming.

"Robbie, why don't you knock off and go on home. We'll catch a taxi. Dutch may sleep all night and there's no sense in wearing you out."

"Yeah, well ... if you guys don't mind a taxi ride I think I will split. I've had enough of hospitals for a while. Man, I'm not looking forward to being in one whenever Colleen has a baby. I'm not that comfortable in these places. They're too *white*, you know what I mean?"

"Too white?" Len frowned, faking annoyance.

"Well, asshole, y'all got a lot of mileage out of my rhinoplasty remark," Jeff Robinson said as he stood and stretched.

"You two can just stop that!" Mariko scolded. "That's enough of that bad boy talk!"

"Yes, mother," Len answered.

"Okay, I'll see you two later. Be sure to let me know if anything changes. Later."

"Sleep tight, Robbie," Len answered as Jeff Robinson turned to leave. "See you tomorrow."

Three hours had passed since Jeff Robinson's departure. The nurses aide behind the counter hung up her telephone and advised Mariko and Len that Dutch had awakened briefly in recovery and returned to his ward where he resumed sleeping. He was doing as well as the doctors anticipated, and if anyone wanted to visit tomorrow, they were welcome to stop by for the afternoon visitation hours.

Len thanked the aide for the information and said to Mariko, "I'll fetch a taxi for us and we can get out of here. Besides having a numb ass from sitting, I'm hungry again. Would you like some dinner somewhere? My treat."

"Real food? Wow! I'll agree to that. Where?"

"Well, how about ... Charley Brown's? Not far from your house, but first, let's find a ride."

On the way back to the Valley, Mariko and Len watched the slow moving rush hour traffic from the back seat of the taxi and quietly discussed their game plan for the evening. Mariko insisted on going to her place first so she could shower and change into something more appropriate. Len agreed, and then he suggested they go to his place so he could do the same.

The taxi parked in front of the quaint Studio City bungalow, which Mariko shared with her two older sisters. Leaving Len, she dashed inside and he took the opportunity to stretch out as much as he could in the taxi's backseat to drift in and out of a fitful nap.

Hearing Mariko's front door close, he opened his eyes and looked out the taxi window. Standing on her front porch and keying the lock, Mariko was startling, a thing of beauty. He looked at her in wonderment as she turned to step off the porch. She smiled as she glided down the sidewalk to the taxi.

Amazed, he was surprised to find his heart in his throat. In mere minutes she had bathed, made up her face, let her flowing black hair down and had totally changed: now wearing a brilliantly flowered blouse with a white sheath skirt over white hose and heels.

"Lookin' good, lady," Len remarked appreciatively as he opened the car door for her. "Driver, please take us to the Villa Casa Grande on Rinaldi in Granada Hills."

When they arrived, Len said, "Welcome to where I live. I'll only be a minute or two. I don't think my transformation will produce the same results as yours, but I'll give it a go. The kitchen is over there, Mariko. Help yourself to anything you like," and he disappeared into his bathroom.

Showered, he wrapped himself in a thick Turkish towel and stepped into his bedroom. To his utter amazement, Mariko, adorned in only her bra and Bikini panties, lay stretched out atop his white comforter, her smooth dark skin accentuated by the white fabric.

"Mariko! My God! What are you doing?" he exclaimed, flabbergasted. "You're practically naked and lying on my bed! Where are your clothes?"

Mariko rolled onto her side and faced him. Propped on one elbow, she looked at him wrapped in his towel. "Well, Boss

... I'm resting," she said, matter-of-factly. "And I didn't wish to wrinkle my things so I placed them in your closet."

Aghast, unable to speak, he continued to stare at her. As his mind reached warp-speed, he found her more than appetizing with her firm breasts pushing against her bra and her long legs parted slightly, provocatively exposing her inner thighs. His breathing became erratic and he felt the uninvited early-warning erotic signals beginning deep within his groin.

"Mariko," he murmured, swallowing hard, "...please, we both know better. You know the department's fraternization rules. What are you trying to prove?"

"Prove? It's not about proving anything, silly. I could suggest that I'm bone-weary and want to stretch out, but earlier you said, 'Help yourself to anything you like', so I'd *like* to have sex with you."

He shook his head in disbelief, his mind wouldn't clear, it wouldn't function. Obviously, his body was functioning; he was becoming totally aroused.

"Now, I know you want me too ... I've been noticing your behavior all week."

"That's probably true, but I'd like to think I have more self-control than to become intimately involved with my Staff Assistant. As much as I might want to, we can't do this. Besides, having sex with a friend is one of the quickest ways to ruin a friendship."

"I know the departmental rules, and I realize how having *bad* sex with a friend could ruin a friendship. I can also see that you're finding me quite appealing right now, hmm?" she said, smiling seductively. Looking directly at the growing bulge beneath his towel, she altered her position to expose her inviting thighs even more.

His flustered mind was ablaze. "We aren't going to do this. Understand?" he murmured, as he sat down on the edge of the bed. "Mariko, we shouldn't..." he said as he inhaled the light fragrance that surrounded her.

"I know we shouldn't too," she whispered huskily as she turned off the table lamp, "but..."

The ensuing ride to Charley Brown's Steakhouse was understandably quiet. Refreshed, Mariko Tanaka sat relaxed as she gazed out her window at the passing parade of shops and stores on the brightly lit Ventura Boulevard.

Stiff-backed and staring straight-ahead, Len drove. With his jaw set and his hands clenched tightly on the Audi's steering wheel, he attempted in some way to dismiss the memory of what had occurred earlier in his bedroom.

She must think I'm some kind of perverted ass now. How in hell can I ever look her in the face again? Stupid shit, Morgan. Why did you have to have sex with her?

Mariko sighed and turned to look at him in his anguish. "Len, don't sit there commiserating. I initiated our lovemaking. I've wanted to since I discovered that Gabrielle was out of the picture."

That remark caused him to divert his attention and glance briefly at her.

"You were vulnerable as hell, Len. I took advantage of the situation and acted *slutty* to get my way. Now that we've been intimate, it's my turn to apologize. Will you forgive me?"

Taken by surprise by her entreaty, he managed to clear his throat before attempting to speak, "Slutty? Hardly, and do I forgive you? Is that what you said? I behaved like a damn animal. I didn't want this to happen with us."

Mariko snickered and shook her head.

"Okay ... that's not exactly true," he said. "In a perverted way I did want it to happen, but you know what I mean. I'm the one that should be apologizing. Can you forgive me?"

She laughed softly, "Oh yes, I do. Moreover, I'm also not concerned about it leading to something more involved, something more permanent. We're good friends and have now shared something quite delightful, okay? Am I truly forgiven?"

He glanced again at her for an instant, then looked back at the road. "Well," he said, "if you'll retract the word slutty. Just know that my response to your advances was not my normal modus operandi. I don't know what came over me."

"Ooh ... unquestionably I know what *came* over me, Mister Morgan."

"Did you have to go there?" he asked plaintively, "I should have picked a better choice of words. I'd hoped it would pass over your head … my remark I mean. Please, can we change the subject?"

Amused at Len's seeming discomfort, Mariko chuckled again.

Arriving at Charley Brown's they left the Audi with the valet and went inside. The maître d' escorted them to a quiet table near a window and they ordered the current special of the house: beef tenderloin tips sautéed with mushrooms and onions. Afterward, they shared a small bottle of Sangria wine and sat quietly staring at one another, waiting for something with which to break the awkward silence.

Len was entranced, still taken with Mariko's appearance, and certainly her physical attributes. He couldn't remember having seen her more attractive, not to mention seeing her naked in his bed. He was still recovering from what transpired earlier.

Clumsily attempting to be all business, he spoke first, "With Dutch in the hospital, it's a foregone conclusion he'll be forced into, or choose, a premature retirement. You mentioned it in the cab."

"Yes. I've been thinking of that too, and I can see you filling the vacancy. Have you thought of that?"

Len sat silently for a minute. "Not seriously, not until today … actually a few days ago Dutch started to mention something but then decided to wait. Truthfully, I don't want his job, I like what I do. I'm a street cop not an administrator. I don't fit well behind desks. I like the give and take out in the real world."

Mariko reached across the table and took his hand. Again, he felt that sudden tingle of electricity in her touch. "You can be a street cop and still be the new Captain. It's not etched in stone how one administrates. Dutch did it his way, as did the Captains before him. It's not a one-size-fits-all thing."

He reached out and rested his other hand on hers. It felt good, comfortable, touching her hand. "If Dutch doesn't return and Commissioner Dansforth appoints me to take his place, you'll be carrying the weight, not me, at least for a while."

She laughed softly and squeezed his hand. "I guess. Dutch has given me more and more tasks to handle lately. It's as if he had a premonition or something. I can't describe it. Anyway, Commissioner Dansforth will promote you. There's no doubt about that, my sweet friend."

She gripped his hand tighter with both of hers and leaned forward against the edge of the table. "Okay, Mister soon-to-be-Captain of Detectives, you will either take me home to my pitiful surroundings, or you will drag me kicking and screaming back to your luxurious bedroom and enthrall me unceasingly. Which will it be?"

He smiled at her light humor, but secretly pondered the exotic wonders and pleasures possibly awaiting him beneath her skirt. "It appears that you have your mind set, Miss Tanaka. As much as I'd like to accommodate, the answer is *no* to your suggestion for a reprise." Oddly, he did want her again: right here, right now. *I guess I've always wanted her*, he conceded.

Standing up, he said wistfully, "My dear, sweet friend, allow me to take you home. Maybe … maybe we could … no," he said, quickly changing his mind, "tonight we sleep alone."

Day 11, 6:55 a.m., Saturday morning, June 15…
"Well, you look rested and chipper as hell considering it's a Saturday workday morning," Jeff Robinson remarked as Len got into the big Ford sedan. "Get a lot of well-deserved rest last night for a change?"

"No, actually, I fussed most of the night," Len explained, casually lying and changing the subject. "I've been worrying about Dutch and how difficult it will be working for you when Commissioner Dansforth appoints you to take his place."

"That's bullshit too. What were you snorting last night? You're Dutch's obvious replacement and you know it."

"Seriously, I don't want his job, not now, not like this. I want to nail Duard van Haan. He's my number one priority right now. Probably yours too?"

"You know it is, Boss; I want his fat white ass on a platter, the sooner the better. Nevertheless, what can we do to make our case? We don't have jack now. It's as the lady DA said, we have a weak case, if any case at all."

"Okay, so let's pretend we're extraordinarily talented homicide detectives and start building a case; is that a plan?" Len asked.

"Right, but after breakfast? You're buying?"

"Sure, I'll buy, just to balance my books because I bought dinner for Mariko last night."

"Where'd you guys go?" Jeff Robinson asked as he pulled into the parking lot at Abbe's.

"Some new place called Ariadde's Greek Gyro Drive-In Restaurant," Len said, intentionally lying again, knowing he had Jeff Robinson's rapt attention. "It's east of the I-5 on Roscoe, kind of a 'home boys' hangout, BUT, one great gyro sandwich, loaded with putrid red onions and some smelly white sauce. Reminded me of your gym socks."

"Holy shit! Are you tryin' to ruin my appetite? Shut up for Chrissakes!" Jeff Robinson yelled, slamming the door of the cruiser.

"Hey! You asked. Is there anything else you want to know this morning?"

"No!"

Devonshire Hills Precinct...
Mariko met Len and Jeff Robinson at the door as they entered the squad room. "First, gentlemen, Captain Dutch had a good night," she said flatly, showing no outward emotion toward Len as she spoke. "He's awake and had a light, liquid breakfast. Second, there's an urgent message from Treasury. Luis Campanera will be moving on van Haan this morning at eight-thirty. Luis requested that you meet with him at the Federal building no later than ten-thirty if you want to question van Haan in regards to the murder. After today, Luis says van Haan will be a scarce commodity, at least that's what the message implied."

"Shit!" Len snapped, setting his jaw, attempting to maintain his self-control. "If ever I wanted to nail a suspect, van Haan's got to be the one. Damn! To hell with it anyway!"

"I'm sorry guys, I'm only the messenger," Mariko said apologetically. "And there's more, Boss. Commissioner Dansforth wants you to call him at home; here's his private number."

Len responded to that request with an uncharacteristic frown.

Jeff Robinson took this opportunity to change the subject quickly. "Miss Tanaka, so how did you like your 'fabulous dinner' last evening?"

"It was great, it was all really great. Why?"

"Damn! Get outta' here woman! The man takes you to some old greasy spoon in the industrial area and you say it was great? I knew it! You got no class, no taste at all."

Puzzled and bewildered at Jeff Robinson's words, Mariko looked at Len, who bit his lip and winked. Saying nothing, he merely shrugged.

"Well, taste is in the mouth of the well fed," Mariko said as she resumed her seat behind her desk. "Maybe you can join us sometime, Robbie," Mariko suggested, winking at Len. "…and we can enjoy a *ménage a trois*?"

"Get outta here!" Jeff Robinson barked. Turning, he followed Len into their office.

Len slid down into his chair behind the small desk, which was becoming as cluttered as Dutch Ryan's. "Damn, I really wanted van Haan first, before the feds gobbled him up and now the Commish wants to chat, probably about wanting me to take over for Dutch. Shit! I hope it's merely a temporary thing."

"Hey, it could be worse … I think," Jeff Robinson said. "Anyway, call the man and see what he wants. Hand your phone messages over to me; I'll sort out the important ones."

"Okay, I'll call him." Len reached forward and tossed a dozen of the pink message slips across the desk, "Have a ball."

14

Still Saturday, June 15...

After leaning back, yawning, and stretching his arms above his head, Len picked his phone up and entered Commissioner Dansforth's home number. After a couple of rings, a pleasant female voice answered. Len responded, "Yes, good morning. This is Lieutenant Len Morgan, Devonshire Hills homicide unit. May I speak with Commissioner Dansforth, please?"

"Yes, Lieutenant, he's outside weeding in the flower garden. Would you mind waiting while I get him?"

"Not at all, Mrs. Dansforth." Len idly tapped his fingertips on his desk and watched Jeff Robinson sorting through the telephone messages. "Apparently the Commish is an early riser; he's outside in his garden already."

The Commissioner picked up, "Len, Harlan Dansforth here. How are the murder investigations going? Got any admissible evidence on that rich guy, the friend of our Mayor? Excuse me a second..." Dansforth coughed, and then cleared his throat. "Damn summer allergies. Sorry, Len, what's his name? Van Horn?"

"Van Haan, Commissioner," Len corrected. "Duard van Haan. I'm sorry, sir, not much at all. We do have confirmation of the scent of cologne in the victim's room, it matches his, but Treasury is moving on him within the hour and we've been cordially invited to join Special Agent Campanera at Treasury lockup at 10:30 a.m."

"Damn it," the Commissioner cursed. Len could practically feel his frustration. "So, what's the status on the

RFK Junior High School killings, the Safety House, Svoboda and the second hooker? Anything new on those?"

"Not a thing, sir. We've hit a brick wall on every case we are working," Len explained. "Excuse me…" Len stifled a dry cough.

Covering the phone with his hand, Len whispered, "Robbie, would you fetch some coffee for us, or whatever it is?"

Jeff Robinson nodded and left the room.

"Additionally, Commissioner, we don't have anything on the Werner Motel shooting either. Our best guess is that we have a phantom assassin running free, possibly back in Europe."

"What about the FBI, anything?"

"I really can't say, sir. They're semi-tight-lipped as usual. Our FBI contact advised Robbie that the assassin might be the notorious terrorist, Yves-Gaston Giroux, a French-Canadian international hit man, based on the still photos we provided. Hit man seems like a huge stretch to me, but that's what we might conclude."

"A French-Canadian international hit man, you say? Kidnapping and killing a hooker? Damn, that is a stretch. Whoever he is, I'd like to find the bastard. Keep working on it. Something will turn up, it always does. As far as taking over Dutch's duties, you and I will get down to cases later. However, you'll be assigned a few of Dutch's everyday chores for now. I hope they don't overload you."

"Thanks, sir. I appreciate your confidence, and a few chores shouldn't be any problem; I was going to volunteer anyway."

Len placed the telephone in its cradle and leaned back into his swivel rocker, suddenly fatigued. As his mind wandered briefly, he stared into the squad room at Mariko, who busily sorting through some papers at her desk. He felt a strange rush of emotion deep within him and he swallowed hard.

He quickly glanced up at Jeff Robinson, who had returned bearing two cups of steaming black coffee. Len hoped he hadn't noticed him. He hadn't.

"Thanks, Robbie. Did you call the lab for any further info on the blood types and DNA tests run on Lorena Reynolds?"

"I did, earlier. They were to fax it over a day ago."

At that moment, Mariko appeared in the doorway, "Robbie, here are the DNA results you asked for. They came in over the fax line last night."

"Just like magic, Boss man, timing is everything. Here, take a look," Jeff Robinson said, and handed the paperwork across the desk.

Len quickly perused the data, then concluded, "Okay, the semen and blood tests show up as type 'O' positive, a fairly common flavor. They're waiting for tests to come back on the specimens taken from Gloria Mitchell to see if they get a cross match. With this, maybe we can add to our slim evidence against Mister van Haan. Saddle up, let's go downtown and visit the Feds and your friend. Any new words on Dutch's condition, Mariko, has anyone heard from his niece?"

"No, no word from his niece. Yes, he's still doing great," she said, grinning. "The same as he was doing earlier when you asked. The nurses tell me he's sleeping like a baby. He did take some pureed food and they said he was being a genuine asshole about that too, not being a nice person at all."

Jeff Robinson had his coat back on and adjusted the knot in his tie, "Go figure. Now who would ever think Dutch would behave like an asshole?"

"Yeah, a prince of a chap that he is, always the kindly, soft spoken, consummate gentleman," Len said, a mild touch of sarcasm in his voice. "I wonder if his niece is a nice person. Or, God forbid, another Dutch Ryan? Keep us informed if anything pertinent comes up with Lana's case, or Tobin's with the classroom shootings, or any of the above, okay?"

"I will," she replied, slyly catching his eye, which caused him to hesitate a split second. "Oh ... one other little detail, a brother of Gloria Mitchell was located and he's in contact with the ME and the DA's office too."

"Good, that's one less detail to be concerned with. One more thing… if an emergency arises today, radio Lana and Wolf and ask them to cover for us while we are in LA."

"Will do. You two be careful out there."

On the way to the elevator, Len's thoughts returned to last night's extraordinary lovemaking and their late dinner date. *That was an incredible evening … a sensational time with one vibrant young woman. I wonder what it would have been like to sleep with her all night.*

"Hey, are you listening?" Jeff Robinson asked, interrupting Len's daydream.

"I'm sorry, Robbie, I was indulging in a little known metaphysical erotic process. I've had too many heavy things to think about; it helps to keep the mind and the pipes clear. What were you saying?"

Shaking his head, Jeff Robinson asked. "Me? I was simply asking if you still wanted me to pick you up Monday morning, or will you be driving? You know, to be here early to do your 'chores'."

"Oh, no, I'll drive. Good thinking though, I'd not considered that. There's no need for you to feel like you have to always chauffeur me around, especially at six o'clock in the morning."

"Good, I wasn't planning on doing it either, *Miss Daisy*," Jeff Robinson chided. "I was already going to suggest that you drive. I've also alerted the traffic division that your operator's license has probably expired, so be on the lookout."

"And you're my buddy? Huh! I always thought you were a jerk and now you have confirmed my suspicions. Enough of that, let's go see Luis and Company."

The Devonshire duo arrived in Westwood at the Federal Building on Wilshire Boulevard at 9:54 a.m. According to Jeff Robinson it was early enough to keep the time schedule Campanera had set for the ten o'clock meeting with Duard van Haan and his attorney.

The two detectives stepped out into the reception area and the same receptionist they recalled from their previous visit greeted them. She remembered them too, and suggested they just go down to Campanera's office and make themselves comfortable. Finding his office empty, they sat down in the small waiting area and stared silently at the plush carpeting.

"This is not the way I wanted this case to end," Len said, reflecting aloud as he examined a scuff on his new loafers. "We're probably going to watch a murderer go into a minimum security country club for a few years, or maybe months, and then be set free to go back to whatever lifestyle he chooses. What a bunch of crap."

"Really," Jeff Robinson said in terse agreement. "But, Len, remember there's no statute of limitations on murder."

At that moment, Special Agent Luis Campanera arrived. He smiled and extended his hand, "Len, Jeff, it's good to see both of you again. Look, I'm sorry to drag you out on a Saturday morning, but we received our orders to move on this guy."

"Yeah," Len muttered. "We heard."

"Sorry, boys. Anyway, we executed a federal search warrant and opened some of those smaller packages. They were full of bad cash, as we'd supposed. Our prosecutors feel we have enough to put him away along with a few others just like him. How's Dutch doing? I was shocked to hear. Is he okay?"

"Dutch is doing fine, according to the nurses at Cedars. And Luis, we do understand how you people have to work; I just wish we had the same preponderance of evidence on van Haan ourselves. We might be close, but I don't recall this ever being a game of horseshoes."

Campanera stood with his hands casually jammed in his front pockets and shrugged. "True. All right, gentlemen, let's go downstairs and see the man and his high-priced attorney. Oh, there's hot coffee down there too, if you need a mid-morning *pick 'em up*."

Van Haan, his attorney, and a federal court stenographer waiting in the interrogation room glanced up when the trio arrived. Ignoring them, Len looked around, taking in the room itself, comparing its stark feel and furnishings to the Interview

Room at the Devonshire precinct, of which he was accustomed. This room had no windows, no one-way glass mirrors, but several surveillance cameras. Unlike Special Agent Campanera's suite, the furniture was austere.

In sharp contrast to the haughty, hard-shell exterior van Haan usually exhibited, today he looked genuinely stunned upon seeing the two homicide detectives again. As the trio of officers entered and approached the conference table, van Haan leaned over and whispered in his attorney's ear. The attorney, in response, concentrated his attention on the two detectives and nodded.

"Do we all know everybody?" Campanera asked, looking at van Haan and his attorney. "If not, this is Detective Lieutenant Len Morgan of Devonshire Hills homicide and his…"

"…his black sidekick, *Mister Tibbs*!" Van Haan shouted, standing abruptly.

Reacting instantly, Jeff Robinson shouted from across the table, "The name is still Jeffrey Robinson, you sorry racist sonnuva-bitch!"

Shocked, van Haan's attorney looked first at Jeff Robinson, then back at his client in amazed disgust.

"That's quite enough, both of you!" Campanera demanded, quickly taking charge. "This is going to be a civil interrogation and that's that! Agreed? Everyone?"

"Fine with me, just so…" Jeff Robinson blurted.

"Jeff!" Len said, restraining his partner. "Please. Cool it and let's get on with this."

Jeff Robinson chose a chair across from the attorney. His dark eyes snapped as he zeroed in on the smirking van Haan. Len sat down at Jeff Robinson's right and Campanera took the adjacent chair.

Len thought, *So, this is what a gangster's attorney looks like today; a thousand dollar suit, physically fit and intelligent … at least so far.*

"Excuse us briefly, gentlemen," van Haan's attorney requested. "Duard, I need a word…." He stood and walked his client to a corner of the large room. There he talked privately, in quiet, even tones in an attempt to restrain van Haan from any further outbursts.

Returning to the conference table, he said, "My name is David Neill, gentlemen. I represent Mister van Haan."

Special Agent Campanera, Len, and Jeff Robinson nodded in acknowledgment. "I sincerely apologize for my client's egregious outburst. It won't happen again," he said, casting a side-glance at van Haan.

"May I inquire as to why we have a team of homicide detectives here for a United States Treasury Department interrogation? It does seem a bit left-handed. Do you agree, Mister Campanera?" David Neill asked, respectfully.

Campanera responded with his patented shrug. "Detectives Morgan and Jeff Robinson have a few questions to pose to your client regarding another matter, Mister Neill. Your client may be a prime suspect in a recent murder in the Valley. Are you aware of that, sir?"

David Neill looked at his client quizzically and shook his head. "No, sir. I'm not aware of that. Please excuse us again, gentlemen. Duard…"

The two men left the table and again conversed quietly. Van Haan showed some definite flushed-face emotion once or twice. Finished, they returned.

It appears that van Haan hasn't been totally honest and up-front with his expensive lawyer. Naughty, naughty, Len mused, watching van Haan's discomfort.

David Neill spoke, "Gentleman, my client is not objectionable to discussing anything that you care to bring to the table. From my standpoint, it's a bit unusual, but this is the twentieth century, right? Now, Duard, my question is a simple one; do you consider yourself to be a suspect or perpetrator of any recent murder?"

"Not at all, David. These two questioned me early one morning at my residence regarding a slaying. Afterward, I simply forgot about it. I'm not involved in any murder. Believe me."

Len looked at his notepad, then at Duard van Haan, "Mister van Haan, if you are as innocent as you claim, then you certainly won't object to answering a few of our simple questions; simple questions that may confirm your innocence in this case?"

"Detective Morgan," Neill interrupted, "if my client has any information that can be of any relevance to your case, I'm certain he will be more than happy to share it with you. Right, Duard?"

Van Haan's face reddened. He scowled at the condescension, but reluctantly nodded his head in agreement.

"Very well," Len said. "Mister van Haan … wait, excuse me a minute, please."

Pausing, Len turned to Campanera, "Will your stenographer be taking recorded notes of our interrogation of van Haan?"

"Yes, and true copies of the transcript will be made available to all interested parties as soon as possible."

Len thanked him and looked at the nearby stenographer who nodded his head in agreement. Satisfied, Len turned his attention back to van Haan, "Mister van Haan. Do you use a brand of cologne known as *Suspicion*?"

"What the hell?" Van Haan bellowed. "Was that goddamn traffic light incident from last week some of your doing?"

"Mister van Haan, a simple Yes or No will suffice." Len said, ignoring van Haan's outburst.

Grasping his attorney's arm, van Haan shouted, "David, they rigged a traffic signal to trick me into running it so their uniformed officers could pull me over and get close to me. I want you to do something about that. It reeks of entrapment. It can't be admitted into…"

"Duard! Please…" an exasperated David Neill demanded, wresting his arm from van Haan's grasp. "Gentlemen, again, please excuse us."

The two men went back into the far corner where Neill did the majority of the talking again while van Haan stared at the floor, reluctantly nodding. Finished, they returned to the table.

David Neill cleared his throat. "Detective Morgan, would you please explain to me what this traffic signal incident is all about? We agreed to be forthcoming today; will you be just as forthcoming and explain that?"

"No problem, sir. On the morning of the murder, two of our police officers, along with a friend of the victim, experienced the presence of a strong cologne fragrance in the room where the murder took place. Being advised that the victim was allergic to perfume and didn't use it, we concluded that somebody else had been in the room recently, and possibly the perfume or cologne scent belonged to the perpetrator."

"Who advised you that the victim was allergic to perfume?"

"A close personal friend of the victim."

"Where does my client fit into this?"

"At that point he didn't. When Sergeant Jeff Robinson and I initially visited your client at his home, we experienced a heavy scent of cologne while talking to him. Based on that discovery, yes, we did a harmless number on Mister van Haan early one morning. Two traffic officers, the same ones from the crime scene, got close enough to your client to identify his cologne as being the same they had experienced at the crime scene."

"What gave you cause to visit Mister van Haan in the first place?"

"We were apprised that the murder victim once serviced an art curator that did business in the Valley. We found Mister van Haan's museum listed in the telephone directory along with several others. His was merely a routine investigatory visit. Coincidentally, while there we experienced the strong scent of his cologne, which obviously piqued our interest."

"Detective Morgan," defense attorney David Neill replied condescendingly, "obviously you are aware of the entrapment laws that protect…"

"Mister Neill!" Morgan roared while staring hard, startling attorney Neill. "Don't presume that I'm ignorant of what we may or may not introduce as evidence in a trial. Give us the benefit of knowing something! Mister van Haan just used the word reek. *He* reeks, sir, *his* cologne would stink up a courtroom just as it is polluting this room. It certainly stunk up the murder scene, giving us a good idea that he had been there on that morning, or is that just too coincidental. We didn't need a ploy to determine that an odor always accompanies your client. We merely needed to identify that specific odor."

Taken aback, Neill answered quietly, "Fine."

Resuming, and turning his attention to van Haan, Len continued, "Now, Mister van Haan, a simple question; do you use Suspicion brand cologne?"

"Yes," he whispered quietly, staring at the gleaming tabletop.

"Thank you. Now, were you in the victim's hotel room on the morning of June 5, the morning of the murder?"

"Duard, no. You don't have to answer that," Neill advised quickly.

Van Haan's face turned red as he turned and glared at his attorney. "I'll answer if I want! Yes! I was there! But, I didn't kill her because she was already dead!"

Len and Jeff Robinson both leaned forward in their chairs upon hearing that unexpected outburst.

"God! She looked so horrible, and the smell of her feces and blood was just ghastly. I ran out of there. Hell, I may have passed the murderer in the hall for all I know. But, just appreciate this, all of you, I may be a lot of things, but I am not a goddamn murderer!"

Len leaned into the table again and looked van Haan directly in his eyes. "And if you didn't go there to murder her, sir, why were you there?"

"No! You don't have to answer that either, Duard," Neill repeated.

Ignoring his attorney again, van Haan replied, "She was blackmailing me and I was paying. I was delivering the regular cash payment we'd agreed to. I was a day late. All I was doing was taking the money to her."

"How much money were you taking to her, Mister van Haan?"

"My client doesn't have to answer that, Detective," Neill again interrupted.

Van Haan, perspiring heavily, sat quietly and didn't respond to the question.

"Fine. All right, sir, when did you first meet Miss Gloria Mitchell?" Len hoped for some small physical response from van Haan that might give him away.

Van Haan didn't flinch. "Who?" he asked, shrugging. "Who is Gloria Mitchell?"

"Gloria Mitchell claims that she knew you, from a year or so ago. She's a hooker, a close friend of the victim. It's alleged that you purchased sexual favors from her in the past. She also claims that you insisted on engaging in bizarre sexual practices. Now do you remember her?"

"No, I don't. But I've known many hookers, of both sexes, I go both ways. What may seem as bizarre behavior for some may be run-of-the-mill for others. If I pay, I want to play. I don't know who she is, why?"

Ignoring van Haan's question, Len continued, "Mister van Haan, what is your blood type?"

"What? What in the hell has that got to do with anything? Why do you want to know that?" Van Haan demanded. "David?"

Looking at Neill, Len shrugged. "I thought we were going to be forthcoming. Is this a problem counselor? Wanting to verify his blood type?"

"It's all right, Duard, answer the detective if you know. Hell, give them a sample if they want."

"Type 'A'," van Haan responded reluctantly.

"Type 'A'?"

"Yes, type 'A'. What's the problem, Lieutenant? Is that the wrong goddamn type?" Van Haan asked sarcastically.

"Not really, type 'A' is as good as any other. One last question, Mister van Haan, why were you being blackmailed?"

Attorney Neill interrupted again at that point, "Mister van Haan does not have to answer that question either. Do you have any further questions, Detective Morgan?"

"One. Mister van Haan, are you familiar with a French-Canadian gentleman named Yves-Gaston Giroux?"

Van Haan's expression froze and he turned pale. "No," he said, swallowing hard.

"Really? Are you certain?" Len questioned, staring intently at the face of one very upset man.

"Detective Morgan, your question was asked and answered. Again, do you have any further questions?"

"Possibly dozens, Mister Neill, but not now. Luis, may I reserve my privilege to question or depose your prisoner later if I so choose?"

"Sure, Len, we'll try to work out something if he's legally available. Any problem with that Mister Neill?" Luis Campanera asked, looking across the table at van Haan's attorney.

David Neill rubbed his chin and paused before answering. "We'll consider it a gentleman's agreement. Fine. No problem."

"Thank you, Mister van Haan, Mister Neill," Len said as he closed his pad and got up from his chair. "Luis, thank you as well. We have no further business here today. Good afternoon, gentlemen."

Luis, again with his hands jammed down into his front pockets, walked to the door with his friends. "Len, Robbie, please say 'Hi' to Dutch for me. I hope he continues to improve. We'll see you both later, for certain."

"Sure thing, Luis. Later."

In the elevator, Jeff Robinson broke the awkward silence. "Len, you can have my shield right now if you want it. I'm really sorry for my infantile behavior in there. It was unprofessional and entirely uncalled for."

Len smiled at his good friend. "No problem. I actually enjoyed it. The over-filled shit; he had it coming. Forget it, okay?"

Jeff Robinson stared at the elevator floor, and then he looked at Len and took a deep breath. "You're a good guy, Boss."

"So are you, Robbie."

Len changed the subject, "Did you happen to catch the stink of shit filling his pants when I asked him if he knew Giroux?"

"Yes, I did. He was definitely affected."

"Yes, he was. He turned absolutely pasty. I wonder why? Maybe at the thought of having two well-placed bullets in his skull?"

"It figures," Jeff Robinson said. "Somewhere there's a connection. I wonder what it is."

"We're going to find out."

The two walked silently to the parked cruiser. As they left the Federal Building complex, Jeff Robinson asked, "What are you doing this weekend? Anything fun for a change?"

"I don't know about fun, but I will visit Dutch again, this afternoon maybe. Then I think I'll go down to Marina Del Rey and putter around my boat. There's a white-haired pussy down there too; I may look her up."

"What? What the hell are you talking about? Pussy? You? White-haired too?"

Ignoring Jeff Robinson's several questions, Len carried on, "The weather is supposed to be fair and brisk. I may take the sloop out for a shakedown, rebuilt engines and all with following seas on the way back. Perfect. What are you doing? Care to come along, you and Colleen? We can go out a few miles, furl the sails and picnic."

"Not if you're gallivanting around with some old white-haired skank! Count us out. Good grief…"

"Robbie," Len interrupted, laughing at his partner, "…it's a white pier-cat: a feline … NOT a skank, all right?"

"Oh … okay, that's different. The sailing and picnic thingy really sounds good, but we're supposed to visit her Aunt Naomi in Valencia. Some fun there, choking down Naomi's *Alpo Helper* casserole. Some other time?"

Len chuckled, "Sure." Then he became serious. "Did you get the impression van Haan was telling the truth in there? That she was dead when he found her?"

"I'd hoped you wouldn't ask. I didn't want to believe what my gut was telling me, but his description of the smell and the gore … his reaction was the same as mine. Yeah, I do, I believe him, damn it."

Len inhaled a deep breath and sighed. "It's funny how you can picture something so clearly, right in front of your eyes, and then it turns out to be a misconception, a false wind."

"What do you mean?"

"When I was a kid back in Wisconsin … age twelve or thirteen give or take, I was sailing on my old board on Lake Geneva. We'd loaded Melissa and everybody else we could find in Grandpa's station wagon and drove to the Big Foot Beach State Park one Sunday for a picnic. I'd lashed my board to the roof rack and wanted to take her out for a quick sail before we ate. The sun was bright, the sky was blue with a fresh breeze out of the southeast, at least that's what my mast feather read."

"Feather? What's a mast feather?"

"A feather is a little windsock of a thingy that rotates on a spindle on the tip of the mast. It tells you which way the wind is blowing, the direction it's coming from. Anyway, about two-hundred yards off shore, as I cleared a point of land covered with a thick stand of tall Red Pines, the boat took an accidental jibe, turned left and keeled over. Instead of the wind being on my face, it was suddenly on my back and all hell broke loose for a second or two as she made that sharp turn. The stern had passed through the eye of the wind causing the boom to swing around and strike my head and the sail to dip abruptly. As the mast pitched sharply, I slid off the deck into the lake."

"No shit, then what happened then?"

"Almost too much. I went under. Fortunately, or so I thought, I was wearing a new life jacket. As it turned out, it wasn't much help. I settled into the clear water and looked up through the rising bubbles. I could see the surface mirrored above me so I stroked with both arms, butterfly style, but nothing happened."

"What? What do you mean, nothing happened?" Jeff Robinson asked, becoming more interested in Len's sailing mishap.

"I mean, nothing. I couldn't surface. Something was holding me down. The hull was turtled, bottom-side up, and right there beside me, but it was too big and slippery to grip so I tried to break the surface again. By now, I'm taking on lake water."

"Did you drown?" Jeff Robinson asked, smiling at his question.

"Yup, I drowned. End of story," Len answered smartly. "No, you silly shit. About the time I thought I was history, something grabbed onto my skinny ass and pulled me from the water, boat and all."

"Someone was there and they rescued you? Is that what happened?"

"Yes, two nearby fishermen in a bow-loading motor boat ... they said they saw me go in and didn't see me come up. They motored over and pulled up next to the exposed hull. They saw my face about a foot beneath the surface and one of them grabbed my life jacket and hauled me into their boat."

"So you didn't drown after all?"

"Not that time. I'll confess, though, when I finished coughing up half the lake, I thanked those two guys like I've never thanked anybody, before or since."

"Fantastic. And those guys just happened to be there and saw you go under."

"Yes, we hear stories folks tell about *angels* rescuing folks in different precarious situations, like those three or four people who came to the rescue of that truck driver in Watts after he was nearly beaten to death back in 1992? I swear, the two guys in that boat were my angels ... I hadn't seen them or their boat out there earlier. So where did they come from?"

"Strange. Before you explain that, what does your story have to do with van Haan, and too, why couldn't you get out of the water by yourself? You were wearing a new preserver; you knew how to swim. Why?"

"As I said, I slid off the deck instead of tipping over backward as you're taught. When I went into the water, my legs tangled with the boom sheet, a small nylon line that controls the attitude of the boom. It slipped from my hand when I slid into the water. The tip of the mast became mired in the bottom mud and the sheet, or line, entangled my right leg, wrapping around it holding me under."

"Had that ever happened to you before? Or since?"

"No. But I learned to fall backward off the deck if ever I got tricked by a false wind again."

"A false wind? Oh … now I get it. You think van Haan is a false wind. Is that it?"

"Yes. I believe he is. Everything we had pointed to him, but he's not our killer."

"Len, you mentioned Melissa and that you were thirteen years old at the time; you two went back a long way, huh?"

"Yeah, we were close neighbors. We grew up about a quarter mile apart and she spent as much time at our place as I did at hers. Our getting married later in life seemed like the obvious thing to do; we were best friends."

"You mentioned once that you two had a baby and her sister adopted it … a girl?"

"Yeah, Bethany Anne," Len said, pausing; a saddened expression beginning to materialize. "It was right after Melissa's accident … I wonder about her at times too. Wondering whatever became of her, but also not wanting to interfere in her life."

Len remained silent for a few seconds, gazing out the window at nothing in particular.

"Well, partner," Jeff Robinson began hesitantly, "...maybe one day your telephone will ring and a voice will say, 'Hi Dad'!"

Len let out a quiet cough. "Fat chance, but that would be interesting. Okay, enough fantasizing, take me home instead of the precinct. I need my car."

The two finished the drive to the Valley in silence.

15

Villa Casa Grande, end of day 11, Saturday, June 15...

After showering and shaving, Len drove to Studio City and picked up Mariko. They then drove to Cedars Sinai to visit Dutch Ryan again. He still looked frail but was in good spirits, having nearly died a couple of days earlier. Len brought him up to speed on that morning's interrogation with van Haan. Then he told him of his visit to Tennessee and the silly fracas that took place in the funeral home. The individual that interested Dutch the most was Aubrey J. Hunnicutt, the Cal Southern football player.

"Call it my feminine intuition, Len," Dutch said, joking feebly, "but I'd keep a close eye on that one."

"I will," Len said, curiously reflecting on Dutch's hunches.

"What's the status on the Safety House murders?" Dutch asked, his voice heavy with sadness and concern.

Len gave him the same explanation he'd given Commissioner Dansforth earlier, "Dutch, we're stymied. We don't have anything going in any of the cases."

Dutch was silent; a look of pain and frustration etched his face.

"Dutch, you're tired and you need to rest. We'll see you later, okay?"

"Fine, Len. Thanks. Mariko, I owe you for everything. I really owe you," he said, the frustration leaving his face. As he let go of her hand Mariko smiled and lightly kissed his cheek, then she and Len departed.

On the way back to the Valley, Mariko broke the silence, "Len, I had an unbelievable time with you last night, and a most enjoyable dinner. It would have been perfect except for one glaring blunder on your part; you took me home."

"Mariko, I enjoyed your company too, maybe too much." He reached over and gave her hand a light squeeze and the electricity resurfaced. "Sweet lady, it would be too easy for me to be seduced again by you, you know? You're an enticing, attractive, intelligent woman, and I'm certain we would be good together ... and the idea of that frightens me to death, but Dutch said something back there that's gnawing at me. He said to keep an eye on the football player, Hunnicutt."

"Great segue, sweets. Smooth," Mariko said, smiling as she reached her left hand across the console and placed it on the inside of his right thigh. "So? What about the football player?"

He looked down at her hand, enjoying the feeling, but disregarded it as best he could, "When you went through the taxi records, do you recall any of them originating in the vicinity of Cal Southern? I seem to recall one in particular that stood out, but my mind was fuzzy when I stopped by the precinct last Sunday; I hadn't gotten a lot of sleep the night before."

"Oh, wow, let me think," she replied, becoming serious, but leaving her hand in place. "You know, I believe there was one fare, a pickup on Vermont Avenue. I can check it out Monday. What do you think ... that maybe the daughter's boyfriend, the college boy, could have something to do with her mother's murder?" she asked as her warm hand crept closer to his inner thigh; her deft fingers playing a fascinating staccato rhythm on his inseam.

"Dutch may be thinking so. So why didn't I suspect the kid too? He and the victim's daughter surely had a colossal interest in Mom's money. Let's go over all of those taxi records again. We may be able to piece something together after all. In fact, I made copies for Robbie to peruse too."

He looked at his wristwatch and lifted her hand from his leg. "Miss Mariko, it's getting late. As much as I'd like to kiss your sweet lips and ravish your wonderful body again, I'll have to take you home, unless you want to accompany me to the marina instead."

"Maybe another time," she replied, and sat back, quietly staring out her window.

Hmm ... that was too easy. Or, maybe she has other things planned.

Dropping her off, he turned the Audi around and drove south to Marina Del Rey to spend the rest of the early evening on his boat, away from pagers, telephones and police business. And, of course, to feed and socialize with Cat, one of his more favorite acquaintances.

Len returned home later and found the red message light blinking furiously on his telephone answering machine. He pushed the 'Play' button and heard Jeff Robinson's recorded voice: *"Len, I tried paging you several times but no response. Right now, it's past noon on Saturday. Luis just contacted the Commissioner looking for us regarding van Haan. I won't go into the details, but when you get this message, page me. I'll call you back. If you get this before noon, get your skinny butt over to the Federal Building, pronto! Later, my man."*

Len instinctively reached for his pager. It wasn't on his waist. "Screw!"

He left the kitchen and went to his bedroom; there it was, sitting on the night table with several earlier calls showing on the LED screen.

Hmm, that 805 area code must be Robbie's Aunt in Valencia, then there's his home number, and this 213 area code ... must be the Federal Building, time says 1:30 p.m. Dammit. What's going on?

Len picked up his phone and called Jeff Robinson at home. "Hello, this is Jeffrey Robinson."

"Robbie, Len here. What's going on? Did van Haan die, or escape? Which?"

"Len! Where have you been? I've been trying to locate you all damn afternoon. No, van Haan didn't die or disappear, on the contrary..."

"Well? What?"

"Luis called the precinct earlier, looking for either of us. Not reaching you, he paged me and I returned his call.

Apparently van Haan received some sound advice from his attorney, what's his name…"

"Neill…"

"Yeah, Neill. Van Haan is turning state's evidence, or whatever it's called when it's federal. I guess he's not that crazy about being in an ordinary lockup with the Russian Mafia connections being what they are these days."

"Stop digressing, Robbie, stay on point and tell me what the hell you're talking about. What is it with you and the Russian Mafia again?"

"Len, wait, listen. What it boils down to is this: van Haan is going into the Federal protection program. He's giving Treasury names, faces, and addresses. The whole shebang; chapter, page, and verse, all the information they need to shut down the entire shitty money business he's been a part of."

"Robbie!" Len interrupted, his patience wearing thin, "What the hell does any of that have to do with us finding a murderer? What?"

"Len, do you remember when he mentioned that he could have seen the murderer in the hall? When he was leaving the victim's room that morning? Well … we, Luis and I, deposed him this afternoon and he testified that he remembered seeing a man in the hallway on the victim's floor. He said it was a bellhop."

"Seriously?" Len asked, scratching his head. "He saw a bellhop in that shit-hole? So … was van Haan able to describe him or could he pick him out of a lineup?"

"Neither. He said the hallway was dimly lit; he couldn't be certain what he looked like. He just got a glimpse of him: tall, fair-haired, average weight and wearing a waist length maroon jacket. That's it. Oh … one other thing."

"Wait! Before you get into that, does the description you just ran past me ring a bell? Does he sound amazingly like our man, Gerot, or do we have several killers in Los Angeles with the same physical description?"

"I thought of that too. I showed him the photos of Gerot; he became very uncomfortable. If van Haan's bellhop is Gerot, he's not about to finger him. At least, that's my take."

"Well, swell," Len replied, obviously disgusted with van Haan's apparent fear of the assassin. "You were going to add something to what you had said a minute ago, you said, *Oh*."

"Yeah, I was. Check this out, he actually apologized to me. He said he was genuinely sorry, and that his bad manners were totally out of line. Go figure."

"He did?"

"Yes, he sure as hell did," Jeff Robinson confirmed.

"Robbie, that's startling. So, did you both do lunch afterwards and share family photos?"

"Screw you."

"Can you meet me after church tomorrow morning at the precinct, about eleven o'clock? I want to go over Miss Tanaka's taxi records again. We both seem to remember a late-night fare picked up near Cal Southern. Can you meet me?"

"Yeah, I can be there. What does Cal Southern have to do with anything? Something new I don't know about? And did you two have lunch again?"

"Lunch? Yes, after we stopped to visit with Dutch…"

"How is he doing?"

"Great. But listen to this hunch of Dutch's. I don't know why it didn't click with me before. The boyfriend of Lorena Reynolds' daughter attends Cal Southern University. When I was at the funeral, it was obvious he was definitely interested as to when the victim's bank account would be accessible to the heirs. The young boyfriend, in Dutch's mind, requires more of our attention," Len explained, staring inside his refrigerator.

"Does Dutch think there's a possibility the boyfriend murdered his future mother-in-law to get his hands on that money? If that's what he thinks, is that what you think?"

"Robbie, I think money makes folks do strange things, and in this instance, there's a lot of money involved, especially if you're a poor boy from Tennessee. Coincidentally, the Cal Southern lad is tall and fair-haired, like van Haan's bellhop, and like Gerot too. Figure that. Anyway, did Luis give you a copy of van Haan's deposition?"

"Yes, I have it right here in my coat. I'll bring it tomorrow, unless you want to see it tonight. I can run it over," Jeff Robinson volunteered.

"No, that's okay, Robbie. Tomorrow is soon enough. Say 'Hi' to Colleen for me, and I'm glad van Haan apologized too. You deserved it."

"Yes, tomorrow. Ciao, bud … and thanks."

Len let out a long exhalation of breath. *Well! This is great. I'm feeling better all ready. Something is finally coming together, and all because of a most unlikely witness, our new best friend, Mister Duard van Haan. All right!*

Len's telephone rang again. Picking up, he said, "Okay, Robbie, what did you forget?"

"Len? It's Harlan Dansforth."

"Commissioner? I'm sorry, sir. I just got off the phone with Sergeant Jeff Robinson. He has some good news for us. Sorry for the mistake, sir."

"That's all right Len, we all make mistakes," the Commissioner replied, chuckling. "I heard about Jeff Robinson's good news too. Mister Neill, van Haan's attorney, called me. Seems like his client is willing to cooperate with the Treasury department now."

"That's what Robbie alluded to, sir. He didn't go into much detail, but he and I were certainly surprised by van Haan's sudden change of character."

"Staring at prison walls and not knowing who your friends are can concentrate one's mind. Apparently, it got to him. That's good. Can you make anything out of his statement?"

"Not having seen it, sir, I can only speculate. However, it may fit together with a hunch Dutch had after I explained something I noticed in Tennessee at the funeral. The victim's daughter has a boyfriend attending college here on a football scholarship. With Dutch's instinct he suggested keeping an eye him."

"Good. Anything else?"

"We have van Haan's statement that he saw a bellhop outside the victim's hotel room. There may be a connection; the bellhop could be the football player. It's a stretch, but one certainly worth looking into. That's about it."

"Well, great, *Captain* Morgan…"

"Sir?"

"Len, I want to be the first to officially wish you success with this thing. As of now, you are our new, permanent Captain of Homicide Detectives. I know you will fill Dutch's shoes and do a fine job for the department."

"Sir… I… I don't know what to say. I'm flabbergasted, sir, but what about Dutch? What's happening to Dutch?"

"Dutch opted for early retirement. He's vested and he told me today that he wants to enjoy life tying flies and fishing. Besides that, he says that you're the best man for the job; Chief Clara says so too. You come well recommended."

Len's mind was spinning, almost unable to comprehend what was happening as Dansforth continued. "As of right now, you're in complete control of the department. You can hire, fire, promote, and turn it inside out for all we care. Just make it all work, okay? So congratulations, perhaps we can do lunch together sometime. I'll catch up with you somewhere. Good night now."

After choking and clearing his throat, Len answered, "Yes, thank you very much, sir. Lunch sounds good."

He hung up the telephone and discovered that the refrigerator door was still wide open. He let out a long sigh, feeling almost light-headed and giddy. Refocused on his refrigerator, he spied a diet-Pepsi, grabbed it and popped the top. He drank half of the contents before coming up for air. The sharp carbonation bit into his throat and tongue, but he didn't feel it.

"So … I'm the new Captain of Homicide Detectives … well, 'Shit the bed, Fred'." He smiled and finished the cola, then picked up the telephone again and called Jeff Robinson.

"Hello, this is Jeffrey Robinson."

"Ah, *Lieutenant* Jeffrey Alonzo Jeff Robinson," Len announced with all the pomp and swagger he could muster. "This is your new Captain speaking.

"And that's total bullshit, too," Jeff Robinson replied. "What have you been snorting today, and you can forget about that Alonzo shit. Did you get too much sun out there on your boat or wherever you were?"

Len laughed aloud at Jeff Robinson's remark. Len's senses finally accepted the inevitable; he was the new Captain of Homicide Detectives and had just promoted his best friend to Lieutenant.

"Robbie, I'm dead serious. Commissioner Dansforth just called. It's true, Jeffrey A. Robinson, and I just made you my new Lieutenant. That's the real deal. Sorry, bud, you be the man now."

Silence prevailed on Jeff Robinson's end of the line. Finally, with uncommon deliberation, he spoke, "Len, this is great news. I … not for me, but you … you are the new Captain. I always knew you would be one day, and now…" Silence again. "Damn, Len. Congratulations! I'm speechless."

"You, speechless? Let me make note of that, a first time for everything. Seriously, Lieutenant, now you get a fancier shield, a pay raise so you can buy that new car you need so badly, and you get a new partner. Maybe that will inspire your hormones to do wondrous things tonight. I'll see you tomorrow."

Man, this is exciting stuff, and I'm too bushed to celebrate. Should I call Mariko? No … no, I'd probably end up wanting to spend the night with her. I'll wait.

With his mind still spinning, he headed to his bathroom and a hot shower. He forgot that he had been in the sun most of the afternoon and that he was slightly sunburned. The blast of hot water set him to wincing and wiggling so he cut the shower short, wrapped a dry towel around his waist and went into the living room. In his favorite recliner chair, he clicked his TV remote device.

Day 12, early Sunday, June 16…
When Len awakened, the room was pitch dark save for the light that emitted from the TV screen. Dashiell Hammett's movie classic, <u>The Thin Man</u>, was playing again. Having seen it several times before he turned it off. Arising from his uncomfortable sleeping niche, he strolled into the kitchen.

The wall-clock read 3:13am He blinked his eyes, reacting to the severe brightness of the kitchen lighting. Unseeing for a while and still half-asleep, he opened the refrigerator door and stared inside again. Eventually he spotted the orange juice container. After shaking it violently, he raised it to his lips and emptied the contents. Satisfied, he headed off to bed.

Daybreak came and Len had overslept. Totally fatigued, he earlier had hit the snooze button on the clock-radio. Now he bounded from his bed, grabbed a quick shower and attempted to shave. Frantically he hurried to keep the appointment made the night before with Jeff Robinson. After drinking a glass of tap water, to wash down yesterday's cold, instant de-caffeinated coffee that he called breakfast, he sped off to the precinct and arrived there at 11:40 a.m. He was late.

As he strode through the squad room toward his office. He smiled and waved at Detectives Paul Tobin and Fred Cooper working the Sunday day-watch.

At the doorway to Dutch's office, he stopped dead in his tracks. There, painted on the clear, plate-glass was his name, *Leonard B. Morgan*, in bold gold-leaf letters shadowed in black. He stared at it unbelievingly, but there it was. Beneath his name were inscribed the words, *Captain of Homicide Detectives.*

"What do you think, Captain?" Paul Tobin shouted from across the room. "Looks mighty nice from here, Boss."

Len stood stupefied and thunderstruck. Then another familiar voice broke his stupor.

"Len! Congratulations, son." It was Commissioner Dansforth, outfitted in his familiar gray pinstripe suit and matching tie. Silver-haired, short of stature and deeply tanned, Dansforth smiled as he came out of hiding accompanied by Jeff Robinson and Mariko.

"Commissioner Dansforth," Len said, extending his hand, then hugging Jeff Robinson and Mariko, "Robbie, Mariko ... good morning. This is a shock. I never imagined my name would be on that door, sir. How?" He asked, catching a quick glance at Mariko, who beamed at him. Smiling back at her, he thought, *Ah … so that's why she let me off the hook so easily yesterday.*

"It was easy, Len. Miss Tanaka contacted the painter and he was available and obliged us. She also tipped me off that you three were going to be working today. It was fortunate in a way that Robbie couldn't reach you, that way, we were able to surprise you appropriately."

Mariko hugged Len again and gave him a big juicy kiss. Smiling and laughing, she kissed him again, this time on his nose.

Jeff Robinson, standing just behind Mariko, stepped forward. "Len, I'm not going to kiss you, not here anyway," he said, "but I want you to know how happy I am for you! This is a great moment." Jeff Robinson gave him a bear hug that had Len gasping for air.

Detectives Paul Tobin and Fred Cooper left their desks and joined the group, "Hey, Boss," Cooper said, shaking Len's hand. "Congratulations!" Tobin followed suit.

Len caught his breath again and grinned. "I'm at such a loss for words…" He turned to Jeff Robinson, "I think I'd rather you kiss me than crush my ribs. Thanks again, Robbie, Paul, Coop, and Mariko. You are my dearest friends. I know that you intended this surprise for me, but late last night, after speaking with Commissioner Dansforth, I rendered my first official function as Captain. Allow me to introduce all of you to a gentleman that we all know and admire, *Lieutenant* Jeffrey Robinson."

The Commissioner slapped Jeff Robinson's back and vigorously shook his hand. Mariko hugged him and planted a big kiss on his face. Jeff Robinson had to retrieve his handkerchief and dab away the tears of appreciation. Smiling, Paul Tobin and Fred Cooper slapped him hard on the back and joined in the handshakes.

Jeff Robinson stood between Len and Mariko with his arms around their shoulders and gathered himself, "Commissioner Dansforth, Mariko, Paulie and Coop, and my good friend Len, what can I say? This is really Len's day, not mine. But to have him share it with me, here with all of you is one of the biggest moments of my life."

Jeff Robinson hesitated for an instant, and then he continued, "I've always said that I wouldn't accept a promotion until I thought I'd reached the competence level of my partner. Obviously, I still have a long way to go, but since it was Len who offered me the job, Hell, I accept!"

"Yes, Robbie!" Len shouted and he put an arm around Jeff Robinson's shoulders, "But we're not finished here. Allow me to introduce our new *Executive Staff Assistant,* Mariko Tanaka. Congratulations, m'lady, both you and Robbie have been promoted."

"What?" Mariko said. "Seriously? I'm thrilled!"

"From now on Mariko, you are officially my right arm."

"Great!" Jeff Robinson said, giving her a hug. "Congratulations, girl!"

Mariko stood with her hands pressed against her cheeks. Tears began to well in her dark eyes. "Len, I ... we ...."

"Good luck, Captain," Dansforth said, frowning and interrupting her as he shook Len's hand again. "Now, everyone, you too, Paul and Fred, shall we go find something to eat? My treat!"

Sunday, June 16, end of day 12…

"Whew! That was some feed," Jeff Robinson remarked, upon their return to the squad room. Smiling, as he rubbed his hands over his bloated stomach, he said, "I may have to call a taxi to drive me home, I've had way too much bubbly."

"Home? What do you mean home?" Len chided, poking Jeff Robinson's ample stomach with his finger. "We still have work to do here, *Lieutenant.*"

"Yes! That's right, I damn near forgot. I did promise to meet you here, didn't I?"

"Yep, and here we are. And *Executive Staff Assistant* Mariko, do you have any pressing plans? We could use another hand, if you'd care to stay."

"No problem, I have all day. What are we doing?"

"First, here are copies of those taxi records you gathered. With Robbie's help, go through them thoroughly again. We're looking for any fares that originated, or ended, on or near the Cal Southern campus and/or the Valley Arms Hotel."

"Okay, that's not a problem; I've nearly memorized those records so far. Anything else?"

"Oh, yes," Len said, placing his hands on her shoulders, "…starting tomorrow, your first administrative duties are to enlist the other Staff Assistants to team up and begin organizing Dutch's hard-files so they make some sense. Completing that, you can bring me up to speed with a review. Then have your Assistants record his files on CDs, categorizing them for future reference."

"Check."

"You will also be responsible for the tedious paperwork Dutch used to handle. As for me, I'm going to remain a beat cop for a while, working outside the office doing what I do best."

"Eating donuts?" she asked.

Jeff Robinson chuckled, "She got you that time, Captain."

"Hush! Both of you! You're going to be an extension of me, 'Miss Blue', the executive brains of the department. I know you can handle it, but enlist a permanent new Assistant to aide you. Congratulations, my sweet friend and good luck." Finished, Len inhaled a deep breath and smiled.

"Len … this is so great." Mariko paused, seeking the proper words before continuing, "You know I'll give it my best but there is something we should discuss."

"Mariko," he interrupted, "I think I know what you want to tell me. Can we postpone that conversation for a while? For now, get on those taxi records, help us find our man."

"Sure, later." she replied, placing her hand on his shoulder briefly, giving him an understanding look before she turned to go.

"Robbie, where's van Haan's deposition?"

"I've got it right here, Boss," he said, producing the paperwork from his jacket pocket.

"Great, I'll look it over while you two review those records. Thanks again."

Len went back to his former office and taking a seat in his comfortable old chair, opened the document and began reading. *All right, Mister van Haan, let's see what you have to say…*

This is good: he's agreeing to 'disclose facts heretofore undisclosed regarding the alleged crime of the murder of one Lorena Reynolds.'

Ah, there's his apology to Robbie. Arrogant bastard; I wonder what he thinks that might get him? Anyway, he apologized; that's a start.

So … he went to her room to pay the monthly agreed upon sum of $5,000. That is a lot of hush money. But apparently van Haan didn't think so.

'When I got to her hotel room, I discovered the door ajar. I pushed it open and entered a few steps, maybe four or five feet into the room. It was early and there were no lights on but I could make out her body lying on the bed, on her back, naked, slashed to bits. It was horrible as I said earlier. The odor emitting from her massive wounds was intense. I retched into my handkerchief and turned, I fled the room, still retching.'

That's interesting, Len thought. *She was already dead as he admitted previously.* As he left the room retching, he *'glimpsed a tall man in the hall wearing what appeared to be a maroon bellhop's jacket … he was either walking or standing a few doors away. It was too dark in the hallway to see him clearly, but he appeared to be a tall, normally proportioned man.'*

Len repositioned himself in his chair and continued reading.

He couldn't estimate his age and didn't recognize the man in the photo Robbie showed him … Gerot's?

Back to the description of the man '... *he might have been six feet tall, maybe taller, didn't know if he was coming or going; didn't see a knife or any other weapon ... just a split-second glance was all he caught.*'

He '*took the money with him and returned it to his safe at home.*'

"Oh, great. Now his libido gets a workout...." '*We always met at her hotel room early in the morning. I always had to awaken her. She appeared to be alone all of those times. Sometimes if I had time, we'd have sex, you know, a freebie.*'

"What an asshole!" Len muttered, then he continued to read, No, '*he had no idea what she was going to do with the money and he didn't care as long as she kept her mouth shut. No, she never mentioned Gloria Mitchell's name.*'

Ah ... so Robbie told him they discovered Mitchell's body in a garbage dump, naked, shot twice in the base of the skull. I wonder what that did for van Haan.

Bingo! The photo he showed van Haan was Yves-Gaston Giroux. I'd have paid good money to have seen his expression!

Finished, Len placed the deposition on his desk and returned to the squad room where Jeff Robinson and Mariko continued to wade through the pile of computerized taxi records.

"How's it going? Finding anything worthwhile?"

"We found only that one fare, the one picked up on Vermont Avenue late on the evening prior to the murder and dropped off at the hotel," Mariko replied. "The cabby's name is Banaji: Sethi Banaji. I'll call Yellow Cab in the morning for his address and telephone number. Other than that, we haven't found anything else."

"Okay, Robbie, maybe Mister Banaji will recognize one of our suspects from our mini-gallery of photos. By the way, you did an excellent piece of work with van Haan. Excellent job. You're a true professional."

"Thanks, Boss, all in a day's work."

"So tell me," Len said, pulling up a chair and stretching his long legs out atop an adjacent desk. "Besides van Haan liking young boys, he also liked ordinary ladies of the night too. But more importantly, what's this fascination again with the Russian Mafia? Now I'm curious."

"Oh ... yeah. Well, according to Luis, after you and I left, van Haan had a major 'Come-to-Jeez-Moment' when he discovered that Treasury was going to put him in an ordinary lockup instead of a country club as we guessed. Apparently, he had an associate that skimmed big bucks off the top too, some guy in Atlanta. And ... I didn't wish to go further into van Haan's sexual practices, sorry."

Len smiled. "No problem."

"Anyway," Jeff Robinson continued, "it's reported that the Russian Mafia boys got to his friend and apparently whatever happened to Jimmy Hoffa would have been kid's stuff compared to what happened to the skimmer; they don't take prisoners."

"I've heard that about them."

Jeff Robinson continued, "Our van Haan may be an arrogant jerk, but he ain't stupid. He asked Neill to negotiate a plea bargain: his testimony for the federal witness protection program. FBI and DEA said fine; Treasury, Luis, reluctantly agreed. Apparently, the Russian Mafia is the major player in this big money swindle, especially the counterfeit stocks and bonds aspect of it. They go for the big stakes and are not to be trifled with."

Len quietly absorbed this bizarre tale and attempted to keep it in perspective as Jeff Robinson continued. "Also, at the end of my questioning, what didn't appear in the deposition may have been the most telling."

"Yes! I was curious about that; tell me..."

Jeff Robinson smiled broadly at Len's curiosity. "When I described Gloria Mitchell's execution with two shots in her skull, and when I showed him Gerot's photo, his expression froze; he became white as those bedsheets you admire, both times. I think he knows the Russian Mafia had her offed. It could be that he may be next."

Len sat silently for a few seconds contemplating Jeff Robinson's words, "My God!" he exclaimed clasping his hands to his head and jumping to his feet, "I think I'm finally beginning to get it! It's starting to make some kind of sense finally!"

"What?" Jeff Robinson asked, staring up at Len.

"Stay with me on this, let me see if I can get it straight. If van Haan used the Russian Mafia's money to buy Lorena Reynolds' silence, those Mafioso types wouldn't look at it as being *his* money, they'd naturally think it was *their* money and they wanted it back. Somehow they discovered that van Haan had paid Reynolds a lot of cash, *their* cash, and they didn't like it."

"Yeah..." Jeff Robinson murmured, with Mariko nodding in rapt agreement.

"With him locked up they couldn't get to him and with Reynolds dead, Gloria Mitchell, holder of the joint bank account, was their next best bet. But we had her tucked away in a Safety House. Enter assassin Giroux; they threatened Svoboda through his aging mother to discover exactly where Gloria Mitchell was. Am I making any sense?"

Both Jeff Robinson and Mariko, sitting on the edges of their respective chairs now, nodded. "Perfect sense," Jeff Robinson said.

Len continued, "The Russians hired Gerot, their assassin, to abduct Miss Mitchell and force her to withdraw their money from the bank. Afterward, with the money safely in hand, Gerot killed her. Then he killed his accomplice, the only one who could finger him. Then he killed Svoboda, the innocent mole and left his gun in the kitchen because his contract work was done."

Finished, Len exhaled. Looking at them, he asked, "Well? What do you think of that flaming-ass, outside-the-box scenario?"

Jeff Robinson sat dumbfounded. "But who killed Lorena Reynolds? Not the Russians..."

"She's a separate entity, I'm positive they didn't kill her; of that I'm ninety-nine per cent certain."

Exhaling, Jeff Robinson said, "Damn ... it makes a lot of sense when you explain it like that. So what about all the sexual activity with Gloria Mitchell? Just passing time?"

Len shook his head, sighed and rubbed his eyes. "Who the hell knows? She was available, and certainly vulnerable. Maybe she was trying to ply her captors with her feminine guile to negotiate a release. I don't know. That's why it's a mystery, Robbie."

"Well," Mariko said, frowning, "mystery or not, having sex repeatedly with someone you intend to murder is sick!"

Len and Jeff Robinson nodded in agreement.

"Listen," Len said, getting their attention, "one of you contact the bank tomorrow and check the balance of that joint account, I'll bet my shield it's empty!"

Mariko turned in her chair and looked at Len. "Could Gloria Mitchell simply walk into the bank and withdraw that much cash, just like that?"

"Sure, either of the women could at any time. Mitchell signed a signature card when they opened the account. Her name on the joint account protects the bank. I'm betting the money is gone, account closed. One of you check it out tomorrow. If the money was withdrawn, ask the bank for copies of their security videos showing who withdrew it."

"Right. But, Len, if the money is gone, then so is your ex-academy-mate Gerot. Why would he hang around?" Jeff Robinson asked. "He's completed his contract; the gun clip theory confirms that. All those bodies were just obstacles between him and the money. Can this be? And, why would the Russians get so excited about a mere $128,000 or whatever it was? I'd think hiring an international hit man ain't exactly cheap."

"We may never know. Maybe it's their ham-handed way of sending a message, who the hell knows? Our problem is this: no one has ever caught up with Gerot, maybe we will."

"That's a huge maybe, Boss," Jeff Robinson said.

"So, what do you think prompted van Haan's sudden change of heart with you? He ate a whole lot of humble-pie to kiss-up to you."

"It's hard to say, but I think he was sincere though. Maybe even the worst of us have some decency left, you think?" Jeff Robinson asked.

"That may well be. Hey! Let's call it a day, it is Sunday after all. Let's get out of here. I want to visit Dutch before his bedtime. Do you two care to join me?"

"I think I'll pass again today," Jeff Robinson replied. "Colleen is at her Aunt Naomi's in Valencia and I have to pick her up, at least I should."

"I caught a cab this morning, Boss," Mariko explained. "May I hitch a ride to Studio City if I go to the hospital with you?"

"Sure, maybe we can even have dinner afterward, at that same great place as before, remember? That really elegant place?" Len asked, smiling at Jeff Robinson.

"Oh, man!" Jeff Robinson yelled in mock indignation. "Are you going to take her back to that slime-bucket, roach invested greasy spoon again? That one out on Roscoe in the middle of the industrial complex? You don't have any class at all, man. Neither one of you do, it's embarrassing for me to even associate with you two."

Len and Mariko laughed heartily at Jeff Robinson's outburst.

"Robbie, we … we confess," Len said. "We played a joke on you. I made up all the stuff about the Greek Drive-In place; it was all a joke…" Len couldn't finish. He took a seat in a nearby chair and continued to laugh as he watched Jeff Robinson's confused expression.

"What?!?!?" Jeff Robinson screamed, "Well, where did y'all eat then?"

Mariko got in Jeff Robinson's face and stared into his eyes. "We ate at Charley Brown's Steakhouse, Bucky. We had succulent prime rib, fine wine with all the trimmings. Even valets."

She put her arm around him and affectionately sweet-talked in his ear, "Look baby, don't you be worryin' none 'bout lil' ol' Mariko now, y'hear?"

"Screw both of you!" Jeff Robinson said, shaking his head in disbelief. "I guess that proves that I'm one gullible dumb-shit, huh?"

Semi-recovered, Len added, "I guess you be." Still laughing, he fell back into his chair.

Cedars Sinai Hospital...
When Len and Mariko entered Dutch's room, they found him sitting up and watching a noisy game show on television. "Len, Mariko! It's so good to see both of you again, let me turn this silly thing off."

"It's good to see you too, Captain," Mariko said, as she bent forward to give him a light kiss on his forehead. "You're looking really good today. Are they getting ready to ship you out?"

Len shook his hand, "Captain, they must be treating you well here, you're looking great!"

Dutch laughed. "The food could be better, but the staff is excellent. The doctor says I may be able to go home sooner than expected, but enough about me, Len, what's going on with the homicide investigations, *Captain*?"

"I..."

Interrupting Len, Dutch raised his hand to his lips, "Hush. Let me speak first..."

Len nodded, "Okay, Boss, fire away."

"Len, If I had ever been fortunate enough to have had a son, I'd have wanted him to be the man I've watched you become..."

"Sir..."

"...now let me finish. I've watched you grow through the years and I absolutely knew in my heart that when it became impossible for me to do my job, you'd be there to replace me. Son, that..." Dutch's voice faltered for an instant. Beginning again, he said, "... knowing that you replaced me is one of the biggest joys in my entire life; and that's the damn truth."

Len looked away for an instant, not wishing to allow Dutch or Mariko see the tears forming in his eyes. Elmer

Dutch Ryan had held Len's hand firmly all the while, which gave Len an obvious out, "Dutch, thank you for that, and by the way you're gripping my hand, it's my guess that they'll be throwing you out of here within the hour."

Dutch chuckled, gave Len's hand a final squeeze and reached for a tissue, pretending he had to blow his nose. "Damn sinus shit."

"Yeah, I know," Len replied. "There's a lot of that going around right now."

Recovered, Dutch asked, "So, Len … what's happening downtown? Anything new?"

Len related Jeffrey Robinson's earlier visit with van Haan and the deposition, mentioning where he explained his brush with a bellhop at the hotel.

"Bellhop? In that shit-hole hotel? You have to be kidding … that flea-infested joint never employed a bellhop!"

"I agree, Dutch. But van Haan swore that he saw a bellhop in the hallway on the same floor shortly after he arrived."

"Have you checked it out with the hotel manager?"

"Not yet, but it's the first thing on my 'to do' list for tomorrow."

The two of them visited a short time longer, but it was apparent Dutch was becoming tired. Mariko bent over and kissed him goodnight. Len advised him to get some rest and keep doing whatever it was that was helping him regain his strength. Saying they'd be back in a day or so, the duo departed.

… … …

Len and Mariko drove north to the Valley and chatted about detective business mostly. Both remarked on Dutch's clarity and intuitiveness, especially with the bellhop issue.

"You know," Len began, "I was becoming apprehensive about how one of us, Dutch or me, would break the ice about me being his replacement. The old guy sure surprised me."

"You were the obvious choice," Mariko said, interrupting, "… and Dutch knew it better than anyone. If he ever gave you a difficult time, it was just his way of mentoring you. That's my opinion anyway."

Sighing, Len replied, "I guess. Well, it's over and done. He's retired, I'm his replacement."

Mariko turned in her seat and placed her hand on his inner thigh again, commenting, "You didn't mention van Haan's connection to the Russian Mafia and their possible connection to the Safety House killings, or your Canadian Mountie friend to Dutch. Was there a reason?"

"Yeah ... Dutch was in such good spirits, I didn't want to revisit the Safety House killings. That may have been a part of his heart problem. Those two Officers were his friends so I chose not to go there. Besides, Dansforth will tell him anyway; he tells him everything else."

As they continued driving they chatted quietly, mostly about Mariko's promotion. "Mariko, when I promoted you, you acted hesitant. Tell me why."

"You mean you want me to explain my less than enthusiastic feelings about being promoted to Executive Staff Assistant?"

"Mariko, if you're thinking of leaving homicide and joining the DA's office, there's nothing I would do to stand in your way. I think it's a great idea. When is it going to happen?"

She reached for his free hand and sighed. "You are too good; your intuition is way ahead of mine, Captain. Actually, I'm still in negotiations with them. We haven't reached a final agreement. Is that good enough for now? Truthfully, at this moment I don't know what to do. And, it's not personal. The DA's office is a great opportunity, but so is the homicide unit."

"It's okay, just keep me informed." He squeezed her hand, and as he looked into her dark eyes, again he felt as though he might melt. "Do what you need to do, Mariko; I'll understand."

"Good, I'm so relieved that you understand. I promise I'll make my decision soon."

"Do you want to stop somewhere for a bite, or some decadent dessert?" he asked, attempting to lighten the conversation.

"Not that kind of dessert." She winked deviously, her eyebrows dancing. "Just take me ... at home."

He gazed at her, attempting to keep his raging heart inside his shirt. "Mariko, sooner or later that attitude will get you into a whole lot of trouble."

"I certainly hope so," she appealed, smiling.

Arriving at her house, Len pulled in the drive and parked. Mariko looked across at him; the lights dancing in her eyes rivaled the stars twinkling in the heavens. Her presence was definitely having its effect on him again.

"I'm happy that you thought enough of my talents to promote me, Len." She leaned over the console and kissed him on the lips, a full, warm, affectionate kiss that lasted several seconds. They both sat for a moment, holding one another, looking into each other's eyes.

Len pulled her closer and kissed her, a short kiss this time. Slowly pulling away, she asked, "Will you come in? My dear sisters went to Santa Barbara and they won't be back until tomorrow. Do you have time? For ... something?"

"Something?"

"Yes, some time with me?" she whispered seductively.

Squirming even closer to him, she kissed his ear. Then she placed her hand inside his thighs and squeezed him firmly. Len gasped, he was becoming aroused.

"What was Mae West's great line? 'Are you happy to see me, or has your shoulder holster found its way into your briefs'?" she asked.

Len choked as he began to laugh. "Mariko ... ever the romantic."

She laughed softly and gently began to massage him. As she did, her breathing became more intense, "I really want you ... please stay with me tonight?"

They kissed again; her soft lips and sweet breath mesmerized him.

"I can't change your mind?"

"Yes," he whispered.

"I can?"

"Yes."

Persuaded, Len surrendered.

Hours later in the dark of Monday morning, June 17...

Len awoke with a start, disoriented for several seconds before remembering that he had gone to bed with Mariko. He looked at his watch in the dim light of her bedroom; it was 1:45 a.m.

Shit! I've got to run!

Reluctantly leaving the comfort of her warm bed, he located his clothes in the dimly lit surroundings, he quietly got dressed. Kissing her lightly, he left and drove away, mentally kicking his ass for staying with her, but justifying it at the same time.

Not that I don't have enough problems right now. And I crave sleeping with her, but making love with Mariko for an entire night could turn into my last on this planet.

He shuddered, savoring the thought.

Granada Hills, 2:00 a.m., Monday, day 13, June 17...

Len parked his Audi in its space beneath the building and took the elevator to his floor. He walked the few feet down the hall to his condominium unit. Entering and going directly to the kitchen, he checked his telephone for messages. The blinking light indicated several were on file. "Amazing, I'm very popular all of a sudden."

Pressing the *Play* button on the answering device, he heard Lawrence Fitzhugh's voice, *"Len, we tapped into Gerot's Vancouver residence telephone lines and subsequently audio-taped a series of what appears to be a sophisticated verbal code sent to him from a pay phone in East Los Angeles. The caller is an English-speaking male and the words* are meaningless on the outside, just words and phrases you might hear every day, that kind of thing. Too, strangely enough, the messages came in at precisely one-hour intervals. Very peculiar. Now, mate, fetch a pen and paper and jot these down."

Fitzhugh's message continued, "*At eight o'clock this morning, we recorded the following, 'One away, two on, two and zero is the count, steal third'. An hour later, this, 'Order takeout from the Abbe's Deli'. An hour later, 'Watch VH-1, Channel 6'. then, 'John Denver, Oh God! Channel 21', then, 'The Hope Tragedy', then, 'The Green Diamond', and lastly, 'Redman'. What do you make of it, anything? Call me at home, regardless of the time.*"

Pressing the *Pause* button, Len quickly called Lawrence Fitzhugh's home number in Ottawa, *Oh, shit... I wonder what the time is there if it's past 2:00 a.m. here, maybe 6:00 there? Boy, will he be pissed.*

A tired sounding Lawrence Fitzhugh answered his phone, "Fitzhugh here, is that you Morgan?"

"Sorry, Lawrence, but your message said to call regardless of the time. I didn't disturb your wife or family did I?" Len queried apologetically.

"I can't say, Len. Allow me to give you her current telephone number and you can ring her up and ask for yourself. She can better tell you if she's disturbed, 'ey?"

Len quietly snickered at his old friend's dry humor.

"Are you two separated, Lawrence?" he asked, feeling very embarrassed. "I didn't know."

"It's not a problem, chap, it happens all the time. I didn't ask you earlier, are you married and happily settled in with kids and all?"

"Sorry, Lawrence. No. I'm an orphan too, marriage-wise at least. I don't do well with the ladies anymore. Maybe it's my deodorant, huh?"

"Deodorant? When did you commence using that? I never mentioned it before, but that may have been the crux of your many problems, 'ey?"

"Really? I never thought," Len said, chuckling. "Seriously, about your lengthy message. What a hodge-podge. I wrote it down as you read it. I'll have my Assistant print it out tomorrow. It may make more sense looking at the words in print. Do you have the Queen Mum's Royal Cryptographers and gendarmes working on it too?"

"Oh, yes, certainly, the entire Royal Encryption staff," Fitzhugh answered, continuing the joke.

"So far, they're wearing a hole in the seat of their trousers from scratching their royal asses. This Jean-Luc Gerot of yours looks damn suspicious, Len. He may not be the international assassin, Yves-Gaston Giroux, but he's up to something highly suspect, isn't he? His Vancouver address is a goddamn mail drop, as I said, and the telephone number is an answering service. He's an international player all right. We prevailed upon a magistrate to issue a search warrant for his past telephone records. So far, we haven't scratched the surface. Tracing ownership of all his incoming calls will take days, perhaps weeks. Locating his whereabouts will be tougher."

"What do you make of the messages, what's your gut tell you," Len asked, settling into a comfortable chair.

"I've been racking my brain for that answer. What does your gut tell you?"

"Sitting here, looking at those messages, I get the feeling he's just been hired to *off* someone else. That's what my gut tells me."

"Another hit? You damned Yankees have such wild imaginations. At any rate, we do have our own people wiretapped to his incoming telephone lines now. The Queen Mum's telephone company was quite accommodating in that regard. We'll route his calls directly through our Ottawa office, day and night. We'll keep up the surveillance on Gerot's father's house in Quebec too. If we spot Jean-Luc there, he'll be pinched. If you can make any real sense from this garbled mess of verbiage we sent to you, beyond your gut feelings, let us know that too, 'ey?"

"I will, Lawrence, this is truly amazing. International intrigue is out of my league. Next time we talk it will be during your workday hours. One more thing, with your permission, I want to include our Federal team players, Campanera from Treasury, and Smith from Justice. Is that all right with you?"

"Quite," Fitzhugh said, yawning. "Well, hello? It's tomorrow already. My bloody alarm clock is going off. I'll talk to you later."

"Right. Okay, Lawrence, later," Len said, yawning as well, discovering that he was still sleepy. "Thanks, and good luck up there."

He stifled another yawn and pressed his *Play* button again. The machine diligently went through five consecutive hang-ups. "Hmm ... oh, well. It's your dime, call me later."

He glanced at the time; it was 2:15 a.m. Scratching his ribs, he padded barefoot to his bedroom, checked the clock-radio alarm, turned back his cool sheets and crawled in. He started to revisit his earlier evening with Mariko, but sleep overtook him.

He thought his head was ringing and spinning wildly, as if he was dreaming again. The unforgiving noise was incessant. Suddenly he awoke; it was his telephone.

Fumbling for it across his nightstand, he picked it up and mumbled hoarsely, "Morgan here…"

"LEN!" It was Sara's voice!

"Sara? Sara? Is that you? What's wrong?" Wide-awake now, he felt the blood suddenly rushing to his head. His mouth became instantly dry and his palms began perspiring.

"Hey pig!" a familiar voice shouted. "I got your little neighbor-woman now, man. She's my woman again!" the angry voice shouted at the other end of the line.

Frantic, Len's mind cleared somewhat and raced wildly.

Is that Armando? Does he have Sara? What the hell? God! What's happening?

"Hey! Pig, remember the *cholo* ... you called a piece of dog shit? Well, this piece of dog shit is ... going to do her again, so before I do, get your ass over here! You ... you and I have a score to settle!"

Confused and becoming frantic, Len shouted, lying through his teeth, "Armando, I'm on an old cordless phone and the damn battery is going dead or something, there's too much static ... you're breaking up, let me get to another phone ... wait! Please!"

Len quickly hit the *Hold* button. Then, he hit his line two button: his fax and computer line. Hurriedly, he punched in the number for Devonshire Watch Command dispatch.

"Ring, damn it! Ring!" he screamed.

One ring ... a pause ... second ring ... a voice, "Valley West Police, please state your name..."

"This is homicide Detective, er ... Captain Len Morgan! This is an emergency! Get a patch on my phone lines forthwith and trace the incoming call for its source! Hurry, it's life or death!"

Not waiting for a response, he pressed the *Hold* button and returned to line one again. "Armando, what have you done to Sara?"

"What kind of hokey ... shit are you trying to pull here," Armando asked, his words thick and slurring. "Your ... phone's going dead? Don't fuck with me, Morgan. I'll cut ... her up if you try to!"

Lying again, Len asserted, "It's no trick, Armando, believe me, my old cordless died. I'm on a different phone now. What have you done to Sara? Are you drunk?"

"Drunk? Bite me, cop. When ... when you get over here, you'll see what I've done to her. After you get here, you can ... even watch us do it again. Does that sound ... sound like a party, asshole? You can watch me do ... her. I'll even do her in the ass for you with my big dick. Then ... afterwards, I'll do your ass with that busted ... busted pool cue!"

Drenched with sweat with his breathing coming hard, Len shouted, "Armando, if you've touched her I'll take you apart, you slimy little bastard! You'll never see daylight again!"

"Look, asshole," Armando said quietly, almost in a whisper, "get over here or ... she's dead. Do you hear me? Now!"

"Yes, but where?" Len asked, his head beginning to clear. "Where the hell are you?"

"Oh, Mister Pig, so now you are ... are getting with the program, huh?" He laughed, "Well, I'll tell you ... where we are, a lot of us..."

"Well, where?" Len shouted, becoming increasingly impatient, praying that Watch Command was tracing this call. "Tell me where you are, I'll be there, and I'll be alone. You let her go and you can have me."

"Well, how noble of... you. Noble indeed, chivalry ain't dead, huh? You'd ... better come alone too or this whole place goes ... up in one helluva big boom and her along with it."

"I'll be alone, but you have to tell me where the hell you are. I can't read your goddamn mind, Armando. Where are you?"

"I'm across ... the Valley, west of DeSoto on Parthenia. Get ... your ass over here so I can slice off your ... shit-caked balls."

"Where on Parthenia?" Len roared, interrupting Armando.

"Oh, Morgan, you're getting so upset. Try to be calm."

"Okay, okay, I'm calm," Len said, sighing. "Where are you?"

"West of DeSoto, west ... of the flood canal. Get over here; park in ... the middle of the street with your ... headlights on. We'll find you."

CLICK

Armando hung up.

Len let out another long exhalation of pent up breath. Totally shaken and frightened out of his wits, he'd soaked through his bed sheets with his nervous perspiration. He stood up and clumsily called Watch Command dispatch again. They answered on the first ring.

"Captain Morgan, this is Officer Longstreet, we copied that transmission, sir. We've traced the address and unit number and fed it into the LAPD's computerized search system. We caught a rare stroke of luck, sir. Their SWAT mobilized late last night in south central LA. They're rolling in our direction now. What's next?"

"Oh, you got SWAT? Great! It looks like we'll have to go in. Have the SWAT Commander call me here ASAP. Keep this off our regular radio transmission channels; keep it covert. And thanks, Longstreet, you did a helluva job, I'll not forget you."

Len ran into his bathroom and splashed his face thoroughly with cold water. Toweling off, he put on a pair of Levi jeans, a dark blue T-shirt, his Kevlar body-armor vest, and his shoulder holster. He removed his piece and racked a round into the chamber, applied the safety and returned the .45-caliber Smith & Wesson semi-automatic to his holster. He grabbed a spare ammo clip as he telephoned for a Yellow Cab.

Then he waited impatiently for the SWAT Commander as he put his Captain's shield on a necklace. Finished, he zipped his windbreaker with the VWPD inscription boldly stenciled in bright yellow on the back.

Come on SWAT! The phone rang, "Morgan here..."

"Hey! What kind of dumb cop game are ... you playing now? Do you think I'm kidding? Do ... you think I'm so lame as to fall for your stupid cop ... tricks? You should've been out on the street by now. Are you ... planning some kind of dumb attack or break-in?"

"God, no! Armando, my own car is in for repair," Len lied, "and I'm waiting for a taxi. You gotta' believe me, I'll be there as soon as I can."

CLICK

"Damn, he hung up again! I hope he believed me. Why doesn't SWAT call back?"

The phone rang again. Len jumped, startled. "Yes, Morgan here."

"Captain Morgan, it's SWAT Commander Ellsworth. We've been apprised of a Code 10-31 hostage situation and we're rolling, maybe four or five minutes away. Backup alerted and on hold, all units operating on Code 10-40, plus radio silence. What's the plan?"

"Ellsworth, am I ever glad to hear your voice, glad you're in on this. I'm awaiting a cab, but it looks like we'll have to use tactical force and go in quickly; I'll let you work out those details. Were you able to pull the caller's location from your electronic data files?"

"We have everything we need. The subject's flat is on the top floor, rear. There's only one other tenant located on that level and they're in the front of the structure. I'll have officers relocate them to a safer level."

"Great!"

"Back-up units from VWPD are on hold and will remain outside a two block perimeter, ME, CSI and EMT units are on a fifteen minute delay. When you and your cab show up, we'll replace the driver with one of ours, probably Officer Ferrell."

"Good man, Ellsworth, you thought of everything."

"It's what I do for a living, Captain. When you two are set, give us a signal and we'll repel into the apartment through the living room windows and the balcony. We'll introduce flash-bangs and tear gas first, if we receive gunfire, we'll use deadly force in return, if that's what you had in mind, Captain. The element of surprise will be in our favor and may be what it takes to save your hostage."

"I trust so, Commander, and that's exactly what I had in mind. The abductor claims the place is booby-trapped. Personally, I think he's full of shit, just talking."

"Yes, and you're probably guessing right. Most folks don't hang around after they've booby-trapped a place. So you called a taxi?"

"Yeah, a Yellow. Have your man meet us at DeSoto and Parthenia. We'll proceed from there. Give him whatever information I need to coordinate with you and your team. Oh, Commander, the hostage is my next door neighbor, a white female."

"Okay … affirmative on that," Ellsworth replied.

"There, I hear the taxi outside now. I'll be there in minutes. Good luck, Commander."

It was a short ride across the Valley and on the way; Len introduced himself to the cabby and told him what was going to take place.

"Stop for the traffic light at DeSoto, here's a hundred dollars for your time thus far. Get out and enjoy a cigarette or two while we commandeer your vehicle. We'll be busy as hell down the street for ten or twelve minutes, then it will be over, got that? If any damage occurs to your cab, the city will make any necessary repairs to return it to its current condition, compliments of the Devonshire Hills Homicide Unit. Clear?"

"Clear as hell, sir," the cabby said, putting the money in his pocket. "I've never been involved in a police action in all my years. This is making me nervous already and I'm going to be blocks away. Are you nervous, sir?" the driver asked, his voice trembling slightly.

"Shit, yes, I'm nervous, but I'll probably get over it. In a few minutes, this should all be history. Just remain here at the intersection until the noise ends, okay?"

"Here's DeSoto, sir, and luckily, we caught a light. Take care now." The cabby disappeared into the dark shadows and a young SWAT officer quickly jumped into the driver's seat.

"I'm your driver, sir. Ellsworth has the tactical squad on the roof at the ready. We came in through the back and relocated the other third floor tenant out of harm's way. We have the exit doors under surveillance and we'll block the driveways when we engage. One two-man team was hiding in place outside when three armed civilians, *cholos*, came out a minute ago and hid in the bushes."

"Great," Len muttered. Like we need that."

"They're likely the ones sent to take you hostage. You and I will attempt to place them under arrest. If they appear hostile and threaten us with their weapons, we will respond. Anyway, a gunshot will be the signal for the main squad to drop in and take the rest of them. Surprise is on our side. Any questions, sir?"

Len forced a nervous grin, "One, have you got a name?"

"Sorry, sir. I'm Officer Jack Ferrell, LAPD."

"Yes, Ferrell, a good Irish name. Okay, Jack; let's begin this thing their way. Drive down the middle of the street and stop. Blink the headlights once and then leave them turned on. Remove your shield from your vest too; you still look like a cop."

"Oops!" Jack removed his shield, attached it to a small chain around his neck and placed it under his blouse.

The taxi rolled forward and stopped in the middle of the block a few yards east of a small bridge that spanned a concrete-walled storm canal that served a heavily populated area of the Valley West's condominiums and apartment buildings.

Sitting in the center lane with the engine idling, Officer Ferrell blinked the headlights again. Up ahead, three men emerged slowly from the shadows of several overgrown, flowering bougainvillea bushes near the street.

Wearing a black tee shirt with a silk-screen likeness of Cuban Communist Che Guevara emblazoned on the front, the lead man, big and armed, motioned for the taxi to move forward. The other two men mimicked him, motioning at the taxi with their gun hands.

"Monkey-see, monkey-do," Ferrell said quietly, letting the taxi slowly idle ahead a few more yards. "Well, Captain, there's three of them and they're all carrying. I don't know about you, sir, but I'm shit-sure not going to surrender. I'll exit the car and give them fair warning, okay?"

"Yeah, but be damned careful, there's a lot of fire power out there," Len cautioned. "This big sonnuva-bitch heading in my direction is holding a .45-caliber. Thank the good Lord for Kevlar."

"No shit. Are you ready, Captain? Curious, have you ever shot a man, sir?"

"No, Jack … I usually go for old women and little kids."

"What!"

"Just kidding, the last time was a while ago … and, yeah, I'm cocked and primed, safety off, one in the chamber. You?" Len asked as he wiped at his dry mouth with the back of his free hand.

"Yeah, I'm fine. Have your window rolled down. I'll jump out and hope for the best."

"Uh-huh.…" Len grunted, sweating heavily as the expected rush of adrenaline surged through his tense, but trembling body.

The taxi came to a slow halt. The big man raised his gun and pointed it at Len as he approached. Ferrell sat calmly behind the steering wheel with his hands raised slightly.

The big man was closer now and Len got a good look at him and his gun. He motioned at Len to get out of the cab.

Inhaling deeply, keeping his eyes glued on that gun, Len slowly raised his right hand, then opened the rear door a crack. The big man was nearly on top of him, so close he could smell the cheap tequila that saturated his breath.

Then all hell broke loose! SWAT Officer Ferrell was outside the taxi shouting, "Freeze! Police! Drop your weapons!"

Thundering ear-splitting reports of gunshots and clouds of sulfur-laden gun smoke filled the air accompanied by screams of pain and the sight of splattering blood as the chests of the two smaller men blew apart. In that same instant, Len slammed the rear door hard into the big man's chest, deflecting his gun and causing it to harmlessly fire twice as Len, squeezing his trigger, yelled, "Enjoy hell, asshole!"

The deafening sound of his own gunfire putting two rapid rounds into the big man's chest drowned out his words.

As the man fell backward, astonishment registered on his face for a split second as his body reacted to the impact of the searing hot lead slugs.

Blood spewed forth from his mouth and his head snapped forward. His wide, unseeing eyes expressed shock and disbelief. His gun clattered onto the warm asphalt as he fell, dead before he struck the pavement.

Catching his breath, Len leaped from the taxi and over the fallen body.

Officer Ferrell was already running through the front entrance of the building. Len took another deep breath and pursued him. Feeling the hard asphalt pavement pounding the soles of his feet, his mind raced crazily.

Shit! This is like a bad dream, I'm running but I'm not getting anywhere ... I hope my old knee holds up ... there's people lying dead back there ... I hear more shooting from inside. God! Run feet, run!

He stormed through the front door and hit the stairs at full stride. The sound of several rapid gunshots echoed from the third level, and then there was deafening silence.

On the second level frightened and confused people poured out into the halls, some screaming, others wide-eyed and simply seeking safe cover while ignoring the pleas of a pair of SWAT officers beseeching them to remain calm.

Len pushed some residents aside and nearly knocked others down as he approached the empty stairway leading to the third floor. There, the hallway reeked of gun smoke and tear gas. He heard men's voices yelling, ordering other men to stay on the floor.

Soaked with sweat and totally winded, he burst into a small smoke-filled living room that resembled a mini-war scene: glass shards covered the floor and the cheap furniture; tear gas canisters emptied their slow yellow spirals next to a bloody, glass-covered body.

"Sara! Where's Sara?" Len shouted hoarsely. With his ears still deafened by his own gunfire, his voice sounded distant and foreign. Getting no answer, he turned from the living room and ran down the center hallway. Stepping over another body, he kicked open the doors, checking every room, finding no one. Thinking he heard his name shouted, he turned.

"Morgan! Captain Morgan! We're in the kitchen. If you can hear me, come back to the kitchen!"

As he retraced his path, his heart pounded fiercely and his burning chest heaved uncontrollably. Desperately needing fresh air, he made another turn and ran headlong into Officer Ferrell. Knocked backward, Ferrell sprawled across the floor but countered instinctively, aiming his weapon directly at Len's dripping nose.

Stopping in his tracks, his eyes opened wide in instant fear. Terrified he gasped, "Uh … partner … lower that big shooter if you will?"

"God! Sorry about that, Captain," Ferrell exclaimed, carefully releasing the hammer. Lowering his gun and hustling to his feet, he said, "How in hell would I ever explain that to Internal Affairs? Blowing off a Homicide Captain's head?"

Len grimaced a tight smile not immediately appreciating the dark humor. "Ferrell, just where do I find the kitchen in this hell-hole?"

"Straight ahead on the right, sir. They're looking for you."

Spitting, gagging, and coughing on the tear gas, Len turned and entered another smoke-filled room. Brightly lit, it featured enameled cupboards, a refrigerator, stove and all of the other necessary accoutrements. "This must be it," he muttered, finally wiping at his dripping nose with his handkerchief..

"Len!" Sara's fragile voice cried out.

Leaving the safety of Commander Ellsworth's arms, she ran to him. "Hold me, Len! Oh, Len, I was so frightened!"

He took her in his arms and squeezed her tightly. Both of them suddenly trembled unashamedly as they huddled together in the smoke-drenched kitchen.

"Let's get you outside where we can breathe," he said, still coughing. "Come on, let's go."

Taking her arm, he led her into the hall and down the stairs past confused, curious, half-awake residents. Excusing themselves, they slowly picked their way to the front entry and outside onto the well-groomed lawn and an abundance of fresh air and curious tenants, standing around in total confusion.

The usually dark side street was ablaze now with flashing red-and-blue lights. Black-and-White VWPD squad cars were wall-to-wall. EMT ambulances, Criminologists and Medical Examiner's SUVs were parked everywhere, expecting dozens of dead or wounded.

The CSI's were busy photographing the three bodies sprawled in the gutter while uniformed cops, with tiny yellow A-frame markers, spotted the locations of the weapons and spent cartridges lying in the street and lawn. EMT crews were attending to two wounded Latino survivors of the shooting in the apartment.

Len looked around and recognized the cabby as he approached; appearing confused and lost as he wound his way through the crowd of law enforcement personnel.

"Cabby!" Len shouted, still coughing, still holding Sara, who clung to him tightly. "Over here!"

The driver approached cautiously, "Holy shit! You weren't kidding about it taking ten or twelve minutes. I haven't had time to finish my first cigarette."

Sara clung to Len as he began to speak. "I'm sorry about your cab. It took some rounds with the first gunshots. I sincerely apologize."

Shivering slightly, more from frayed nerves than the early morning temperature, Len asked, "Do you have a name? Normally I'm not so rude."

"Gerald, Gerald Bauer. Just call me Gerald."

"Thank you, Gerald Bauer; your able assistance was greatly appreciated." Len shook Gerald's hand and explained, "For the moment your taxi is evidence of a gunfight, so we'll have to take it back to the motor pool tonight and repair that and any other damage. We'll have it back for you tomorrow."

Gerald frowned, and squinting his eyes, said, "Well, if you don't mind, I really need it now, bullet holes or not, sir, to get back home with. It still runs doesn't it?"

"I suppose so, Gerald, the damage is to the right rear door or rocker panel mostly…"

"Sir, I live over in North Hollywood. Would it be all right if I drove it to the motor pool tomorrow morning, after I see if I can rent an alternate cab?"

"Sure, Gerald, whatever is convenient for you … as soon as our CSI criminologists here are finished with it. When you're there tomorrow, leave your name and address with the motor pool manager. We have special commendations for people like you, Gerald. And thanks again for everything. Goodnight."

Len turned and looked into Sara's swollen blue eyes. He still saw a major amount of fear remaining there. Holding her close, he said, "Sara, I was so damned scared and confused when Armando called. I nearly went out of my mind. I just didn't know what to do or how to save you. I'm so damned sorry that you had to go through this, so sorry."

"Len, it was horrible!" Between sobs Sara explained, "He treated me so badly; he put tape over my mouth and then raped me in the living room twice … drunk, right in front of all those men…" Holding her hands over her face, she broke down.

Angered and wondering where Armando might be, if he's dead or alive, Len held her close, attempting to be of some comfort.

Still sobbing, she continued, "He was out of his mind with rage and hatred, and he said later he would rip all of my clothes away and all of them could take turns with me ... it was terrible."

"Unbelievable! None of them touched you, did they?" Len asked, a look of anger and major concern on his tired face.

"No, but he said they were going to, all of them, after he killed you in front of me ... oh, God!" she sobbed, catching her breath. "It was so horrible. I'm so glad you're here."

"Well, it's over, Sara," he said, setting his jaw. "But, right now I'm going to have you taken to Valley General Hospital. We'll get you examined, treated, and sedated and in a warm bed for some much-needed rest. I'll come by tomorrow, later today. Is that all right? It's the best thing to do. You really need to go with the EMT crew and get looked after."

"But, Len, I can't go! I can't! I need you to stay with me, please! I don't want you to leave me again..."

"Sara, I still have police business to finish here, and really, the hospital is the best place for you now, to get you as far away from this place as possible. Until you can rest and unwind, they can best take care of you. Please go?"

She sniffled and wiped at her nose with a tissue she had been squeezing. "All right ... yes," she said. "I guess that's a good idea. You'll be sure to get me later? You won't forget?"

"No, I won't forget, and yes, I'll get you. Now go."

The attending EMT ambulance driver took Sara's arm and gently led her away to his white and orange bus. Slowly snaking its way through the crowd of vehicles and personnel, with flashing lights only, it quietly sped away.

Len walked back toward the apartment building and looked for Commander Ellsworth. He was standing in the entryway, flanked by Ferrell and a local television newscaster. Ellsworth finished with him and the newscaster departed.

"Ellsworth, got a minute?" Len asked, as a sudden chill caused him to zip his windbreaker again. "Do we have any media concerns we need to address tonight? Oh ... I almost forgot, was the place wired for explosives?"

"No, to both questions," he replied. "And I already handled the media. For their information, a nameless SWAT source allowed Cable News One to presume that one gang abducted another gang's woman. The reporters bought it. I see you sent your neighbor away, and she's all right? Man, she went through a ration of shit in there, huh?"

"She's shook up as hell, but seems about as right as one can be after being raped several times by the bastard. What a hellacious nightmare to go through." Len paused, coughing again. "Is he, the bastard alive?"

"No, Captain," Ellsworth replied.

"Shit. I'm sorry to hear that. You did a fine job, Commander; your plan worked to perfection. What's the body count, how many survived, did you have any casualties or wounded?" Len asked, nervously rattling off questions.

"Whoa, slow down, Captain, one question at a time. Everything came off as we planned. We lowered four men outside the windows and awaited your signal shots. Four more were on the roof waiting to drop when we observed your neighbor through an unlocked skylight, tied up and curled in the corner of a back bedroom. That open skylight was pure providence so we made use of it. We just 'dropped in'," Ellsworth explained, smiling at his presumably clever remark.

Len, catching his breath finally, hung his head wearily and smiled too. "So what transpired with Armando, their *jefe*?"

"I'm told he has a date with the Coroner along with the three cholos you and Ferrell took out down here along with one other unfortunate soul from upstairs. Altogether, there were seven of them, five didn't make it. The two that did will live and I've sent them to the hospital for treatment. VWPD will meet them there. My boys are spitting tear gas, but that's life. One of my team tore his shirtsleeve going through a window. That was our casualty, one shirtsleeve. It was a well-coordinated operation."

"Yes, it was, a helluva fine job, Ellsworth. Thanks for handling the media too. I really didn't want Sara's name and face all over the morning news reports; that's the last thing she'd need on top of everything else. We'll help them do a good spread with the info they have now, maybe it will scare off any other would be gang-bangers for a while."

"Let's hope so." Looking about and seeing his team waiting, he said, "Captain Morgan, it's been a pleasure, if I can ever be of service again, you know where to find me."

"Say, now that you mention it, you certainly can be of service, I need a ride home." Len checked his watch. It read 4:15 a.m. "Better, if you and your team have the time, I'll buy breakfast."

"Breakfast?" Ellsworth smiled from ear to ear. "Captain, you're a man after my own heart. We've been hard at work since midnight. Hey, boys! Breakfast is on the new Captain. Saddle up; let's move 'em out!"

Minutes later, the black step-side police van, with Officer Ferrell driving and Len riding shotgun, turned off Ventura Boulevard and into the parking lot of a small, twenty-four hour restaurant. Len, Ferrell, and Ellsworth led the way, the balance of the team followed. The two-way radio clipped on Ellsworth's hip snapped static and squawked mildly as he opened the restaurant door.

Len brought up the rear after the team had entered. *This is a night to remember. It started out with Mariko, then we rescued Sara from Armando, and he's dead now. I shot a man, and he's dead. My temporary partner Ferrell shot two men, they're dead along with one other. But the entire SWAT is alive, I'm alive, and Sara's alive. I guess that counts for something.*

The hostess pushed several tables together. With a big smile, she ushered the entourage of tired blue uniforms into the comfortable dining room where the mixed aroma of sizzling bacon, eggs, and hot coffee tantalized their senses.

Officer Ferrell, took a seat beside Len, and smiled back at the hostess. Noticing the exchange, Len mused, *Live for the moment I guess.*

18

Later on Monday morning, day 13...

The big SWAT van stopped and parked at the curb in front of the Villa Casa Grande condominium complex. Len looked into the back at the assembled SWAT team and hollered, "Hey, gentlemen! It's been a real pleasure! Thanks a lot. And Ellsworth, that was a great job, I'll definitely mention you in my report. You get high marks for this one, friend. Thanks."

Turning to his new pal, Jack Ferrell, Len grinned broadly, "Partner, thanks for leaving my face in place. I know it's ugly but it's the only one I have."

Ferrell laughed and reached out to shake Len's hand. "No problem, Captain, I only had a couple of rounds left, you'd have probably lived." Chuckling, Len stepped out onto the street and waved a last farewell.

The first rays of the morning sun were beginning to crest over the adjacent rooftops. It would be daylight soon and he was beat. But, tired and exhausted as he was, he must soon begin his normal workday. Afterward, make that mandatory visit to Internal Affairs to surrender his weapon and then get mired in the usual bog of senseless political questioning afterward.

"Nothing personal, Captain Morgan, it's just our routine procedure…" Len muttered, mimicking IAD.

His mind raced through the past few hours beginning with Armando's calls, Sara's frantic screaming plea, his own initial frustration and feeling of helplessness, and the fatal shooting of the lead man in the darkened street.

Suddenly he felt a growing queasiness in his stomach and lower abdomen accompanied by cramping and that warm, salty rush of saliva in the mouth and throat when the glands go into hyper-drive.

Oh shit, no ... I'm going to throw up!

He bent forward and rested his hands on his knees. With sweat beginning to form on his face and neck he wished for the sick feeling to subside. It didn't.

Staring into the gutter pan in front of him, he felt the first sickening surge of bubbling bile beginning to make its way up and out.

Unhhh ... unh ... oh shit! Shit, I hate this!

His acrid stomach emptied. His legs trembled so much that he became unsteady. Not wishing to lose his balance, he dropped to a kneeling position with his knees resting on the rough curb, his hands to either side. With his churning stomach nearly emptied, he retched, gagged, and spat, expelling as best he could the rest of the vile tasting foodstuffs he'd consumed so robustly minutes earlier.

Spitting profusely and still coughing, he staggered to his feet. With legs still shaking, he reached into his back pocket for his handkerchief to wipe his mouth and chin.

At that moment, across the street in his line of sight, an older woman was out for an early morning walk with her dog. Having seen Len vomiting in public, she stared at him in contemptuous disbelief. She shook her head in a typical parental scolding manner.

Seeing her reaction, Len weakly raised his hand, as if to explain that it was not what she thought. He didn't get the opportunity. She had turned her head and quickly strode off in a fit of self-righteousness leaving him to his misery.

Well, fuck you, old woman, and your ugly dog too. Haven't you ever seen a worthless bum lose his cookies in the gutter? Give it a rest! Things aren't always as they seem..."

With his physical bearings somewhat regained, he turned and walked slowly into Villa Casa Grande and upstairs. He couldn't remember a time when he stunk so badly, or when his mouth tasted so foul. Stripping completely, he carried his sweat-soaked clothes back to the laundry room and stuffed them in the washing machine. Then he remembered the condition of his bed sheets. He retrieved the sweat-dampened sheets and pillowcases and returned to the laundry room where he set the water temperature on 'boil' and cut it loose.

Whew! I'd better do that to me too, he thought as he padded nakedly to his awaiting shower. *Man, I'm ripe. Rotten is way too polite to describe this, phew!*

Lathering up in the warm shower, he watched all of the previous night's excitement seemingly spiral down the drain. Except one, his mind kept returning to the lead man's expression as he sent him to meet his maker.

I suppose I'll see his ugly face on everything I look at for the next year. The dumb bastard, why did he have to hang out with Armando anyway? I wonder if he was with Armando that morning Robbie and I stopped at the pool hall. Funny. Aren't minds a wonderful thing? Too bad they don't come with a toggle switch.

Dried off and still naked he limped around aimlessly, suddenly hobbled by major shin-splints making their nagging presence known after all the stair climbing and running from the hours before. Then he remembered the mental plans he had made for this morning had he enjoyed a normal night's rest. Picking up his telephone, he called the precinct and asked the switchboard operator for Traffic Division Officer Duane Josephs' telephone number. Writing it on a notepad as he called, he yawned and listened to the ringing: it went on for what felt like minutes, finally, "Hello, Duane here."

Josephs' voice on the other end of the line startled Len out of a daydream, "Yes … sorry Duane, this is Morgan, Homicide, did I wake you?"

"No, sir, I was showering and didn't hear the phone ringing. What is it, sir?"

"Duane, let me ask; do you own a dark suit and muted tie, or more than one of each?" Len's senses were beginning to function again.

Taken completely off guard by the offbeat question, Josephs hesitated for a second, "Er … ah, yes, I do. More than one of each in fact. Do you need a full inventory of my closet, sir?"

Len clasped his palm over the receiver and laughed aloud at this fresh, smart-ass attitude; one he wouldn't have guessed existed inside this usually quiet young man.

Regaining his composure, Len responded, "Seriously, Officer Josephs, we need to fill a spot in the homicide department, but our new recruit can't show up in a blue polyester uniform. That's why I asked you if you owned any suits and ties ... so, what do you think?"

"Pardon me, sir, but did the Lieutenant have too many drinks last night?" Joseph asked, his voice relaying no expression whatsoever.

Len cleared his throat and continued, "Officer Josephs, I rarely drink and I'm dead serious."

The silence on the other end of the telephone was deafening. For a moment, it was as if the connection had severed. "Excuse me, Detective Josephs, are you all right? Is there a problem?"

"No, sir ... but are you telling me that I'm a homicide detective now, and that you want me to report today wearing a suit and tie?"

"Real close, you're now an *apprentice*, a rookie, a new homicide detective junior grade. We'll give you a shot at it, so wear a dark tailored suit, a medium blue starched shirt, and a muted red silk tie, got that? Black loafers too, not your beat cop oxfords. Just don't show up looking like a poorly dressed cop pretending to be a smartly dressed used car salesman, okay?"

"Yes ... yes. I understand. What time and where, Lieutenant?"

"Seven o'clock sharp on the second floor of the precinct. Report to my ex-partner, Lieutenant Jeff Robinson. Be sure you call in and promptly advise your traffic Captain too, let him know you have received a promotion and a transfer to homicide. The proper paperwork will be forwarded to him later today."

"Ex-partner? Lieutenant?" Josephs questioned.

"Yes, he's my ex-partner, and your new partner. And, Detective Josephs, it's *Captain* Morgan," Len said, smiling.

"Sir! I mean, yes, sir, Captain Morgan." Josephs paused a second, slowly digesting this, then continued, "Sir, may I ask when all this took place?"

"It's still taking place, Detective," Len said. "Actually, it's been just the last day or so. Why?"

"Wait! Captain," Josephs interrupted, "…on TV right now! They're reporting a gang-banger shootout in the Valley West overnight. It's all over Cable News One! LAPD SWAT took out five gang members. Wait, it was a hostage situation too. One gang had abducted another gang's woman."

"Well, isn't that amazing … some of the things that go on in your own back yard?"

"Yes, sir."

"Also, Detective Josephs, I appreciate all of the *sir* shit, but it's too *academy* for the homicide unit. Will you lighten it up? And, when you see Robbie, tell him that you are *it:* the *anointed one*. He'll understand and I know he'll be thrilled. Then have him page me. I'll probably be busy with Internal Affairs most of the morning. Will you pass that along to him too? And don't answer 'Yes, sir'…"

"…uh, okay, Captain, I'll pass that along. May I inquire why you will be busy with Internal Affairs, in case Lieutenant Jeff Robinson asks?"

"Tell him that I shot and killed an armed gang-banger in a Valley West shoot-out overnight. Now be certain to have him page me. Congratulations, *Detective* Duane Josephs. I'll see you later, goodbye."

Len hung up and then called directory assistance for the number of the Valley Arms Hotel on Sepulveda Boulevard. After calling and waiting through a few rings, he heard a tired response, "Hello, Valley Arms."

"Sir," Len said, "how many bellhops do you have employed at this time?"

"What? …fuck off!"

CLICK

Hey! That's not nice, Len hit the *Recall* button and waited for the man to answer again. He did.

"Sir, this is Captain Morgan, Devonshire Hills Homicide, let's try this again. How many bellhops do you have employed at this time?"

"Captain? Was that you a minute ago?" the voice asked, more cordial this time.

"Yes, it was. Do you always rudely hang up on people seeking information?"

"I'm sorry, Captain, I've had a tough night, actually, a day and night. I'm the manager here and I just worked a double shift. I'm bushed. Sorry."

"I think I know the feeling. Now, how many bellhops?"

"Captain, that's almost funny. You've been here, you know what kind of a dump this is. How many bellhops have you ever seen around here? None, zip, nada. What? Did we just get bought by the Ritz or the fuckin' Waldorf-Astoria chain?"

"I'm not *fuckin'* aware of either," Len said, mimicking the manager. "To your knowledge, has anyone resembling a bellhop been seen in your hotel lately?"

"Not to my knowledge, Captain. Sorry I can't be of more help."

"Well, I asked. Thanks for your time. Get some rest and have a nice day."

Dutch was right again. Van Haan's man in the maroon jacket didn't work in the hotel, but may have been checked in as a guest. More snooping and digging for Miss Mariko.

Len checked his watch, 6:30 a.m. He decided to get dressed and visit Jim's Corner Coffee Shoppe. *Some of his low-viscosity, high-octane coffee might be just what the doctor ordered. That'll keep me awake and wired, that's for certain.*

Dressed and ready to go, he made certain his pager was functioning and attached it to his hip. He locked his door and favoring his newly acquired shin splints headed out to visit with Jim.

The early morning California sun was beginning to put out some major BTU's as he entered Jim's Corner Coffee Shoppe.

"Hey! You!" Len called out to his old friend whose back faced the front door.

"You talkin' ta' me?" Jim asked, in his thick Brooklyn accent. Turning around, he smiled, "Hey! Where ya' been hidin' man? It's been a week hasn't it?"

"I think it has. It took me that long to get that last cup of your coffee out of my system," he said, grimacing playfully. "But hell, give me another one, Jim, I'm tough."

"I can prob'ly do that. This ain't 'Big' bucks, but I can get ya' a good cup of java. Here." Jim handed Len a paper cup filled with his every day, scalding black brew. "I knew that was going to be ya' choice today and I had it all prepared. D'ya' want a lid fa' that, or a fork, which?"

"That's a tough decision," Len answered, squinting as took a sip of the hot brew. "Ouch. 'Big' bucks? Don't you mean…"

"Nah," Jim interrupted. "I mean Big bucks. J'eva' buy a coffee there?"

Len nodded, agreeing with his friend.

Staring at Len's face, Jim asked, "How much sleep didn't ya' get last night, seriously? Ya' look like something what the cats covered over. Bad night?"

"That bad?" Len asked, sipping the hot liquid. "Just between us, Jim, I was in that Parthenia Street shoot-out last night. I got in a couple of hours sleep earlier, but I've been up since eleven or midnight, I can't remember."

"Uh-huh," Jim murmured, nodding. "That was gang related wasn't it? That's what the TV and radio said today."

"Between you and me again, Jim, it involved possible gang members, more like *amigos* of the abductor."

"What? Abductor?"

"The press initiated the gang theory so our public relations staff decided that story was believable enough to live with. It started with a kidnapping/hostage combination involving Sara, my next door neighbor," Len confided. "Keep all this under your white paper hat, okay?"

"No, not ya' pretty lady neighbor? Ya' don't mean the little gal with the nasty boyfriend do ya'? Was she the hostage?"

"You can refer to him as her *late* nasty boyfriend. He bought it last night along with several others."

"Jeez, did ya' see any action, Len? Did ya' mix it up?"

Len stared out the window and continued to sip the hot coffee, ignoring his friend's question. "Why am I drinking this shit anyway? It's almost eighty degrees outside."

Taking Len's cue, obviously he wasn't going to discuss the previous night's activities any further, Jim answered, "Because it's so flavorful an' chock full'a nutrition?"

Having just taken another swallow, Len choked on it while trying not to laugh, "Wrong on both counts, Jim. Hey, buddy, I gotta' go. Ciao."

Len tossed a couple of dollar bills on the counter and left Jim's to limp back to the condominium and his Audi. On the way he remembered another telephone call he'd overlooked. Stopping at the pay phone on the corner, he called the Valley General Hospital to check on Sara. The switchboard transferred his call to the restricted ward where she was resting and a woman's voice answered.

"Good morning," Len said. "This is Morgan from Valley West Homicide, please let me speak to any police officer standing guard in the hallway."

A couple of minutes later Len heard a voice answer, "Officer Remboski here, what can I do for you?"

"Good morning, Remboski, Captain Morgan here. Can you tell me how Sara Dunlap is doing?"

"She's still sleeping like a baby, sir. To my best knowledge, she hasn't moved a muscle since last night. Shall I wake her, to let her know you're on the phone?"

"No! Let her rest. Tell me, have the press or broadcast media been giving you a bad time, wanting any particulars?"

"Just the normal kind of crap, sir. They're hangin' out in a nearby hallway, watchin' and waitin', but we're used to them. I deflect their questions, you know, the I know nothin' kind of thing, like old Schmaltzy in Hogan's Heroes used, you know. Both of us are tellin' them to contact PR at the precinct."

"Good man…" Len said, quietly chuckling at Remboski's gaffe. *"Schmaltzy?" Good grief, who is this guy?* "Well, keep up the good work, Officer." Pausing, his curiosity getting the better of him, Len asked, "Wait, what's with this 'we' and 'both of us' stuff?"

"Yes, sir, the two wounded Latinos are on this floor too, and under police guard across the hall from Miss Sara. Didn't you know that, sir?"

"No, I shit-sure didn't!" Len answered coldly. "Remboski, contact Watch Command for me. Tell them I want the guards doubled on their rooms. Also, ask Command to advise the hospital that visitors are a definite no-no for those two. Don't allow anyone other than cops or hospital staff in that ward until those two are healthy enough to be moved to our lockup, no one. Got that?"

"Well, it's not rooms, sir. Both of them are sharin' one room now," Remboski advised.

"Well, that's total bullshit too!" Len yelled, his energy level rising. "I want them in separate rooms, Remboski, and right now! What kind of sloppy-ass horseshit routine are we running? And remember, no media, no visitors, no nothing in those corridors. Put an airtight lid on those bastards. And Sara too."

"Y... yes, sir."

"Do this too, while you're at it," Len added, calming down. "Here's my pager number, I'm going to be busy for a while. When Sara awakens, ask her to page me. And again, keep the reporters and TV camera people away from her. It's damned important that she isn't made visible to the media. We'll continue letting them believe she was one of the gang and let it drop from there, got that?"

"Yes, sir. I'll radio Watch Command right away, and also see that Miss Sara gets your number."

"Fine. Thank you."

"Captain, before you hang up, let me say that I admire the way you took the bull by the horns, goin' in with SWAT like you did. Anyone else would have been fillin' their shorts, probably still tryin' to negotiate with those bastards. You did good, sir. Really good."

"Thanks, that's greatly appreciated, Remboski. I did what I thought best, and I have some recriminations too. Maybe on a different day I would have done something different, but thanks. I'll talk to you later, and excuse my attitude; I'm a bit frayed around the edges this morning."

Len hung up and loosened his tie. The heat radiating from the sidewalk and the asphalt street was causing him to perspire through his clothes. Walking slowly, still feeling the effects of the shin splints, he entered into the underground parking garage taking as much advantage of the cool shade as he could and enjoying the change in temperature. Keying the ignition in his Audi, he backed out of his parking space and left the building to drive to the precinct for his ensuing meeting with the ever-ominous Internal Affairs Department.

As he pulled into the precinct parking structure, his pager went off. It was Jeff Robinson. *Must be Josephs made it to work.*

Len walked slowly, still limping slightly, to the elevator. As he entered the squad room a loud, rousing cheer greeted him from his compatriots, "Hey, it's Len, guys! He's here! Great job last night, Captain, great job! Good man!"

"Hey, relax, it's just me," he said shyly. "No biggie. Is Robbie here? Where's Robbie?"

Jeff Robinson pushed his way through the small mob scene surrounding his new Captain, still busily fending off questions about the shootout.

"Look, you guys, I'll give you the whole story later. Right now we have a major amount of business to take care of, maybe a murderer to catch. Robbie, Lana, Wolf, Mariko, please come into Dutch's office. New Detective Josephs too, where are you Duane?" Josephs appeared, raising his hand in answer to Len's question.

Inside his office, Len took a seat on the corner of his new desk. "Robbie, I trust you have discovered who your new partner is this morning?" Len asked, smiling at his old friend.

"You know, Boss, last night after you hung up, I was fearful you might be promoting Lanny Boyle from Vice. Then my better sense took over. What a relief when Duane walked in and said he was the *anointed one*," Jeff Robinson wisecracked, using Len's term. "Believe this or not, somehow I knew that he would show up wearing a blue shirt and muted, red silk tie. He's an excellent choice, green-as-grass, but we'll make a detective out of him."

"I agree with our new Lieutenant. We saw the end result of his work at Cal Southern. You made an excellent choice, Boss," Svetlana Belanova said, smiling broadly with Wolf nodding his head in agreement. Josephs blushed modestly.

"So, Duane … you're the green rookie *blue* with the nose of a black-and-tan-hound?" Wolf Mueller asked, smiling at his color-filled remark that resulted in a few less than impressed facial expressions from his associates. Mueller continued, "You picked a good one, Boss."

Josephs continued to blush, but nodded his head in response to Mueller's compliment.

"Thanks, guys," Len said. "I'm certain 'Green' Duane appreciates all that and I do too. We'll give him a good run at it and see how it works out. So, Duane, no black dress loafers?"

"Sorry, sir. I'll go shopping this afternoon."

Len smiled. "Okay, let's get down to business. We have another young man that needs our full attention this morning, a possible murder suspect named Aubrey Hunnicutt. He's enrolled at Cal Southern University, and he may be one of our murderers. We have a witness that may have seen him outside the hotel murder scene a week and a half-ago. Robbie will fill you in on those details."

"Oh, yeah," Belanova mumbled, "the one at the Valley Arms Hotel, the slashed up hooker."

"Right, Lana, that's the one. Our witness may have described the fellow we're going to close in on today. He's here from Nashville, Tennessee on a football scholarship. My understanding is that he's living on campus, supposedly in the athletic dorm. His girlfriend, coincidentally, happens to be the well-endowed fifteen-year old daughter of the hotel victim."

Belanova nodded, "That's more than a coincidence, at least in my opinion."

"Well," Len added, "it's one connection we have. I met this youngster. He's a cocky, well-built athletic type. Be careful, he's big."

"What's the plan, Len," Jeff Robinson asked, shifting in his chair.

"The plan is this: first, Mariko will call Cal Southern Administration and have Hunnicutt's picture faxed over here so all of you will know what the kid looks like. Silly me, I have a fistful of enlarged glossies taken in New Lebanon, but they're at home on my kitchen counter."

"Anyway," Len went on, "Robbie, you and Duane will take photo collection along with his photo and that of Gerot and see if the cabby can ID either of them. Also, Mariko, have the university give you all the information they have on Hunnicutt: his dorm and room number, his class schedules including football practice, his place of employment, his jock size…"

"What?"

"Kidding, just kidding, Mariko! Any medical records will be helpful too, that kind of thing, everything."

He continued, "Lana and Wolf, contact Miss Deborah Rosen, our Assistant DA, and have her contact Judge Shepherd's office requesting a first-degree murder arrest warrant and a search warrant for Hunnicutt based on the taxi driver's expected confirmation of Hunnicutt as his fare. Have the search warrant include the whole damn university for all I care. We want to look over everything connected to this kid. When you have the warrants, radio Robbie and meet him at the university. You guys work out the location."

"Will do." She replied.

"Then you and Wolf toss his room, his closet, look through all his clothes, and look especially for bloodstained clothes, especially a maroon jacket. If so, get the jacket to CSI. Look in his athletic locker and his car, if he has one, and his workplace if he has a job on campus."

Detectives Belanova and Mueller nodded. "Gotcha."

"Robbie and Duane, after you contact the Cabby and show him the photos, if he makes Hunnicutt, radio Lana and arrange to get the arrest warrant from her. Move in at ten-o'clock. Arrest him and book him on murder one about the same time that Lana and Wolf's search is going on. By the way, for the record his full name is Aubrey James Hunnicutt."

Taking a breath, Len continued, "Robbie and Duane, I want you to stay in radio communication with Lana and Wolf, keep your radios turned on. Wolf, Lana, if by some freak of fate you happen to run into Hunnicutt during the search, place him under arrest for murder, you know the routine, cuff him, read him his 'Miranda' and then shoot him in the ass…"

The room exploded with laughter.

"Should save the county taxpayers some major trial expense, huh?" Jeff Robinson suggested.

"Uh-huh," Len grunted. "Okay, girls and boys, I've got to run so get on your ponies and ride! I'm obliged to visit with Internal Affairs this morning. I may have to turn in my shield and piece after spending some quality time with them today. Good luck to all of you. Please be careful out there, I'll see you later."

"Right, Boss, later," was the group's collective answer.

As he departed, his pager beeped. It was a number he didn't recognize, other than recognizing the exchange as being one in the Valley West.

Sara? It must be. She's awake early enough. Reaching for a nearby telephone, he entered the number; it rang once.

"Len?" It was Sara.

"Hi, yes, it's me. How are you? You're up early enough; did you rest?"

"Yes, Len," she responded. "Can you come get me now? I want out of this place. When can you come get me?"

Thinking frantically, he apologized. "Sara, I can't right now. I'll have to send a car over to take you home. I'm scheduled to meet with Internal Affairs this morning; in fact I'm running late. I'll send two of my officers to get you."

"But you promised. Why can't you come get me?"

"Sara, I know I promised and I'm sorry. I would if I could, but I have to do this thing. It's a departmental procedure and I'll be in a batch of trouble if I ignore procedure. Understand?"

"I guess…" she said, pouting.

"I'll have a couple of suits come get you. We need you out of there ASAP to keep you shielded from the media; they're still on a feeding frenzy."

"Bummer." Surrendering to the inevitable, she replied, "Okay, send over those suits. Will anybody be in them or are they just empty suits?" she asked, resigned to the fact that Len wasn't going to be her rescuer this time.

"I think someone should be in them; if not, call me. I'll see you later. And remember, Sara, it's important that you do everything the suits tell you. We'll play a small trick on the media, okay?"

"Okay. Goodbye."

Turning, he saw two of his homicide detectives sitting at their desks. "Paulie, Coop … I have a mission of mercy for you. Are you busy?"

"No, not that busy. What have you got?"

"Go to Valley General Hospital and pick up my neighbor and take her to lockup. Make it look like she's a prisoner and you're taking her in. You guys can make a big deal out of this charade, have her head covered, handcuffed, etc. You know the routine. Officer Remboski is guarding her hospital room so tell him to leave there and meet you at the lockup. Have him waiting there to take her out through the back door and drive her to my condominium; *my* unit, not to her place. Tell him to stay there with her until I arrive, okay? Here's the key. Remember, keep her covered so no one can get a picture or video of her, that's important."

"We got it, Boss. No one will have a clue who she is," Paul said, with Fred nodding in agreement.

Catching Mariko as she was going into his office with some paperwork he said, "Mariko, this is a dumb long shot so don't snicker. Get a list of all guests registered that night from the Valley Arms. This is not a big priority."

"Got it. Good luck down there."
"Thanks…." *Now, Internal Affairs, here I come, ready or not!*

Mid-Monday morning, June 17…

Mariko stuck her head into Len's office where Lieutenant Jeff Robinson was explaining to the team of detectives what Duard van Haan witnessed moments after the murder. "Excuse me, Robbie, Cal Southern just faxed the data so don't dash off. Give me a minute to collate it and I'll run off some copies for you."

"Fine, Mariko, we'll be right here."

Jeff Robinson then continued with his briefing, relating everything that was pertinent to the case starting with day one.

A few minutes later Mariko returned, "Here you are, gentlemen, Hunnicutt's picture, his class schedule, his football practice schedule, his dorm and room number, and his place of employment. He's a busboy and backup waiter over at the Campus Dining Room, which may explain van Haan's concept of a 'bellhop' in the hallway. For your convenience, Cal Southern also sent over a map of the campus along with the size and brand of his jock…"

"What?"

"I'm kidding too! But, they were quite cooperative today."

Snickering, the troop of detectives examined the paperwork and discussed the various aspects of Hunnicutt's background.

Svetlana returned to the room and joined the group, having been on the telephone with Assistant DA Deborah Rosen. "Hey! The Unabomber, Ted Kaczynski, was indicted on ten counts yesterday, according to our lady DA. That's one bad-ass off the streets. She also said Judge Shepherd will issue the warrants this morning, pending a confirmed ID on the suspect from Robbie's cabby. Then Wolf and I will meet Robbie and Duane at the campus. Main gate, Robbie?"

"Suits me. We'll be there."

"After that," she continued, "we'll check out his room while he's at morning football practice, hopefully getting arrested."

"That works for us," Jeff Robinson said. "Worse case, if we don't get confirmation of Hunnicutt's ID from the cabby we can regroup back here. Does anyone have any questions? If not, time's a wasting!"

"I have one." Josephs reached inside his coat and pulled out a bulky .38-caliber 'Special' revolver. "This antiquated bad-boy is too big to be carrying under my coat. Where can I stow it until I procure something more appropriate?"

Jeff Robinson took Josephs' gun and whistled softly as he hefted it. "Man, that is a big one. Where did you get that thing, from the Wyatt Earp collection?"

The other detectives chuckled.

Josephs blushed.

"Son, stow it in our cruiser, in the trunk for now. If we need it we can get it. We'll get you outfitted with something more appropriate later. Are we all ready to rumble? Do y'all have your radios? Let's go, good hunting."

As the troops left Len's office, Mariko called out," Hey, *Junior Dete*ctive Josephs, congratulations, and take care out there."

"Thanks Mariko. Er ... sorry, I mean *Executive Staff Assistant* Tanaka. The same to you, congratulations."

"Mariko," Jeff Robinson asked, approaching her desk, "has anything else come in that we need? Do we have everything now?"

"You've got it all, baby. Hey! Robbie, after this is over maybe we can all go 'industrial' and do a quickie lunch at Ariadde's Greek Gyro Drive-In, huh?"

"Woman, so help me…" His voice trailed off as the double glass-doors closed behind him. As soon as they closed, he backtracked and reentered, returning to Mariko's desk.

"Mariko, I forgot; would you call the hooker's bank like Len asked and see if their joint account was closed, and if so, request videos showing who made the withdrawal? Let him know what you find?"

"Will do," she replied.

Jeff Robinson disappeared into the awaiting elevator where Josephs waited, patiently tending the door.

Valley General Hospital…
Detectives Paul Tobin and Fred Cooper pulled into the steamy hot parking lot behind the hospital and parked next to one of the huge, roll-off refuse containers.

Tobin opened the trunk of their cruiser and retrieved a blue, police issue parka with VWPD stenciled in bright yellow on the back.

"Are you cold?" Cooper asked. "It's crowding ninety-degrees right now."

"No, you dumb shit, this is to conceal the pretty lady so the nosey reporters and camera crew won't get a look at her."

"Ah… good thinking," Cooper said, looking around. "It's quiet enough back here today, hot as hell but quiet. Let's see what's happenin' inside."

The duo entered the hospital, took a turn through the kitchen and crossed over to the freight elevator. Getting off on the third floor, they turned right and approached the nurses' station.

"We've got company," Tobin observed. "Look, two cameras."

"Yeah, well, let's ignore their ass and find Remboski. There he is, that must be her room, huh?"

"Must be. Hey, Remboski," Cooper said, smiling and extending his hand. "How is it you get all the easy-money, air-conditioned gigs?"

"Hi boys. Fancy meeting you two here," Remboski said, shaking their hands. "Coming to relieve me?"

"In a manner," Tobin answered. "The Captain wants you to leave now and boogie over to lockup. We'll take the lady, and with you attracting those cameras out there, we'll escort her outta' here. You wait for us at lockup, inside by the back door. This is a big theatrical production, Remboski, mainly for the media geeks."

"Theatrical?" Remboski asked. "No problem, I used to be a thesp….."

"Pay attention," Tobin interrupted. "Captain says for you to then take the lady to *his* condominium and stick around until you are relieved. Here's the key. Captain wants you two to stay there, *not* at her place. He says it's really important that she doesn't go back to her place for anything. Got it?"

"So Morgan wants me to take her to his place, is that it?"

"You got it," Cooper replied. "Why, did you think he wanted you to take her to your place? Jeez, Remboski."

"Hey! She's a looker. I could do a lot worse."

"We know, man, and you probably have," Paul Tobin offered, chuckling. "All right, are we ready to blow this pop-stand?"

"Let me knock on the door first," Remboski said.

Hearing the knocking, Sara answered, "Is that you Remboski?"

"Yes, ma'am, are you decent? May we come in?"

Inside the hospital room, Remboski introduced Sara to Paul and Fred and they explained the procedure they were going to follow.

"Oh, great. I can go home now, take a shower and get into some fresh clothes. Where's Len now?" she asked.

"Right now, ma'am," Paul Tobin explained, "the Captain is probably involved with the Internal Affairs board of review. Not a happy place to be, ma'am. Also, the Captain doesn't want you going back to your place. He specifically ordered us to have Officer Remboski take you to his condominium. You can shampoo and shower there just as easily, right? We can stop briefly at your place for a change of clothes."

"I suppose," she said, her curiosity beginning to get the better of her. "Whatever, it's no big deal. It'll work out."

Tobin handed Sara the over-sized police parka and struggling with it, she pulled it over her head. It came nearly to her knees and left her hands and arms concealed well up into the sleeves.

Tucked inside the parka's hood, with just her eyeballs exposed, she asked, "Why does he have to go before the review board, or whatever it's called?"

"It's official departmental procedure, ma'am," Tobin explained. "Anytime an officer fires his service pistol, especially if he uses deadly force causing a death, that officer must relinquish his weapon temporarily and face possible suspension until the review board clears him, or makes whatever disposition they choose to make."

"No kidding? So even if the officer uses his weapon in self-defense, or in the line of duty protecting a civilian, he has to go before this review board?"

"Yes, silly as it seems," Tobin said, "that's how it works around here, ma'am. Okay, Remboski, you take off and bait the media folks. We'll duck down the hall to the freight elevator. Sorry, ma'am, before we leave, we need to put the cuffs on you to make you appear to be our prisoner. It's part of the Captain's game plan."

"Great." She frowned as she placed her hands behind her back, "Okay, I'm ready if you are, let's go."

Remboski left the trio in the hallway and on the way out noticed the door to the two fugitives' room was unguarded. He checked it and found it locked. He stopped at the nurses' station. "Has anyone seen the other officer in the past few minutes?

The nurses' aide answered, "I saw him escort one of the fugitives down the hallway toward the back stairs. Is there a problem?"

"Oh, he's probably taking them over to lockup then," Remboski offered.

The nurses' aide didn't speak, being confused by his remark, knowing that no one except Sara Dunlap had been discharged this morning.

Remboski thanked the aide and casually continued on his way past the gathered press corps. With their eyes focused on him, neither the reporters nor the cinematographers gathered had paid any attention to the trio leaving by the alternate route. Reaching the elevator Remboski pressed the button to summon it. As the door opened, the arrival bell sounded as he stepped inside.

Alerted and seeing Remboski entering the elevator, the reporters and cinematographers leaped to their feet and raced to the door in an attempt to reach it before it closed. They were too late.

Inside, Remboski pressed the button for the second floor. Reaching there, he pressed the button for the first floor and left the car. He walked casually down the hall and entered the Men's Room. He relieved himself at the urinal and smiled, knowing those media fools were probably on the first floor by now, curious as to where he disappeared.

Detectives Tobin and Cooper, with Sara in the cumbersome parka, made it undetected from the freight elevator and outside without incident into the sweltering heat of the back lot. They loaded Sara in the rear seat and asked her to kneel on the floor.

Tobin threw a police blanket over her, apologizing profusely. "Please hang in there, Miss Sara. When we get clear of the hospital you can surface and take advantage of the air-conditioner."

Cooper got in behind the wheel, veteran Tobin rode shotgun. With everyone in place, the trio sped off in the direction of the lockup.

Devonshire Hills Police Precinct...
Len walked into the Office of Internal Affairs lobby at exactly 8:30 a.m. The desk officer easily recognized him and smiled. "Captain Morgan, it's good to see you. Congratulations on your promotion, sir. They're expecting you. Just go back to Lieutenant Woodward's office on the right."

"Thanks, Officer, thanks very much." Len could feel the beginnings of butterflies stirring in his stomach as he walked down the hall. He paused at the open door with the freshly painted words, *Lieutenant Charles L. Woodward, Chief Investigator, Internal Affairs Unit.* He knocked quietly on the doorjamb.

Woodward, seeing Len standing in the doorway, motioned to him, saying, "Come in Morgan, you're right on time. Have a seat."

Pressing his intercom button, he spoke, "Come in Payne, Morgan's here." Pressing another button, he said, "Flossie, bring your dictation device to my office now."

Len stood in front of Lieutenant Charles L. Woodward's desk, removed his service pistol from its holster and carefully extracted the clip and ejected the round from the chamber. He repeated the last procedure to ensure the chamber was empty. Satisfied, he carefully placed his .45-caliber Smith & Wesson pistol on the desk with the other items.

"If you examine the clip, Lieutenant, you'll notice two rounds are missing," he explained as he took a chair. "If you have the Medical Examiner's report you'll note they lodged in or near the gangbanger's heart."

Woodward placed Len's gun and clip in a large manila envelope and without comment wrote out a receipt. He stared back blankly as police veteran Lieutenant Lester Payne, a long time Internal Affairs investigator, entered and took a chair beside Len.

Woodward asked, "Was that remark to be construed as humorous, Morgan?"

"Excuse me, Lieutenant Woodward, before we continue, if this is a formal hearing, sir, you may address me as *Captain* Morgan, thank you. And no, it wasn't meant to be construed as humorous, merely concise."

Lester Payne pulled his chair closer to Len, "That was some fracas out there last night, Len. May we have your side of the story?"

"Wait for Flossie, Lester," Woodward said abruptly. "She's getting her dictation machine. She'll be just a minute. When she arrives *I'll* conduct this interview,"

Len looked at Lester Payne and replied quietly, "Off the record, Lester, yes, it was quite a fracas. Short but intense."

Flossie Perkins, a buxom young uniformed police stenographer entered with her stenotype machine. Nodding at Lieutenant Woodward, she sat down in a straight-back chair in the corner facing Len and Lester Payne. "I'm sorry I'm late, sir. I'm ready, anytime."

Woodward nodded. "Let us begin. For the record, this interview is being conducted with Captain of Homicide, Leonard B. Morgan, in reference to a fatal shooting that took place in the early morning hours of 17 June 1996. Captain Morgan, will you give us your rendition of what transpired last night? Take as much time as you like. We have all day."

I'll bet you do, Len thought as he unbuttoned his suit coat and got more comfortable.

"It began when I received a threatening telephone call early this morning, sometime around two-thirty, maybe later…"

"Be precise, how much later?" Woodard interrupted.

"Charley," Lester Payne said. "Please, let's let him tell his story uninterrupted. Afterwards we can ask him to amplify or expand if need be."

Len looked appreciatively at Lester Payne and nodded. "Thanks. Anyway, the principal on the other end of the telephone line indicated that he was holding my neighbor, Miss Sara Dunlap, hostage. I knew he was telling the truth because when I initially answered the telephone, I heard Miss Dunlap scream out my name. Excuse me; may I trouble you for a glass of water?"

Lester Payne got to his feet. "Of course, Len. Wait a second, I'll fetch a pitcher and some glasses for us. Would you like some water, Charley? Flossie?"

"Thanks, no, Mister Payne." Flossie answered.

Woodward chose not to respond and instead, sat motionless, quietly staring at Len.

Len noted his staring too. *What is this fresh punk's agenda? A new kid on the block enjoying his first power trip? I'm acquainted with*

Lester Payne, he's a solid veteran with a reputation of being fair. Charles L. Woodward is new, young and an unknown quantity.

Payne returned, poured two glasses of water and handed one to Len.

"Thanks, much obliged, Lester," Len said and took a long swallow.

"Continue, Captain Morgan," Woodward said.

"Yes. As I said, the principal advised me that he was holding my neighbor, Miss Dunlap, as hostage and that he wanted me as well. I was at a loss for a split second, not fully knowing how to react. After I focused, I stalled him by virtue of having a second telephone line at my disposal. I put him on hold for a few seconds and called Watch Command Dispatch. They put a patch on my lines, traced the calls and alerted Los Angeles PD SWAT, which fortunately had been active earlier in south central LA."

At that point, Woodward made a detailed notation on his yellow legal pad. "Go ahead."

"I called for a taxi, took it to Parthenia and DeSoto, traded drivers with a SWAT officer and got scoped on SWAT's plan of attack and tacitly approved it."

Again, Woodward made another notation on his pad.

Noting that, Len continued, "We took the dark street toward the apartment complex where the abductor had quarters on the third floor. SWAT had removed the only other resident from the third floor level to a safer location. Several officers were in place on the roof above the principal. Two additional officers were stationed in the second floor hallway."

"Captain Morgan," Lester Payne said, as he leaned forward, closer to Len, "do you know why there were officers stationed in the halls?"

"I believe it was a precautionary move made by SWAT Commander Ellsworth to prevent unnecessary panic from the second level residents when the shooting began. That's my best guess, Lester."

Lester Payne nodded and leaned back in his chair.

Len cleared his throat and continued. "The SWAT driver parked the taxi in the street as we had been directed by the principal."

"The driver's name?" Woodward asked.

"Officer Jack Ferrell."

"Two 'r's?"

"I suppose; I really don't know." Woodward made another note on his pad.

Len continued, "At that time three men armed with handguns came out of the bushes and approached our vehicle. SWAT officer Ferrell jumped from the cab and ordered them to 'Freeze'. Surprised at first, they began shooting at us. Officer Ferrell and I returned fire taking them out. Following that exchange, we entered the building. Upon hearing our gunshots, SWAT immediately followed with their flash-bangs and tear-gas. They broke into the principal's apartment through the windows and an unlocked skylight. Returning a minimum of gunfire, they quickly disposed of two armed Latinos, rescued my neighbor and it was over."

"A *minimum* of gunfire, Captain? Define minimum if you would."

"Less than a lot?"

"Captain Morgan, be specific."

"Okay ... as I was negotiating the stairs and the hallway, I didn't hear that much as far as gunshots: maybe two automatic weapon reports of three shots each? It wasn't much. Don't you have CSI's report? They photographed every empty, spent casing at the entire scene."

"I'll ask the questions here, Captain. So you and this Officer Ferrell shot and killed three young Latino men in a street fight, and two other young Latinos were shot and killed on the third level following SWAT's entry? Is that accurate?" Woodward asked.

Becoming irritated by the incessant interruptions and haughty attitude, Len answered, "Yes, five men were killed. This entire action took maybe five minutes. SWAT took the proper steps to ensure no civilian injuries beyond being frightened or deafened temporarily by the gunfire. The hostage, Miss Dunlap, who had been raped repeatedly by the principal, was transported to Valley General Hospital as were the two wounded men."

Woodward looked at his pad of paper, "Anything else, Captain Morgan?"

"Well, SWAT suffered a torn shirt sleeve. The two surviving gang members went to Valley General Hospital for treatment, as I said, and are currently in lockup facing arraignment in Superior Court. The hostage, Miss Dunlap, highly traumatized by the entire sequence of events, remains under professional care."

"Is she all right today, Len? She must have been horrified," Lester Payne said.

"As far as I know she's doing okay. I've spoken with her briefly. She will be going back to her condominium soon under police guard."

"Captain Morgan, can we get back to cases and let the homilies wait?" Woodward asked impatiently. "You say you don't know precisely what time the call came in last night. Why not?"

"Why not?" Len asked sarcastically, pausing for a moment to stare indifferently at Woodward. "I don't know why not, sir. I have no precise recollection of the time when the call came in. It was about two-thirty, or maybe three o'clock, give or take, and I was sound asleep. If it's that important, we could request my LUD records."

Woodward studied Len from behind his desk. He took a deep breath, and continued, "That's not necessary. Again, what measures did you take to stall the principal, as you claim?"

"I lied to him. I told him my cordless telephone was acting up. I actually put him on hold while I called Dispatch. The principal bought it. He was highly suspicious, but he obviously bought it."

"I find that totally amazing," Payne said, chiming in. "So you put him on hold long enough to contact Dispatch. Weren't you fearful that he might take desperate measures against your neighbor if he thought you were being deceptive?"

"Hell, yes, Lester. I was out of my mind with fear. I knew this man personally from a previous experience involving him and my neighbor. He was a psycho and extremely dangerous in any setting; a loose cannon and totally unpredictable. I had to use any device at hand to trick him, outwit him, to take him and his friends by complete surprise. It was a difficult choice, but it was the only feasible choice. In this instance it worked."

"Captain Morgan, do you think that your fear possibly caused you to take thoughtless measures in order to rescue your neighbor?" Woodward asked, staring intently at Len.

"Not at all."

Woodward cleared his throat, "Why didn't you just drive over to his apartment complex instead of summoning a taxi? I understand that we are spending departmental time and resources to repair it today. Is there a reasonable explanation for that?"

"The reasonable explanation is because the taxi took some bullets, Lieutenant Woodward. But, I think the answer you're looking for is this, I needed to buy some time to ensure that this plan was going to be semi-successful. Had I driven I would not have had the advantage of an armed SWAT officer with me. That stratagem probably saved my life. If the cost of repairs is a problem, sir, I'll personally cover it."

"It isn't that much of a problem. Now, what prompted you to take such thoughtless measures in this situation? Five young Latinos are dead, Captain, because you decided to invade a residential domicile last night," Woodward expounded, staring directly at Len. "What authority do you have to order a SWAT team into action and risk the lives of innocent civilians as well as those of police officers?"

Len nearly came out of his chair. He stared hard at Woodward, "Sir, I take personal offense at your presumptions. Five armed and dangerous *men* are dead today, but not because of my 'thoughtless' measures! Five *me*n are dead today because one idiot decided to break the law, kidnap and rape an individual and hold her hostage, all to possibly extort his perverted revenge on me. He instigated the action; I merely retaliated, sir, to do what I could to save a woman's life. Also, I strongly reject any notion you may harbor because of the dead men's racial heritage, of which you seem locked on."

Woodward sat silently, unblinking.

"As far as authority," Len continued, "I'm a twenty-five year veteran of this police force, sir. I hold the rank of Captain of Homicide and authority comes with the rank. I didn't have time to call the Chief of Detectives, or the Governor, or Bill Clinton. There wasn't time for protocol, I had to act. It required drastic action, not 'thoughtless', your word; I took it."

Woodward shrugged and replied, "You said you tacitly agreed to the SWAT Commander's plan. Why tacitly?"

"What would you have me do, Lieutenant? Get out of the taxi with a goddamn bullhorn and discuss the covert operation with the SWAT Commander while he's standing on the rooftop?" Len asked, catching a glimpse of Lester Payne out of the corner of his eye. "Officer Ferrell related the plan to me in the taxi; it looked sound and we implemented it."

Payne shook his head and chuckled quietly, apparently enjoying the remark regarding the 'goddamn bullhorn'.

"Revenge," an obviously irritated Woodward repeated, "you mentioned the word 'revenge' earlier, Captain Morgan, and of having had a previous experience with the principal. Explain that?"

"The principal used to date my neighbor, the hostage…"

"He dated her?" Interrupted Lieutenant Woodward, "and you claim that he raped her repeatedly while she was his hostage? I find that totally ludicrous."

Len stared at Woodward and exhaling loudly, replied, "Ludicrous or not, those are the facts. If I may continue; one evening I heard a loud fight ensuing from her condominium and I went next door to investigate. It appeared that he had been beating her. I told him he could leave or stick around and I'd arrest him. He left. My neighbor told me where he usually hung out so the next morning I visited him at a pool hall in the Valley. I talked to him 'like a father' in front of his *cholo compadres*. I embarrassed him. That's it in a nutshell."

Payne leaned forward. "Was last night your first contact with him since that encounter in the pool hall, Captain?"

"Yes."

Woodward shifted some files on his desk and asked, "Captain Morgan, why did you shoot a young man in cold blood on a public street last night? Wasn't there a viable option available, such as placing him under arrest?"

Len paused a few seconds before answering. He expelled a long breath again and out of exasperation explained, "That 'young man' and two others with him were armed men. They approached us, their weapons in plain sight and aimed at us. Regardless of their age, or heritage, their intention was to take me hostage and deliver me to their psychopathic friend. My intent was to defend myself and rescue my neighbor. I had a loaded gun pointing directly at me by a man with bad intentions, sir. Have you ever been in that situation?"

Woodward looked daggers at Len and didn't reply.

"When he cocked the hammer, the infliction, or threatened infliction, of serious physical harm to me seemed apparent. We gave them fair warning and identified ourselves, but they insisted on firing at us. In that split second it was not feasible to give the gunman in front of me further warning and I shot him. If I hadn't, perhaps he would have shot me."

Woodward's eyebrows rose, "Do tell, Captain."

"Gentlemen, do you have any further questions?" Len asked impatiently, taking a final swallow of water. "I've a murder case I want to wrap up today."

"A few more; I won't keep you much longer," Woodward advised, watching as Len reluctantly settled back in his chair. "Captain, you decided to rush the apartment while your neighbor was inside being held hostage by armed and dangerous men, as you describe them. Again, did you actually consider, perhaps, that your thoughtless action might endanger, or possibly be fatal for your neighbor?"

"You used that word 'thoughtless' again, and I'll answer your repetitious question again. I certainly considered her safety as I explained earlier. It was uppermost in my mind. As I have also explained to you, my choice was the only rational choice I could have made at the time, considering her captor's mental state. In my opinion, her life wasn't worth a plug nickel in that apartment with him there. Also, negotiation was totally out the question, totally. The principal didn't have the mental capacity to reason…"

Interrupting, Woodward asked, "How did you come to that conclusion?"

"Because he was blind with rage, perhaps drunk or high on drugs when he called me. Who knows? Time and surprise were our best weapons so I decided to rush. I'll take total blame, or total credit, for the consequences. If Dispatch recorded our initial conversation on the telephone, you could listen and judge his frame of mind for yourself. He didn't have a frame of mind in my opinion; he was out of his mind."

"We have listened to the recording," Woodward replied haughtily, "dispatch provided it for me earlier."

"What? And you're sitting here questioning *my* judgment? Give me a goddamn break!"

"Giving a 'goddamn' break to cops who indiscriminately kill people is not what this department is about, Captain, as you'll soon see." Lieutenant Woodward got to his feet, "All right, I am through with you for now…"

"Fine!" Len said, getting to his feet. Standing and looking at Woodward, Len was surprised at how short he was. *He must have been sitting on a cushion, 'Little big man'.*

"Go chase your murderer with the time you have left." Woodward said. "However, commencing at noon today, you are on a mandatory thirty-day suspension without pay until further notice. Feel free to appeal this ruling in writing if you choose. Your appeal period would extend your official paid time on the job for an additional ten workdays. After that, stay at home, understood?"

Frowning, Len nodded, choosing instead to say nothing further, he watched as Woodward turned abruptly and strode from the room.

Len took a deep breath and stared blankly at Lester Payne. Woodward's words, putting him on mandatory suspension weighed heavily as he extended his hand. "Lester, if it wasn't so early in the day I could use a stiff drink. Thanks for your consideration. I'll see you later I guess. Thank you too, Officer Flossie."

As Len passed through the reception area, the desk officer stopped him and handed him a note, "Captain Morgan, you have a message, sir." Taking it, Len read:

CSI ran fingerprint matches through the FBI's database. Victor Vasquez is actually Armando Alvarez. The other survivor is Jose, aka Pepe, Hernandez. VWPD will transport Alvarez and Hernandez from Valley General Hospital to County Hospital today to await arraignment. Additionally, the bank funds from the joint savings account of Reynolds and Mitchell are depleted.

Mariko Tanaka.

Still day 13, but earlier that Monday...

At 6:30 a.m. at Valley General Hospital on the day following the SWAT detachment, the sound of a male orderly entering their room, accompanied by the ever-present police guard, with their breakfast awakened Armando and Jose. The orderly placed the food-trays on the adjustable tables beside their beds and, followed by the guard, quietly left the room.

"Look at this shit, Jose," Armando said, sneering. "They feed better slop to hogs."

"Well, it looks good to me, man. I'm going to eat it."

"I hope you puke, man." Armando responded. "Hey, we gotta' figure a way outta' here, and soon, man. They'll probably be shipping us to lockup this morning."

Jose nodded in agreement as he wolfed down the food on his plate. "Armando, you sure you ain't gonna eat yours? Give me it, I'll eat it."

Armando pushed his tray table over as far as he could, close enough for Jose to reach.

"Listen, Jose, the stupid cops probably have only that one pig outside the door. We could take him easily enough and get his gun too, you think? Then we can go out the back stairs to the parking lot and cop a ride. You with me on this?"

Jose, his mouth full of scrambled eggs from his second breakfast, nodded his head. Swallowing the last bite, he said, "How are we gonna handle the cop? We got no weapons, man."

"I'll think of something, don't worry, *muchacho*."

"Yeah, Armando, that's what I dig about you, man. You're cool, and you're *muy intelligente* too, but what about clothes, man? We got none, just these shitty gowns with sleeves and no buttons. We gotta' have some real clothes."

"Yeah, yeah, clothes, maybe they put our clothes in the closet. Take a look, see what's in there," Armando ordered.

Jose pushed his tray table back from the bed and walked slowly toward the closet. His wounds from the night before consisted mostly of minor cuts from window glass. Jose had been asleep under a large window on a sofa at the time. Offering no resistance, he escaped being shot.

Armando, however, suffered a gunshot wound to his shoulder as he barely escaped into the back of the apartment when the first wave of SWAT blew through the living room windows. He took refuge in the bathroom and a stray round perforated the wall and hit his shoulder. Afraid for his life or being shot again, he remained crouched in the bathtub behind the shower curtain.

SWAT Officer Jack Ferrell discovered him scared and bleeding, hiding in the tub. Lying to Ferrell, Armando gave him a fictitious name, then claimed, "...*el Jefe* was killed in the first seconds."

Jose opened the closet door and muttered a curse under his breath. "What is it?" Armando asked, "Do we have any clothes? Jose?"

"Just our Nikes. Now what?"

Armando sat in thought, his brow furled. Sitting up, he stifled a moan as made an effort to get out of the bed. His shoulder wound made moving very painful. He bit his lower lip as he slowly turned to let his legs hang over the side.

Jose had gone into the bathroom to relieve himself and was returning.

"Armando, if we can surprise that cop, I can knock him out with my fist, *no problemo*, man. I've done it a lot of times. Anyway, there's nothing in this room that we can use for a weapon. What do you think?"

"What? You will just hit him with your fist and take him down? No way, man. We'll open the door very quietly and grab him. That will be the most dangerous time. Someone may be out there with him, or just walking by. If that happens, we're in deep shit, man. Then we'll be stuck."

"So, if we open the door and if he's alone, I'll just hit him with my fist. What's wrong with that?" Jose questioned.

"I'll tell you what's wrong with that, it won't work. When we open the door, you will grab his head and put your hand over his mouth real hard. Then drag his ass back into the room. I'll take his gun and smash him. That *will* work, *comprehendes*?" Armando asked, smiling at his own brilliant idea.

"Okay, man, then we put on our shoes and boogie out of here wearing these little flowered gowns with the butt-crack clear to our necks? That shouldn't attract too much attention, huh? We need clothes, man, to get out of this place."

"Hey, *amigo*, chill! I'm still thinking. Wait a minute, okay?" Armando, tested his equilibrium for the first time and stood up.

Jose retrieved their shoes from the closet, sat in a visitor's chair and began to lace his.

"Jose, there has to be an employees' closet on this floor somewhere. Maybe it's between here and the back stairs, or by the freight elevator or something. Anyway, we'll have a *pistolo* so if we see anyone in the hall we'll just take their clothes. They won't argue with us, especially with us carrying a piece, huh?"

Armando silently complimented himself again for having solved another sticky problem.

"Well, it's getting late, when do we do this?" Jose asked, standing with his ear pressed against the door.

"Right now," Armando whispered as he crept in behind Jose. "No better time than right now, *amigo*. So, we open the goddamn door now. Remember, you grab him and cover his mouth quickly so he can't make any noise, okay? Now!"

Making no sound whatsoever Jose quietly turned the lever handle and slowly opened the heavy door a crack as Armando crouched behind him. The lone guard was standing with his back to them and hadn't heard the door open. Jose surveyed the hallway quickly, the coast seemed clear; no one was there that he could see.

Moving with the speed of a panther on the attack, he reached out, grabbed the guard's face with his huge hand and dragged him back into the room. Armando, having closed the door, unsnapped the guard's holster and smashed the struggling officer hard across the temple with the gun barrel. The guard moaned and collapsed onto the tiled floor.

"Jose, look at that! You two are almost the same size. Put on his uniform, quick! Then you can escort me down the hall and no one will be the wiser, hurry!"

It took Jose mere minutes to suit up and change shoes. Now he looked like any other VWPD cop on the force. He slowly opened the door again and peeked out, not a soul in sight. Officer Remboski would normally have been on duty outside Sara's room, but he was currently at the nurses' station, talking to Len Morgan on the telephone.

In the corridor, the two fugitives locked and quietly closed the door. Turning left, they headed for the back exit stairway. On the way, Armando spotted a door marked, "Staff."

"In here, quick," he ordered.

The door was unlocked. Inside were shelves stacked high with the green scrub garb worn by the various hospital nurses and orderlies. Armando threw his gown on the floor, grabbed a pair of slacks and a blouse and quickly put them on. He looked over the array of accessories and found a green cap and green slip-ons that fit over his Nikes.

He laughed as he added a surgeon's facemask that he tied loosely around his neck.

"*Caramba!* Officer Jose, how do I look? Am I a double for Ben Casey or what? Okay, let's split and snatch a ride."

The unlikely looking pair made their way unhindered down the back hall to the stairs and outside to the rear parking lot. "Find an easy one to hot-wire, Jose. You know," Armando ordered, "…and hurry for Chrissakes!"

"Here's one," Jose said excitedly, "and the *boboso* left the windows open. Must be he didn't want the inside to get too hot or something, huh?"

Jose opened the door of a faded green Ford Pinto and crawled in behind the wheel. A professional part-time car thief and familiar with hot-wiring, he bypassed the ignition switch and pulled the wiring harness loose from under the dashboard. He quickly connected the right set of wires and the old car's motor started immediately.

"*Caramba!* Let's boogie," Armando screamed in glee. "And don't get no silly traffic tickets either."

Smiling self-assuredly, Jose, albeit 'Officer Jose' now, jabbed the accelerator with his newly found right shoe and the little car leaped forward heading in the direction of Granada Hills and Len Morgan's condominium.

A few minutes later, as they were nearing the neighborhood, Jose asked, "Which one is it? There's so many and they all look alike, man."

"Take a right turn up there on Rinaldi; it's on the left about a block away. It's called Casa Grande or something, some fancy Spanish words to describe what it ain't. Turn here, there it is, over there on your left. Drive into the parking garage. I've got the security combination memorized. We'll be safe in there. They'll be looking for this wreck soon and they sure as hell won't be looking here." Armando laughed, self-satisfied with his plan.

"Armando," Jose said, "you are so *intelligente*. Why are we parking in there again?"

"We'll wait for the pig Morgan in there where it's cool and dark. We'll ambush his ass this time! Then we'll find Sara again. We need to talk, talk a lot," Armando said, his dark eyes cold as ice.

The stolen car turned into the drive and stopped at the security gate. Armando relayed to Jose the sequence of numbers to key in. Seconds later the big iron-gate quietly rolled back to conceal itself within the brick and masonry outer wall of the parking garage. They drove inside and parked in a place with a wide-angle view of the entrance gate as well as the elevator and stairway doors. Jose shut off the engine and they slouched down to await the arrival of their quarry.

Heading toward the Hollywood Freeway…
Jeff Robinson and Josephs left the precinct and headed east on the Ventura Freeway toward the Hollywood freeway with Josephs driving. "Traffic is sure light for this hour of the day," he remarked. "It's moving pretty good so far."

"Fortunately for us that it is," Jeff Robinson replied. "We have some miles to cover if we're going to be at Cal Southern by ten o'clock." Glancing at his wristwatch as he spoke, he noted it was just past 8:30 a.m. "It was good that Mariko got in touch with Banaji the cabby before he got out onto the streets or we'd have missed him."

"I agree. Do you think he'll be of any help, trying to ID a picture of a fare from over a week ago?" Josephs asked.

"Help or not, we still gotta' ask him, and if he does, we gotta' radio Lana and Wolf to pick up the warrants."

"Right."

"This case has been stingy as far as gathering any evidence. I'll take anything I can get right now. Hey! There's the Hollywood Freeway coming up, make sure you're in the through-lane and we don't end up in Burbank, okay?"

"Sure enough. So, this may be a silly question for a seasoned vet like you, Robbie. Are you a a little nervous about maybe pinching this Hunnicutt kid? Do you ever get nervous?"

"Nervous … no. Well, not yet anyway. I think excited fits better. Some things make me nervous, but this morning I'm more excited. I have a feeling that we're going to be arresting our murderer."

Jeff Robinson and Josephs arrived at the Yellow Cab taxi barn in East Los Angeles and parked out front. Inside they spied the dispatch room and entered through the open door.

"Good morning," Jeff Robinson said cheerfully. He removed a departmental calling card from his coat pocket and handed it to the dispatcher seated behind a desk in front of a large, round microphone. "I'm Lieutenant Detective Jeff Robinson and this is my partner, Detective Josephs. We have an appointment to meet with Sethi Banaji. Is he available?"

The dispatcher looked at Jeff Robinson's card and pushed an alternate button on his microphone, "Sethi Banaji, you've got official company. Oh, Sethi, could you bring me a reheat of coffee too? I owe you, sir."

The dispatcher looked back at Jeff Robinson, "He'll be just a minute. Oh…" he said nervously, obviously embarrassed at his oversight, "I'm sorry, would either of you care for some coffee?"

"Thanks, we're running a little tight on time today, thanks anyway. Did you want a cup, Duane?"

"No, thanks, I'll pass. I could use a restroom though, is there one close by?"

"Through that door, you can't miss it," the dispatcher said, pointing.

As Josephs opened the door, a dark-skinned, middle-aged man approached him carrying two cups of steaming coffee. *Apparently this is Mister Banaji,* Josephs thought, holding the door open.

The man nodded, entered the dispatch room and set the hot coffee on the dispatcher's desk. Turning to Jeff Robinson, he introduced himself. "I am Sethi Banaji, sir. How may I be of help today?"

Jeff Robinson removed a group of mug photos from his suit coat pocket and handed them to Banaji. "Sir, I'm Lieutenant Jeff Robinson. I have some photos I'd like you to look at. Do you recognize any of the men pictured here?

Records show that you may have picked up one of them on Vermont Avenue late at night on the evening of June four. Your stop was the Valley Arms Hotel in the Sepulveda district. He may have been wearing a short-waisted maroon jacket."

Sethi Banaji looked at the several pictures. He placed one over the other and stared again, then nodded quietly. Handing the photos back to Jeff Robinson he said, "Yes, I do remember this one; he is in the photo I placed on top. He paid his fare with single dollars and much silver; nickels, dimes, quarters, that kind of change."

Jeff Robinson looked at the top photo and his heart nearly stopped beating. It was him: Aubrey James Hunnicutt.

"Are you absolutely certain of this, Mister Banaji? Would you be willing to give sworn testimony to that effect in a court of law?" Jeff Robinson was barely able to conceal his excitement.

"Yes, I do remember him, as I said, paying in small bills and silver, and that is fairly common. But, seven or eight dollars in pocket change does not happen every day. You also mentioned his jacket. Yes, it was dark-red or wine in color."

Jeff Robinson smiled excitedly and extended his hand. Sethi Banaji accepted it. "You may have helped us bring a vicious killer to justice, Mister Banaji. We'll be in touch, count on that. Expect to receive a subpoena from the county, just a formality, Mister Banaji. Thanks again, sir."

Josephs returned to the room as Banaji replied, "Oh, that is no problem, send it over, Detective. Anything to support the law and order."

"Thanks again, sir. Come on Duane, we've got a pinch to make!"

Jeff Robinson's feet barely touched the ground as he and a curious Josephs returned to the cruiser. "So, am I to assume that our taxi driver identified the suspect?"

"More than that, Duane. That taxi driver could have just sent Hunnicutt to the gas chamber. Let's go; I want his ass."

Jeff Robinson buckled himself in and pointed straight ahead. "Get this tank moving, Detective, we gots us a criminal to apprehend!"

Keying the two-way radio, he contacted Svetlana.

Svetlana's two-way radio squawked; it was Jeff Robinson. "Lana, the cabby fingered Hunnicutt. Advise the Judge and pick up the warrants. We're heading for the University. If we don't make contact, we'll arrest Hunnicutt and catch up with you and Wolf later. Clear."

"Great! Roger that. Clear."

Sergeant Svetlana Belanova and Detective Wolf Mueller entered the reception room of District Judge Shepherd's office located in the County-Municipal Building Annex and introduced themselves to the paralegal seated at the front desk.

Smiling, Svetlana said, "Good morning, we have positive confirmation that a Mister Aubrey James Hunnicutt has been identified as the prime suspect in a murder case. Our department called earlier to inform the Judge of that possibility. With his identity confirmed, we are here to obtain an arrest warrant for Mister Aubrey James Hunnicutt, a student/athlete residing at Cal Southern. We also requested a separate search warrant for his dormitory room, his athletic locker and occupational premises."

"Yes, Detective, we have the warrants prepared. I'll have the Judge sign them and you can be on your way," the paralegal answered.

Moments later, she returned with the paperwork. "Here they are, the warrants are signed and ready for you. Please sign this receipt and include your shield number. Good hunting," she said and handed the documents to Svetlana.

"Thanks, we truly appreciate the Judge's cooperation and expediency on this one. Goodbye now."

"Now that was one fine looking female," Wolf observed as they left the office and walked back to their cruiser. "Why do I always end up with some flea-bitten skank?"

"That's probably a rhetorical question, right, Wolf?" Svetlana suggested dryly.

The two detectives left the parking lot and headed south to the Cal Southern campus. Belanova radioed Jeff Robinson.

"Robbie, we have the arrest warrant in hand and will try to catch up with you at the campus entrance, main gate. Clear."

Standing at the IAD reception officer's desk, Len was numb with shock as he stared unbelievably at the message from Mariko. *That little bastard survived after all and he's in the same hospital across the hall from Sara! Dammit!*

He thanked the young IAD officer and ran to the elevator. Upstairs in his office, he called Watch Command. "This is Captain Morgan, Devonshire Hills Homicide. Were more uniformed officers sent to Valley General Hospital this morning to guard the two survivors from last night's shootout?"

"Captain Morgan, we've been trying to reach you concerning that. No one has been sent as yet; Chief of Detectives Rogers wanted to speak with you first…"

"Connect me with her then," Len interrupted, as he impatiently paced the floor.

He waited on hold a few seconds, then a familiar female voice answered, "Chief Clara Rogers here; is that you Len? How are you?"

"Chief Rogers, ma'am, right now I'm having a cow. One of the two survivors of the incident last night and later admitted to Valley General Hospital was the perpetrator, Armando Alvarez. I want an armored unit over there as soon as possible and move him and his partner to county medical or to our lockup. I want them moved, Chief, and to hell with their wounds or other conditions. Alvarez is a deranged bastard … uh, sorry, ma'am. Both are extremely dangerous; they're capable of anything."

The Chief frowned. "I didn't know the circumstances; certainly … wait a minute, I've just been handed a message. Hold for a sec?"

After reading the note Chief Rogers said, "It's getting more serious, Len. We found the officer guarding their room subdued and stripped of his uniform and weapon. The two fugitives have allegedly stolen a car and are on the streets. I'll put out an APB and a BOLO immediately. I'm sorry, Len. I'll keep you informed, you do the same."

Len slumped, all of his strength had sapped away. *This is unbelievable. Armando is at large and armed.*

Detectives Paul Tobin and Fred Cooper, with Sara in tow, parked in front of the VWPD lockup. Paul opened the rear door of the cruiser and beckoned the disguised prisoner to step from the car. As they accompanied her into lockup, the officers made certain the huge police parka completely shrouded her face.

The ever-present media were on hand, alerted that one of the surviving gang members might be arriving soon. The two detectives kept Sara concealed from the prying eyes of the reporters and TV cinematographers as they escorted her into the building. Once inside and into a secure room they removed the handcuffs from her wrists.

"Dear God! This is too much!" She exclaimed, impatiently struggling to discard the hot, heavy garb. "Can someone get me a towel or something so I can dry off? This is way too damn much!"

Fred Cooper retrieved a clean towel and handed it to her. "Ma'am, we were under strict orders to keep you concealed and away from any press and photographers. We're sorry the weatherman didn't cooperate."

"I know, Detective," Sara said apologetically, taking the towel. "Normally, I'm not such a cranky bitch, but I've endured too much the last couple of days. Thanks for the ride boys and for getting me out of the hospital. Where's Officer Remboski? I want out of here."

Remboski waiting nearby answered, "Right here, Miss Sara. At your service."

"Remboski, take me home."

Len's conversation with Chief Rogers and the news of Armando's escape left him frustrated. Hopeless, he stared at his desktop. *Shit. I'm screwed! I can't do anything. This is crazy. No shield, no gun, and Sara's out there in the Valley, the possible target of Armando again. I have to locate her.*

He picked up his desk phone and called the lockup. A voice answered immediately and Len asked, "Are Homicide Detectives Paul Tobin and Fred Cooper still on site?"

"I'm sorry, sir, they left minutes ago."

"Damn! Is Officer Remboski there? He was attending to a young lady."

"No, Sir. They left too."

Shit! He thought, frustrated. "Thanks, Officer."

He sat silently, his hands gripping the edge of his desk. Stupefied, he absent-mindedly opened the center drawer and saw a potential answer. *Dutch's Smith and Wesson; it's still here!*

He removed it from the drawer and hefted it. *It's an identical match for my own, even to the cross-checked nylon grip the FBI prefers.*

He closed the drawer, ejected the ammo clip and checked it out. Ten rounds, it was full. He replaced the clip, racked a round into the chamber and clicked on the safety.

What the hell am I thinking? I'm on suspension, or nearly so. His brow furrowed, his mind spun wildly. *If I take Dutch's gun and have to use it, I'm going to be in really deep-shit! Probably fired ... I couldn't legitimately call for back up either. I'm so screwed.*

His breathing became heavier; his palms perspired. He stared at the weapon in his hand and pondered, searching for an answer. He weighed the remaining options, torn, not immediately finding a satisfactory resolution.

What should I do? "Screw it! To hell with good judgment," he muttered. Surrendering, he holstered the gun inside his coat. "Much better," he said, exhaling a deep breath. "I think…"

Leaving his desk, he strode into the squad room. Seeing him, Mariko got his attention. "Captain, Cal Southern just sent over copies of the medical records from Aubrey Hunnicutt's file. FYI, his blood type is type 'O'."

"Type 'O' again … really, maybe a match with the Reynolds murder scene semen. I gotta' run, Mariko. Armando is loose and Sara Dunlap is unaccounted for. I'll be at my condominium in a minute. Hand me a two-way radio, I may need it later. How busy are you right now?"

"Not very … why? And aren't you on suspension? And if you are, why are you still carrying your piece?"

Ignoring her questions he said, "Contact IAD, the Commissioner's office and Chief Clara Rogers; advise them that I have opted to appeal the findings of Internal Affairs, and the required documentation to that effect will arrive on their respective desks today. Please prepare those for my signature. I'll return later."

"Gotcha', Boss…"

"As a separate thought, prepare a requisition to the powers-that-be for outfitting the entire homicide department with personal, top of the line radio-phones too, okay? Thanks, wish me luck."

Minutes later, Granada Hills, Villa Casa grande complex…
Len parked his Audi next to the curb in front of the complex and glanced at his watch, it was only 9:30 a.m. *I'm still legal for another two and a-half hours. That's good.* As he stepped out of his car he was immediately made aware that the temperature in the Valley West was rising drastically.

Whew! Must be well over one-hundred degrees now. Scanning the street for a police cruiser, Len wondered impatiently, *Where in hell are Remboski and Sara? They've had plenty of time to get here.*

Unaware of the potential ambush that awaited him below in the parking garage, he noticed a blue sedan approaching. It parked behind his car. Sara and Officer Remboski were inside.

She leapt from of the passenger's side and ran to him, crying, laughing and hugging him for all she was worth. "Len, I'm so glad to see you. What's the matter, you look alarmed?"

"I am alarmed! Armando is alive! He escaped from the hospital early this morning. He's armed and his whereabouts are unknown. I want you and Remboski to go to my condominium right now. Stay inside and don't come out for any reason, got that?"

Sara and Remboski nodded. "Oh, no!" she murmured, clasping her hands to her face.

"By the way, Remboski, where did you commandeer this unmarked car? Narc Squad?"

"No, Captain. I thought if we were trying to keep Miss Sara away from inquiring minds, we'd do better in a plainer car. We drove to my place and switched. This is mine. Is it a problem?"

"Oh ... no. Good move. Now, let's go inside where we can talk."

As they turned to leave the hot sidewalk, one of the residents of the condominium drove up beside the trio. The driver lowered his passenger's side window and leaning over said, "Len, I may be paranoid, but two men I've never seen before are in the parking garage slouched down in an old green car. They're not doing anything, just sitting down there in the shadows. I saw you and thought you might want to know."

Len stiffened, *Armando!*

"Thanks, Ed. I appreciate knowing that. I'll check them out. Take care now." The neighbor waved and drove away.

Len turned to Sara and Remboski and said, "Okay, you two, get upstairs while I check out the parking garage."

Len followed them into the foyer. "Remboski, when the both of you get to my place, lock the door and don't open it for anyone but me; that's an order. I'll be back in a few minutes, don't worry. Go!"

"Yes, sir," Remboski answered.

"Len!" Sara cried out as Remboski ushered her to the elevator, "Please be careful!"

Len took a deep breath, nodded and left for the stairs leading to the parking garage.

21

Still Monday morning, June 17...

Jeff Robinson and Josephs arrived at the Cal Southern campus' Main Gate at approximately 10:10 a.m. "Dammit, Duane. No sign of Lana or Wolf. Well, hell, let's do it," Jeff Robinson said, nervously. "They have the arrest warrant. We'll get it later on the way to the precinct."

"Sounds like a plan to me, Boss." Josephs answered, noting the out of character nervous edge in Jeff Robinson's voice.

With the aid of the map provided by the Cal Southern Administration office, they drove directly to the football practice field where they parked the cruiser and entered through the open gate of the cyclone-mesh wire fence. Inside, they walked across the lush green turf and headed toward a large group of young players huddled together in the center of the field.

As they walked, Jeff Robinson asked, "Are you nervous, Josephs? I think I am now, a little anyway. I knew you'd appreciate hearing that."

Josephs looked at Jeff Robinson, laughed and gave him a reassuring jab on the shoulder. "Yeah, the cheeks of my ass may be a little tight right now, but don't worry, I can take care of myself."

The two detectives approached the group of about thirty heavily perspiring young athletes who, upon seeing them, moved apart. The Coach, squatted on one knee in the midst of his players, stopped speaking and looked inquisitively at Jeffrey Robinson, "Is there something I can do for you gents?"

Jeff Robinson flashed his shield. "Excuse us for interrupting, Coach. We're looking for one Aubrey Hunnicutt, is he with you in this group?"

Removing his cap and wiping at his brow, the coach got to his feet and said, "No, detectives, um … I think Hunnicutt's with the red-shirts and freshman over there." He pointed to the opposite end of the practice field. As he did, one of his players nodded.

"Yeah, officers. He's working out with the red-shirts," the player said, following his coach's lead.

"Thanks, thanks too, Coach. We appreciate your help. You boys have fun now." Jeff Robinson and Josephs turned and headed in the direction of the smaller group.

"Think those young kids are enjoying themselves out here today, scrimmaging under this hot sun with full pads?" Jeff Robinson asked, beads of gleaming perspiration forming on his tense face.

Josephs loosened his silken tie and wiped his forehead with his handkerchief, "I can't say, but for me on a day like this, my choice would be the beach. Wait a minute, Lieutenant, my shoelace is untied…"

Jeff Robinson, taking a cue from his young partner, removed his handkerchief, wiped his sweaty forehead and watched as Josephs finished lacing his shoe.

"There, done," Josephs said.

"Good, let's see what this next bunch shows us."

When they neared the group, a couple of the players turned and curiously stared at them. "Excuse me," Jeff Robinson interrupted, as he entered the small circle of players. "We're looking for one Aubrey Hunnicutt. Is he in this group?"

The players shuffled about as they looked around their small circle. A well-built, sweat soaked young man stepped forward and removed his shiny, dark crimson helmet. "I'm A. J. Hunnicutt, nigger. Who are you two?"

Jeff Robinson flashed his shield and stared at the big, imposing athlete, "Aubrey James Hunnicutt, I'm Lieutenant

Detective Jeffrey Robinson. I'm placing you under arrest for the murder of Lorena Reynolds. Please turn around and place your hands behind your back. Read him his rights, Detective Josephs."

A sudden hush fell over the coaches and the perspiring young players who had gathered around, encircling Hunnicutt and the detectives.

Aubrey Hunnicutt, sneered a half-smile and replied, "Well, nigger, that's such a bunch of bullshit. Who'd you say I'm supposed to have murdered?"

"Please turn around, Mister Hunnicutt, and place your hands behind your back..."

"Yeah, yeah, cop, I'll turn around..."

As Hunnicutt let his helmet fall to the ground, he spun quickly, executing a karate style elbow-jerk to Jeff Robinson's temple. The sharp blow struck the surprised Jeff Robinson full force and left him stunned, almost out on his feet.

Jeff Robinson staggered and tried to regain his balance when Hunnicutt whirled and placed a vicious reverse leg-kick to the side of Jeff Robinson's head. Dazed and nearly unconscious, he collapsed onto the ground with his scalp and mouth bleeding.

"Duane, pull your gun..." Jeff Robinson's words were slurred. "Get him under control; pull your gun ... quick!"

Instead, Josephs crouched and slowly backed away from his fallen partner. Still crouching, he stared straight ahead at the menacing Hunnicutt, who now, mimicking Josephs, crouched in a Karate attack mode.

"Remember, Robbie, we locked it in the trunk. I don't have it."

"Great," Jeff Robinson managed to grunt, struggling to remain conscious while attempting to loosen the two-way radio from his belt at the same time.

Shocked, Hunnicutt's practice mates and the assistant coaches silently backed away in disbelief; to helplessly allow Hunnicutt and Josephs plenty of room for whatever violence was about to ensue.

"I can handle this 'boy', Robbie; try to call for an additional unit and an EMT bus."

Hunnicutt watched and continued to mimic Josephs' crouching Karate posture as both of them slowly circled counter-clockwise.

"You puny pantywaist," Hunnicutt said, sneering as he wiped a hairy forearm across his sweaty face. "I'm gonna' hand your silly shit-filled head back to you and then this 'boy' will finish off your old nigger buddy. Ready sissy?"

"As ready as I need to be, shithead, unless you plan to run your silly-ass mouth all day," Josephs taunted. "I'm not a helpless hundred-pound woman. Today you'll have to deal with a man."

The nearby players and coaches murmured, confused and questioning, wondering exactly what was going to take place.

Suddenly Josephs stood erect, raising his left knee to the front of his chest with his toe pointed toward the ground.

Concentrating totally, and taking Hunnicutt by surprise for an instant, Josephs balanced on the ball of his right foot, his knee bent slightly. With both arms raised high and spread apart above his shoulders, his hands dangled on limp relaxed wrists. He stood poised, motionless, in the classic Karate Crane posture.

"Shit," Hunnicutt said, sneering. "Who d'ya think you're kiddin' now?"

He lunged at Josephs, who with lightning-like quickness, leaped, catapulting vertically, clearing the ground for a millisecond with both knees tucked. His left foot found the turf as his strong right leg shot forward in a powerful scissors kick. The hard toe of his shoe connected solidly with the chin of the onrushing Hunnicutt! It caught him full and sharp.

Hunnicutt's head and upper body snapped back violently with the impact of the powerful kick. Nearly stopped in his tracks, the momentum of his rush carried his heavy legs and lower body forward. He fell backward and collapsed clumsily atop the calf of his right leg, subdued and unconscious.

The hush that previously befell the young football players suddenly ended. They murmured noisily among themselves, standing in collective awe at what they had just witnessed.

On the ground, Jeff Robinson, still dazed, was on the radio to Watch Command Dispatch. "Code-three, code-three… Officer down, needs help, Cal Southern football practice field, alleged murder suspect in hand. Send EMT and additional unit … Jeff Robinson, clear."

Racking a round into the chamber of Dutch's .45-caliber pistol, Len entered the unlit stairway leading down to the parking garage and noticed immediately that the burned out light bulbs hadn't yet been replaced. *This is a break. I could kiss that forgetful old maintenance man right now.*

Reaching the bottom of the stairs, his heart raced wildly as he cautiously peered into the parking area. Perspiring heavily now, his breath came in short shallow gasps. He scanned the various parked cars, the few vehicles remaining there on a hot Valley Monday.

Is it still Monday? His over-active mind mused. *It feels like it's been Monday for a week.*

Reacting to the chatter of his own busy mind, he thought, *Good grief! Can we just shut the fuck up? There's work to do here, plenty of time to dissect the calendar later.*

Suddenly he saw it. *There it is!* Again, his insistent mind chattered, *The old green car and two guys in it! It must be Armando and Jose!*

Hidden from sight of the two fugitives, Len now wondered, *How can I coax them out of there and safely into custody? I suppose I could just casually step out and empty the gun at them, but that wouldn't be too sporting. Besides, I might not disable either of them. Guess I'll have to be heroic and expose myself; make them think I don't know they're here. And knowing Armando, his machismo will definitely force him into making a big play.*

Sighing and bracing himself for the reality of the moment, Len checked the gun and quietly released the safety. He wiped his sweaty palms across his suit front and placed the gun in his *off* hand, his right hand, close to his quivering leg and out of sight of the two men in the green car.

Sighing again, he licked his parched lips and attempted to swallow, but his mouth was dry as Texas sand. Feigning casualness he took another deep breath, "Okay, Morgan, here goes nothin'," he whispered.

Faking indifference, he stepped out of the stair opening and into the well-lit parking garage. There, with his senses going wild, he stopped, intentionally exposing himself to the fugitives sitting in the old car fifty feet to his left. With his nerves reaching warp-drive, he scratched his head, pretending to be looking for something, anything. *So far so good, they haven't taken a shot at me yet. My God! Why am I shaking?*

Feeling their eyes on him, he forced himself to look to his right, away from them as he took a deep breath. At that same instant, he heard a car door hinge creak. He turned quickly in the direction of the noise and saw Armando, gun in hand exiting the car in his stolen hospital scrubs. With a grace belying his bodily wounds, Armando leaped across the old car's hood. His mouth was open and he screamed words that were beyond Len's adrenaline-deadened comprehension.

Len broke and sprinted across the drive-lane. Suddenly everything became a surreal, slow-motion dream. The hard, shiny floor slowly floated up to meet him as he extended his arms in a headlong, twisting dive toward the sanctuary of the row of parked cars.

Armando fired!

"Aaarrgh!"

Len felt the hard sting of sharp pain as the hot slug slammed into his left hip simultaneously with the explosive echoing report of Armando's gun. The hard, shiny floor hit him hard on his ribcage and right elbow, nearly knocking the breath from his lungs. He skidded across the polished floor, stopping when his head slammed hard against the left front tire of a parked car. He rolled onto his back.

"Ungh! Sweet Jeez … that hurt!"

In that same split-second, he aimed his gun in the general direction of the fast charging Armando and instinctively squeezed the trigger.

BAM! BAM! BAM!

"Ummph!" Armando, nearly knocked from his feet, grunted loudly. The three .45-caliber rounds struck his abdomen causing dark red blood to pour immediately from his stomach wounds saturating his stolen hospital scrubs. As he gripped his waist with his free hand, his lifeblood ran down his arm and onto the shiny concrete floor. Severely wounded, bleeding profusely, he staggered, screaming wild incoherent obscenities and came to a stop standing nearly atop the fallen detective.

With eyes half-closed, Armando's contorted lips quivered, but no sound came forth. He shook crazily as he struggled feebly in an attempt to raise the stolen revolver.

With Dutch's semi-automatic in his left hand now, Len winced and fired one shot, point blank.

Armando's throat exploded, sending blood and sinew across the garage and onto the adjacent cars. Blood spewed from his open mouth. The stolen police revolver fell from his limp hand and clattered noisily onto the shiny concrete driveway. Lifeless, his body fell backward. His head struck the hard concrete floor with a sickening thud.

In intense pain, Len struggled to get to his feet when suddenly he saw a large uniformed police officer cautiously approaching from his right. Not recognizing him, Len took quick aim at the officer's eyeballs.

"Freeze! Who the hell are you? Wait, you're not a cop! You have to be Jose, or Pepe! Whoever, *alto!* Stop, right where you are!"

It was Jose, and he stopped. Raising his hands slowly above his head, he glanced at the dead Armando, then furtively at the police revolver lying on the concrete floor mere feet away. He glared first at Len, who was now standing and leaning against the front fender of a car, then quickly back at the revolver.

"Jose? *Ciadado!* Relax!" Len exhaled heavily and shifted his weight, trying to attain a modicum of comfort.

Smiling a slow but pained smile, he watched Jose's darting eyes.

"Damn. You know, watching you looking so wistfully at that *pistolo* makes me think about Clint Eastwood, except I know there are several rounds left in my gun. You can't feel that lucky. Can you?"

Jose snorted and looked away saying nothing. Then he hung his head, the fight was gone from him.

"Len!" Sara's voice suddenly shrieked, echoing loudly off the hard concrete walls and floor of the parking garage. "Are you all right?" she asked, screaming as she ran toward him with Remboski following, panting and out of breath. "Len? Answer me!"

"Stop! Right there! Don't you come any closer! I have a dead man here and another man at gunpoint. There may be others..."

Sara stopped short and clasped her hands over her mouth as she stared at the enlarging pool of blood surrounding her former lover's lifeless body. Tears of fear ran down her quivering chin. Unhearing, she tried to comprehend the situation.

"For Chrissakes, Remboski," Len screamed, "...get her the hell out of here! Now!"

Officer Remboski took her gently by the arm. As he led her away, she continued looking back at Len, stark fear and disbelief etched across her face. With Remboski escorting her, they disappeared from sight, back into the safety of the darkened stairway.

Len kept Jose in his sights throughout that sequence with Sara, his gun held on him the entire time, discouraging Jose from considering any further thoughts of bad intentions.

Feeling dizzy and weak, Len slid down the front of the auto to the cool concrete floor and stretched his legs out in front of him. He switched hands with the gun and with his sticky, blood-covered fingers, retrieved his handcuffs.

"Jose, I know you've probably had enough of this cops-and-bad-guys horseshit for one day; me too." Still in pain, his breathing was becoming more normal now.

"Fortunately, unlike your buddy here, you're still alive, so I'm going to toss my cuffs to you. Take them over to that concrete column. Wrap your arms around it and cinch the cuffs on both your wrists, *comprehendes*? Snug 'em up good, don't try to be a hero."

Jose nodded, retrieved the cuffs from the floor and did exactly as instructed. With his hands cuffed together, he hugged the cool concrete column. Relaxed, but perspiring profusely through the heavy polyester police uniform, he pressed his forehead against the hard cement column.

With both of his hands free now, Len put Dutch's gun aside and reached for his two-way radio. Just as he keyed it, he heard Jeffrey Robinson's faint voice: *"Code-three,Code-three… Officer down, needs help, Cal Southern football practice field, alleged murder suspect in hand. Send EMT and additional unit … Jeff Robinson, clear."*

"Robbie, Oh no! Not my Robbie!"

Len's mind raced crazily. Keying his radio, he called Watch Command dispatch. A female voice responded, Len yelled at her, "Code-three! Send additional unit and an EMT bus to Cal Southern forthwith for Lieutenant Jeff Robinson!"

He took in a deep breath and continued, "While you're at it, you have another Code-three. Officer needs help forthwith, me. I need a unit at the Villa Casa Grande parking garage on Rinaldi Street in Granada Hills: one fugitive dead, one in custody. Send EMT, crime unit, medical examiner, you know the routine. Morgan out, clear."

"Captain Morgan, EMT and additional unit confirmed and are underway to Cal Southern now. How bad is your injury? What is your condition?" the concerned dispatcher at Watch Command asked.

"I think I'll live, I'm fine, just took a bullet … okay, maybe good enough for the condition I'm in," he mumbled, attempting to make a joke. "Patch me over to Commission Harlan Dansforth, if you can. I need his counsel and guidance."

"Yes, sir, one minute, sir. What was the last part of your request? You faded on me."

"Dammit! Just tell Dansforth I need to talk to him! Clear."
"Yes, sir!"

The blood continued to ooze from his wounded hip covering his left hand, saturating the leg of his trousers and the surrounding floor. He was concerned with that and of his increasing weakness.

Minutes passed and he sat staring at Jose. Feeling light-headed and faint, his mind crazily wandered back in time to a hazy spring day on a flat field when his Grandpa George was plowing behind their old horses, Bill and Molly, pulling a single-bottom plow.

Little Len ran barefoot in the new, cool furrow, inhaling the musky scent of the newly turned ground, feeling the cool dampness of the fresh, black Wisconsin dirt on his grimy feet.

The furrow gleamed and shone brightly as it came off the plowshare but quickly lost its sheen as it dried under the bright spring sun. He'd stop and watch intently as the exposed earthworms wiggled, sorely aggravated by the intruding plowshare as they attempted to seek shelter from the heat.

"What?" Len mumbled hoarsely, "Grandpa? Are you here?"

"Len, where in hell are you? What happened?" Police Commissioner Dansforth shouted frantically, attempting to get Len's attention. "Where are you?"

"I shot myself in the foot, sir," a dizzy Len Morgan joked. "Seriously, I just killed Armando, one of the escapees from the hospital and with a gun I'm not supposed to have. I took Captain Ryan's gun. I know I shouldn't have but I took it from his desk. My bad, sir."

"What?"

Len's voice faltered, his words slurred, "I know, sir, if I survive this … I should be fired on the spot…"

"Len, don't try to speak! EMT is on the way and they'll be there in minutes. Save your strength. And any trouble you think you're in is nothing compared to what you've just been through. Understand? Len? Dammit, Len?" Frustrated and fearful, the Commissioner screamed loudly into the dead telephone, "Why can't you answer me?"

Duane Josephs knelt over his stricken partner, using his body to shade Jeffrey Robinson's face from the hot morning sun. The coach of the freshman squad and two of the biggest football players pulled a dazed, weak-kneed Hunnicutt to his feet and held him securely to prevent him from inflicting any more damage on anyone.

Jeff Robinson stared through blurry eyes at his new partner, "Jeez, rookie, I … I didn't know you were a Karate expert. When? I mean, where in hell did you learn that?"

"Don't speak anymore; your jaw appears to be dislocated. Hush."

Jeff Robinson nodded.

"If you promise not to tell anyone our secret," Josephs confided quietly, "I learned it from watching Ralph Macchio in the Karate Kid movie a dozen times. Satisfied? Now relax, don't try to talk and don't move. Hey, there's Lana and Wolf. You guys! We're here! Over here!"

Detective Sergeant Svetlana Belanova and Detective Wolf Mueller took Hunnicutt from the grasp of his former teammates and watched as Josephs read him his rights. Wolf Mueller handcuffed him and put him in shackles he'd retrieved from the trunk of their cruiser. Secured, subdued, and soaked with stinking sweat, young Aubrey Hunnicutt, still groggy, sat silently on the ground, to await the additional unit and the ride to lockup.

EMT arrived and hustled Jeff Robinson away to Valley General Hospital for treatment and observation.

Josephs, using Jeff Robinson's two-way radio, advised the additional unit that the situation was well in hand, but they needed to get over here and take custody of Hunnicutt.

Svetlana Belanova smiled approvingly as she looked first at Hunnicutt's heavily bruised chin, then back at Josephs. She nodded her approval. "Duane, it appears that you ate that smartass' lunch. I'm proud of you, kid!" she said, slapping Josephs' sweat-soaked back. "Oh … and here's the arrest warrant from Judge Shepherd. You'll need it."

"All in a day's work, ma'am," Josephs replied, blushing.

At that moment, the additional cruiser arrived. The three detectives kept watch of the subdued Hunnicutt while the uniformed officers crossed the playing field to meet them.

"Hi," Josephs said to the first uniform on the scene, "I'm Detective Josephs, homicide unit. It's good to see you. This is Aubrey Hunnicutt in the restraints, and here is his arrest warrant. Book him on murder one with malice, resisting arrest, assaulting an officer with malice and intent, battery, and misconduct generally unbecoming a Cal Southern football player. That should cover it."

The uniformed officer grinned at Joseph's remarks and took the accused by the arm. With his battered head still hanging, Aubrey Hunnicutt walked unsteadily across his last practice field to the awaiting police cruiser.

Josephs reached down and picked up the shiny new helmet Hunnicutt had left on the turf. Svetlana Belanova said, "Well, Detective, that should make a nice memento for your first collar. I doubt the university will complain."

"Yeah, maybe not. Thanks."

"If you're interested, we still have a search warrant to implement. When we heard Robbie's emergency radio call we beat a fast path over here. We have to finish so would you care to join us? It's a good experience, learning how to totally trash a suspect's place properly, you might even enjoy it."

"Yeah, I might at that," an interested Josephs answered. "Let me throw this souvenir and my sweaty coat in our car. Lead the way, I'll follow."

The EMT crew arrived at the Villa Casa Grande parking facility garage and discovered the iron security gate had them locked out. They unsuccessfully attempted to lift it in order to gain entry. Frustrated, they radioed for assistance from the FDVW.

Agonizing minutes later the fire department and EMT crews arrived in force. After several unsuccessful attempts, they managed to physically lift and remove the heavy wrought-iron security gate from its tracks. Setting it aside, they rushed in, hoping they were not too late.

Knowing that time was of the essence, the initial EMT crew raced quickly into the subterranean parking area and found Len Morgan, seemingly unconscious, lying in a pool of blood. They gathered him up and with a terrified Sara Dunlap accompanying them, rushed him to Valley General Hospital.

Underway, the EMT driver radioed ER, "Be ready at the door when we arrive. The subject is unconscious and non-responsive; BP is dropping rapidly. Subject's vitals are marginal and he is in shock, three minutes out. Clear."

Aware now of the action that had taken place in the last several minutes; a shaken Mariko Tanaka nervously poured a hot cup of coffee for herself and reached for her telephone. With quivering fingers, she called Colleen Jeff Robinson. "Colleen? This is Mariko Tanaka of Devonshire Homicide."

"Hi Mariko, what's up?"

"Colleen, I'm sorry to have to tell you, but Robbie has been injured."

"What? A car accident? Or has he been shot? What happened?"

"No, he wasn't shot, but Captain Morgan was."

"What?" Colleen interrupted again. "No! How?"

"Please, let me explain," Mariko interrupted. "Robbie got in a major scuffle while arresting a football player at the university. He's been taken to Valley General Hospital for observation. Captain Morgan was in a shootout at his condominium in the parking garage. He is at Valley General Hospital too. Neither conditions are life threatening. Hello? Colleen? Are you still there?"

"Yes, I'm here, Mariko. This is unbelievable. I just returned home from the gynecologist, I'll leave now. Thanks." She hung up.

"Well, I will too." Mariko said as she replaced the receiver.

At the hospital and out of the emergency room, the orderlies carefully lifted the tall, semi-conscious man from the gurney and gently placed him in the hospital bed.

The attending nurse looked at him and then over at Jeff Robinson, "Detective Jeff Robinson, meet your new roommate, Detective Morgan."

"What?" Jeff Robinson mumbled, turning his bandaged head to see. "Len? Is that you? What the hell are you doing here?"

"Hi Robbie," Len said, his words slurred, "I've been shot in the ass, no biggie. It's good to see you again and to share these fine accommodations with you."

"Shot in the ass? No biggie? Forget it, I don't want to know."

"Good…"

"Anyway, Captain, I got here first, so rank be damned. I keep the bed with a view." His words went unheard. Len was fast asleep.

Several minutes later, Jeff Robinson awakened in almost a dream state. Though his eyes remained closed, he sensed a familiar presence near him. Carefully peering out through his bandages with the eye that opened fully, he saw Colleen, his wife, looking back at him from inches away. A soft smile etched her face.

"Robbie, sweetheart," she whispered, "It's me, Colleen. You don't need to talk if you want to rest. Just know that I'm here with you."

Reaching his hand out, searching for hers, Jeff Robinson whispered, "Why are you whispering?"

Colleen covered her mouth, stifling a chuckle. "I guess because Len is sleeping over there with a visitor."

"What?" he asked incredulously. "He's sleeping with a visitor in the other bed? What a pig! Doesn't he have any pride? Someone needs to tell him this is a hospital, not a brothel."

"Robbie, shush, such language! He may hear you. I misspoke; Sara is the visitor's name and she isn't *in* his bed, she's beside it." Colleen said softly, trying to keep from laughing at her husband's apparent confusion. "We just met. Did you hear me? She's sitting beside his bed while he's sleeping. Understand?"

"Oh, I get it. Sorry, Sara. You're Len's neighbor?" Jeff Robinson asked in a semi-normal voice.

"You are sorry," Len mumbled, waking but still groggy from the anesthetics. "...and yes, Sara is my neighbor. I've been listening to the both of you. Is Sara here? I can't make my eyes open. They feel like they're glued shut."

Sara squeezed his hand, and whispered, "I'm here, Len. Now get some rest, you've had a big day."

"Why are you whispering, Sara?" Len whispered, forcing his eyes open. "Because they are whispering?"

Both Sara and Colleen bit their lips to keep from laughing. Regaining her composure, Colleen, cleared her throat and said, "If both of you big men are awake enough, I have some good news for a change."

Jeff Robinson looked back at her through his facial bandages. "What kind of good news? *Good*, good news, or just good news?" he asked, placing emphasis on the first *good*.

"Well," Colleen replied, hesitating, "how about *great* good news, *Daddy*?"

Total silence filled the room for an instant until Jeff Robinson came bolt upright in his bed. "Ouch! Damn, that hurt. Honey, what did you call me? Daddy? Are you saying that you're pregnant?"

Colleen put her arms around Jeff Robinson's neck and hugged him hard. "Yes, my love, we are going to have a baby!"

Len, quiet all this time, stared in disbelief for an instant, and then he nodded and smiled.

Following Colleen's announcement, the door opened and resident Hospitalist Dr. Burt walked in. "Well, it looks like our two heroes are recovering. How are both of you feeling this afternoon?"

"I'm fine, Doc," Jeff Robinson replied, lying back and returning his attention to Colleen. "Except I have to get out of here and back to work soon, Colleen's going to have a baby."

"Really?" Dr. Burt asked, looking at Colleen, "not for a while, I presume?"

"Not for a while, Doctor," she said with a big smile.

"So, Mister Jeff Robinson..." Dr. Burt began, "tell me; how are you feeling?"

"I have a splitting headache, Doc," Jeff Robinson said, "...and the right side of my face feels like every tooth had major dental work without benefit of a painkiller. Is that normal?"

Dr. Burt nodded, "You may have a mild concussion, Detective. That condition may keep you in bed another day. Your jaw was dislocated too, and we reset it, which is probably why your teeth hurt. Being kicked in the face might have a bit to do with your discomfort."

The Dr. turned and peered intently into Len's eyes. "Are you still dizzy, Detective Morgan? Any vertigo? You hit your head hard too. Not a concussion, but you may experience some dull headaches and dizziness for a few hours. Besides your wound, you also bruised your ribs and right elbow."

"I don't feel any vertigo or dizziness, Doc, but I am lying flat on my back too. Did I lose a lot of blood from my gunshot wound? I think I passed out a couple of times in the garage. Frankly, I was getting worried."

"Worried? He was scared absolutely shitless, Doc ... believe me." Jeff Robinson added.

"Go to sleep, Robbie." Len responded.

Amused at the repartee, Dr. Burt continued, "You lost about two pints and we replaced it. Two pints is not enough for concern. You were beginning to go into shock in the garage, and you were physically depleted, probably from a lack of solid food, liquids and adequate rest I'd guess. Do you remember when you last had any nourishment or hydrated?"

Len thought, not answering immediately. "No, I can't honestly remember. Is it still Monday? I know we ate a Sunday morning brunch with the Commissioner and several friends, and I had a light dinner some hours afterward. Oh ... a daybreak breakfast with SWAT that ended up in the gutter in front of my place. Is that enough?"

"When you are running on your nerves, as you were, your body releases a lot of toxins. Anything can happen. In your case, you became weak, dizzy, and you passed out. Your gunshot wound is relatively minor, considering you were shot at close range, but it's a gunshot wound none-the-less. We removed the bullet, luckily for you, not a hollow point, which had penetrated to your hipbone and stopped, not far and there was no damage to the bone. If you are a fan of the old western movies, the cowboys used to say, *'It's only a flesh wound'*. You'll be out of here by Wednesday night, guaranteed. We'll keep you on that IV and catheter a while longer. Now get some rest."

Dr. Burt then turned back to Jeffrey Robinson, "Detective Jeff Robinson, you'll probably be out of here tomorrow. When you return home, eat a lot of Colleen's chicken noodle soup. Avoid chewing gum or solid foods for forty-eight hours or more. I expect that your jaw will calm down in a couple of days."

"Thanks a lot, Doc," Jeff Robinson replied.

Dr. Burt stopped as he reached the door and looked back. "I don't know if you two are aware, but you have a small mob of cops gathered outside waiting to visit with you. I can let a couple in but I want you two to rest and not become agitated. Are you up to it?"

"Sure, if you are. Len?"

"Send 'em in, Doc," Len said.

Valley General Hospital, Monday night, ending of day 13…

Dr. Burt opened the door, "Folks, they're both awake. Only two of you can visit for a while, and don't stay too long, Doctor's orders."

The group assembled outside the room in the hospital corridor had waited patiently for Dr. Burt's cue but understood his limiting instructions. Commissioner Dansforth and

Executive Staff Assistant Mariko Tanaka were the logical choices and they bid goodbye to the others and quietly entered the room.

After waving at Jeff Robinson and Colleen, Commissioner Dansforth and Mariko stopped by Len's bed. Commissioner Dansforth, his face serious, spoke, "Ladies, please give me a few moments in private with Captain Morgan?"

Mariko answered, "Certainly, Commissioner," and she went to Jeff Robinson's bedside followed by Sara.

Commissioner Dansforth stood with his back to Jeff Robinson's bed. "Len," he said quietly, "…first it's good to see you alive and on the mend. Second, since I was the one that appointed you as my Captain of Homicide Detectives I'm not about to throw you under the bus."

His face was unsympathetic. He paused to take a deep breath, and then continued, "I am forced to say that you knew that borrowing a weapon and entering into a deadly situation involving a fire-fight without proper backup is not departmental policy, or professional, or smart. Stupid is not how we do things here; we aren't vigilantes."

Dansforth paused again, "…but you did what you did and fortunately things worked out, except for your being shot."

"Sir…." Len interrupted.

"Please allow me to finish!" Dansforth demanded, sternly. "As of noon today Internal Affairs had placed you on suspension, supposedly to go home. I knew when they caught wind of what transpired before noon in the parking garage they would ask for your immediate resignation…"

"Sir, I…"

"Would you please shut up? So the Chief of Detectives, Clara and I pre-empted that. By the way, Clara Rogers is a good friend to have, in case you ever wondered. Anyway, we met with them on your behalf, to nip-in-the-bud the possibility of your termination from the force. With some heavy-handed persuasion from Clara, and my explanation of the facts, they agreed to amend their initial ruling and they reduced it to Administrative Furlough with full benefits and pay, unless you formally appeal that is. For the time being you will remain on furlough for thirty days, or as long as you need to rehabilitate…"

"Thank you, sir. I."

"I'm not finished," Dansforth insisted. "If you choose to appeal their ruling and waive the furlough, you may function as normal and conduct your duties as Captain of Homicide Detectives for the next ten days, beginning today. After that, you are positively on the outside and your furlough begins. No exceptions. It's your option."

"Sir."

"One last thing, Captain, there will not be a second IAD hearing regarding the shooting in the parking garage." Finished, Commissioner Dansforth shook Len's hand.

"Commissioner, sir, thank you. I really don't know what to say except that I sincerely apologize for my recent actions. More, I appreciate all you've done, and again, I realize what I did was the height of foolishness and poor judgment. I am deeply embarrassed."

"Well, Chief Rogers and I merely explained the facts to that fresh Lieutenant Woodward and Lester Payne. You have a good friend with her too, by the way. Clara suggested that while they were comfortably discussing your previous case among themselves, you bravely played loose cannon in a parking garage, alone, outnumbered, and involved in another shoot-out with two escaped fugitives who were armed and dangerous. Again, you risked your life to protect the well-being of your neighbor. Is this the young lady, Len?" Dansforth asked, nodding at Sara, who had returned to Len's bedside.

Startled, Sara blushed. "Yes, Commissioner, I'm the damsel that gets him in trouble so frequently. He is a dear, sir. I don't deserve a friend like him."

"She's the one, Commissioner. It seems that I'm always around when the situation demands," Len answered.

"Well, let me know your decision, Len. I'll visit with Robbie for a few minutes and then leave for home. Nice meeting you, ma'am."

Dansforth left Len's bedside and Mariko returned. Ignoring Sara, she turned and clasped Len's hand and squeezed it hard. Then she bent over and kissed him lightly on the forehead.

"Boss man," she whispered as tears began to form, "I was terrified when I heard you were in a shoot-out with those two fugitives. You sure know how to screw up a girl's workday."

He squeezed her hand, hard, "Hey, none of that! I'm the only one that gets to cry in here. I actually began crying when Colleen told us Robbie was pregnant."

"Robbie? Colleen?" Mariko squealed and turned quickly, smiling at the two of them.

Mariko gave Len another light kiss and squeezed his hand again. With a concerned smile she said, "I hope you get out of here soon, Boss. The office isn't going to be the same without you. Get some rest now. Good-night, Sara."

Len smiled at Mariko as she turned to leave.

"I think you have a definite fan there, Captain," Sara observed.

"Yes … indeed."

"How are you doing, Sara? Have your nerves settled somewhat?" Len asked, concerned for his neighbor.

"I'm beginning to rid myself of the shakes I guess. These hours of non-stop hell have definitely taken their toll. I'm not as accustomed to it as you guys. I don't know how you do it day after day."

"We aren't accustomed to it either," Jeff Robinson said, eavesdropping. "We just pretend we are. He pretends he's tough and can handle it. Secretly, he soils his boxers like the rest of us."

"Hey! I only did that once so knock it off," Len scolded, looking for something to throw at Jeff Robinson.

"It only takes once and then you're branded for life," Jeff Robinson retorted.

"Go figure," Len said, surrendering.

"I'm ready to leave and let these two heroes get some sleep," Colleen suggested. "Do you have a ride, Sara? If not, I can drop you off."

"No, Mrs. Jeff Robinson, I don't have a ride. I came here with Officer Remboski so I guess I'm afoot. Thanks, I will take you up on that. I should leave too; it is getting late and they need their rest."

"Will you two visit tomorrow?" Len asked.

Bending over, Sara kissed him lightly on the forehead. "Wild horses couldn't keep me away. Yes. I'll be here." Then Sara went over and kissed Jeff Robinson's cheek, congratulating him one more time. "I'm so happy for you guys."

Smiling, Colleen gave Len a love pat on his cheek. "Did you enjoy my Aunt Naomi's casserole the other night, baby? I can bring some for you; there's plenty more where that came from."

"Yeah, Len. You may as well eat it, she'll just throw it out or give it to the neighbor's dogs anyway. Help yourself." Jeff Robinson said.

"Robbie! That's terrible," Colleen scolded, frowning.

"I know. Len said it was terrible too."

"You two are what's terrible," Colleen said, getting in the final word. "We'll see you tomorrow, boys, sleep tight now."

Colleen and Sara got in the shiny new compact sedan that Jeff Robinson recently purchased. "Nice car, Colleen," Sara remarked as she closed her door. "Ah ... I do love the smell of a new car."

"Thank you. Robbie bought it for my birthday. He picked out the car; I picked out the color. Our old one was a wreck and falling apart so he decided it was time. With the baby coming now, I know I'll be more at ease with the reliability of this one."

Colleen turned onto the boulevard and headed east to Villa Casa Grande. On the way, she asked, "It's none of my business, but are you two guys getting serious? You and Len?"

"Serious? Not at all, we're just neighbors. Frankly, I can't see Len Morgan getting very serious with anyone. Can you?"

"Oh, I don't know," Colleen answered. "He had in the past, but his past romances didn't work out that well. He is available you know."

"No, I didn't know, but so much has happened in the last two days, it's been so frightening. Not frightening between Len and me, just the horrible events of the past few hours. I'm not certain that I can even handle staying alone tonight. I was so scared when Armando and his smelly buddies approached me Sunday afternoon. They forced me to stop my car in the street outside my place in broad daylight. He and one of his scumbag pals jumped in and made me drive to their dirty apartment where Armando, stinking drunk on tequila, bound and gagged and raped me at knife point on the floor while his dirty, drunken bastard friends sat around watching!"

"Oh, no!" Colleen gasped.

"Yes," Sara said, breaking into tears. "He said, 'Submit', and if I tried to resist or scream he'd cut my face! I was terrified and wanted to die, Colleen, it was so damn horrible! I felt so dirty, scared shitless and ashamed too!"

Pausing, Sara blew her nose, wiped at her eyes and took a deep breath. "After Armando finally got a hold of Len, he said he was going to let all of them have me while Len watched. And if Len became aroused, he'd use that knife and … and cut him! Colleen, it was so horrible. I thought, 'It must be a nightmare'. I thought I'd wake up any minute. I actually prayed that Len wouldn't come and that I'd just die!"

"Sara, I can't begin to imagine how horrible it must have been for you," Colleen said, attempting to be of some comfort.

Suddenly Sara screamed out! "Oh, shit! I forgot! My car is still parked there!"

Startled at Sara's outburst, Colleen asked, "What? Your car is still at that apartment building? Do you want to get it now?"

"No, no! Not tonight," she said, wiping her eyes again with a tissue. "Although I hope it's still there I don't want to get it now. Tomorrow, when its daylight … I'll get it tomorrow and run it though an auto wash-and-detail shop; to rid it of the stench of those smelly bastards."

Sara shuddered slightly and clasped her arms around her shoulders as she recalled the nightmare. "My nerves couldn't stand it tonight; I'm sorry."

"Honey, don't you be frightened," Colleen said. "It's all over. You'll perk up. Get a good night's rest and things will look better tomorrow."

"Maybe, but I don't know if I can still handle being around Len anymore. It's plain to see his work is his life. I grew up living with that. I didn't like it then, I don't know if I could adjust to it now."

Puzzled, Colleen asked, "What do you mean, if you continue being around Len? Are you considering breaking it off? Why?"

"Colleen, my dad was a traffic cop in Denver. His younger brother, my Uncle John, still is; he's a detective. As a kid, I never saw that much of my dad because he worked hard, all hours of the days and nights. But back then if a man supported his wife and family, he was considered a model husband. It didn't matter what kind of father or husband, he really was."

Sara wiped at her eyes with a tissue again and continued. "Dad would come home late at night, usually drunk. He'd always yell a lot and argue, or beat Mom or us kids. Then he'd go off to bed to sleep it off. Mom put up with it because I guess it was expected of a cop's wife."

"Then he was killed in a high-speed chase. Some dip-shit robbed a liquor store and Dad, who was off duty, heard the call on his scanner and gave chase, trying to be a big hero, maybe get a promotion. You know, sucking attention, wanting recognition, to be as good a cop as Uncle John. Such bullshit…."

Sara paused and stared out of the car window. "After his funeral, Mom never adjusted to him being gone. It wasn't that hard for me; I really hadn't seen that much of him anyway, except for the occasional drunken beatings. Do you see what I mean? I don't want to repeat the same mistake my Mother made."

Sara began to cry again, the tears flowing easily. "I'm sorry; I don't mean to be a baby. My life has been such a mess lately, Colleen. I need to get out of Los Angeles. I really do."

Startled, Colleen looked at her and asked, "Sara, does Len have any idea? Does he know about your father, and how you grew up? He needs to hear that from you, dear, especially if you're serious about leaving. It's only fair. I mean you can't run off somewhere and leave him hanging can you?"

"I don't know. I don't know how to begin telling him. I know I can't stay here, I have to leave this place."

Sara cleared her throat and dried her eyes, "That became clear this afternoon in that garage with Armando all bloody and lying dead at his feet, and Len lying on the cement, bleeding, with his gun on that fugitive. Tell me, have you ever seen Robbie in a situation like that? It made a lot of things change for me and I just can't handle it; I'm not that strong. I'm sorry."

Colleen didn't answer for a moment. "I've never seen Robbie in any kind of action. I don't know how I would react, but how can you just leave? That isn't right."

"Maybe, but trying to explain it to him and failing to do so, then ending up staying here living in despair and confusion, that isn't fair to me either. I refuse to do it."

Colleen parked in front of Villa Casa Grande. "Sara, do you want me to walk you in? I can stay with you for a while; if you want, I will. I'm in no hurry."

"Oh, Colleen, I'd really appreciate that a lot. I really don't want to open that door by myself. But are you sure you want to?"

"Girl, I've got all night and nothin' else to do! Let's go."

Tuesday, June 18, Day 14…
At the hospital, Colleen got off the elevator and walked down the wide corridor to the room where her husband, Jeffrey, and his friend and partner, Len, were resting. She opened the door and peeked in, "Are y'all catatonic?"

Len heard her voice and lifted his head, "Hi, Colleen," he whispered, "I'm awake. Robbie may be napping. Is Sara with you?"

Before she could answer, Jeff Robinson turned his head slightly, "Hey, you two, what's with all that whispering again? What do we have, a cheap, back-alley love affair going on here?" he asked, feigning suspicion as he rolled over on his side in order to see Colleen.

"Cheap back-alley affair? You have a nasty mind," Colleen said, giggling and kissing her half-awake husband. "You should be ashamed of yourself. Our affair is open and public, so shame on you. And, Len, Sara should be right over. I drove her to that apartment so she could get her car. She was going to take it somewhere for a detailed scrubbing."

"Good. Hey, I'm interrupting. I'll take a nap, then; nice seeing you again, Colleen." Len rolled over and was asleep in seconds.

Colleen and Jeff Robinson spent the next hour or so chatting quietly, mostly about their new baby that would soon become such a presence in their lives. When the door opened Colleen turned around expecting to see Sara entering, instead it was the day nurse.

"Good morning," she said. "How are we all doing?"

"Fine here," Jeff Robinson answered, "just a hint of a headache this morning."

"And your mouth and jaw, do they hurt today?"

"Fine, no problem."

"Then you're the winner, Mister Jeff Robinson! You gave the right answers. Doctor Burt said if your jaw was okay and if you experienced no major headaches, you would be free to check out this morning. You're a free man again," the nurse said with a smile, "… as soon as I replace the bandages on your face."

"What about Len?" Jeff Robinson asked, sitting up and looking at his friend sleeping in the adjacent bed.

"We'll let him sleep. I'll come back at noon and remove his IV and catheter. Afterward, Doctor Burt needs to examine his wound. For now, we'll let him rest a couple of more days."

"I see. Do a favor for me?" Jeffrey Robinson requested as she carefully replaced the bandages on his bruised face. "Ask him to page me after he wakes? I don't want him to think I abandoned him."

"I understand," the nurse said, securing the new wrappings. Then she checked the closet for his clothes, "Your things are in here. Take it easy after you leave us today, Mister Jeff Robinson. You can remove the wrappings tonight and leave them off. But don't overdo, nothing physical. I'll send an orderly with a wheelchair, okay?"

"Fine," Colleen said. "I'll take him home and have him rest in bed for a day or two. Right, honey?"

"You're the boss," he answered, smiling as he turned to get out of the bed. He slowly let his feet touch the floor and cautiously stood upright. Minutes later, fully dressed, he stopped beside Len's bed.

"Get your rest, buddy," he whispered hoarsely, lightly touching Len's arm. Turning, Jeff Robinson took Colleen's hand and sat in the awaiting wheel chair.

The midday sun shone brightly on the big oak shade trees outside the hospital window. A gentle tugging on his arm awakened Len from a hard sleep. Squinting his eyes, trying to focus, he mumbled quietly, "Wha ... what's happening?"

"It's me, Mister Morgan, your day nurse. It's time to remove the IV and the catheter. Let me adjust the window blinds first."

Returning, she took his arm and deftly removed the needle. "There, now it's gone. Hold this cotton swab against that for just a minute, Mister Morgan, and take a deep breath...."

Taken by surprise, Len blinked his eyes as the catheter was extracted, "Whoa ... that was interesting," he said, more to himself than to the nurse.

"Are you all right?" she asked, replacing his covers. "Let me come around the bed and change the bandages on your wound."

Len, still slow to awaken, looked at the face that belonged to the voice. *It is a gentle face,* he thought, *not beautiful, but gentle. Perfect for a nurse.* Her gentleness extended to her adeptness in changing his bandages too. She was finished in minutes.

"There. The wound is doing very well, Mister Morgan. Two or three more days and you won't need those bandages."

"Good." Suddenly aware that he was the only patient in the room, he asked, "Where's Robbie?"

"Mrs. Robinson came by earlier today and took him home. Doctor Burt gave him a clean bill of health to leave."

"Oh. Did the good doctor say anything about me getting out of here?"

The nurse nodded her head. "Yes, Mister Morgan. I think I heard Doctor Burt mention that he would release you in a day or two. Mister Jeff Robinson also left word for you to page him when you awakened."

"What day is it, ma'am? I'm confused; they've all been running together lately."

"It's Tuesday, the eighteenth, and past time for your feeding. We let you oversleep so today, lunch or breakfast, it's your choice. What's your favorite, I'll have the kitchen prepare whatever you want."

"Anything at all?" Len asked, bemused. "I am hungry."

"Anything you want. Name your poison," the nurse said, removing a pen and a small note pad from her pocket. "Shoot."

"Shoot? Uh … probably not *shoot*, ma'am. I've done enough of that lately. However, I will tell you what I'd like. Can you round up two eggs over easy on crisp hash browns and diced onions?" Len asked, animated at the thought of real food. "Maybe some bacon too? And strong black coffee?"

"Give us a few minutes. Would you like a fruit juice or a V-8?"

"Both if that's possible. And sourdough toast with raspberry jelly?"

"You are hungry. But first, you must take these pills Doctor Burt prescribed for you. One is for pain, the other is an antibiotic."

Len popped them into his mouth and took a couple of swallows of water. "Did you just bribe me with the promise of breakfast?"

The nurse chuckled, "No, the breakfast is a reality."

Len watched as she left the room. *She's a nice person,* he thought, *not the average over-worked hospital type.*

He looked at the telephone on the table next to his bed. Drowsy again, he considered calling Jeff Robinson but thought better of it. His eyelids became heavy and in seconds, he was sleeping soundly.

A female orderly entered Len's room, pushing a serving cart loaded with various sized stainless steel covered plates. The aroma of the bacon and hot coffee quickly awakened him. He watched impatiently as she adjusted his bedside tray-table.

"This is great, ma'am," he said, diving in, licking the bacon grease from his fingers, "...how were they able to get this kind of food at this time of day?"

"Most of the *getting* is in knowing the names of the cooks. Do you like it?"

"Like it? Ma'am, this is the greatest," he said, wiping his mouth with a big white napkin. "I don't know how to thank you, but this spread is great. Give yourself and the cooks my sincere thanks. Do you do this for everyone?"

"Not all the time. They prepared that *spread* as you call it, because you'd missed both your regular breakfast and lunch, you must have been starving. Now, that you're finished eating, get some rest."

Still Tuesday, day 14...

The late afternoon sun created the cooling shadows of the plentiful oak trees that engulfed the west wing of the hospital. A soft breeze filtered through the open windows inundating the room with a pleasant calming effect.

Inside, Len was still sleeping when Mariko Tanaka quietly opened his door. Going over to his bedside, she pulled a chair closer and sat down. She looked at him lying there, sleeping peacefully. She gently took his left hand in her own, laid her head on the bed beside him and closed her eyes. She squeezed his hand softly and waited.

He stirred somewhat when he felt her presence, her soft, warm hand on his. "Mariko?" he murmured as he attempted to open his heavy, sleep-laden eyes.

Mariko felt him stirring, "Len? Hi baby, are you awake?"

"Hi, Sweetness," he said, shaking the sleep from his mind. "For a minute, I thought I was dreaming again. What's up? You look so serious."

She sighed deeply, and squeezed his hand again, "You mean it shows? Poop."

"Slightly. What's on your mind?"

Taking a deep breath, Mariko began, "I didn't want to become more involved in your personal life because I don't know how tight you are with your neighbor Sara."

"Whoa! Trust me, we aren't *tight*." Len said emphatically. "And more involved in what?"

"I'm really happy to hear that, Boss. I wasn't certain about Sara. Anyway, Colleen went back to your condominium building early this afternoon, to find Sara actually. She didn't answer her door. Then when Colleen visited the precinct for some of Robbie's things, she told me about the talk she had with Sara last night."

"About what?" Len asked.

"About Sara. Colleen drove Sara home and they talked."

"So?" Len asked, softly massaging the back of her neck.

"Len, I'm sorry, but this is totally nuts! And I'm pissed!" she said, blowing her nose on a tissue, and then burying her head in the bedding beside him.

Len stroked her long black hair, noticing that she was wearing it loose today, not pulled back in its normally tight bun. Confused and perplexed by her behavior, he waited for her to continue.

"Mariko, when you come up for air will you please explain this? And *pissed?*"

Raising her head, Mariko blurted out, "She's gone. Sara's gone! She told Colleen last night that she was leaving Los Angeles and she did!"

Seeing her intensity, Len sat quietly and allowed the gravity of her words to sink in. "How do you know this?"

"Paulie gave me your house key to return so I visited your condominium today. I thought you might appreciate some clean pajamas, that sort of thing. I stopped and knocked on Sara's door first. There was no answer."

Len watched and digested her words as she took time to blow her nose again. He became more curious, wondering where this might be going.

Mariko continued, "Then I went to your door, taped to it was a note. I did a terrible thing, Len. I read it. It was from her."

Len ran his hand through her hair and gently caressed her scalp. As he did, he pondered, *Maybe Sara had left. If she left, why in hell would she leave without saying goodbye, or thanks? Something? Where would she go?*

"Len, I'm sorry. Here, I brought the note." She took a wrinkled paper from her purse and handed it to him.

He touched a finger to her soft lips, "Shhh, it's all right, Mariko. Put your head back down and rest."

As he contemplated the short note, the words seemed foreign, as if written by a stranger, and from a place Len didn't know existed.

Dear Len,

This is difficult for me to say. I must leave Los Angeles and you. The past two days have been really difficult and hard on me and the recent events reminded me of too many things from my past, things I've tried to escape from, to put behind me. I know I'm weak, I can't help that, but I know you are strong and will survive. Please forgive me for not having the courage to say goodbye.

Sara

Len finished reading the note. Bewildered and frowning, he crumpled it. Then he looked at Mariko, who was quietly staring at him. Face-to-face, she placed her arms around his neck and kissed his lips softly. It was a long soft kiss. She let her cheek slide past his. Embracing him, she held him tightly.

"Len, I watched you tough it out after Gabrielle left, and I am watching you now with this. Sara blew out of town without even saying thanks. Not too gracious. I know, I'm being judgmental, but even if the two of you weren't close, as you say, she could have at least been appreciative enough of you to seek you out and say goodbye."

He held her tightly, feeling her warm breath on his neck. Then she whispered in his ear, "This is never going to happen to you again. Never ... never again. I love you, Len Morgan."

Startled, Len looked at her, his dear friend and recent lover. Looking into her dark eyes, her face was more serious and intense than he ever remembered.

She reached out and touched his unshaven face. Brushing his cheek with the back of her fingers, she kissed him again, this time with more intensity, more passion. Pulling back from the kiss, she gazed deep into his blue eyes. She kissed his cheek and then the corner of his mouth, then spoke, "Boss, you may think I'm crazy but I really do love you. I have almost from that first day we chatted."

Len held her close and pressed his forehead hard against hers, his eyes closed tightly, unable to respond, desperately wanting, but unable to express his growing feelings and his own love for her.

Wednesday morning, June 19, Day 15...
The sound of an approaching ambulance siren awakened Len from a hard sleep. He switched on his bed lamp and checked the time; it was 5:02 a.m.

Sitting up and gathering himself, he filled his drinking glass with water from the pitcher beside his bed and took a long slow drink.

Well, that activated the old bladder. Let's try hitting the deck and practice some walking, he thought as he lifted his bed covers and slid his legs out of the bed. As his feet touched the cold floor, he cautiously put his full weight on his legs. *So far, so good.*

The night before, he required assistance to walk to the bathroom. It embarrassed him. Today, he was intent on making it on his own. *I need to get out of this place, wounded hip or not, there's too much to do and too little time to get it done. I can't be wasting away in here.*

Mariko Tanaka had visited Len the evening before. Along with some clean pajamas and Sara's goodbye note, she brought a copy of the series of the telephone messages from RCMP Commander Lawrence Fitzhugh. Additionally, news had it that Aubrey Hunnicutt opted for a public defender and the Judge appointed Len's ex-wife, Carole Bullock, who pled Hunnicutt not guilty at his arraignment.

Professionally, defense attorney Carole Bullock and Len went back a long time. She was a highly capable defense attorney with an above average record when it came to getting an acquittal for her clients. She was also a sensible attorney who knew when the odds were not in her favor and quickly made the best deal possible for her client.

Len needed to get out of the hospital soon and meet with Assistant District Attorney Deborah Rosen to discuss the merits of the case before she and Carole Bullock met in an adversarial setting.

In the bathroom, with his early morning rituals nearly satisfied, Len tried to sense what his physical condition was. Spitting out the mouthwash and rinsing his mouth with clear water, he cautiously walked across his room to his bed.

To hell with the bed, he thought, and reached for the notepaper on which the coded telephone messages were printed. He pulled a straight back chair closer to the bed lamp and sat down to study the mysterious collection of words taken from Jean-Luc Gerot's answering system.

"What a bunch of shit," he mumbled. "What's the key to this?" Len continued to stare at the note that challenged his intellect. Suddenly, one part of the note stood out in spades.

"VH-1?" Len questioned aloud.

He reached for the telephone and quickly called Jeff Robinson's home telephone number. After several rings, a sleepy voiced Jeff Robinson answered, "This is Jeffrey..."

"Robbie? Did I wake you?"

"No, dip-shit, I had to answer the phone anyway. What the hell time is it?" he asked, attempting not to yawn. "Forget about it, I don't want to know."

"I'm sorry, buddy. How are you feeling? I'm so used to calling you when I need help. Are you healthy enough to work today?"

"Healthy? And work? I'm okay, healthy enough to go to do some light lifting, why, what do you have in mind? Excuse me," pausing for a second he said, "It's just Len, Colleen, go back to sleep."

"Robbie, remember that day after the stakeout when I was half-asleep and you explained van Haan's personalized license plate to me?"

"VH-1?"

"Yes. What did you tell me about that?" Len asked, adjusting himself in the straight chair.

"Let me get to another phone, Len. I'll put you on hold, okay?"

"Fine." His hip began to throb so he adjusted his position in the straight chair again.

Len waited for a few seconds, and then Jeff Robinson spoke, "I'm back. I explained to you that VH-1 is a major cable TV musical program. Pop music, not the classical stuff you prefer. Why, are we going to a rap concert now?"

Len ignored the question. "I have this garbled mess of phrases that my Mountie friend in Ottawa got from Gerot's phone when the RCMP tapped his line. The letters VH-1 are part of the message."

"Well, Captain. That certainly could be referring to van Haan. Is that what you're suggesting? Wait a freakin' minute, if Gerot's telephone line is receiving a message with a reference to van Haan in it...."

Len interrupted, "That might mean van Haan's ass is grass?"

"Seems highly likely. Why else would an alleged international hit man get such a message? But, a series of ordinary phrases alone don't mean 'jack' unless you know what it takes to decipher them."

"Exactly, Robbie, so I need to get out of here, now. How long will it take you to get here?"

"To the hospital? To get you out? Man, are you on drugs or something? I guess that question is obvious; someone shot your ass. Anyway, you can't just get up and walk out of the hospital!"

"Hey, bud! I've been up and walking around a lot this morning, fed well too, but I really need to get out of here. I can survive. As far as being shot, Doctor Burt himself said it was just a flesh wound and that I'd probably be released today anyway. I'm just accelerating the process a few hours. All I need are a few extra bandage pads to have on hand, you know, to change and replace; *farshtain*?"

"I *farshtain* that crap all too well, but Doctor Burt removed a bullet from your ass and now you are trying to convince me to drag that same skinny ass out of the hospital. What does the Doctor think of this stunt? Have you considered asking him? You're under suspension anyway. What about that?"

"Administrative furlough," Len corrected, smiling, "…and with pay. I'm going to file an appeal to my suspension, which gives me ten active work days to rescind. Besides, I can't afford to stay here any longer. Look, if you're too busy, I have a dime, I'll call a cab."

Pausing, sensing that Len was deadly serious, Jeff Robinson responded, "Save your screwin' dime, I'll come get you. Do you have any clean clothes?"

"Not really, but you can take me home and I'll get some."

"Shit, and I thought my days of chauffeuring *Miss Daisy* were over. My new partner is not going to respect me, Captain. He may think I'm just your butt-boy again."

"Detective Josephs? Just pull rank on him, Robbie. If he complains, tell him he can go back to wearin' the polyester blues. That'll slow his flow, and he won't be dissin' you."

"The blues? But what about his muted red ties?" Jeff Robinson asked, playing the old game and enjoying it.

"Fine. He can wear his red tie with his polyester blues."

Jeff Robinson laughed so loudly that it forced Len to move the telephone away from his ear.

"Sheee... that's too much, Captain. Okay, I'm on my way. Be ready to scramble."

"Thanks, Robbie. I owe you."

"Damn straight you do. Later."

Len put the telephone back on the table and stood again, assessing his situation, *Standing isn't a problem, walking isn't a problem. The part most frightening is the 'in between', the part between the standing and taking that first step.*

Jeffrey Robinson opened the door and entered the hospital room. Though his cheek remained slightly swollen, he was free of facial bandages.

Len sat in the straight chair, dressed in the same disheveled and bloody clothes he'd worn following the parking garage shoot-out the previous Monday.

"Well, my, my, aren't we all wrinkled and snazzy looking this morning." Jeff Robinson remarked, a slight hint of sarcasm in his voice. "Straight out of GQ, huh? Did you talk with Doctor Burt? No. No, you didn't."

"Take my arm. When I stand up, I can walk, it's that first step that terrifies me. Let's go."

The two detectives walked slowly down the quiet corridor. As they approached the nurses' station Len was disheartened to see a familiar face staring back at him, a face looking at him in total astonishment.

"Detective Morgan," the day nurse implored, "what are you doing out of bed, up walking around and dressed like a street bum? You should be in your bed. Who is this person with you, and really, that suit is a total mess."

"Don't scold me, mother, I can explain..."

"You had better explain, sir, and be quick about it because you are going straight back to your room."

"Maybe ... but first, let me introduce you to my good friend and long-time partner, Lieutenant Jeffrey Robinson. Earlier he told me the same thing regarding the suit so you two have something in common..."

"Well, in common or not, you can just turn around, Mister," the nurse interrupted. "Lieutenant Jeffrey Robinson can accompany you back to your bed. Right now, Captain Morgan."

"With all due respect, ma'am, I can't do that. We have to leave here now," Len insisted, concentrating on the unrelenting face of his nurse. "In doing so, we may prevent another needless killing. It's that important. Will you advise Doctor Burt of the urgency of this, please?"

She stood staring at the unlikely pair. Distressed, she asked, "Is he really telling the truth, Lieutenant Jeff Robinson? Is this a life or death situation, or is your Captain tired of our cooking?"

"Ma'am," Robinson began, "in my lifetime, I've never seen him tired of anyone's cooking. And yes, this has all the earmarks of being a life or death situation. The Captain speaks the truth."

The day nurse threw her arms in the air in surrender, "All right, Captain, I'll get yelled at for allowing this charade, but will you at least let me change your bandages and give you your pain meds before you leave? I was on my way to wake you to do it anyway. It will only take a minute."

"My place or yours?" Len quipped.

"Yours, your room, if you don't mind lying back down on your bed for five minutes," she said, "...just to change the bandages." Smirking, she glanced at Len and winked. "Smart-ass."

Shrugging, Len looked helplessly at Jeff Robinson, "Back to the drawing board?"

After she made short work of the bandage replacement Len got up from the bed and again pulled on his wrinkled, bloodstained trousers.

"Thanks, ma'am, you're a real sport. Where can I get a few pain pills and more of these bandage-pad thingies? How frequently should I change them?"

"At your local pharmacy, or better, let's go back to the nurses' station. I'll give you a full package. And I should call for a wheelchair too…"

Len looked at her face. Now she looked almost beautiful, no longer uncompromising and imposing. "Thanks, no, I need the exercise, and you're a sport. I appreciate this."

Len and Jeff Robinson left the room and stopped at the nurses' station for the bandages. Bidding the day nurse a fond adieu, they slowly made their way to the elevator.

As he rode across the Valley with his old partner, Len read and reread the list of code phrases again. "This is mystifying, Robbie. VH-1 is the only thing that makes sense so far. What do you make of the baseball jargon?" he asked, studying the paper.

"Okay, 'One away', there's a one," Jeff Robinson said. "Then, 'Two on', now there's a one and a two. 'Two and zero is the count, steal third'. Looks like a 1-2-2-0-3 sequence. Okay, what in hell is a 12203? A zip code?"

"Could be. What about the 'Hope Tragedy' followed by the 'Green Diamond'? Odd … the Hope Diamond was blue, and linked historically to tragedy with anyone connected to it. I just don't get it," Len mumbled.

"That doesn't make much sense either, unless the 'Green diamond' has something to do with baseball again. Green baseball diamond?" Jeff Robinson questioned. "You know, like a green grass infield? Hey, here we are at your place. There's your Audi, too, still parked on the street. Looks like they left all your tires and wheels."

"Good, I was concerned about that. Will you pull it inside while I change my clothes?"

"Hell, why not? Anything else you want me to do, *Massah?* Y'all want me to fetch some of old Jim's liquid gunpowder too?"

"*Fetch?* Sure, are you buying?" Len asked, chuckling at Jeff Robinson who used one of his favorite old words.

"Why not, Boss. But spot me a ten; all I have on me is my Visa."

Len reached into his soiled trousers pocket and frowned, "All I have is a fiver."

"That's okay, I'll trust ya' for the rest," Jeff Robinson said

Amused at his wise-ass ex-partner, Len said, "Some things never change." He laughed quietly as he took the elevator to his floor. Walking past Sara's door, he noted that he didn't feel any emotional pangs. *That's progress,* he concluded.

Inside his condominium, he went back to his closet, took out a change of clothes and placed them atop his bed. Stripped naked, he grabbed his shaver and made short work of his three-day-old beard.

Jeff Robinson walked in as Len was struggling with his tie. "Here's your poison and your fiver; the coffee's on Jim. This shit should wake you up. If nothin' else, it's hot."

Len took the hot coffee and winked at Jeff Robinson. "Thanks, *partner.*"

"Partner, huh? Just like old times. What's it been, two, three days? You're too much. Where to now? Soleh's Deli, then the office?"

"Soleh's Deli first, then the office."

"Yep, just like old times," Jeff Robinson chuckled as he locked the door and followed his former partner down the hallway.

In the cruiser, Len read the coded phrases again as they backtracked across the Valley to Soleh's. Folding the paper, he returned it to his shirt pocket. "Robbie, when we get to the office, get with Mariko and have her generate a copy of this on a computer screen. Then you two and Josephs dissect it thoroughly."

"Gotcha'," Jeff Robinson replied

Len keyed the two-way radio. "Watch Command Dispatch? This is Captain Morgan."

"Dispatch here, Captain. Quick recovery, sir. It's good to hear your voice."

"Thanks, Officer. Can you call Assistant District Attorney Deborah Rosen's home number and patch me in?" Len asked.

"Will do, sir."

"Robbie, I instituted another order of administrative business earlier; I had Mariko put in a acquisition for top of the line personal radio-phones for the department. Radios are okay, but we need the improved phones too," he muttered.

A minute or so later, he heard a recorded female voice speaking: *"This is Assistant DA Deborah Rosen, please leave a message. I'll return your call."*

"Great," Len grumbled. "This is Captain Morgan, Devonshire Hills Homicide Unit, Miss Rosen. If you get this message before you leave for work..."

"Yes, this is Deborah Rosen," a voice interrupted. "Detective Morgan? Sorry, it's *Captain* Morgan, now. Is that really you?"

"It's really me, Miss Rosen. Am I catching you at a bad time? I know it's early."

"No, not really, but I thought you were in the hospital. That was a quick recovery. What can I do for you?"

"It's my understanding that defense attorney Carole Bullock is representing Aubrey Hunnicutt. Are you aware of that?"

"Yes, I found out earlier. Why? Is that a problem?"

"No, not at all, Miss Rosen, not at all. Have you spoken to her since? And if not, I'd like to schedule some time with you first to review our evidence book and explain what we've collected so far on Mister Hunnicutt. Are you free sometime this morning?" Len asked, as Jeff Robinson pulled into Soleh's parking lot.

"I believe so. I'll call you as soon as I get to my office, Captain. Will that be soon enough?"

"Sounds good to me. I'm having breakfast now; we'll be in within the hour, say eight o'clock?"

"I'll call you at eight."

"So much for that, Robbie," Len said as he slowly got out of the cruiser.

Their early morning bill of fare was light: tomato juice, fresh warm bagels with cream cheese, a large rasher of thick bacon, cottage fries with minced onions and eggs over easy. The conversation was heavier: Aubrey Hunnicutt's case.

"Two days away from the office and I feel as though I need to be retrained. Did Lana and Wolf contact you after they tossed Hunnicutt's dorm room?"

Jeff Robinson, caught with a mouthful of bagel, quickly swallowed and wiping his mouth, answered, "Yeah, I talked to them a couple of times. Hunnicutt owned a dark crimson waistcoat; actually three of them were in his closet. They're at the CSI lab, all of his clothes in fact. Forensics should have something this morning."

Len's brow furrowed, "Is that all we have? Questionable clothing?"

"Oh, no. No, we have an exact clone of the steak knife used to murder Miss Reynolds, 'on loan' from the Cal Southern dining room kitchen," Jeff Robinson added between bites.

"Did Lana interrogate Aubrey? Does she have a statement?"

"No. No one has talked to him except Ms. Bullock and the judge at the arraignment. Maybe that's good, him sitting there in lockup doing nothing. That might be all it takes to soften his hard-ass exterior, think?"

"Maybe; we'll see. Are you finished? I'm antsy, I need to see my desk again," Len declared, slowly getting up from the booth.

"See *your* desk again? So which desk is it now? My new one or Dutch's old one?"

"Damn. A cop without a desk or a gun," Len said, leaving a tip for the waitress. "I wonder what happened to Dutch's gun that I borrowed. I hope someone returned it from the parking garage. It is his, he might want it back."

"Yeah. Harlan Dansforth sent it back. It's cleaned, reloaded and in the center drawer of your desk again."

"Great!"

They were the first to arrive at the precinct squad room. Len went to his old desk and began the process of cleaning out the drawers. The transition from his old office to Dutch's previous office took about twenty minutes, during which time the other day-watch detectives arrived and pitched in, lending a helping hand.

Jeff Robinson then made an unexpected announcement, "Captain Morgan, if I might direct your attention to the squad room, the entire Devonshire homicide squad chipped in and we have a surprise for you. Go get it boys!"

"What?" Len questioned, taken by surprise. "What the hell are you talking ... oh, my God! Are you kidding me?"

Wolf Mueller and Fred Cooper carried in a sparkling new coffee maker and placed it on an empty desk. Svetlana Belanova followed with a new coffee grinder. Behind her was Paul Tobin with a large box of Arabica Blend coffee beans. Mariko and Flossie stood to the side, watching and applauding loudly.

"You mean I have to make the coffee now? No more 'La Brea Tar Pit' concoctions?" Len asked.

"If you want coffee, Boss, that's the way it looks to me," Jeff Robinson answered.

Flossie, spoke up, "Captain, we'll leave it out here in the squad room and all take turns; each day one of us will see that it's made fresh so you can relax. It's my turn today, whenever you are ready."

"Thanks, Flossie, thanks, all of you. What a perfect surprise. The only thing I dreaded about returning was the precinct coffee."

The group chuckled and went on their way.

Settled in, Len sat down behind Dutch's desk feeling totally out of place. One thing came to mind, he'd never seen this desktop so void of papers and trash.

Impatient, he looked at his wristwatch; it read 8:05 a.m. "Hmm ... time's a wasting. I'll call Miss Rosen."

A voice answered, "District Attorney's office, may I help you?"

"Yes, this is Captain Morgan, Devonshire Hills Homicide Unit, is Miss Rosen in?"

"One minute, Captain."

Seconds later. "Captain Morgan. This is Rosen. I was just going to call you. What do you have?"

"You are probably privy to most of this, but from the beginning, Aubrey Hunnicutt is in custody." Len explained. "We arrested him on the strength of an eyewitness that saw a man of his size and build, wearing a maroon jacket in the hall outside the victim's room within minutes of her murder. Coincidentally, he owns three such jackets."

"Has your eyewitness picked Hunnicutt out of a line-up?" Rosen inquired.

"Hardly, our *eye witness* is currently cooling his fat ass in lockup with the United States Treasury Department. He's unavailable to attend a line-up session or much of anything else for that matter."

A concerned Deborah Rosen responded, "That's disturbing. Are you telling me that you arrested Hunnicutt based on three maroon jackets and an alleged criminal's testimony?"

"No," Len answered quietly. "We arrested Hunnicutt based on many things, and our search warrant has produced hard evidence. Forensics has his clothes and they will determine if any traces remain of the victim's blood. Additionally, we have an exact match for the murder weapon that we found at his employ. I didn't mention an East Indian cabby who will testify that he drove Hunnicutt to the crime scene the evening before."

"That's it? That's all you have?" Rosen asked coldly.

"Miss Rosen, if you are looking for a smoking gun, please forget it, the victim was stabbed to death," Len said, sarcastically. Catching Jeff Robinson's glance, Len winked.

"*Touché*," Deborah Rosen replied, her voice becoming more professional. "I'd still prefer a smoking gun and more hard evidence than you've produced. This is a weak case to present in court if we expect a conviction."

"Conviction aside, Miss Rosen, if you are half as clever as I think you are this case won't go to trial. A confession would suffice. Would you accept Hunnicutt's voluntary confession?"

"Is Hunnicutt going to confess?" a more focused Deborah Rosen asked. "Do you have knowledge that he will willingly confess?"

"No, Miss Rosen, but if you will allow me to choreograph a scenario, let's begin by putting a message on Carole Bullock's voicemail right now and state that we want to interview her client at nine o'clock today. After you get the jump on Attorney Bullock, call me back. I'll fill you in on how we play the old poker game. Okay?"

"This better be good, Captain. I'll do this based on your years of wheelin' and dealin'. I'll call back."

Len leaned back into his chair and stared at the ceiling. *It's time to be up and moving around again; I can't afford to become a cripple now.*

He stood slowly and paused for a moment to get his bearings. Satisfied that he wasn't going to collapse, he made his way to the Men's Room. Following that short trip, he poured a final cup of the steaming black precinct coffee from the fabled *La Brea* coffee pot and returned to the squad room where Jeff Robinson, Josephs, and Mariko were studying their respective computer screens.

"Well?" he asked, as he gingerly took a seat on the corner of a nearby desk, "How are we doing?"

"Not a lot of progress, Boss," Mariko responded, glancing back at him. "How's your hip? You should be in the hospital, you know, resting. Shame, shame on you, Captain. Besides, you're supposed to be on suspension. What's the deal?"

"*Mother* is right, Boss," Jeff Robinson agreed, looking up from his computer.

At that moment, Josephs interrupted. "Excuse me, have either of you compartmentalized this pattern of words on your screens?"

"If I knew what you were talking about maybe I could answer," Jeff Robinson said.

Mariko shook her head. "No, not yet, have you?"

"Yeah, this is interesting," Josephs explained as he maneuvered his mouse on the pad. "I just finished. Look, I've made a rank and file 'Tic-Tac-Toe' pigeonhole arrangement, segmenting each of the individual words into their own little box."

Interested, Len got up and limped over to see what Josephs was doing.

"I hear you're clever with your feet too, Duane," he said, shaking the hand of his rookie detective.

"I told Robbie that I could take care of myself, sir. I didn't elaborate on how. Actually, I was scared shitless too, sir. Aubrey Hunnicutt is a big guy, and quick. Look at Robbie's face, you can understand."

"Where did you learn Karate? Not at the academy, that's for sure. What are you, a Black Belt?"

"Not yet, sir, I have a ways to go." Josephs explained. "Actually, I was an extra during the filming of Karate Kid, the first one. I doubled for Ralph Macchio several times doing some minor stunts. Most of the extras on the set were Karate geeks and we all spent a lot of our spare time practicing that Crane kick while standing on a caisson. I got lucky with Hunnicutt."

"I appreciate what you did. But carry a side arm next time, it's much easier, and besides, you won't soak your suit through with perspiration."

Josephs grinned. "All right, first thing tomorrow, sir."

"And Josephs, didn't we have an understanding about that academy *sir* stuff?"

"Uh ... sorry, Captain."

"Great, now what have you got going here?" Len asked.

"I've made this simple, Captain," Josephs said, winking smugly. "Most people understand simplicity; it's far less complicated."

Len smiled and watched quietly for a few moments. Sipping his hot coffee and staring hard at Josephs' monitor screen, he suddenly erupted in total disbelief. "Holy shit! Look at that, Duane! Read that second column of words in your grid from top to bottom!"

Josephs began reading aloud, "One away, two, takeout, VH-1, Denver, Hope, Green, and Redman ... Jeez! Take out

VH-1! It sounds like a hit! A sanction! Is VH-1 van Haan? And they want van Haan killed?"

All of them hovered over Josephs' shoulder and peered at his monitor. "Look at that," Jeff Robinson exclaimed, pointing. "Big as hell. Take out VH-1! That's got to be van Haan!"

"But what does 'One away and two' have to do with anything?" Mariko asked. "More hits?"

Josephs answered, "I think it has to do with leaving out the first word of the entries in the code and using only the second word sequence. That's how it worked out anyway."

Fancy," Jeff Robinson replied, "but Denver? Why Denver? Is van Haan being moved to Denver?"

Len reached for the nearest telephone and assured them, "I'll damn soon find out!"

Still Wednesday, still day 15...

In the Westwood Federal building, Special Agent Luis Campanera's telephone rang. "Hello, Campanera here."

"Len Morgan here, Luis. I have a simple question. Where is Duard van Haan, is he still in Los Angeles?"

Campanera, taken off guard for a second, said, "What? Len, you know I can't tell you that or anything about him; he doesn't legally exist anymore. Anyway, that was two questions. What's the deal?"

"Okay, Luis, be picky. *If* he did exist, here's another question, maybe two or three; how many of your people, or any other federal agents for that matter, know where van Haan is, or where he's going?"

"A short list, just a few. Again, why?" an agitated Special Agent Campanera asked.

"Let me cut to the chase." Len's tone of voice became serious and out of character. "If I told you I thought van Haan was in Denver and that Gerot knew it, what would be your first response?"

Campanera became completely silent on the other end of the line, seconds passed. Finally, he took a deep breath and responded, "If you weren't a cop and a good friend I'd have you arrested within the hour. Where did you get that kind of that information?"

"It's a long story, Luis, maybe not so long, but convoluted as hell," Len suggested.

Campanera sighed. "Besides yourself, how many of your people are aware of this?"

"Just the four of us here at Devonshire, unless the RCMP cryptographers in Ottawa have cracked the same encoded message. Now, tell me, how many of your people know of van Haan's whereabouts?"

Sighing again, Luis Campanera answered, "Me, and two others. And the Royal Canadian Mounties? How in hell did they get involved?"

"How? Only that they did. Listen, *amigo mio*, I'm recovering from a small gunshot wound. I got shot in the ass and should still be in the hospital, okay? Basically, I'm bedridden here in my office and I can't jet down to Los Angeles this morning so can you come up here today, like right away? I'll tell you the whole blazing story, Mounties and all."

"Shot in the ass? Do you have a 'copter port? I'll fly up."

"Close to the ass. Yes, a bona fide heliport right on the roof; it's well marked. You can be here in twenty minutes, maybe less. Anyway, thanks. Oh … this is my distrustful mind petitioning this, please swear on your Mother's grave," Len requested emphatically, making it more like an order than a suggestion. "…do *not* mention this conversation to anyone, no one, not even your own people, okay?"

"Right. I think I get it. Twenty minutes? I'll be there. Alone."

"All right, boys and girl," Len said, addressing his detectives, "…Luis will be here soon and we'll get the scoop."

Len's telephone rang. He excused himself from his not-so-royal band of cryptographers and limped into his office to answer it.

"Captain Morgan, this is Deborah Rosen. Phase one worked out. I left my request on Carole Bullock's answering machine before she arrived at her office. She returned my call and is agreeable to holding a joint interview with Hunnicutt. However, she wants to converse with him first. I agreed. We'll meet in your precinct's Interview Room at nine-thirty. Is that good for you?"

"Nine-thirty is just fine. I'll be there. Now let me explain my plan to you…"

Len and Assistant District Attorney Deborah Rosen's chat lasted for several minutes. Satisfied that the plan would get the results they sought, they hung up and Len rejoined his decoders.

"You know, y'all qualify for a fancy Buck Rogers decoder ring now, provided you have enough box-tops and the twenty-five cents."

"Whoa," Jeff Robinson whispered softly, feigning infantile excitement, "I can't wait to get my hands on that."

"Look," Mariko said, pointing, staring intensely at her monitor screen. "This number six and the number twenty-one. Would the sixth month, twenty-first day do anything for any of you besides it being the first day of summer?"

"It does for me," Luis Campanera announced to the astonishment of the assembled group of crime fighters as he entered the squad room.

"Luis," Len said, smiling, extending his hand from his seat on the corner of an empty desk. "Fast flight. It's good to see you again. Please sit down. Robbie will walk you through what we've put together so far. But first, tell me, what about the sixth month, twenty-first day?"

"The sixth month, twenty-first day, or June twenty-one, is classified information, but since you innocently brought it up I can't arrest you ... yet," Campanera said with a big smile. "Seriously, June twenty-one is this Friday. It's when van Haan arrives in Denver. The fact that you know this blows me away. It's scary. What else do you know? And how do you know it? This was classified information. How's your ass, too?"

"My ass is fine," Len said, smirking a little as he folded his arms. "Go ahead, Robbie."

"Luis," Jeff Robinson began, "we know that French-Canadian Jean-Luc Gerot, AKA, international terrorist Yves-Gaston Giroux, knows this too. Len's old LAPD academy mate, Jean-Luc Gerot, looks too much like the international hit man to be a coincidence and we've concluded they are one and the same. Another of Len's academy mates, the Canadian Mountie, tapped Gerot's Canadian phone lines, ergo this garbled bit of nonsense."

"Where is the coded message, Robbie?" Campanera asked. "May I see it?"

"Sure. Take a look on Detective Josephs' monitor."

Everyone watched quietly as Campanera studied the maze of words on the screen. Reading it, he stopped in mid-sentence, his face blanched. "Len, they know the address of our pick-up and drop-off location in Denver! We call it Hope Green. It's a secured location in the residential southeast side of town. Hope Green is a generic feminine name we contrived for a mailing address. How do they know this, whoever the hell they are? Damn!"

Len sat silently, letting the gravity of Campanera' last statement sink in. Exhaling, Len replied, "Perhaps a mole, or your telephone lines aren't secure? Do any of the other words have any meaning for you?"

Campanera stared at the monitor, not speaking. Then he shook his head and replied, "No, except that 'Redman' is a comparable slang term for Native American..."

"Or like *chew*," Detective Josephs suggested. "You know, Red Man was a brand of chewing tobacco my granddad used to buy."

Both Len and Campanera realized it intellectually at the same instant, but Jeffrey Robinson verbalized it, "Chiu, Special Agent Andy Chiu ... sonnuva-bitch!"

The shocked group sat stunned. Len asked, "Luis, is Andy Chiu one of the two agents privy to your classified information?"

Completely shaken, Campanera nodded his head. "Yes. Goddamit!" he said, cursing and throwing his hands in the air. "Why Andy? He's a good agent." Campanera paused for an instant. "Maybe he was *too* good an agent. This explains a lot. I'll have to alert Washington right away. We'll have to arrest Andy before we relocate van Haan."

"No!" Len shouted, slamming his hand hard on the desktop. "Excuse me, Luis, but let's leave Washington the hell out of this! We can't have you nabbing Andy too soon! This is much bigger than saving a piece-of-shit like van Haan!"

Shocked, Luis Campanera stood now and faced Len, curious where he was taking this.

Lowering his voice, Len continued, "Okay, I know, I know, van Haan's a major witness in your bad money bust, but we have an opportunity to capture an international criminal, a hit man, one that I'd personally like to introduce to our California penal system. Let's leave Washington out of the loop for the time being. Do you see what I'm saying, Luis?"

"Do I see a big bait-and-catch in the making?" Campanera asked, a slow smile beginning to form on his previously confused countenance. "Is that what you're saying?"

"*Si, mi amigo*, I think we're on the same page, and I hate that stupid expression."

Len extended his hand to his friend again, "Let's sit in my office for a bit and see what we can cook up to catch our hit man, and to keep van Haan alive at the same time. Mariko, before I forget, did you send a memo on my letterhead to Internal Affairs and Commissioner Dansforth advising them of my appeal until further notice?"

"I did. They should have it by now."

"Thanks."

Mariko smiled and responded with a thumb-up.

Completing their private conversation, Len accompanied Campanera to the roof top heliport for his return hop to Los Angeles. As he took the elevator back to the second floor, he mentally reviewed their conversation and the plans for an upcoming trip to Denver.

The plan was simple enough, and dangerous, but satisfied that this plan was as good as it gets, Len thought, *It's going to be interesting to see which of us is the more surprised, Jean-Luc or me.*

As he exited the elevator, he noticed a woman dressed in a suit standing in the squad room chatting with Mariko. Seeing him approaching, Mariko motioned for him to come over to her desk. As he did, the woman turned and smiled.

So, this might be Deborah Rosen, he surmised, returning the smile. *She's certainly not a librarian. And smells better than most attorneys too. Nice.*

Deborah Rosen was the new Assistant District Attorney recently assigned to the Devonshire Hills district. Though she was tall, her high heels accented her height even more. Of moderate build and average proportion, she wore her dark blue suit professionally. Extremely attractive, her closely cropped dark hair, dark eyes and red lips enhanced her flawless complexion.

"Captain Morgan, I presume? I'm Deborah Rosen from the Office of the District Attorney. It's good to see that you are recovering."

Still smiling, Len extended his hand, "Thank you, Miss Rosen. It's good to see you and to place a face on a name. Does your schedule allow us time to discuss a plan of attack before we meet with opposing counsel and the defendant?"

"Yes, we have a few minutes. As I mentioned, Ms. Bullock wanted to confer with her client beforehand. Shall we use your office?"

Gesturing, Len said, "Yes, it's right over here. Please come in and have a chair."

He closed his office door, limped around his desk and slowly sat down. "Please excuse my slow-footedness, if that's even a word."

Rosen took a seat, adjusted her skirt and crossed her shapely legs. "I understand completely, Captain Morgan, it's a wonder you are on your feet at all, and so soon. We heard of your exploits at our offices earlier. It's more a wonder that you are still alive. Your Staff Assistant also explained your choice to appeal your suspension."

Len didn't comment, instead he blushed slightly and idly moved some papers away from the center of his desk. "Miss Rosen, I view my pending furlough actually as a long-awaited vacation, nothing more, but I want to take it on my timetable."

He looked up at her; she nodded. "Please tell me about Carole Bullock, is she tough?" Rosen asked.

"She is more than capable. On a personal side, she is my former wife."

Rosen's head snapped around, "Sir?"

"We were married for about two years back in the mid-seventies. Our careers always seemed to be at odds: her being a defense attorney, me a detective. So both being rational adults, we decided to call it off and we have remained good friends. That's it."

"Really? That's it?"

"Well, not totally … Carole met and began dating one of my best friends a few months later. They married and moved to Ohio for a decade or so. Then Bob, my friend, her husband, took ill and they came back to California. We lost him two years ago."

"I'm sorry to hear that."

"Yes, thank you." Len cleared his throat. "So back to the case, I think if we play our cards right, we can possibly get Aubrey Hunnicutt to voluntarily confess. In my heart, I truly believe he killed her, but I'm not certain a jury would convict him based on my intuition. You've had some time to digest my suggestions since our phone conversation, what do you think?"

"Captain, your plan is a good one, and if you can pull it off and persuade Hunnicutt to confess … more, to persuade your 'ex' to allow Hunnicutt to confess, I would be more than satisfied as you would be."

At that moment, Len's intercom buzzed; it was Mariko. "Captain Morgan, Carole Bullock and her client are waiting for you and Ms. Rosen downstairs in the Interview Room."

"Thanks, Mariko, we're on our way."

Len stood, walked slowly around his desk and opened the door for Assistant District Attorney Rosen.

"Have you dealt with your ex-wife in an adversarial situation before, Captain? Besides your divorce proceedings?"

"Yes, a number of times, and pre-empting your next question, it has never been a problem."

"Good, let's keep it that way."

The two of them took the elevator to the first level of the precinct building where he stopped briefly for a swallow of water from the drinking fountain. He followed Deborah Rosen inside the interview room where Defense Counsel Carole Bullock greeted him, "Captain Morgan, it's good to see you again. I trust you are recovering from your recent injuries?"

Len smiled and nodded at his friend, his former wife.

Carole Bullock, a Harvard Law School graduate and noted public defender, was pure professional. In her mid-forties, she wore her silver-streaked hair neatly pulled back into a soft upsweep. Her gray suit nearly matched her intense eyes; eyes outlined by metal-framed reading glasses, which she kept, balanced on the end of her straight nose.

"The pleasure is always mine, Carole. Allow me to introduce you to Deborah Rosen, our Assistant District Attorney."

The two females shook hands and took their respective chairs. Len took a seat at the head of the elongated conference table; Deborah Rosen sat at his left with her back to the high windowed outside wall. Carole Bullock sat on his right, facing the one-way mirror. The defendant, a shackled Aubrey Hunnicutt, clad in a bright orange jumpsuit, sat to Carole Bullock's right, with a uniformed officer standing nearby. Hunnicutt stared sullenly at the top of the table, exhibiting his usual half-sneer.

Carole Bullock began, "Assistant District Attorney Rosen, Captain Morgan, for the record, I have been duly appointed by the court to act as legal counsel to represent the legal interests of my client, Mister Aubrey James Hunnicutt."

Turning to Aubrey Hunnicutt she continued, "Aubrey, this is District Attorney Rosen. I think you may have already met Captain Morgan."

Still sneering, Aubrey Hunnicutt nodded and looked straight ahead at the tabletop.

"Good morning, Mister Hunnicutt," Deborah Rosen said as she retrieved her reading glasses from her leather briefcase.

"Hi again, Aubrey," Len said quietly. "I'm sorry we have to meet under these conditions."

Aubrey Hunnicutt didn't respond.

"Officer, please remove Mister Hunnicutt's handcuffs. And Ms. Bullock, may I call you Carole?" Len inquired.

"You may, Detective Morgan," Carole Bullock answered. "It's not like we haven't been here before, is it?"

"Right," Len observed. "Carole, let's not waste each other's time. We have a tight case against your client, the defendant. As a result of the murder of Lorena Reynolds, several other killings have taken place…"

Carole Bullock interrupted, "I sincerely pray that you aren't intending to charge my client with those other crimes, are you?"

"No," he said, leaning forward, "we may have another suspect or two in mind for those. What I'm saying to you is this, I think enough people have died already, and Ms. Rosen concurs." Deborah Rosen nodded in agreement, as Len spoke.

"And?" Carole Bullock shrugged as she adjusted her glasses.

"And, we would like you and Aubrey to consider the possibility that if he goes to trial, the probability of his being found guilty is extremely high. As you know, if he, as an adult, is found guilty of a capital offense with special circumstances, he will likely be sentenced to death in the California gas chamber."

"Obviously, you think you have a good case against my client. Let's see what you have first. Perhaps a jury would find my client not guilty; have you considered that?"

"Carole, I've considered the age-old rumor that California will fall into the ocean someday, but I hardly believe it."

Carole Bullock chuckled. "Are you implying that California will be under sea water before a judge or jury would acquit my client?"

"Exactly. I firmly believe Aubrey will be found guilty, and with that finding comes the nasty sound of the cyanide tablet splashing into the acid." Len's eyes narrowed and he stared directly at Aubrey Hunnicutt, who was returning the cold stare. "It's the last sound you will ever hear, Aubrey."

"Len!" Carole Bullock scolded, her eyes narrowing. "That language is not necessary, not necessary at all!"

Len shrugged and stared directly into Hunnicutt's hate-filled eyes again. "Maybe not necessary, Carole, but I believe Aubrey understood exactly what I said."

Hunnicutt turned away, preferring not to look at Len any longer.

"Len, before we go any further, let's discuss what you have in the way of a tight case, then we'll consider the direction I perceive you to be taking." Carole Bullock's expression became more serious as she tapped her pen on her legal pad.

"Fine with me, our complete evidence book will be available to you later today through the normal discovery process. Where do you want to start?" he asked, grimacing and shifting in his chair, trying to find a more comfortable position. "Do you have more than one legal pad with you today? You may need it."

"Just get on with it, please," Bullock answered. Her expression softened as a slow smirk formed. "Ever the comedian."

"Excuse me," Deborah Rosen interrupted, "Ms. Bullock, do you want a police stenographer present?"

"No. No thanks, Ms. Rosen. I don't see any need for a stenographer or a recorder now. My client has nothing to say today. All right Len, I'm ready. Let's hear your evidence, all of it. Start with a motive first."

"Fine, usually a motive is not considered as hard evidence, but I'll happily share my opinion with you. It's all about money, Carole, a lot of money."

At the mention of the word *money*, Aubrey Hunnicutt's eyebrows raised and he glared across the table at Len.

"How does an interest in money enter into this?" Carole Bullock asked, taking note of her defendant's reaction. "What money? Whose money? How much?"

"Allow me a minute to 'Tee up', Carole," Len said, shifting again in his chair. "Aubrey is currently courting the murder victim's fifteen-year old daughter, Laureen. When I attended the funeral service in Tennessee last week, both Aubrey and Laureen showed a curiously abnormal interest in the money left by the victim. No remorse that Lorena Reynolds was dead, no interest in how we were progressing on the case or with the search for the killer, just 'when do we get the money'?"

Noting Carole Bullock's rapt attention, Len continued, "Lorena Reynolds had a considerable amount of money in a joint savings account shared with a friend of hers…"

"A friend?" Aubrey Hunnicutt interrupted loudly, "Shit, she's just 'nother dirty whore!"

Carole Bullock's head snapped around. "Mister Hunnicutt. You will please remain quiet until I ask you to speak. There will be no further outbursts from you today, is that understood?"

"Yes'um," Hunnicutt said, blushing, avoiding eye contact.

"I'm sorry, Len, please continue," Carole Bullock bid as she adjusted her glasses.

"Lorena Reynolds and her friend had a considerable amount of money in a joint savings account. Together, Lorena and her friend were planning a future move to San Francisco: to begin a bed-and-breakfast venture. As I said at the funeral service, the knowledge of that money captured the focus of both Aubrey and Lorena's daughter Laureen."

"The ol' woman wanted to git her greedy hands on it too!" Aubrey Hunnicutt loudly protested, coming out of his chair.

"Sit down, Mister Hunnicutt!" Carole Bullock ordered, moving to the edge of her chair seat. "You will do well to remain silent and *not* speak nor make any further noise until you are asked. Do you understand me?"

Staring at the tabletop again, Hunnicutt merely nodded.

Ignoring the outburst, Len cleared his throat and continued, "My contention is that your client and the victim's daughter knew about the money and maybe guessed they knew where some of it was kept."

"Stop … back to my initial question; 'the money'. You keep mentioning it. How much money are you talking about?"

"Uh … in excess of $128,000.00, which was previously held in a joint account; previously, because it's not there now."

Aubrey's head snapped around, "Well, where the hell is it?"

Carole Bullock glared at him again. "Mister Hunnicutt, just shut the hell up! And Len, *previously*? Not there?"

"We have no idea where it is. That's a fact. May I continue?"

"Please do."

"We contend that Aubrey visited Lorena Reynolds the night before her death in order to get any money she had, or a portion of it. When he was unsuccessful and obviously capable of rage, as we've seen here today, he murdered her. He does exhibit a temper. Do you agree?"

Leaving Len's question unanswered, Carole Bullock countered. "I think your motive is lame, it's total conjecture. What substantial evidence do you have?"

"We have more than enough to persuade a jury to send Aubrey to the gas chamber. We have witnesses on both ends of the chronology that place Aubrey at the hotel…"

"*At?*" Carole Bullock questioned.

"Yes, at," Len answered. "We also have his clothing; specifically incriminating trousers and waistcoats. Some tested positive on the criminologist's spectrometer for the victim's blood splatter, a conclusive match with Lorena Reynolds' blood type. Additionally, the FBI lab has Aubrey's initial DNA findings, and they match with the abundance of seminal fluids recovered from the victim and her bedding. Further DNA comparisons will tighten that noose. Excuse the metaphor." Pausing, he studied her impassive expression, waiting, hoping for some glimmer of understanding.

Carole Bullock paused briefly in her note taking and looked blankly at the one-way mirror behind Deborah Rosen, then at her client. Releasing a sigh, she said quietly, "Go on."

"We have the actual murder weapon and a duplicate match of the weapon: a steak knife from the Cal Southern University dining room kitchen where Aubrey is employed as a waiter/busboy. We have a cabby who immediately picked Aubrey out of a group of pictures. The cabby will testify that he drove Aubrey to the hotel on the night before the murder and how Aubrey paid his fare, in mostly small bills and change; change that a waiter/busboy would accumulate. We also have a near eyewitness to the crime, one of Lorena's regular clients, a 'John', who provided us with a sworn deposition before being called out of town."

Carole Bullock's curiosity seemed to rise with that statement.

Noting that, Len continued. "Our eyewitness, the 'John', will testify that he saw Aubrey in the hotel hallway outside Lorena's room that morning, minutes, and maybe seconds after the killing."

"Excuse me, Len, have either men, the cabby or the 'John', picked my client from a lineup?"

"As I said, the cabby immediately identified Aubrey's face from a collection of a dozen random photos. Our second witness has not been readily available. We are waiting for a time convenient to both witnesses, and then we'll place Aubrey in a lineup."

"Who in hell's gonna' believe a lyin' blackmail victim?" a red-faced Aubrey Hunnicutt screamed as he jumped up, his fists clenched white with rage. He looked at his astonished attorney, then glared at Len, who stared back, unimpressed, but aware that the police officer guarding Hunnicutt was about to subdue the defendant. Seeing the responding expression in Len's eyes, the office relaxed and backed away.

"Who mentioned blackmail, Aubrey? And sit your ass down!" Len ordered brusquely.

Carole Bullock glared at her disruptive client and shouted, "And don't you say another word! Sit!"

"Ms. Bullock," Deborah Rosen asked quietly, "do you want a stenographer now?"

Not answering, Carole Bullock took a deep breath to regain her composure and stared at her written notes. She exhaled, more of a sigh, and said quietly, "Let me first advise my client of his options."

A confused Aubrey Hunnicutt looked at his attorney, "Advise me of what options?"

"Mister Hunnicutt, as a criminal defendant in the state of California, you have the right to be represented by legal counsel, and if you cannot afford an attorney, the court will appoint one to represent you. The Court appointed me to represent you. If for any reason you want to replace me with a different defense attorney, all you have to do is ask the Court to consider your request. In essence, you may fire me. Do you understand what I have just explained?"

"Yes'um," Hunnicutt replied, serious now, listening politely.

"And?" Carole Bullock asked.

"Uh … ma'am, I'd be obliged if you might could stay on," a considerably chastened Aubrey Hunnicutt answered.

Looking back at Len, Carole Bullock asked, "What else? What other evidence do you have?"

Len shifted in his chair again to relieve the discomfort in his throbbing hip. Inhaling deeply he continued, "We have a partial print on the murder weapon, more of a smudge, a computer enhanced smudge now. We will also compare Aubrey's right hand with the imprint left on the victim's bruised throat. Forensics stated the killer was left-handed, as is Aubrey. Me too, for that matter, anyway, we have numerous hair and fiber samples taken from the bed and the crime scene. Forensics will take a sample of Aubrey's pubic hair for further DNA comparison. That, along with the semen samples taken from the victim, and the bedding, will conclusively put him in the victim's bed where she was murdered."

"Thank you, Len." Carole Bullock placed her pen atop the legal pad. She turned to Hunnicutt, took another deep breath and placed her hand on his arm. "Mister Hunnicutt, after listening to the preponderance of real and circumstantial evidence presented here, it's my opinion, not a fact, just my opinion, that if you go to court and stand trial, your prospects of reaching middle-age are slim. The state could convict you of murder one. That's first-degree murder. Do you understand what I just said?"

Swallowing hard, Hunnicutt said, "Yes'um, but I didn't go there to kill anyone. I just wanted her money…"

Exasperated, Carole Bullock explained, "But Mister Hunnicutt, you took a damn steak knife with you. That reeks of pre-meditation. Do you understand?" Sighing, she continued. "If you are convicted by a judge or jury, there is a good chance of your being sentenced to the gas chamber, as Captain Morgan so indelicately described. Do you understand that, Mister Hunnicutt?"

Hunnicutt nodded his head and stared at the tabletop directly in front of him. He rubbed his perspiring hands together.

"Earlier, the state tacitly implied that if you willingly confess to this crime, there's a likelihood that your sentence would be reduced to life in prison with little or no possibility of parole. Do you understand that?"

Tears formed in Hunnicutt's eyes and ran down his tanned face. He nodded his understanding.

"Ms. Rosen, do you bring the authority to grant my client a reduced sentence short of the death penalty?" Carole Bullock asked.

"No, Ms. Bullock, I don't," Deborah Rosen answered flatly, removing her glasses and placing them atop her briefcase. "We can't foretell what a judge will rule after reviewing the evidence. I can say this: if your client is agreeable to show and express remorse, and to confess solely of his own accord, and if he does so today, as well as allocute before sentencing in the presence of the Court, our office will strongly recommend a life sentence. My guess is that a judge would sentence him to life without parole as opposed to the gas chamber."

"Carole, we'll step outside and let you discuss this with your client," Len said as he rose from his chair. "Signal us when you're ready." That said, Deborah Rosen and Len left the interview room.

Outside in the corridor, Deborah Rosen said, "Captain, you're a complete scoundrel. You know as well as I do that van Haan can't pick anyone from a lineup, and when did this smudged print suddenly become tangible? I didn't see that in the forensic report."

Len merely shrugged. "I know these things and you know these things. We both know that van Haan can't help us beyond what he's done so far, but she doesn't. The smudge? There is a smudged print on the knife that we can computer enhance. Again, it may not be conclusive, but in either case the important thing is this, they aren't cognizant of what we don't know and can't prove. Look, Carole's signaling to us."

They returned to their chairs and Deborah Rosen asked, "What is your client's decision?"

"My client will confess to murder-two, with a guarantee of a life sentence, no gas."

"Sorry, Ms. Bullock, no way," Deborah Rosen rebutted coolly as she removed her reading glasses again and returned them to her briefcase. "He either confesses to murder-one or takes what he gets from the Court; we spend the people's time and money to guarantee his trip to gas-pellet land."

The room became deathly silent.

Gas-pellet land? What a choice of words, Len thought, as his hip began to throb again. *Funny about this damn hip. While we were going hot and heavy in here, no pain, no strain. Now... ouch!*

Hunnicutt looked pleadingly at his attorney. Then he nodded and began to sob quietly. Holding his head in his hands, bitter tears trickled down the backs of his bare forearms.

"Yeah, I killed her."

25

Still Wednesday afternoon, June 19, day 15...

Len quickly reached for the nearby telephone resting on the Interview table and called a familiar number. "Miss Tanaka, please have a precinct stenographer join us. Thank you."

While he was on the telephone, Deborah Rosen excused herself and left the Interview Room. Len remained seated, quietly contemplating the events of the past couple of weeks, that and recalling his off time spent with Mariko. He called her a second time and asked that Detective Lieutenant Jeffrey Robinson attend as well.

Minutes later, Jeff Robinson opened the door for Deborah Rosen as she entered holding several cans of cold colas. Right behind them, Officer Flossie, the steno from the Internal Affairs Department, appeared in the doorway. When everyone was in the room and seated, Len made the introductions.

"Carole, you remember Detective Lieutenant Jeffrey Robinson. Robbie was instrumental in the arrest of your client. Our precinct stenographer is Officer Flossie, whose last name, I regret to say, is lost to me right now."

"Perkins, sir, Officer Flossie Perkins," she said, smiling. "...actually, now it's Devonshire Homicide Unit steno."

"Hello again, Robbie, Officer Perkins," attorney Carole Bullock said, nodding. "It's always a pleasure to meet with the law enforcement community."

"It's our pleasure to meet again with the public defenders as well," Jeff Robinson answered.

"I presume you remember my client, Aubrey Hunnicutt, Lieutenant?" Carole Bullock said. "Officer Perkins, my client, Aubrey James Hunnicutt."

Len helped Officer Perkins with her stenotype machine and plugged its cord into a nearby electrical receptacle. "I thought you were with Internal Affairs, Flossie. Did you just transfer to our department?"

"Yes, almost, sir, it's effective tomorrow."

"Do tell," Len said, smirking, remembering his recent encounter with the Internal Affairs officer, Charles Woodward.

"Yes. 'Do tell'," Officer Perkins said in return, winking.

Deborah Rosen distributed the cold colas around the table and resumed her seat beside Len.

"Thank ye', ma'am," Hunnicutt muttered, nodding appreciatively at Deborah Rosen, who nodded in return.

"Carole, you have the floor," Len advised, gesturing to her.

Carole Bullock waited for Officer Flossie Perkins to adjust herself in her chair and make ready her transcribing machine. The rest of the group waited quietly. Aubrey Hunnicutt fidgeted nervously in his chair and sipped at his cola.

Carole Bullock began, "Know all men by these presents: Aubrey James Hunnicutt will be sworn and deposed on this day, June nineteen, nineteen-ninety six, knowingly admitting to his guilt in the slaying of one Lorena Reynolds, on the morning of June five, nineteen-ninety six. Are we ready?"

"Aubrey, raise your right hand," Carole Bullock intoned. "Do you swear that the testimony you are about to give is the truth, the whole truth, and nothing but the truth, so help you God?"

"Yes'um, I do," Hunnicutt whispered.

Attorney Bullock continued, "First, state your full name, place of birth, and occupation. Then relate your story, please."

Clearing his throat, Hunnicutt declared, "I'm Aubrey James Hunnicutt. I was born on March nineteen, nineteen-seventy-seven in Gatlinburg, Tennessee. I work at the University Dinin' Room at the Cal Southern University campus. I'm a student with a football scholarship; I mean I was a student...."

Seeing her client faltering, Carole Bullock poured him a glass of water from the pitcher. "Take your time Aubrey. We aren't in any hurry. Proceed whenever you are ready."

Hunnicutt took the glass of water, drank all of it and continued. "I killed Mrs. Reynolds. Afore that I'd know'd her a long time from me datin' her daughter, Laureen, back in New Lebanon. Laureen'd told me about her ma's plans to move to San Francisco and open a restaurant or somethin'. Laureen said she and her granny would be leaving New Lebanon when her ma moved. She told me once that her ma had a lot of money saved up, that she kept some of it hidden away in her room. The rest of it was in a bank." Pausing he asked, "Would you pass that water pitcher, please?"

Jeffrey Robinson pushed the pitcher across the table within Hunnicutt's reach. Drinking another glass, he continued. "I don't remember exactly when it was that she told me about her ma gettin' them big blackmail payments; it must'a been after one of her visits to California. I know when Laureen came back home, she was all decked out in nice clothes and all. It must'a been around last Christmas time, I don't rightly recollect."

Len interrupted, "Aubrey, how did you know the money came from blackmail payments?"

Aubrey Hunnicutt stopped speaking and looked at Carole Bullock, seeking a response.

"Aubrey, we don't expect you to remember every detail of your life, just relate the details that involve the slaying," Carole Bullock advised him as she removed her glasses and pinched the bridge of her nose. "What about the blackmail?"

"Well, ma'am, Laureen told me all about that money first, and then how her ma had blackmailed this rich guy that was willin' to pay to keep her mouth shut. I thought she was kiddin' when she said how much money her ma had. I come from a poor family. My kin scraped to put me into Brentwood Academy so's I could play major high school football. We ne'er ever had enough money. I figger'd if Laureen and I were fixin' to get married one day some of that money might could be ours. I figger'd if I knew when she collected the blackmail, I'd be waitin' there one day and get it away from her, 'splainin' how Laureen and I were gonna' be needin' it and all."

"Aubrey," Len asked, "how did you determine when the blackmail payment was made? How did you learn that?"

Hunnicutt looked at Carole Bullock again, Bullock nodded, Hunnicutt answered. "Laureen's ma left some bank statements out one night when she, Laureen, was visitin' here and she took 'em. The bank papers told how much money was in the bank and the dates when she, her ma, made the big deposits. They was always made the fifth day of the month, 'ceptin' for Sundays, so's I thought if I got there on the fourth, I'd have a good chance of gettin' the money from her before she got it in the bank."

Hunnicutt paused, took a deep breath and continued, "I called her number on the mornin' of the fourth. I disguised my voice to sound like, you know, a 'John', and I made a date to sleep with her that night. I said I'd be gettin' into town late and would be there like ten-thirty or eleven o'clock. She said to bring two hun … two-hundred dollars and plan on stayin' the whole evenin'."

"Aubrey, what part of this plan did Laureen orchestrate, or contribute?" Len asked. "Wait … let me rephrase that: did Laureen help you put this plan together? This plan to obtain money from her mother?"

"No, sir!" Hunnicutt answered emphatically. "Laureen didn't have nothin' to do with none of it. None, sir, all she did was volunteer some helpful information. This was all my own idea."

"I see," Len said, frowning skeptically. "Remember, Aubrey, you are under oath here and you must state the truth. Again, did Laureen have anything at all to do with this scheme?"

"No! Nothin'!"

"All right," Len said, frowning again, not completely satisfied. "Please continue."

Hunnicutt nodded and poured another glass of water. After drinking from it, he continued. "I called me a taxi and went to the Valley to her hotel right after I got off work from the dinin' room. When she opened the door, well, she was sure surprised, I'll tell you, seein' it was me. I went in."

Pausing, a faint smile formed on his ace as he recalled the moment. "She was all pretty and wearin' a flimsy little gown; she smelled good too, like right after a fresh shower or somethin'. She said she was expectin' a visitor from out of town so's I'd have to go before he arrived."

Pausing a few seconds to recollect, Hunnicutt continued, "Sure, I knew better, but I said I'd leave when he got there. So then we drank some wine and talked some. I made up a sorry story about how much I loved little Laureen and all, and how young she was, and how bad I wanted to sleep with her, but that I respected her too much and she was too young for that. I told her ma how hard it was, playin' football with all them pretty girls on campus watchin' and wantin' to get you in their bed and stuff, and how horny and worked up I was gettin' and all. That trick worked pretty good on her. She said her visitor must have shined her and now she was feelin' sorry for me, I guess, so's she helped me undress and took me off to bed."

Pausing again, he looked at Carole Bullock and asked, "Do you want ... you know, the details of that? I mean what we did and stuff, or anything?"

"No, Aubrey, please spare us those details. Just answer me this, did you and Lorena Reynolds engage in voluntary sexual intercourse?"

"Uh ... yes'um."

"More than once?"

"Yes'um, four times."

Shaking her head in utter disbelief Carole Bullock asked. "After the fourth time, what did you do? What happened?"

"It was real early, maybe five o'clock I think, just gettin' light outside. When we'd finished the last one I dressed n'asked her if she had any spare money so's I could catch a taxi home. She said she didn't. I knew she was a liar an' I got real mad at her. I knew she had that five-thousand stuck away somewhere in that room and I told her I wanted it. We yelled and screamed and she told me to get out. I hit her … hard, near knocking her out … she was naked and so little. She fell onto the bed. I jumped on her and grabbed her throat and I stabbed her hard, then I stabbed at her again. I don't know how many times. I was real mad. I just wanted that money. I figger'd it was mine…"

Sobbing, Hunnicutt stopped talking and clasped his head in his hands again. His shoulders convulsed involuntarily.

Assistant District Attorney Rosen waited for Hunnicutt to regain his composure. "Aubrey, why were you carrying a knife from the university dining room kitchen that night?"

"For protection, ma'am," he said, sniffling and wiping his nose on the back of his hand. "The neighborhood 'round the campus is bad. Not safe like on the campus. People are gettin' mugged and killed 'round there all the time. I figger'd I needed some kind'a protection if I was goin' off campus at night."

"After you stabbed her, what did you do, Aubrey," Len asked as he shifted uncomfortably in his chair.

"I left the room. Then I heard someone on the front stairs, so I hightailed it the other way down the hall. I heard her door openin' and thought for a minute it might be the rich guy with the blackmail money so's I turned to go back. Just then, he blew out of the room pukin', and a coughin'. I turned and took the back stairs outta' there."

Len looked first at Carole Bullock, then at Deborah Rosen. Jeff Robinson caught his glance and merely raised his eyebrows. The two women's expressions remained stoic.

Hunnicutt wiped at his eyes and continued, "I ran down the back alley and must'a lost the knife some'rs, I know I didn't have it later. Then I saw an ol' bike leanin' against a back fence so's I took it. I rode it all the way back to campus and pitched it away in a dumpster. When I got to my room, I took off all my clothes and showered, then went to the laundry room. I laid low until the funeral. That's it, there's nothin' more."

"Thank you, Aubrey," Carole Bullock said, shaking her head again.

"I'm terrible sorry for what I did, ma'am."

"Aubrey, do you understand you gave this statement under your own free will?" a bone-weary Carole Bullock asked.

Hunnicutt nodded.

"And ... and with your full and complete understanding, and that you are of sound and disposing mind and not acting under duress, menace, fraud, misrepresentation or undue influences whatsoever?"

"Yes'um, I guess so," Hunnicutt answered, nodding glumly.

Carole Bullock looked at Len and Deborah Rosen and announced, "Captain Morgan, Ms. Rosen, this is murder two, that's all. Agreed?"

Deborah Rosen nodded in agreement.

"Very well, Aubrey will sign this document after Officer Perkins prepares it for my review. I'd like the names and signatures of everyone here listed as witnesses."

She turned and looked at her client and rested her right hand on his shoulder, "Aubrey, go back to your cell. Get a good night's rest; you aren't going to the gas chamber. When the paper is ready, I'll review it with you; then you may sign it. I'll see you tomorrow morning. Good-day everyone."

The group stood and one by one filed out of the Interview Room. The uniformed officer waited and took Aubrey Hunnicutt away while a dour Carole Bullock strode quickly down the empty corridor to the main lobby.

Len, Jeffrey Robinson, and Deborah Rosen waited as Officer Perkins gathered her belongings.

"Gentlemen, thank you for an exceptional job of police work," Deborah Rosen said. "It's really a pleasure to win one."

"Thank you, Ms. Rosen, it feels good to close a case too," Len added, "especially this one. However, this particular case seems to be evolving, it's created a few spin-offs. We'll talk again soon, goodbye now."

Jeff Robinson and Len took the elevator to the squad room level. As they entered, Mariko looked up, "So? What happened? Did he crack?"

"I guess," Len said, carefully taking a seat on the corner of a desk again. "I don't know if crack is the operative word. Let's say we overwhelmed him as well as his attorney early on, like an irresistible force or something. Whatever, he confessed."

"Good," Mariko said, "because you have another *séance* scheduled for tomorrow, Thursday, with Jose Hernandez's illustrious defense attorney, Mister Frankie Santini, who wishes to meet here with you and the DA at ten o'clock."

"Did you notify the DA," Len asked.

"Yes. Ms. Rosen will be back tomorrow."

"Fine. Now, Robbie, I need a ride home," Len said. "It's been too long a day, I'm pooped."

"All righty, *Miss Daisy*, we'll take y'all home now," Jeff Robinson said, gently taking Len's arm.

Standing up, but not immediately moving, Len said, "Mariko, child, I'm brain-dead anymore. Will you contact Commander Fitzhugh in Ottawa? Advise him only that we cracked part of the code and Gerot is likely in the states. Don't elaborate beyond that."

"Consider it done. Oh..." Mariko said, recalling something she had forgotten. "Another surprise to add to the new coffee maker, bean grinder, and the radio-phones that may be in the pipeline; motor pool has a brand new cruiser ready and waiting downstairs for you, Captain. They retired Dutch's car to the City Building Inspection department, or something."

"Great!" Jeff Robinson said elatedly. "We can drive your car, Boss. I'll break it in for you tonight and bring it back tomorrow."

"Whatever," Len said, agreeing. "Just take me home."

Len and Jeff Robinson got off the elevator at the parking garage level and walked to the motor pool, the precinct's vehicle service and repair center.

"She's over there, Captain," one of the veteran mechanics shouted. "She's a hot one, sir," he added.

"Thanks, Curly. Keys in it?"

Curly nodded his head.

"Whoa! Now, that's my idea of a fine looking ride," Jeff Robinson remarked, admiring the sparkling new black Ford

Crown Victoria sedan that gleamed under the bright overhead lights. "My, oh my. Such a pretty thing. Look! Shiny aluminum wheels too; not black rims and silly hubcaps. Perfect!"

"Just because it's black," Len snorted, settling into the plush front seat.

"Big, black, and smells good," Jeff Robinson corrected smugly. "Like me."

"That's so much bullshit," Len deadpanned. "Now take me home, *Morgan*, and try not to hit anything."

Out on the street, Jeff Robinson reflected, "It was strange sitting in there watching Hunnicutt telling his story. I felt sorry for his silly ass. Even if he did damn near kick my head off. Did you feel the same way? Am I getting soft in my old age? I mean, first it was van Haan I got soft on, now Aubrey."

"I felt something too, Robbie. I'm not sure if it was sympathy, but it was close. I mean … he's so damn young. He might have been all-pro one day if he hadn't been so eager to make a fast buck. And he's not rocket scientist material, you know, that's apparent."

"Yeah, it's as though some misguided code made it all right for him and his Laureen to maybe think that some of the money rightfully belonged to them."

"I got that too. Or maybe it's a regional thing, although the folks I met in Tennessee were the salt of the earth, straightforward, honest. Even some of the cops."

"So, Boss, do we need to stop at a drug store for any meds or bandages?"

"No. I can probably handle it myself. Aspirin, new bandages I've got at home; it's sleep I need. I've been awake since five this morning."

"Oh, really? And who was the dummy you called at five-ten this morning?" Jeff Robinson asked. "Who was the dummy that rescued you from the hospital and that nice nurse?"

"Okay, so do you want to crawl in the sack with me and take a nap too? There's room, and I'll be alone tonight."

"You're not my type," Jeff Robinson answered as he parked in front of Villa Casa Grande. "Here we are. Are you taking the elevator or do you want to do the front stairs?"

"I'm tough, I'll take the stairs. Anyway, I must have a ton of junk mail to pitch. Remember to pick me up tomorrow morning, and be damn sure you take care of this car." Pausing for a second, looking appreciatively at his longtime friend, Len added, "Thanks for everything, bud."

"It's nothing. Seven o'clock? I'll be here, Captain."

Len got out and closed the door of the gleaming new cruiser. *Nice, solid, it sounds just like my refrigerator ... right now, anyway.*

In the foyer, he checked the mail, lots of it mashed into the small mailbox. "Junk, junk, junk ... and more junk," he mumbled, standing at the trash container, pitching it in, piece by piece. "Okay, another little something from Sara." Opening it, he read:

Dear Len,
I presume you found my note on your door. I am truly sorry for the abrupt way I left. I'm visiting Denver, staying with my Uncle John. Later, when I feel better I'll call. If you like, maybe we can discuss my problems.
S.

He noted the Los Angeles postmark and the date. *She must have dropped it off on her way out of town. My being in Denver will be handy though. Maybe I'll look her up when I arrive Friday. Maybe I won't, too. Who needs it? Still no appreciation.* Crumpling the note, he pitched it into the waste container.

He took the stairs slowly, one-step at a time. The pain wasn't as nagging as he imagined it would be. Most of his problem was fatigue; he was one tired man.

In his bedroom, he stepped out his clothes and stood naked. Eyeing the day-old bandage-pad on his hip, he was relieved to note that it didn't show any evidence of seepage. *Damn, maybe I'm healing. Let's see if it can survive a hot shower. It's been forever since I've had one.*

Ten minutes later, he was toweling off and the bandage was soaked but remained in place. He dried himself and patted gently at the bandage. Wrapping himself in a clean, dry towel, he reached for his robe. His bed looked too good to resist and in seconds, he was flat on his back atop his comforter and sound asleep.

In what seemed like seconds later, the distant ringing of the doorbell penetrated his groggy consciousness. He sat up quickly. Lightheaded but becoming oriented he arose and limped slowly through the living room. He opened the door, it was Mariko dressed in athletic sweats and holding an ovenware bowl full of something that smelled enticing.

"May I come in or shall we just eat out here in the hall?" she asked, kissing his cheek. "Sisters and I concocted this for you. I sampled a small cup before coming over and I want more. If I say so myself, it's great!"

"Come in," he invited, smiling excitedly and gesturing for her to enter. "It smells scrumptious, what is it?"

"Chicken noodle soup, middle-eastern style ... well, sort of. We got the original recipe from Tsibia, our Jewish bobbeh and housekeeper when we were growing up. It's more her recipe than anything else. We just added some stuff over the years. Whatever, Tsibia would say, *'It can't hurt'*."

Mariko followed Len into his kitchen where he placed a couple of soup bowls, condiments, napkins and spoons on the table. With everything arranged they proceeded to eat an early evening meal of the heartiest chicken noodle soup he had ever experienced.

"I really like these huge noodles, where do you buy these guys?"

"We make our own," she explained. "It takes longer, but ... you can't buy noodles like this off the shelf. So, how was your day, love? Did your bullet wound give you a lot of problems?"

He shrugged. "No, not really. You saw me hobbling around. Sitting is the worst, because sooner or later I have to stand up."

Mariko giggled.

"I need a small favor, Mariko, would you replace the bandage on my hip before you leave? I have a package of them the nurse gave me this morning."

"Sure, that's no biggie. If you're finished with the soup, we can do it now, and Mister, I'm *not* going home," she said matter-of-factly as she covered the remaining soup and placed it on one of the barren shelves in Len's refrigerator.

"Oh really? Great! How silly of me. So where do you want to do the bandage? On the sofa, the floor? On top of my bed or does somewhere else make more sense?"

"No, your bed is fine. Lead the way," she directed. "Where are the bandages?"

"In there, on the pullman counter in the bathroom," he pointed, holding onto her arm as he limped slowly to his bedroom.

"Pullman? You mean the vanity?" she asked, looking in the bathroom.

"I guess," Len said, agreeing. "It took me ten years to get used to the word *Pullman* instead of vanity. I always thought a Pullman was part of a train."

Mariko found the bandage pads and taking out a fresh one, sat on the edge of the bed beside Len, who stretched out on his side.

"Scoot over, hon. I need a bit more room." she said, as he adjusted himself on the bed. "Okay, fine, that's fine. Do you want to undo your robe, or shall I?"

He untied his robe and Mariko stared quizzically at the bath towel wrapped around his waist. "I suppose that's all you're wearing, a bath towel?"

"Yep. That's it, I'm nearly *commando*. Just a minute, I'll undo it. Now don't look, okay?"

Mariko sat smiling at this big overgrown child of a man. "Are you shy, my Captain?" she quizzed, watching in wonderment as he fussed, struggling with the heavy towel entangled with his robe.

"Shy? Probably, I'm just not accustomed to having a beautiful young woman sitting on my bed watching while I attempt to preserve my dignity. Know what I mean?"

"Oh, good grief, let me undo that towel before you hurt yourself," Mariko said. "It's not like I'm going to see anything I haven't seen before."

Len chuckled, blushing slightly as he watched her deft hands untangle the thick towel. After tucking the free edge in between his thighs concealing his manly virtue, she rested her hands on her hips. "There, is that all right? Can you roll over onto your side now?"

Doing so, he watched as she carefully removed the dampened bandage from his hip. "Hmm… the skin is all pink and puckered, maybe because it got wet when you showered, but the wound looks good, as good as it can I guess. How often should we replace these bandages?" she asked, looking intently at the wound.

"As long as there's any chance of seepage. The nurse said the flesh damage wasn't that extreme, it just bled a lot initially. Look, it's kind'a scabbed over already. Not a sign of seepage since she put that bandage on earlier today. Great!"

Mariko rose and went into the bathroom. Returning, she brought a small dark colored plastic bottle and uncapped it. "This won't hurt, sweet Captain, if anything, it may tingle."

"Right, tingle. The last time I heard the word *tingle* I nearly passed out. What is that stuff? Is it mine?"

Mariko nodded as she soaked a small pad of cotton with the liquid, "It's just hydrogen peroxide. See? No pain at all, just bubbles and a little tingle."

Len was lying propped on his elbow. "Whoa!" He jerked instinctively as she applied the dampened wad of cotton to his wound. "That is cold!"

Mariko laughed softly, looking as her big man flinched at the touch of the damp compress. Opening one of the thick bandage packs, she gently applied it to his hip. "Is this feeling better now?" she asked as she pressed the tape against his leg, attaching the bandage compress delicately.

"Fine, you're doing fine, kid." Len looked over his shoulder and winked at her as she knelt over his recumbent frame.

Finished, Mariko smiled and reaching behind her head, unfastened the ribbon holding her ponytail. She shook her head and her thick black hair cascaded across her shoulders.

"Roll over on your back, get comfortable," she cooed, another slow smile beginning to form on her red lips as her black hair enshrouded his face.

He obliged. Looking up at her, he placed his arm around her shoulders and pulled her close enough to kiss her mouth.

Mariko responded eagerly, returning his kiss as she snuggled against his warm body. He kissed her again, feeling her kissing him back. They pulled apart and gazed wistfully at each other.

Len spoke first, "I recall something that Ernest Hemingway once wrote: *'Remember, everything is all right until it's wrong. You'll know when it's wrong'.*" Pausing for a moment he continued, "Mariko, I know what we're doing may not be right, but it sure is nice."

"I know," she said, reaching for the switch on the nearby table lamp.

Thursday, June 27, day 16...

The slow rhythm of the classic slow rock music that awakened Len on other days repeated itself today. This time it caused him to awaken abruptly from his dreams. His bed was not cold and empty as in many previous mornings.

Mariko was still there and awake. "What station is that? I like it," she asked quietly. "What time is it?"

"KLVU-FM I think. It's nearly six o'clock, why?" he asked, lightly kissing her lips.

Returning his kiss, Mariko pulled him against her warm, voluptuous body. In moments they were again experiencing each other's eager response. After a while they paused and simply gazed at each other.

"Len, fraternization rules or not, I want to be here with you again tonight, and forever too, if you don't mind. What do you think?" she asked, almost shyly.

Len felt this sudden, intense surge of heat welling within his chest. "I'd love to have you stay over, always," he answered, meaning every word. They kissed again, then kissing her nose, he suggested, "But, let's save this."

"Yes, for tonight!" Mariko answered, giggling. "I'd better run now. I need to return my sister's car. I'll shower at home and see you later?"

Nodding in agreement, Len jumped out of bed. Stopping to take inventory of his hip, he limped into his bathroom as Mariko pulled on her sweats.

Out of the shower, he put on his robe and padded out to the kitchen. He took a container of juice from the fridge and pondered the previous night in his mind as he filled his glass. *Well*, he thought, *I survived an entire night with Mariko. Not bad for an old fart I guess. Poor baby, I don't know for the life of me why she's so attracted to me, but it's not difficult to see why I'm getting more and more attracted to her.*

Rinsing his glass in the sink, he returned to his bedroom and quickly dressed, remembering that Jeff Robinson would be waiting outside soon. Hitting the stairs at full stride, he noted that his sore hip and leg were becoming a fading memory.

Maybe it pays to have an in-house nurse, he thought as he stepped out onto the street.

Seconds later, Jeffrey Robinson arrived in the new cruiser and stopped next to the curb. The big black Ford Victoria gleamed brilliantly in the morning sunlight.

"Great timing," Len remarked, getting into the passenger seat. Looking at Jeff Robinson, he let out a scream, "Jeez wept! What in Mother Mary's holy name is that all about?"

Jeffrey Robinson sat smugly erect behind the wheel wearing a black-leather chauffeur's cap, white gloves, and oversized chrome-framed sunglasses.

"Where to, *Miss Daisy*?" he asked pompously.

"Hah. Just aim us toward Soleh's, *Morgan*, and if you have to check out the lights and the siren on this thing, can you please wait until we clear the neighborhood?"

The shiny black cruiser roared away from the curb forcing Len hard against the backrest. On the way across the Valley, Jeff Robinson did take advantage of the lights and siren to run one very safe traffic light.

"This is a much nicer car than mine, Captain. When do we poor Lieutenants get ours upgraded?"

"Robbie, you only get a new car after you've been shot in the ass," Len said, chuckling. "And y'all don't get no white chauffeur either."

"Yeah, bummer," Jeff Robinson replied, unimpressed. "Say, you looked unusually spry coming out of your building this morning. Must be those bandages are working."

"Yes, it's the bandages," Len said, his eyes twinkling.

Having finished his breakfast first, Len sipped his coffee and watched as Jeff Robinson finished the last of his. "What's the latest word on the RFK case, Robbie? I haven't talked to Paulie and Fred for a while. Anything new?"

"Nothing that I know of. That killer kid just vanished. He must be an out-of-towner, or a newbie to the Valley. His face doesn't appear anywhere on any school records."

"Strange, isn't it?" Len reflected. "Hey! Did I tell you that you're accompanying me to Denver?"

"Denver, like in Colorado?" Jeff Robinson asked, taken aback, stopping between the last bites of his omelet.

"Yes, the fabled Mile-High City. I'm going to become van Haan's double for a day and you can be my *Mister Tibbs*."

"Forget it." Jeff Robinson said, wiping at his mouth with his napkin. "What kind of crazy crap are you talking about now? Is this the plan that you and Luis discussed?"

"Yes, it is. We'll be part of a combined effort of several law enforcement agencies: Treasury, FBI, Denver Police, and our own VWPD; one big happy cop family zeroing in on Jean-Luc Gerot. We hope."

"Explain this *plan*, if you can, in thirty words or less," Jeff Robinson suggested. "I'm more than interested, but this plan sounds like some bad shit to me."

"Surprise, Robbie, surprise. Surprise is our best weapon. It sure as hell worked for us last Sunday night at the apartment shoot-out. Hopefully, it will work for us again."

"Hopefully? Are you bringing SWAT along too?" Jeff Robinson asked, pushing his empty plate away. "I don't like that word hopefully. It's like saying rarely, as in 'I rarely get shot'. So what's the magic plan?"

"It's a good one, and simple too. Treasury is delivering van Haan across Denver in a two-vehicle caravan. Originally, the object was to deliver him to a halfway house, the Hope Green Safety House as it were. From there, the US Marshals were to secrete him into some obscure, God-knows-where, witness protection community."

"Never to be seen again, I suppose?"

Len nodded. Finished with his coffee and getting the passing waitress' attention, got a quick refill. "You and I will be in a second look-alike, two-vehicle caravan on the Interstate in Denver. We'll follow a block or so behind the one transporting van Haan. I'll be disguised to look like him. You'll just be along."

"You will be disguised to look like van Haan? No way. That wouldn't fool anyone, especially Gerot."

"Wait a minute. FBI will have Van Haan disguised too, to look like me. You know, in case Agent Chiu gets word to Gerot so he knows what to expect. We'll both be wearing a dark hat, dark glasses, and a dark long-coat. None of the things he normally would wear. I'll be dressed the same way, except I'll be wearing two or three layers of Kevlar body-armor under my coat, to make me appear to be as stout as him, and for various other reasons too," Len explained, winking.

"Wink at some other fool, fool. Will you be wearing any Kevlar on the back of your stupid head? Jeez! Gerot shoots people in the head, remember?"

"Really?" Len remarked sarcastically. "We are hoping … no, we're *confident* that he won't be able to get behind me. That's where you come in, partner."

"Yeah, partner," Jeff Robinson grumbled disgustedly, "like I want to hear this."

"Gerot always uses a nine-millimeter pistol, you know. He'll want to be close enough to take me out with it first and then put his signature in the back of my skull. You're going to be hiding nearby when I greet him. I'll simply say 'Hello', and politely take him out before he inflicts any damage on anyone, especially me. Afterward, it's your responsibility to make certain he behaves."

"Oh, hell, and I thought this was going to be dangerous," Jeff Robinson retorted sarcastically. "Listening to that hare-brained scheme, I think you should go back to that hospital and get your silly head examined."

"I like the plan, Robbie. Besides, it's the only one we have," Len explained as he finished his coffee.

"What if Gerot is tipped off first? By Andy Chiu? Then what?"

"The chances of that happening are slim to none. Just you and Luis are knowledgeable about this. Special Agent Andy Chiu will be totally out of the loop. When the time comes, Luis will have given instructions to the FBI agents to handle him before he could alert anyone. At that point, Van Haan will be spirited away, like you said, 'never to be seen again'. Care to kiss him goodbye first?"

"Huh! I'd rather kiss your bleeding white ass first," Jeff Robinson snorted. "Seriously, there are better guns around than me. Why do you want me to back you up?"

"I don't need your expertise as a marksman. I want you there to observe how a real cop gets his man. Watch and learn," Len chided. "It's sorta' like ol' Don Imus once said, '*If Gerot wants to play big-time froggy with me, jump on, baby!*' "

"Shee-it! You are one sick puppy," Jeff Robinson scoffed. "All right, I'll come along. Should I bring the video camera too?"

"You do that. Okay, let's go. I have to meet with our ADA and Attorney Frankie Santini in a minute or two. Are you through eating?"

Winking, Jeff Robinson replied, "Well, no. I haven't had any pie."

When the well-fed duo arrived at the Devonshire Hills precinct, Detective Duane Josephs was busily chatting it up with Officer Flossie and Mariko, still sitting at her old desk.

"Good morning, Captain, Lieutenant," Josephs said. "It appears that you're moving better today, sir, not so gimpy."

"Thanks, Duane, I think I am. Isn't it absolutely amazing what a hearty bowl of homemade chicken noodle soup will do? Good morning, Flossie, Mariko. Has Santini arrived, or am I early? And looking at the curiosity on your faces, I had the soup catered last night."

"Oh, okay ..." Mariko answered, showing no hint of their escapades following the chicken soup entrée. "Anyway, you are early, Captain, and Santini will be late if he maintains his usual pattern of punctuality. We were just going over the transcript of Aubrey Hunnicutt's statement. You did a fine job of leading him. Good job."

"It was nothing, I had help," Len answered.

"Help? Who helped?" Josephs asked.

"Hunnicutt helped. I couldn't have done it without him. His short fuse and big mouth made it relatively easy. I just rode along. Flossie, if you have a minute, will you join me?"

The two of them went into Len's office, "Please have a seat, Flossie. I need to get to know you better since it appears you are a part of our homicide staff now. Would you like some coffee or ice water?"

"No thanks, Captain, I'm fine."

"First, welcome aboard, Flossie, and if you don't mind, tell me a little about yourself; finite details excluded...."

Flossie snickered, then she said, "Excuse me, sir, as compared to many others here, my life is a composite of finite details."

Len smiled. "Go ahead."

"I was born and raised in Kearney, Nebraska. I attended the Denver Academy of Court Reporting, graduating three years ago. Anything else?"

"Kearney, pronounced phonetically as 'car-knee'. So how did you, a Colorado native, end up in California?"

"Oh, yeah, a girlfriend from the Academy was from here so I visited her on vacation two years ago. She lived in Venice Beach. I fell in love with everything about it and I eventually moved here. I hired on a few weeks later with the county and they reassigned me to the Devonshire Hills precinct. Here I am. And when did you learn how to pronounce Kearney?"

Len smiled, "Not a lot of non-western Flatlanders know the difference, hmm? Ten, eleven years ago, I was driving I-80 back from Wisconsin and blew a tire. My spare was one of those undersized, midget types, so I limped into Kearney and found a tire dealer located downtown on the main drag."

"I know that place…."

"So I bought two new tires, spent the night at the local Ramada, which was an interesting experience, and left the next morning for the coast in a raging blizzard. Anyway," Len continued, "I'm sure you will enjoy your new job here. Between you and me, you may be replacing Mariko, although she hasn't made her decision to leave official as yet. Our secret?"

"Yes. Our secret. Thanks, Captain."

As Flossie left his office, Len looked up and watched as Assistant District Attorney Deborah Rosen entered the squad room. It was difficult not noticing her. Today she was wearing a red suit, white blouse, white hose, and dark sunglasses that matched her jet-black hair.

Len stood as she entered his office, "Good morning, Ms. Rosen. This isn't a Lady-in-Red-John-Dillinger thingy today is it?"

"Funny you would mention that," she replied, removing her sunglasses. "Donald Trump wears red power ties; I thought a completely red suit might intensify the power. What do you think? Too much red?"

"I like red. It may not be suitable for open court or the legislature, but in here, with Frankie Santini, he may be delighted. Look, there's our Frankie now. Let's go meet him."

Enter Francisco, 'Frankie', Santini, Esquire, Attorney at Law. His entrance was a work of marginal black-velvet art. He swaggered in doing his best Anthony Franciosa impression ... gray silk tailored suit, heavily tanned, chewing gum, and smiling broadly at everyone.

Stopping squarely in front of Deborah Rosen, he gave her his best 24-carat smile. "I'm Francisco Santini, Esquire, and very pleased to meet you, whoever you are."

"Frankie," Len interrupted disdainfully, "please allow me to introduce Assistant District Attorney Deborah Rosen. Ms. Rosen, Francisco Santini, representing Jose Hernandez. Right, Frankie?"

Santini was too busy smiling and shaking Deborah Rosen's hand to notice Len. "It's always a pleasure to meet our prosecutors of law and order, Ms. Rosen. May I call you Deborah?" Santini asked with a wide smile.

"The pleasure is mine, Mister Santini, and you may call me *Ms*. Rosen, thank you," she answered, her voice taking on its normally cold professional edge.

Santini snapped his heels together and lowered his head, nodding, "Yes. Thank you. Shall we proceed?"

Gesturing toward his office, Len invited them to enter. Santini followed Deborah Rosen with Len bringing up the rear.

Mariko, sitting at her old desk with Officer Flossie, covered her mouth to keep from laughing aloud at the magnificent put-down just administered by Deborah Rosen. "He's kind of cute, but why does stupid have to accompany cute?" Mariko asked. Officer Flossie nodded in agreement.

Len sat in his chair behind his desk and looked across at Santini. "So what are we doing here today, Frankie? Your client has a rap sheet a foot long and I personally made the collar at the point of a gun."

"You were in possession of the gun, Captain. My client was unarmed."

"Non-responsive, sir. Your client was wearing a stolen police uniform taken from a fellow officer, a friend of mine. An officer who has a concussion as a result of your client's bad intentions," Len added.

Attorney Rosen sorted through her briefcase and looking up, she asked, "Mister Santini, what is your client's name again, also, what is his docket number?"

"I represent Jose 'Pepe' Hernandez, Madam Prosecutor, and his docket number is…" he paused while he opened his briefcase. "Yes, his number is D, as in Devonshire, 9762. D-9762," he repeated.

"Thank you. And again, do call me *Ms.* Rosen. There's no need for that *Madam Prosecutor* shit around here," she said icily.

Swallowing hard, Santini replied, "Thank you, Ms. Rosen, yes."

Len watched this interesting sparring match and was highly amused. *Ms. Rosen two, Santini zero.*

"Mister Santini," Deborah Rosen began, looking at a paper from her briefcase. "Let's cut to the chase. Your client is looking at some bad time. He's been accused of some major work, sir: kidnapping, accessory to rape, auto theft, involved in a two shoot-outs. I don't see a plea bargain here; I don't see anything at all. So, why are you here?"

"I thought the same thing myself, before one vital piece of information became available to me. To background: Jose was a late arrival at the apartment where Miss Dunlap was held captive following her abduction and her assault, or rape as you suggested. He didn't arrive in town until later in the evening. Jose is guilty of merely being in the apartment when SWAT arrived. The facts, the police report, show that he was sleeping on a sofa under one of the windows when SWAT broke through. He wasn't armed, nothing."

"Is your 'vital piece of evidence', as you refer to it, tangible?" Deborah Rosen asked.

"Yes. I would call it tangible. It's a true copy of a traffic citation my client received outside of San Diego earlier that evening. Here, take a look," he said, handing Deborah Rosen a Xerox copy of the citation. "You will note the time and date indicated show that Jose was north of San Diego at 11:48 p.m.

I haven't clocked the exact mileage from the Del Mar-Via De La Valle exit, but I would guess it's close to two hours driving time, even if you speed."

"Len, what time did SWAT log in their report? What time did the shootings take place?" Rosen asked.

"We know that Sara Dunlap was abducted earlier in the evening, but there is no record of time. It's my recollection, too, that the shooting started well into the morning, 3:15 am or thereabouts. Also, I make that drive to San Diego occasionally. The junction Frankie identified is roughly two and one-half hours from here, with good time that is. May I see the citation?"

"Please continue, Mister Santini," Deborah Rosen directed, handing the citation to Len.

"Thank you. I contend that Jose was a late arrival to the crime scene. He was sleeping when SWAT came through the windows. The police report backs that up. The glass wounds to his face and neck confirm that as well."

"What is your point, Mister Santini?"

"It's simple; my point is that Jose is guilty of car theft, nothing more. That's my point," a frustrated Santini said. "I will move that the other charges be stricken."

"Frankie," Len began, "besides vehicular theft, Jose, is also charged with battery on an officer of the law and impersonating an officer. He's also looking at felony menacing and he is certainly an accomplice to attempted premeditated murder of a police officer, me. Think it over before you embarrass yourself by filing a weak motion."

"Lieutenant, my client did not assault your officer with his own weapon. Your forensics lab informed me that fingerprints lifted from the weapon belonged to the officer and to Armando Alvarez, now deceased. Armando struck the officer."

"Damn it, Frankie! Get serious!" Len yelled, his patience with Santini wearing thin. "Your client physically restrained and subdued the officer long enough for Armando to remove the gun from the holster and strike him. On top of that, he's an accomplice to attempted premeditated murder in the parking garage when Armando shot me. Jose is in deep doo-doo, Frank. Sorry."

Wide-eyed, Deborah Rosen stared at Len, surprised at his loud outburst.

"Pardon my lack of manners, ma'am." Len said, noticing her expression.

Exhaling, Santini paused. Cocking his head, he asked, "Okay, fine. Would either of you like to know the whereabouts of the kid who shot up RFK Junior High School?"

The surprised expression in Len's eyes suddenly met Deborah Rosen's; it was electric. They both stared back at Santini, who began to fidget nervously in his chair, taken aback by their joint reaction.

"Sir, how long have you possessed any information of that magnitude?" Rosen demanded, looking Santini directly in his eyes and holding her stare.

"Why, uh... not long at all...."

"Counselor!" Deborah Rosen snapped, "Are you aware that this borders on..."

"Just a minute," Santini interrupted excitedly, reaching for his handkerchief. "Let's not go there! I only learned of this today when I visited Jose. I'm not guilty of withholding anything. You can't accuse me of that!"

"Sir, I can accuse you of what I can prove. You waltz in here today, smiling, running your slick, infantile suave number, then you go into an idiotic song and dance and attempt to nibble away at the state's case, all the while withholding vital evidence that can possibly bring an alleged child murderer to justice? You're such a fucking disgrace!"

Slamming her briefcase shut, and removing her reading glasses, she continued, "I strongly suggest that you make whatever evidence you have available and do it now, Mister Santini ... that or hire an attorney to represent you."

Déjà vu! Len thought. *That's a class act she has going with the briefcase and glasses.*

"But ... but my client may be in jeopardy if I break the client-attorney privilege," Santini whined, wiping at his neck with his rumpled handkerchief.

"You opened this can of worms, sir. Your client is in custody and is quite safe. Produce your information right now," Deborah Rosen demanded, "...or I'll have Captain Morgan place you under immediate arrest. Understood? Captain?"

Looking across the desk at Santini, Len awaited his response.

Sweating heavily, his once perfectly starched collar having wilted under the stress, Santini blurted out, "The shooter lives with his grandmother. Somewhere in Reseda I think. Anyway, it's just off Reseda Boulevard north of Ventura, in one of those small apartment houses in *Gifilte Gulch*."

"Is that it?" Deborah Rosen demanded, "You have no street address?"

"Jose has the address, or phone number, maybe both," Santini said quietly, looking out into the squad room, not wanting to face Deborah Rosen's wrath again. "Talk to him."

Len hit his intercom switch, "Mariko," he said quietly, "please have Robbie and Josephs join us." Turning back to Santini, "Frankie, accompany my detective to lockup and get all the information Jose has on this kid. If we make an arrest, we'll resume this conversation later."

"But..."

"No," Len said firmly, waving him off as Jeff Robinson and Josephs entered the room. "Robbie, have Detective Josephs escort Mister Santini over to lockup for a privileged attorney/client interview, then I want you to stick around here for a minute, your flight plans have changed. Goodbye, Frankie. Keep your nose clean."

"I'll be leaving too, Captain," Deborah Rosen said as Santini departed Len's office. "Keep me informed?"

"I shall. Nice work too," he said, grinning and extending his hand. "You know, you do that briefcase and glasses shtick as well as anyone I've seen."

"Captain, it was bad enough *schlepping* my ass over here to listen to that Philistine's *dreck*. I have no patience for that." Shaking his hand, she winked, turned and walked away.

Smiling, Len sat down and leaned back in his swivel chair. Jeff Robinson watched Rosen's departure and commented, "I think I understood what she meant, but I sure as hell didn't understand what she said."

"Robbie, she said what you thought she said. She doesn't consider Santini a *mentsch,* that's for certain."

Alone with Jeff Robinson now, Len rose and closed the office door. Resuming his seat, he said, "Robbie, I need you to catch your flight to Denver today as soon as you can make arrangements. If we're going to risk our asses tomorrow it's important that we know as much as possible about the neighborhood."

Jeff Robinson nodded in agreement. Arising they both went out into the squad room.

"Now, make your telephone calls and get out of here, Robbie. I need a nap," Len said. Turning to Mariko he asked, "Where are Paulie and Freddie? Are they close by?"

"I'll check and let you know. Do you want to see them or just speak with them?"

"Yeah, if they aren't eating lunch or something, have them get back here. We may have a break in the Stamos case."

"Oh, that's great! I'll bring them in right away," she answered, keying her two-way radio. "Oh Len, Dutch's niece, Mary Katherine, is in town and will be taking him home today. Doctor Malcolm released him."

"No kidding?" Len said, grinning widely. "That's great. Must be his fabled rhinoplasty operation worked out then."

Mariko let out a scream! "Stop it!" she yelled, laughing so hard she nearly dampened her panties. Jeff Robinson, on the telephone in his office looked up, untouched by the hilarity he was missing.

Len chuckled too, and returned to his office where he busied himself going over the Stamos case files. There was so little to go over it was nearly an embarrassment. Remembering today's pending press conference, he called Watch Command Public Relations and got an answer on the first ring.

"Hello, Miss Kay, this is Morgan in Homicide. What kind of media pressure are you enjoying today? Any?"

"Well, if it isn't Captain Leonard B. Morgan," Kay Lehner, the Departmental Spokesperson, answered. "It's good to be talking to you again. Yes, we do have a press conference scheduled today. Are you healthy enough to join us? Your presence would be greatly appreciated, as you might guess."

"I'd love to join you. I presume that you have something newsworthy for the local, underfed news hawks?"

"Yes, if you are referring to the Reynolds case? The media cornered defense counsel Carole Bullock last night, but she wasn't agreeable to reveal anything. I received word this morning that her client would be signing a confession and I wanted to call you for any details, but I didn't know how much work you have taken on since your return from the hospital."

"I'm almost up to full steam. It's good, too, that Carole didn't leak any information. I'll call her now to make her aware of what we intend to do. See you at one-thirty."

Getting to his feet, Len called Carole Bullock's number and waited for her receptionist to pick up. "Hello? This is 'him' at Devonshire Homicide. Is Ms. Bullock in this morning?"

"Just a moment, Captain Morgan, I'll ring."

"This is Carole Bullock. Is that you, Len Morgan?"

"Yes, it's me, dear, your favorite adversary and ex-husband. I understand you hosted a short encounter with the press last night. Who won?"

"It wasn't much of an encounter, sweetie. I decided to let your people tell the department's side of the story. I really didn't want to spend any more of my time on it."

"I think I understand. Care to elaborate?"

"Not really. I often try to practice something I learned from Bob: Wrap it up and move on."

"Yes, Bob was a smart man, Carole, good and decent too. He comes to mind frequently. All of us lost a good one…"

"Yes, and this weekend we'd have celebrated our wedding anniversary so I'm taking a little private time to reflect."

Pausing briefly, Len replied, "I always appreciated his humor. He did love to laugh."

"Yes, he did, Len. I'm curious … you may enjoy this, did Bob ever relate a silly yarn to you about a correspondence he exchanged with a young punk adversary when we lived in Ohio?"

"No, I don't recall. What was it about? I'd like to hear it."

"At the time Bob was a senior partner in a four partner firm in Columbus; a well-established firm with high class, respectable clients. You know the routine. Anyway, he was representing a client for some insignificant thing or another and the opposing counsel, a brash, ill-bred mouth-breathing type, sent Bob a horrendously distasteful letter. Bob said, ethically speaking, it was the worst piece-of-shit he'd ever received from any opposing counsel in all of his years of practicing law."

"No kidding. So, what did he do?"

Carole Bullock began to laugh aloud … composing herself, she said, "Something totally unlike Bob, you know how laid-back he was, or seemed to be, this was new ground for him. So he sat down and composed what later became known around the local legal circles as *The Bullock Letter*." She began laughing again.

Waiting a few seconds, Len asked, "What did it say; can you tell me?"

Gathering her wits, Carole continued, "I'm sorry. He began dictating it very properly to his paralegal, deliberately adding the word 'Esquire' following the opposing attorney's name and including all of the acceptable and proper legal flourishes. And he ended it very properly, as he always did…"

"Yes? Go on.…"

"The message he wished to convey, to the wet-behind-the-ears- jerk, he situated squarely in the center of the page with ample white space above and below… in upper case type it read: 'FUCK YOU'!"

With that, both of them burst into howling laughter.

Gathering herself again, she continued, "Below that exclamation he added, 'Stronger letter to follow' and signed his name." Again, she burst out laughing.

Len took several seconds to regain his composure as well. Wiping at his eyes and struggling to contain himself, having never experienced that type of behavior from his good friend Bob, Len said, "Carol, that's the funniest thing I've ever heard! And Bob actually sent that to the opposing attorney? He did that?"

"Yes, and apparently one of the two paralegals privy to the correspondence faxed a copy of it to every other legal secretary in the county, ergo, *The Bullock Letter*. It's anyone's guess where it ended up afterward."

"Wonderful. I'd have never thought … anyway, m'dear, back to the business at hand. Are you comfortable with the outcome you settled for in Mister Hunnicutt's case?"

"Yes, this has been fun, Len, very enjoyable. Mister Hunnicutt, not so much."

"How so?"

"Actually, you know, I really never liked that sneering little boy. I didn't like his arrogant attitude from the first time I met with him. When it came out that besides murdering his future mother-in-law, that he'd also screwed her all night, that just about did it for me; I nearly walked. And that's off the record."

"I appreciated you staying and toughing it out, Carole. You did a good job for him, though, under very trying circumstances. At least he will probably avoid the gas chamber."

"I'd almost prefer that he didn't. I'm sorry Len, but his kind makes my ass ache. That's putting it mildly. And, again, dear, all of this chit-chat is off the record."

"I understand, better luck next time, Carole. Stay in touch."

"Thanks, you be safe now; we'll do lunch again in a year or so, right? And reminisce?"

"Sure."

"Goodbye."

As soon as he hung up his intercom buzzer went off; it was Mariko. "Boss, we have a guest out here who wishes to speak with you."

Walking into the squad room, Len noticed a middle-aged female standing next to Mariko's desk. *I wonder who that is? I guess we'll find out soon enough.* "Yes, good morning. I'm Captain Morgan, how can I help you?" he inquired, extending his hand.

The woman took Len's hand in both of hers and smiling warmly, replied, "Captain Morgan, I'm Mary Katherine Riley, Elmer Ryan's niece. I'm so happy to find both you and Mariko here today."

"Yes, Mary Katherine," Len responded. "We heard that your uncle was going to be released later today, so what are your plans; anything special? Is there anything we can do?"

"No, no special plans other than to get him home where he will be relaxed and comfortable. Then feed him properly and get some weight back on his bones."

"Now that sounds like the perfect plan to me," Mariko said. "Your uncle is such a dear and we were really worried about him…"

"And if it hadn't been for you, Mariko, we might have lost him."

Len nodded in agreement.

Mary Katherine continued. "I wanted to thank you personally for your help and all that you've done. Obviously, both of you are busy so I'll be going now. Just feel free to visit Uncle Elmer when your time allows. Thanks again, both of you."

"We appreciate that, Mary Katherine," Len said. "And thanks for stopping by. Now that Dutch … uh, your uncle … we call him Dutch. What I'm trying to say is, with you in town, we know he will be in good hands. Take care now."

Mary Katherine smiled, nodded and left.

Mariko raised her eyebrows, "Well, Boss … she is a tad more reserved than her feisty uncle, agreed?"

"Yep. Much more so. While I'm standing here starving, do you have lunch plans today?"

"My only plan is to have lunch, Captain. What did you have in mind?"

"The cafeteria sounds good to me. I need to stay close. I have a lot going on and I have to attend the press conference at one-thirty. Soup and salad?"

"Sure," Mariko said, stretching her arms out above her head, expanding her chest and amplifying her capacious breasts.

The two lovers ate a light lunch and discussed the fast changing events of the past week. Eventually Len broached the subject of their fast growing, albeit short and torrid relationship.

"Mariko, I need to tell you something ... something heartfelt. You have become the dearest, closest person in my life, with Robbie running a close second. For me at my age, it's a sad commentary to look back and discover how few good friends I have. On the opposite side of that coin is the quality of the friends I have. I don't want anything to ever sour our friendship."

Mariko squeezed his hand.

"This is very difficult," he continued, "...I'm not well versed in expressing my emotions." He looked into her dark eyes; eyes that reflected the love expressed for him. He whispered hoarsely, "Mariko, I know you once said there was a guy you had your eyes on, but I have to tell you this, I'm falling in love with you."

Mariko looked to see if anyone could see her and squeezed his hand again and smiled, a small tear glistened in her eye, "I'm so happy," she whispered, "... and you are so sweet, my Captain. I love you too. And the *other guy*? He's *you*, sweet man--I had my eyes on you from the first day I saw you in the squad room. There was something about you and I felt it immediately."

"So it was *me* all along?"

"Yes, just you." She squeezed his hand hard and released it. "You know, that last night in the hospital, I wasn't certain how you felt about Sara and then there was the unceremonious way she left town. It made me sad, and I was jealous too. When she split, I became irritated. No goodbyes, no thanks, nothing, and after you personally risked your life twice for her, all that on top of how shabbily Gabrielle treated you earlier. I wanted you to know that I love you, Len Morgan. That's all."

Len gazed into her eyes, "I wish I could kiss you right now."

"Me too ... let me finish. Last night ... actually, I didn't stay with you to share my feelings, I didn't know if I ever wanted to tell you again. Now we both have and I'm really happy."

"Someday soon we'll go out for an extended stay on my sloop. We'll furl the sails, crack a cold beer, kick back, drift and talk. I'll divulge my deepest and darkest secrets. If you still want to hang around after that, you'll be more than welcome. Deal? Oh ... are you allergic to cats?"

Mariko looked at him, her dark eyes not betraying her inner feelings. "Cats? No... so, it's a deal? When? I need a break," she said, impatiently seeking an answer. "I need to get laid again soon too, maybe in the good Captain's berth?"

"Good grief, sweets, not too blunt. We'll set sail while I'm on furlough. Is that a deal, then?"

"You got it," Mariko affirmed, smiling. Then, taking a deep breath, she said, "But, I have to tell you something first…"

"Mariko, you're not pregnant are you?" Comprehending his sudden outburst and its possible ramifications, he looked around the room to see if anyone was listening.

"Be calm, silly boy, this is about my professional career thingy now. I have decided to tender my resignation from the department and I've accepted the prosecutor's offer. I'll be assigned to their investigative section, rather like being a detective, hmm?"

"Mariko, great! But you know I'll miss you like crazy around here, how could I not?"

"Well," she went on, "I really think it would be best if we weren't working together, you know what I mean. I want us to be together, but away from here and this will be perfect."

Len sat quietly. "That's fine, it will be perfect," he said, staring at the vibrant young woman who was becoming such a force in his life. "When are you leaving me? Us?"

"I'll never *leave* you, you're stuck with me, but professionally, I have my accumulated vacation time which I'll be taking. My last workday in homicide is a week from tomorrow and the Commissioner advanced his blessings on that."

"Professionally, I'll surely miss you, lady, but you have my blessings as well. You know that."

"Thanks, love. I know you think you'll miss me, but Flossie is catching on quickly and she will do just fine. I've learned a lot working with you, with Dutch, and Robbie and the others too, but I want something different. The fraternization word convinced me that this was the right choice. I don't want to ever lose you. Still, I don't want to work beside you, not here, not this closely."

"I understand, Mariko. Completely. Okay, now what?"

"Well, back to work," she said, smiling. "And you have to beat it upstairs for a press conference, right? Oh, about tonight? You and I originally had a date planned, remember?"

"Yes, no changes. Now I'd better get upstairs. We'll talk later."

Thursday, end of day 16...

Following his conversation with Mariko, Len strode into the crowded, noisy pressroom, experiencing an inner lightness he hadn't enjoyed in years. As usual, the many reporters accosted him, asking their inane questions. As always, he merely smiled and said nothing. Kay Lehner waved at him, catching his eye as she went to the microphone where she introduced herself.

Adjusting its height, she spoke, "Good afternoon everyone. Are we ready?"

The noisy reporters quieted somewhat and the answer was affirmative from those that chose to answer. Lehner introduced herself and, waiting for some semblance of order, she began reading from her typed notes describing the Hunnicutt confession of the previous day. Sticking closely to her written notes, she ignored the occasional interruptive questions from the reporters.

Moving on, Kay Lehner read, "I'd like to tell you that we have good news regarding the RFK Junior High School shooting case. This case is one that I'd personally like to see closed. If we had our druthers, we'd wish it weren't a case at all, that it never happened. It was senseless and brutal; a waste of two innocent worthwhile lives, plus it permanently scarred the lives of dozens or more of our precious youngsters."

"Do you have any suspects?" one of the reporters shouted.

"The most I can tell you today is that we are continuing to receive bits of information and we're piecing leads together regarding the shooting. We have direction and we are following it. At this moment, the entire homicide team is actively working this case. That's all I have for you today, thanks for your patience, ladies and gentlemen, now I have to leave."

Kay Lehner turned to her right, stepped off the raised platform and disappeared into a side hall away from the media.

Len started for the elevator when suddenly, one of the print reporters saw him and yelled, "Hey! There's Morgan! He knows what's going on! Morgan, stop...."

Len turned and looked back in the direction of the loud voice; it was no one he recognized. The reporter rudely pushed his way through the other reporters and got in Len's face. "We demand to know what the facts are with the RFK shooting and you know what they are, Morgan! What the hell gives anyway?"

Highly irritated, Len stepped back, "Whoa, man ... use a breath mint once in a while. As far as facts, when we get them, you'll get them. As far as demanding? Here's a big fat suggestion for you; demand in one hand, shit in the other ... see which fills up first! Now please get the hell out of my way."

The reporter refused to step aside, instead he foolishly grabbed Len's arm. "I said you know the goddamn facts, now spill 'em!"

Len wrested his arm free and got in the reporter's face. "Touch me again and I'll put the cuffs on you! You seem to have forgotten that you're our guest here, now step aside ... I said NOW!"

Getting that message, the rude reporter nervously blinked and slowly backed away, "Yeah ... sorry."

As Len returned to the squad room, Mariko asked, "How did it go today, Captain?"

"Not bad," he said, still fuming slightly. "Mostly disorderly, impolite, no big change I guess. But it's always easier when we have something newsworthy to say. I don't always appreciate how hard those media people have to work for the scraps of meat we occasionally toss at them. I couldn't do it. Today, some of them seemed fairly happy to hear something newsworthy, some didn't."

"Paulie and Coop are on their way back from lockup," Mariko said. "They met there with Josephs and Santini. They should be here any second."

"Good, did they get what they wanted?"

"Apparently," she answered. "They said Jose gave them some really good information." At that very moment, the detectives walked into the squad room, all of them smiling happily.

"Gentlemen, come into my office, talk to me, talk to me," Len invited as he sat down at his desk.

"Captain," Detective Paul Tobin began, "we got the message and met Duane at lockup. The prisoner, Jose Pepe Hernandez, claims he knows where the killer of Georgie Stamos is and he furnished us with an address. On the way back, we radioed Watch Command, they made the address for us. It's in the Reseda area in a small apartment house crammed in one of those narrow side streets north of Ventura Boulevard. How do you want us to proceed, sir? Blow out the door?"

"No," Len answered, simply. "We've waited too long for this lead. If the killer is still living there, let's make damn certain we know he's in the building before we move. We don't want to possibly flush him out into the underground. We'll take him alive, but with enough force on hand to ensure that he doesn't escape. I want a stakeout on the building immediately. Commandeer a room across the street, stake out the back alley too, put our good people in there. We have the composite picture; did you show it to Hernandez?"

"Yes," Tobin answered. "He said it was a good likeness."

"Good. Did Jose volunteer what his connection was to the kid?" Len questioned. "Does he know who he is?"

"Yeah, but hang on," Fred Cooper said. "This kid is Jose's cousin, an illegal … up here from Guadalajara to do a paid hit."

"A hit?" Len exclaimed, leaning forward in his chair, "A hit on a fifteen year-old school kid?"

Cooper continued, "Len, the irony is that Georgie Stamos *wasn't* his victim. That's what Jose said anyway. Something about another Latino kid using the name George. Actually, his name is Jorge, a smart *Cholo* punk who runs drugs at RFK and other schools. Apparently Jorge, who calls himself George, had been skimming, holding out on a Mexican cartel. Jose's cousin was sent here to take him out and to do it in such a way as to make an example for the 'other Jorges'."

"Shit. And he mistakenly shoots an innocent kid whose name is really George? The Stamos kid wasn't even a Latino for Chrissakes … not even close. What the hell do we have here, an idiot hit man? Damn! What a piece of work!"

"It ain't over," Tobin added. "The word is Jorge, the skimmer, knew he was a target and somehow managed to spoon-feed the killer kid the bad identity information. Now, Jorge is waiting for the killer kid, Jose's cousin, to go public and while he's out, he'll sanction him."

"Yeah," Cooper said, "now Jose's cousin is scared shitless to venture out into the open, afraid of taking a cap by Jorge, the guy he was supposed to do in. Is that justice?"

Len leaned back in his chair and stared at the ceiling. "It's too bad this killer kid is so damn stupid. It's difficult to guess what his next move would be."

Tobin and Cooper nodded in agreement.

"Okay, let's get some people out there. Have Mariko or Flossie get a phone tap request into the DA, and get arrest and search warrants too. The killer kid may order takeout, or a pizza delivery, that would put us right in his face, borrowing a trick from our French-Canadian Gerot. Did Jose give you his name?"

"Ernesto Hernandez Diaz," Tobin replied. "Like I said, he's only fifteen, this was his first trip to California, and his first hit. Maybe it was his Initiation?"

"Fifteen?" Len muttered incredulously. "That is so sick."

"That's what Jose said too, Len," Tobin added, rising from his chair. "You know, Boss, Jose seems like a fairly average guy to me. His cousin's actions pissed him off big time. Want us to bring in Jorge? Jose gave us his address too."

"Yes, definitely him," Len affirmed. "But do it covertly, no media. We don't want Ernesto to discover it's safe now to make a dash for the border."

"Okay, will do," Tobin said.

"Charge him with conspiracy for now. The killer kid Ernesto was just the messenger. Did anyone bother to inform the DA's office of Jose's cooperation?"

"I'm about to make that call right now," Tobin replied.

"Good, maybe Jose needs a break for a change. He did seem like a good sort. He just picked the wrong crowd."

The trio, including Josephs, left Len's office. He watched them get on the phones as he hit his intercom, "Mariko, did Robbie catch his flight to Denver, and do I have a seat assignment for tomorrow morning?"

"Yes, to both, *my* Captain."

He nodded, enjoying Mariko's sly wit as he looked through his glass partition at nothing in particular, "Thanks." He stood, stretched, shut off his office lights and walked out into the quiet squad room.

Mariko looked up, "Captain, I know what you and Robbie are up to tomorrow, and I know the weight you must be carrying right now. You be careful, please?"

Len nodded, and laid his hand gently on her shoulder, "You know how Robbie and I are; we're both big cowards. Playing it safe is all we know so don't worry. For now, help Tobin, Cooper, and the others to nail that killer kid, Ernesto. Will you do that for me while I'm gone? I'll be back Monday and fill you in on the details."

"Bullshit!" she blurted out, surprising him. "You can just find a telephone and call me from Denver when this shit is all over. That's what I expect."

Conceding to her wishes, he replied, "Yes, I will, I will. That's a promise."

Len turned away and left the squad room.

Mariko watched him, sadly wondering if she would see him alive after tomorrow.

Later, at the Villa Casa Grande, he parked the shiny Crown Victoria cruiser in the garage guest spot and took the elevator to his floor.

To hell with the junk mail, it will have to wait.

Denver International Airport…

Jeffrey Robinson walked down the jetway bridge into the crowded concourse. Luis Campanera, waiting, promptly greeted him. "Robbie, how was your flight?"

"It got bumpy as hell ten or fifteen minutes out. Other than that, it was cake. What's the plan?"

"We'll get a car for you first, and then you can follow me to Hope Green. We have plenty of food and anything else you'll need. Two other agents will be staying with you, a female, and a male. We attempt to give the place a normal appearance," Campanera explained, "…for any of our neighbors that might question our presence. Oh, and Len wanted us to have the combination screen door removed from the front entry. It's done if you remember to tell him."

Outside the terminal in the bright Colorado sunshine, they went immediately to an awaiting car parked at the curb. Campanera took Pena Boulevard and headed to a nearby auto rental agency where Jeff Robinson's car was waiting.

"Take this two-way radio, Robbie. It's tuned to our Federal frequencies. The Denver Police will also have a radio team monitoring us and providing a sharpshooter to work inside with you and Len. Any questions?"

"Yeah, I'm puzzled. How does the jurisdictional thing work? How do Len and I, as California law enforcement officers, waltz Gerot out of Denver and Colorado after we catch him?"

"If he's arrested on our property, at the Hope Green house, he's technically on Federal property," Campanera explained. "The city and State authorities have no jurisdiction and don't want any. US Treasury will *waltz his ass* onto the plane and accompany him back to California. Once we land in LA, on California soil, he's all yours. The State of California wants him for greater crimes than we do, he's all yours."

"That's simple enough. So what's with a Denver PD marksman?"

"Back up more than anything else, and it puts a Denver officer on the scene if there are any jurisdictional questions later."

"Hmm, okay ... so you're assuming we'll have no problem taking Gerot tomorrow?"

"Robbie," Campanera reflected, "I think you and Len are excellent cops. You guys will do what it takes to get this guy. What I appreciate most is the element of surprise that Len built into this pinch. It looks plenty good to me."

Not impressed or satisfied with the 'plenty good' plan, Jeff Robinson opted to change the subject. "So, Luis, what is the deal with Andy Chiu? Have you discovered anything new that you didn't know beforehand?"

"Yes, we did. Once we discovered he was dirty, we did some covert overnight snooping and discovered a boatload. From the beginning, Andy Chiu led us and the agency to believe that he was a political defector from northern China. One who'd escaped into Russia and into the west via their version of the Asian 'underground railroad'. His story was all bullshit."

"Really?" Jeff Robinson said. "Is there really an Asian underground railroad?"

"Yes. But our Andy turned out to be a highly educated, Russian-born Korean, who dealt in various illegal narcotics in Shanghai, China. He'd immigrated south with other ethnic Koreans from eastern Siberia. Somewhere, maybe in his Shanghai narcotics business, he made contact with the Russian Mafia. Seeing a potential mole, they put him on the payroll and shipped him to the United States."

Jeff Robinson shook his head in amazement. "Luis, that's absolutely incredible. So how did he ever land a job in Treasury? Do you accept walk-ins like at the corner barbershop?"

"He applied for federal employment as a multi-lingual interpreter and translator, being fluent in Russian, Korean, Mandarin and English. The FBI, having no real way to do an in-depth background, grabbed him up in a heart-beat."

"But he worked for you, in Treasury."

"Yes, but technically, he is an FBI Special Agent; now soon to be ex-agent."

"Yeah, ex..." Jeff Robinson said, nodding. "But where is he going to end up after tomorrow, if I may ask."

Campanera, smiled, "You may ask. He will disappear into the ethers as a result of a fatal automobile accident."

"What? You're actually going to kill him off? Do you guys do that?"

"No, Robbie," Campanera said, smiling impishly. "We'll just make it *look* like we killed him off. Satisfied? Here we are. There's your car, follow me into Denver."

Jeff Robinson stared at the big sedan, a replica of Len's new Crown Victoria cruiser back in the Valley, a replica except for one thing: "Great color, Luis, white, my favorite."

Campanera chuckled, "Sorry, Robbie."

The late afternoon Valley sun created long dark shadows and gave some relief to the oppressive July heat. Detectives Paul Tobin and Fred Cooper pulled the big yellow and white furniture mover's step-van up in front of the small, flat-roofed two-story apartment building located off Reseda Boulevard.

Outfitted in furniture mover's coveralls, they were the picture of innocence and commonplace. One difference was the false partition installed in the box of the van behind the cab. Inside the hot cubicle, Detective Duane Josephs staffed the radio along with the wall-mounted speaker that was wiretapped to the telephone line of the suspect's apartment.

"Duane, are you all set? Do you have a signal?" Tobin asked.

"Right as rain here, bud," Josephs replied, adjusting his headset. "Let me see if this peephole is working, maybe to let in some fresher air. In case you didn't know it, it's stifling in this little box. Thank God for that battery powered oscillating fan, guys."

Reaching up, Josephs slid a small, thin wall panel to the right. On the inside of the van, it looked like a sliding panel. On the exterior of the van, it appeared as a solid black dot, part of the logo of the moving company.

"Looks good," he said. "So, are you two going to set up inside now?"

"Yeah," Cooper replied, "we'll carry in a batch of those cardboard boxes. It will look like we're going to begin packing. When we're set, we'll signal you to see if our equipment is working. Keep cool."

"Cool? In here? Smart ass!"

"Sorry Duane, just let us know when the team behind the apartment is in place, they'll give you a signal. Take care, too," Tobin added.

Tobin and Cooper got out of the truck's cab and went to the rear of the van. They opened the doors, removed several empty boxes and went inside the vacated second floor apartment to set up surveillance across the street from the young fugitive, Ernesto Diaz.

Josephs' radio squawked, it was Svetlana Belanova, "Point Guard, this is Backdoor Trot, we're in place and comfortable. We got pizza, cold beers, hot male strippers; everything is *jake* here. Let us know when it's over. Clear."

"Roger, Backdoor Trot, clear." Josephs replied. "Silly shits."

At home, Len tossed his coat at the big recliner chair and collapsed on his sofa. He felt the soft cushions absorbing the weariness from his tired body. His mind began to shut down, slowly blurring the myriad thoughts and plans made for the following day. Eventually he slept.

Friday, June 21, day 17…
The slow rhythm of the classic slow rock music that awakened Len on other days repeated again today, this time from a dream-free sleep. He looked beside him where Mariko was sharing a major part of the bed. She arrived at Len's condominium late last night, toothbrush in hand and unearthed him from his sofa and they went to bed. Eager for each other, they made love into the night. Now she was asleep on her stomach in the middle of the queen-sized bed.

He checked the time; it was nearly 4:30 a.m. If he rose now there was plenty of time to shower, grab a juice, and drive to LAX and catch his 6:38 a.m. flight to Denver.

Or is it at six o'clock? He thought. *I'd better check that out.*

Naked, he padded into his living room and retrieved the note showing his flight information. *Ooops! My flight leaves LAX at six o'clock, it arrives in Denver at nine-fifteen central time. Oh shit, I have to move.*

While he was showering and shaving, Mariko rose and made coffee. Len reluctantly kissed her goodbye several times, finished his coffee and ran for the elevator. She stood in the doorway and waved sadly at the back of his head, feeling the same empty feeling of dread that she felt earlier.

Will I ever see him alive again?

Len caught the Friday-morning-lite traffic on the I-405. At LAX he parked and ran to his terminal. Catching the escalator, he made it to his gate with minutes to spare. In his seat and buckled in, he wondered if he had been followed or observed.

This international intrigue and Russian Mafia hit man scenario is beginning to make me paranoid. The big plane rolled slowly from the jet bridge to the taxiway. Len yawned and closed his eyes, *Screw it. I'll deal with the subterfuge when I reach Denver. I'll fantasize about Mariko now.*

Arriving at the Denver International Airport in Denver, Len spotted Jeff Robinson waiting, leaning casually against the glass partition next to the moving walkways that divide the concourse.

"Good flight?" Jeff Robinson asked.

"Relatively, some nasty bumps out there, maybe fifty miles out I'd guess. Do we own a car?"

"Yeah, a snazzy white Victoria sedan and a two-way G-Man radio."

"Where do we rendezvous with Luis?" Len asked, as they rode the escalator to the underground shuttle.

"At the Federal car-pool garage near lower downtown. We have a while before we need to check in with him. Want to get something to eat?"

"Sure, got a place picked out?"

"Yeah," Jeff Robinson answered. "There's a Denny's just north of the new baseball stadium, just off the interstate and close to our rendezvous with Luis. Let's eat there."

"Really? At Denny's? Fine with me," Len deadpanned, "...your poison, you buy."

Outside the multi-tented main terminal building under a clear blue Colorado sky, Jeff Robinson had followed Luis Campanera's lead from the day before and parked at the curb. The approaching security guard nodded when Jeff Robinson flashed his shield. Inside the car, they buckled up and sped away toward downtown.

They sat in the small restaurant, sipping black coffee and chatting. The three-egg Western omelet filled Len to the brim, having eaten on the plane earlier.

"If I keep eating like this, I'll be as stout as van Haan and won't need three layers of Kevlar," Len said. "Any suspicious characters skulking around Hope Green?"

"No, just a couple of neighbors across the street comparing their hedges and flower beds. It's a quiet neighborhood, not far from a small college. Ordinary folks."

"Are you nervous," Len asked, becoming unquestionably nervous himself.

"I think I was more nervous when Josephs and I went after Hunnicutt. Of course, Josephs was green as hell, at least as far as I knew. Although I'm not wild about your crazy plan here. You and I have been down roads like this before; I have some idea what to expect from you. With Josephs, it was a learning experience."

"Right. This may turn into a learning experience as well. I've never tangled with an international hit man before. This is all new to me. Oh, did you call Mariko? Did the boys and Lana have any luck with the Diaz pinch last night?"

"Yeah," Jeff Robinson said, beginning to smile. "And I talked to Josephs this morning too. He was the radioman."

"Cooped up in the box with no air-conditioning?" Len asked.

"Yeah ... he complained that he must have sweat off ten pounds. It seems that Ernesto's grandmother called for a pizza delivery about eight-thirty or so. Lana intercepted the pizza delivery-person, a female, a block away. Lana conned her out of her blouse, her hat, and the freekin' pizza."

"Damn," Len said, chuckling. "That's rich. Then what?"

"Paulie and Coop went in through the back of the building and waited for Lana to appear in the upstairs hallway. Josephs and Mueller covered the entry and back doors. There ain't no one going to get in or leave the building until Ernesto is in custody."

"Any gun play?" Len asked.

Now Jeff Robinson commenced laughing. He quickly regained his composure and continued, "No. Lana knocked on the door and waited. Ernesto himself came to the door with the *dinero*, Lana took it, handed Ernesto the pizza box and then flashed her shield. He freaked out and dropped the pizza. Lana took the cue and with one of her classic ballerina moves, kicked the *putz* ... squarely in the nuts!"

The two men laughed so loudly that it drew the attention of half the patrons in the restaurant.

"That's hysterical," Len said, wiping at his eyes with the back of his hand, "but highly effective. So what did Ernesto do then?"

"He puked all over the place," Jeff Robinson said, howling again and reaching for a napkin to wipe the tears that flowed freely down his cheeks. "...and all over the spilled pizza too!"

Still enjoying the laugh, Len, asked, "So, did Ernesto's public defender make a big deal out of Miss Lana's obvious roughhouse tactics on Diaz's bruised stones?"

Jeff Robinson, collected himself again, "Lana innocently told her that Ernesto resisted arrest when she produced her shield so she merely 'persuaded' him to cooperate. Go figure?"

The two of them laughed even harder at that explanation. Len waved off the waitress who returned with yet another coffee refill. He left a couple of dollars on the table as he and Jeff Robinson, with their sides hurting from all the laughing, made their way to the cashier's counter.

Outside, Len stopped and inhaled the thin air of lower downtown Denver. *Ah, yes... it smells a bit like South Central Los Angeles on a bad day. Suppose that would piss off the environmental purists around here if they knew that?*

The two detectives got into the rental car and headed for the Federal car-pool garage to meet Luis Campanera. "So, did we get a tight pinch on Ernesto? Who read him his rights if he's a national?"

"Now who do you think?"

Len paused, shaking his head. "Detective Junior Grade Duane Josephs I presume?"

"Ol' bilingual Duane, yep."

"Well, swell," Len said with a snicker. "What a catch. He's a covert Karate Brown-belt and speaks fluent Spanish too. I better keep an eye on him, he'll be wanting my job before long."

"Before long?" Jeff Robinson questioned, "Hell, he wants it now."

Len smiled.

As they proceeded to their rendezvous with Campanera, Len gazed at the passing buildings. "Robbie, if this all goes totally wrong today, my Last Will and Testament is in the center drawer of my desk. I left everything I own, bank accounts, the whole batch to Mariko … and to you."

Jeff Robinson's head snapped around and he stared hard at Len who was looking intently back at him exhibiting an expression he'd never witnessed before. Jeff Robinson quickly returned his gaze to the road and saying nothing, nodded.

Len reached across and squeezed his arm. "I knew you'd understand. Thanks."

Still June 21, Day 17…

Len and Jeff Robinson pulled up in front of the Federal garage and parked. The two detectives went inside and found Luis Campanera waiting for them.

"Hey! Len, Robbie. Over here, we need to hurry." Campanera took them into a small room he had requisitioned for the morning. In the center of the room was a table piled with a variety of men's clothes.

"Len, today, we have van Haan outfitted in a lightweight black raincoat, dark glasses and a Colorado Rockies baseball cap over an ugly black wig. He's our veritable 'Man-in-Black'. Try on this Kevlar armor and a coat. We'll see how you compare."

"Fine," Len answered, putting on the armor vest. Then adding the coat and hat, he postured, turning slowly, pretending to model the ensemble.

"He needs more bulk," Jeff Robinson indicated, shaking his head. "He's not as portly as van Haan."

"Very well," Campanera replied. "Put on another layer of Kevlar. That should do it."

Len did as directed and put the raincoat on again, "Well?"

"Mah-velous, you look simply mah-velous," Jeff Robinson retorted attempting to imitate comedian Billy Crystal's impression of Ricardo Montalban. "Will your forty-five fit in the pocket of that coat?"

"I'm not carrying, Robbie. I don't want a gun, and no, these pockets are too small anyway."

"Len," Jeff Robinson implored, "you need a piece of some kind, this guy is dangerous."

"Robbie, I have a plan and I don't need a piece." Quickly changing the subject, he said, "Damn, this outfit is getting hot already. When do we leave?"

"As soon as you put on the ugly wig," Campanera said. "Follow me, guys, our rides are arriving as we speak. Robbie, are you armed?"

"Yes."

"All right," Campanera said, "let's do this thing."

Len nodded, saying nothing.

The two-vehicle caravan of white SUVs made good time crossing through lower downtown Denver on the southbound Interstate-25 Valley Highway. The commuter traffic increased as they neared the Santa Fe Drive split. Following the lead suburban, Len's driver stayed in the number three lane, driving slightly faster than the posted speed limit.

"There they are, sir, up ahead of us on the right," he said, pointing. "Good timing is everything."

Looking ahead about two city blocks Len saw the other white SUVs approaching the Broadway Street off ramp.

"Chet, the driver in the lead vehicle, has his radio keyed to our frequency so we can monitor what he's doing, sir. We'll be able to hear the conversations going on when he fakes the engine trouble. The witness is in the second vehicle with Special Agent Chiu."

Suddenly the radio squawked, "Shit. Blue Jay, sir. This is Red Robin. I have a mechanical situation going here; follow me off the freeway. Dammit, I'm experiencing some engine problems and losing acceleration. Sorry. I'm going to have to exit here on Broadway; follow me down into that RTD parking lot on the right. Over."

"There he goes," Len's driver said. "Just as we planned. Chet is faking engine problems now. The second vehicle with the witness and Special Agent Chiu will follow him off the highway. Sit tight while I speed up and take their place in the traffic."

While Len's driver was explaining this, another voice responded over the radio, "Roger, Red Robin. This is the Blue Jay. We copy and will proceed to RTD lot. Ten four."

Both of the lead SUVs left the I-25 freeway and Len and his entourage continued southbound.

Following the lead SUVs off the I-25 were two unmarked black sedans that stopped at the bottom of the off ramp, successfully blocking the intersection and preventing any following traffic from following the SUVs containing the van Haan entourage.

As the second SUV pulled into the RTD parking lot, Andy Chiu asked, "What's his problem? I don't see any smoke from his tail pipe."

The driver answered, "It may be electrical, or a fuel pump failure, who knows? We'll check him out, sir. It's probably nothing." Saying that, the driver of the second SUV carrying Chiu and van Haan pulled up and parked next to the disabled suburban.

Andy Chiu immediately jumped out and ran toward the vehicle. Suddenly he stopped. Surprised, he slowly raised his arms, startled by two armed FBI agents with their guns aimed at his face.

"Place your hands behind your head, interlock your fingers and turn your ass around," the lead FBI Agent ordered. In shock, Andy Chiu obliged.

"What's the meaning of this?" he demanded. "What the hell is going on?"

"You're under arrest." The agent said as he frisked Chiu. Locating Chiu's two cellular phones and his weapon, the agent handed them to his partner. "Come along."

At the same time, two US Marshals from the first SUV jumped in with van Haan and his driver. "Swing over to the south side of the lot, Chet. We'll switch vehicles and take it from here."

Turning to van Haan, the Marshal explained, "Mister van Haan, we experienced a situation temporarily but everything is under control. Relax now, you can remove your disguise and don't ask any questions."

White faced and soaked through with perspiration under his black garb, an agape van Haan merely nodded.

In the meantime, Len's caravan proceeded south through south Denver. Staying on the Valley Highway, they followed the same route the original caravan would have taken and exited onto eastbound Evans Road. Farther on they turned into a fashionable residential neighborhood consisting primarily of immaculate townhouses shaded by mature trees.

"We're close, *Mister van Haan*." Jeff Robinson said.

"Why thanks, *Mister Tibbs*," Len added, admiring the attractive townhouses as they passed by. "Nice neighborhood Robbie, did you get any inquiring glances from the white folks when you arrived here?"

Jeff Robinson smirked, but remained silent, ignoring Len's smart-ass question.

The SUVs pulled over to the curb in front of an ordinary looking brick-faced townhouse on a tree-lined cul-de-sac. The agents from the lead vehicle came back and accompanied them into the house.

"Luis," Len observed, stopping on the sidewalk. "Who are those two men across the street, see them? There, the ones trying to look like gardeners. Are they your people?"

"Yes, but how did..."

"Get them the hell out of here," Len snapped. "They're not Latino and they're wearing street shoes. Gerot isn't an idiot. If I spotted them, so would he. I can handle Gerot alone, trust me."

Len looked over the entire neighborhood and stepping onto the front porch, checked out the front door, "Ah… good," he muttered. "The storm door has been removed." Satisfied that the rest of the arrangements looked natural and serene, Len and Jeff Robinson left Campanera outside and proceeded into the house.

"We'll leave you here with our two resident agents and Denver Police Sergeant John Dunlap," one of the special agents said. "We have Sergeant John on loan today from Denver PD. Good luck."

Len nodded and the agent disappeared out the front door. He climbed into one of the SUVs and drove away.

Len looked at the stocky, graying, police sergeant. Extending his hand, Len queried, "Sergeant John Dunlap … is it possible that you have a niece by the name of Sara Dunlap, one who recently lived in Los Angeles?"

Mildly surprised, the sergeant replied, "Well … yes, as a matter of fact, I do. Do you know her?"

Finishing the handshake, Len nodded, "I knew Sara. Los Angeles is such a unique place; most of us out there know everyone else."

Sergeant Dunlap, questioning Len's off-hand remark said, "I really can't believe that's the truth, sir. How do you know her anyway? She just moved back here."

"Sergeant Dunlap, may I call you John?" Len asked.

Dunlap nodded, "Sure."

"Actually, John, Sara and I lived next door to each other in the same condominium complex. I'm Len Morgan, her former neighbor."

"Well, no shit," Dunlap uttered in amazement. "Sara did mention you. It's a small world, huh?"

"So it seems, especially when we're all jammed into one room. How is she doing?"

"She's fine. She's arranging to transfer from the bank in California to their subsidiary here in Denver. She couldn't handle the hectic California lifestyle I guess."

"Pity. Well, tell her hello for me. By the way, John, why are the Denver Police on the job today?"

Dunlap explained, shrugging, "I'm a sharpshooter, that's one reason, that and to officially observe since this is still inside the corporate limits of Denver. I'm not on duty in an official capacity, other than for observation. The Feds requested me, I'm on loan."

"Good. I appreciate your talents, John, but I pray that we don't need your expertise. In the event we do, though, take out his gun hand, his right hand, disable him but don't kill him, understood?" That said, Len removed his dark glasses and looked intently into Dunlap's eyes.

"Oh shit, oh shit... " Jeff Robinson announced excitedly. "It looks like we may have company. A brown International Parcel Service delivery van just pulled up. It looks like Gerot to me; he's wearing an IPS uniform. He's on the street now and coming around the truck. He has a flat package..."

"Great! Good!' Len exclaimed. "This is good, getting down to cases this soon. I didn't want to wait around forever and get all strung out."

Len glanced at the two resident FBI agents, "You two go into the kitchen and wait, this won't take long at all. Robbie, you hide in that small powder room. Use the mirror on that foyer closet door to observe what's going on out here. John, you stand in the sitting room ... over there where you can see Robbie. If you see Robbie making a move, follow him as fast as you can. Are we set? Safeties off? Rounds chambered?"

Jeff Robinson and Dunlap nodded. They deployed their guns, released the safeties and took their places.

Intense but nervous, Len took a deep breath, put on his dark glasses and peered through the white-lace curtains on the sidelight of the large front door. He watched as the faux IPS man casually approached on the front walk.

Len felt his palms tingling and sweating again, the adrenaline surged just like those last times waiting in the taxi with SWAT Officer Ferrell and standing in the parking garage at Villa Casa Grande.

Len took another deep breath and frantically wriggled his sweaty fingers in a vain attempt to settle his nerves. "That's our man, gentlemen," he whispered quietly. "That's definitely Jean-Luc Gerot, big as shit, same MO with a package atop his right hand again … probably his Glock hidden under the package. Some things never change. Jean-Luc, I can read you like a cheap novel."

His voice scratchy and hoarse, Len cleared his throat and swallowed. His legs began to tremble nervously, his entire body was tense with anticipation and his coffee filled bladder was suddenly demanding relief. *God! I really don't need to piss my pants now!*

He took a final deep breath and gripped the doorknob with his sweaty right hand and watched as the faux IPS man, package in hand, stepped lightly onto the concrete stoop. There he paused for a moment and appeared to check the address label on the package. Satisfied, he walked nonchalantly across the porch to the front door.

As Gerot reached for the doorbell, Len abruptly jerked open the door. Caught by complete surprise, Gerot froze, startled at the sight of the tall imposing figure in black that loomed large in front of him.

That split second of hesitation was all Len needed. Lunging at Gerot, he struck down and away at his right arm, knocking the package across the porch stoop and exposing the nine-millimeter handgun. In the same instant, he grabbed Gerot's right wrist and slammed his gun-hand hard against the doorjamb while grabbing Gerot around the neck with his right arm and kneeing him unmercifully in his unprotected groin.

Gerot's eyes bulged in excruciating pain. His face contorted as he strained to exhale a long, agonizing groan deep from the bottom of his lungs. Len quickly applied his knee into Gerot's groin a second time. As he did, the nine-millimeter gun suddenly discharged!

"Argh! Shit! No!" Len screamed!

The gun fell to the porch floor, clattering harmlessly away. Writhing in mortal pain, Len fell against Gerot and collapsed against him. With their bodies entangled, they rolled off the concrete stoop into a flowerbed.

Terrified for his partner's well-being, Jeff Robinson screamed and rushed outside. John Dunlap pushed Jeff Robinson away and was atop both Len and Gerot in a flash. He grabbed the moaning, convulsing Gerot hard around the neck and wrestled him away from Len, now sprawling and moaning loudly in pain amidst the crushed flowers.

Powerless now, Gerot remained in a tight, painful fetal position with his hands clasped tightly over his genitals, still vomiting profusely and offering no resistance.

Sergeant John Dunlap, breathing hard, hauled him coughing and choking to his feet and finished cuffing him just as the two would be 'gardeners' arrived, running from their hiding place across the street.

In the meantime, Len was still writhing in what appeared to be mortal pain, grasping his left leg with both hands. Perplexed, Jeff Robinson hovered over him, definitely confused as he tried desperately to locate his friend's wound

"Where are you hit? Where? I don't see any blood!"

Still grimacing Len rolled over on his back. Clenching his knee, he sat upright and attempted to get to his feet. "Damn football!"

Breathing a sigh and relieved that his best friend hadn't been shot, Jeff Robinson carefully assisted him to his feet just as Luis Campanera and the other FBI agents drove up in the SUVs.

Sweating and breathing heavily, with his arm around Jeff Robinson's shoulders, Len steadied himself and stood looking at his thoroughly subdued former police academy classmate from a different life, now a former international assassin-taken-prisoner, Jean-Luc Gerot.

Still reeling from the sharp pain in his knee and the emotional and physical exertion, Len's chest heaved as he panted hard, catching his breath. Between loud inhalations he said, "Jean-Luc, it's really good seeing you. But I don't care to meet like this again if you don't mind. Please, come in the house and sit down."

Inside, a sullen, silent Jean-Luc Gerot sat in the parlor in a straight-backed chair while an FBI agent placed him in shackles. Gerot stared inquisitively at Len as he removed his dark glasses and sweat soaked wig.

"Who in hell are you?" Gerot demanded between coughs, his voice hoarse. "And how the hell do you know my name?"

"I'm an old classmate of yours from the Los Angeles Police Academy, Jean-Luc. And look what you have become, a whore killer among other things."

"Yeah, so what?" Gerot grunted.

"So what? Well, Jean-Luc, when we get your ass back to California, you'll be looking at the death penalty. That's what."

Unresponsive, Jean-Luc Gerot looked away, preferring to sit quietly.

Len pulled a chair up in front of him and sat down. "That is, unless you decide to cooperate with us and fill in some blanks, like who hired you and why."

The two adversaries stared silently at one another. Gerot broke the silence first. "You will believe what you choose, but I don't know who hired me, in most cases I never know, nor do I care. It's business, *monsieur*. My telephone rings or I get a telegram. I answer and give them an offshore account number and a day certain when I'll complete the sanction. They pay. That's how it works."

"And you always maintain your schedule? You never fail or screw up?"

Gerot snorted contemptuously and looked away.

"That is until today, outside on the porch," Len said.

"*Oui*, I became careless today," he responded. "This was going to be too easy. *C'est la vie*."

"Easy, like the Safety House in the Valley?"

"*Oui*, just like it."

"Dipshit."

Luis Campanera appeared in the living room, grinning excitedly from ear to ear. "Everything went better than planned, huh?"

"Yeah, Luis," Len said as he got to his feet, leaving Gerot to brood. "We're ready to fly back to Los Angeles as soon as we can get *Monsieur* Gerot back to DIA. I've experienced enough of him and Mile-high Denver for a while."

Jeff Robinson sat down in the chair in front of Gerot and turned to Len, "May I have the honors, Captain?"

"Help yourself, Robbie. While you're at it, see if he will tell you what was so important that he had to kill all those people. Was it to retrieve a lousy $128,000?"

Disgusted, Len threw his sweat soaked hat, long coat and Kevlar armor vests onto a nearby sofa. Running his hands through his thick mop of damp hair, he limped to the stairway, sat down hard on the carpeted landing, and watched impassively for a minute as Jeff Robinson read from the Miranda card in his hand.

Len took out his handkerchief and wiped the beads of perspiration from his face. Still sweating, he rose and limped outside to the front porch into some fresher air. He could hear Jeff Robinson's steady voice droning inside. Len winced, flexed his leg and carefully stepped from the porch onto the sidewalk. There he gazed at the mature trees, the manicured lush lawns, and mused, *Such a placid setting for the apprehension of an international killer. Who'd a thought?*

Luis Campanera and Sergeant John Dunlap came out of the house and joined him. "Captain," Dunlap said, "that was some piece of work. When I heard his first grunt I knew exactly what you'd done. There's not much defense against a well-placed knee to the balls."

"Thanks, John," Len said, agreeing and looking appreciatively at Dunlap and Campanera, who were standing on the front porch. "It seems to be our department's latest method of apprehension anymore. I can't wait until he has to piss. I love the sound of a grown man screaming."

The three men laughed heartily at Len's crude remark.

"And Luis, I got what I wanted today. I wanted to repay him personally for the three cops that he murdered, three cops from my precinct and all friends of mine. I wanted his sorry ass really bad. And, I wanted to be unarmed. I was, and with Sergeant John and Robbie's help, we took him out. Thanks again, guys, for being here."

Suddenly a muffled noise followed by some kicking sounds ensued from the back of the IPS van parked at the curb. Len and Sergeant Dunlap heard it at the same time. Dunlap raced to the curb, followed by Campanera while Len hobbled along behind. They opened the sliding side-door and looked inside. There, bound, gagged, and wearing just his undershorts, was the owner of the vomit-soiled brown IPS uniform that Jean-Luc Gerot was currently wearing. Dunlap untied the partially dressed driver and got him outside into the fresh air.

"Are you all right?" Dunlap asked.

"I think so," the shaken driver said, rubbing a knot on his head, "What in hell is going on?"

"Oh, some mild excitement," Dunlap explained, looking inside the van for Gerot's clothes. Finding them, he said, "Follow me, we'll get your clothes back."

"You're a lucky young man," Len added, walking tenderly behind the trio as they entered the big house. "Most of this fellow's helpers find themselves the recipient of a couple of caps in the back of their head."

"Shit," the IPS driver uttered.

"Robbie, John, please help *Monsieur* Gerot out of those borrowed clothes and into his own. If he gives you any shit, squeeze his balls."

The clothes swap took only a few minutes, with Jean-Luc Gerot offering no resistance. The IPS driver went outside and hosed off his soiled shirt. Hastily wringing it out and putting it on still wet, he went on his way after first promising Sergeant John Dunlap that he would yet today make a complete report to a local Denver Police station house.

In the process of swapping clothes, Jeff Robinson and Dunlap discovered a motel room key in the pocket of Gerot's trousers.

"Where's the Hamlet Motel, John?" Jeff Robinson asked. "The key tag says it's on Colorado Boulevard, how far away is that?"

"The Hamlet? Maybe fifteen minutes from here. Want to take a look?"

"Len? Do we have time?" Jeff Robinson asked.

"Sure, if afterward Sergeant John will drive you to DIA. We still have a plane to catch."

"DIA's not a problem," Dunlap said. "I'm not doing anything else today. In fact, I'm finding this most enjoyable."

Campanera nodded, "No rush, we have two hours to catch our plane. Also, Len, we've commandeered the entire first-class compartment, compliments of the Secretary of the Treasury."

"Great, maybe I can get some sleep," Len said. "Luis, may I borrow your cell phone?"

"Help yourself. All right, boys, let's get ready to fly. If *Monsieur* Gerot is cuffed and shackled let's get him into the SUV. Put one of those high-collared Kevlar vests on him too. I don't want to risk a last minute assassination attempt on our assassin."

Len waited impatiently for Mariko to answer. "Homicide, Devonshire Hills precinct, Miss Tanaka speaking…"

"Hi, kid," he said quietly. "We got our man, not much pain, not too much strain. It went way better than we expected. We're on our way home, meet me at LAX later?"

Speechless for an instant, and definitely relieved, Mariko didn't immediately respond. Finally, she let the pent-up emotion release and with tear-filled eyes replied, "I was so worried, Len … oh, honey, my God! What a relief. I'll tell the boys right away!"

"Mariko, also tell Lana that I borrowed some of her ballerina thunder, I kicked Gerot in the balls, twice! Tell her that for me?"

He could hear the laughter in the background as Mariko relayed his message. Then she said, "You'll be happy to know that we arrested young Jorge this morning and we're holding him on murder one and conspiracy. Just so you know. It looks like we finally have a clean slate, Captain."

"Wonderful! That's great, really great. Hey, babe, I will see you later, huh? Dinner at a quiet place after we land? Overnight on the sloop?"

"Yes, yes! I can't wait! Fly safely, goodbye now."

Len thanked Campanera and returned his phone. He looked back at the house and waved goodbye to the two smiling Treasury agents and gardeners. Feeling relieved and relaxed, he turned and walked slowly to the street to join Campanera's group readying to head for DIA.

They waited in the warm afternoon sun outside the white-tented DIA main terminal building for Jeff Robinson and John Dunlap to show up. Twenty minutes later the pair arrived in Dunlap's police cruiser complete with flashing lights and wailing siren in full operational mode. Jeff Robinson smiled as he exited the cruiser. He turned and saluted as Dunlap sped away after waving back at Len and Campanera.

Jeff Robinson approached carrying a leather overnight bag.

"What did you find?" Len asked. "Anything worth keeping?"

"Oh, some nine-millimeter ammo clips, another new Glock, peppermint flavored toothpaste, Hanes BVDs, some weird trinkets, $128,000 and change ... that sort of thing," Jeff Robinson answered, winking and grinning broadly.

"The money? No kidding!" Len exclaimed. "Is it all there?"

"I didn't count it all, but in round numbers, it appears most of it is here. So, shall I check it with a porter or shall we try to sneak it through security?" Jeff Robinson winked again.

"Good question. Let's not advertise the fact that we recovered the money. Maybe the department can contact the victims' attorneys and maybe they can quietly deposit it somewhere safe."

"Good idea, Boss ... I haven't seen you to mention, too, that after I read Gerot his rights, I asked him why he of all people was sent to retrieve the Mafia's money. He said, like you mentioned, it was more to send a message; one helluva loud and clear message to anyone else connected with the Russian Mafia's businesses."

"That and to retrieve their money?" Len asked.

"No, Gerot said they agreed that once he had it, he could keep it. It was his to do with as he liked. The message was the main issue."

"That is interesting, incredible too. This money has cost enough time and lives so far. But right now? Carry it aboard," Len said, beaming. "We're up-town dudes now, flashin' our tin and travelin' first class, let's fly."

The contingent of law officers seated in first class were quiet and mostly subdued as they flew back to California. Jean-Luc Gerot sat alone, bundled in his protective Kevlar armor-vest. He stared straight-ahead, silent, shackled hand and foot, his seat belt keeping him restrained.

Across the aisle, Len managed to sleep while Campanera and Jeff Robinson chatted. Two other Treasury agents read magazines or worked the NYT crossword puzzles, but kept a watch on Gerot.

The big plane made a smooth landing at LAX, as opposed to the landings at DIA earlier. As it taxied to the gate, Campanera advised his men, "San Fernando Valley West has a security contingent and a police van waiting on the tarmac. Take Gerot off the plane into the jet bridge, then walk him down the outside stairs to the runway and deliver him into Devonshire Hills precinct's truck. Get a receipt."

The big plane rolled to a stop, the jet bridge glided over and made contact with the fuselage. The flight attendants quickly opened the door and the troop filed out as the waiting passengers on board watched in wonderment.

Two federal agents, with Gerot in tow, led the way as Campanera had instructed. Len and Jeff Robinson nodded their appreciation to the smiling flight crew and followed Campanera. As they left the jet bridge, they stepped into the large concourse and paused; bedazzled at the amount of bright lights, cameras and the chorus of raucous deafening noise that greeted them.

"Good grief! This is unbelievable," Jeff Robinson said, standing beside Len.

Len saw Mariko first. He winked and smiled. She winked, smiled back and blew him a kiss. Surrounded by screaming newspaper and broadcast reporters, still overwhelmed by the bright lights from a dozen TV cameras that nearly blinded him, he heard Kay Lehner yelling his name.

Shouting above the din, he asked, "Is this some of your doing Miss Lehner?"

"I wouldn't have missed this for the world," she yelled as she pushed Len and Jeff Robinson toward the screaming, roped off media. "Tell 'em what came down in Denver today, Captain."

Len smiled back at the rowdy assemblage of local and national press and broadcast media. Waving his hand, they quieted somewhat as he was handed a wireless microphone.

"Good evening, everyone! Let me say this first, California has never looked so good!"

A loud roar went up that would be reminiscent of Dodger Stadium when an injured Kirk Gibson came off the bench to pinch-hit the winning homer in game one of the 1988 World Series.

Len waited for the crowd of assembled cops, media types, and ordinary folks to quiet down. "Second, both Lieutenant Jeffrey Robinson, my friend and homicide partner for the last twelve years, and I are very tired, maybe beyond tired. We both need a hot shower, trust me on that!"

"It's been a long trying day," he continued, "but a highly successful day for our department. I'll give you a statement, but I won't take any questions now. Fair enough?"

It obviously wasn't 'fair enough' if the volume of noise was any measure of their opinion, but he continued, "Last night here in the Valley, our San Fernando Valley West homicide team arrested the alleged murderer of young Georgie Stamos. Georgie, you may remember, was the student at the RFK Junior High School who, along with his teacher, was the victim of a brutal killing. All I can give you, pending any future relaxation of the district judge's current gag order, is that our suspect is also a minor. He is currently being held in juvenile custody, charged with one count of murder one with special circumstances, and one count of murder two."

The throng went crazy, wild-eyed news reporters screamed questions at Len from all sides, but he merely waved them off, shaking his head.

"I can't speak to any more than that now. Why? Because for once, I don't know any more than that, except this..."

He waited for a few seconds as the crowd quieted down.

"...early today our San Fernando Valley West homicide team arrested yet another minor; the alleged perpetrator behind the RFK Junior High classroom shootings. He, too, is being held in custody at Juvenile pending arraignment on conspiracy to commit murder one. Again, I can't speak to any more than that, sorry."

The disgruntled mob of shouting media types became less interruptive when it became apparent that Len was not going to answer any of their questions.

Len motioned for Jeff Robinson to join him at the microphone. "Lastly, friends, today in Denver, with the able assistance of the Denver Police Department and the United States Treasury Department, we apprehended a fabled international assassin. He is currently in the custody of the San Fernando Valley West Police Department. His name is Jean-Luc Gerot, spelled, G-E-R-O-T, alias, Yves-Gaston Giroux."

Dozens of flashbulbs exploded and a sudden hush fell over the assembled reporters who recognized the last name as that of the notorious European terrorist. Then the volume of noise intensified as more questions came forth, forcing Len to wave them off again.

He cleared his throat and raising his voice, now becoming hoarse, continued, "Jean-Luc Gerot will be charged with the murders of fellow San Fernando Valley West Police Officers Farley, Beck, and Svoboda, as well as Ms. Gloria Mitchell, and his thus far unidentified accomplice. Tomorrow, Departmental Director of Information Kay Lehner will fill you in on any additional details we can release along with anything else the presiding judge will allow us to release on the Stamos case."

Len paused and looked across the crowd where he spied Mariko again and smiled. "Also, after due consideration, I will happily begin my long-awaited suspension as of midnight tonight. That, following a long hot shower and a quiet steak dinner with good company; good company during the dinner part only. Unfortunately, my shower stall is too small for visitors."

He smiled. The huge crowd responded with laughter. "Thanks for the great welcome home, folks, we appreciate it. Good night."

Len and Jeff Robinson waved back at the roaring crowd and stepped down from the platform. With the help of a dozen uniformed LAPD officers, they struggled slowly toward the concourse exit amid the swollen ranks of noisy reporters, flashing cameras and curiosity seekers in general. Smiling and ignoring the endless questions and congratulatory pats on the back, they made it through the mob and into the noisy, traffic-filled street outside the LAX terminal.

Alone and away from the previous confusion, Len stood and looked at Jeff Robinson, his tired but happy friend, his partner in life. "I guess we both drove, huh?"

"Looks that way."

Jeffrey Robinson, somber now, glanced down at the grimy sidewalk; dampened by the encroaching marine layer. He raised his head and looked again at his friend. "I haven't said this yet, I didn't know how, but you made me damn proud today. You're a credit to the profession." Then he hugged Len hard and pulled him tight against him. "You're the man, Len, my man. Now go have a quiet weekend with Mariko and enjoy that paid furlough. I'll buy breakfast when you get back."

Len's throat tightened as he returned the hug of his longtime friend. "Thanks, Robbie. You're the best too. See you at Soleh's?"

...to be continued in Detective Len Morgan Novel #2,
titled, **His Father's Sons**

His Father's Sons
A Detective Len Morgan Novel #2

Circa 1996 – San Fernando Valley, California...
Len Morgan, Valley West Police Department Homicide Captain, returns to work, following a two-week furlough spent sailing his sloop on the blue Pacific, and finds his department knee-deep in the investigation of a mysterious car explosion that left the victim charred beyond recognition. Len later gets word from his mother that his father, declared MIA in Korea 46 years earlier, has resurfaced and sent her a huge sum of money.

This leads Len to a bizarre reunion with his estranged father and his two Asian half-brothers, all of whom he learns are international criminals involved in a murderous and deceptive high-tech scheme to infiltrate and destroy our current system of government, and to cleverly frame him for a diabolical murder.

About the Author, John Wright~

I retired as a Project Superintendent from commercial construction in 2001 and decided to fulfill a life's ambition-- to write detective-fiction novels. I'd had the urge for most of my adult life. In high school, one of my literature teachers once commented that I should pursue a career in journalism.

Ever the skeptic, I finally heeded his challenge decades later in part and spent years writing hundreds of published Political Blogs and Letters to the Editor.

In 1997, I began writing *A Scent of Suspicion* at the suggestion of an Internet friend from Utah. Self-published in 1999, it became the first in the Detective Len Morgan Series followed by the sequels: *His Father's Sons, A Passion for Revenge, CHAOS ...and Cops!, INSANIA INTERRUPTUS* and *In Pursuit of Phantoms.*

In 2013, I took a short break from fiction writing and put together a compilation of my earlier political Blogs and Editorial Letters and published an opinionated nonfiction book: *Prodigious Political Ponderings & Prognostications ...a sobering glance back; slouching into the early Obama years.*

All of these books are available at the Createspace eStore.com/ and as Kindle eBooks at Amazon.com.

John Wright

Made in the USA
Middletown, DE
01 July 2017